THE MISTRESS

By the same author
THIS TOWERING PASSION
Volume 1: The Lovers

THE MISTRESS

Volume Two of the
This Towering Passion saga

by

VALERIE
SHERWOOD

This title first published in Great Britain 1991 by
SEVERN HOUSE PUBLISHERS LTD of
35 Manor Road, Wallington, Surrey SM6 0BW.
This first hardcover edition published in the U.S.A. 1992 by
SEVERN HOUSE PUBLISHERS INC of
475 Fifth Avenue, New York, NY 10017

British Library Cataloguing in Publication Data
Sherwood, Valerie
   The mistress.
   I. Title
   813.54 [F]

   ISBN 0-7278-4290-0

Printed and bound in Great Britain by
Billing and Sons Ltd, Worcester

DEDICATION

In loving memory of beautiful Tawny, our graceful shorthaired cat whom we named for her lovely coat. To Tawny, valiant and unshakably loyal, whom we found starving in a snowy barn in northern Virginia, waiting endlessly for an owner who had died and was never coming back to her, to Tawny of the long legs and the long claws and enchanting ways. To Tawny of the enormous intelligent light green eyes and the tawny fur and the delightful purr, Tawny who brought us gifts (for example, a dead mouse carefully carried into our bed and deposited between my husband and myself!). To Tawny the roguish and brilliant and all too human (once she found herself trapped in a loft above the milkhouse at Thorn Hill and couldn't make it down the wall ladder, so we propped a long board up so that she could run down it to safety, but it was so shaky that when she leaped upon it she gave an almost human scream of despair – and then ran down to arrive shaken and with great relief!). To charming Tawny of happy memory, whose time with us was all too short, this book is affectionately dedicated.

Valerie Sherwood

All that I am, all that you were,
The love we left behind
In wonder now has found us
With golden ties that bind!

Contents

BOOK I

THE MISTRESS

PART ONE

THE TOAST OF OXFORD

CHAPTER 1

The wind, whipping across a white winter landscape, had brought a biting cold, but the Christmas season at Oxford was as merry as Lally had promised. For Lenore, however, it was a terrible Christmas, all the gaiety and gladness shadowed by fear.

In defiance of the law, a dozen of the merriest Oxford youths (all of them with Royalist leanings) went together and purchased a Christmas goose, which was stuffed with chestnuts and oysters and roasted by Mistress Watts's cook. To this feast, Mistress Watts generously contributed a large plum pudding and Geoffrey, who had come back from his mysterious, snowy ride in funds, furnished chestnuts to roast before the fire. Young Michael brought sweetmeats his mother had sent him from their manor house south of Coventry, while most of the others arrived laden with wine.

Lenore's sense of doom had returned and pervaded what should have been a wonderful day, heightened as it was by callers and the giving of gifts. Lenore felt quite overwhelmed, for Lally arrived early, bringing her a pair of gay red wool stockings, and a new pair of gloves from Ned. Both gifts were badly needed and gratefully accepted, for her own stockings were much-mended and her hands in her threadbare gloves were near to freezing these days.

She presented Lally with an orange plume for her hat. Geoffrey had told her earlier that they had enough money to buy presents for everyone and they had rushed out, banging on closed shop doors and getting surprised tradesmen to come downstairs and open up for their late-bought gifts. Ned's gift of a pair of gauntlets must be given to him later, for now that the snow had stopped and the roads were passable, he was spending Christmas Day with his Marston lady.

Lally exclaimed impressively over the lovely plum velvet hat and muff Geoffrey had given Lenore as she whirled about the room modeling them for her. But Lally fell silent at sight of the enameled ring Geoffrey sported. Lenore knew what she was thinking—that a ring would not hold Ned, that perhaps nothing would hold him. Quickly she urged on Lally another glass of Christmas cider—hastily procured, along with sweetmeats, from Mistress Watts downstairs. Lally accepted the cider, but Lenore hadn't missed her sad, envious glance.

Lenore had a bad moment when Gilbert arrived bearing the muff he had promised. He looked startled to see Geoffrey, but he rallied and presented the muff with a flourish —it was of marten and very soft. Lenore had steeled herself to face him—the first time since that hot, shameful encounter in her bed. In silence she accepted this bitter gift. The soft brown fur seemed to sear her hands; she yearned to hurl the pretty muff into the fire. But . . . they were all watching—Geoffrey sardonically, Lally with narrowed eyes.

Gallantly Lenore lifted her head and gave Gilbert a cool, impersonal smile. "It's very lovely," she said in a lightly distant tone.

"As you are, Mistress Lenore." Gilbert fetched her a handsome bow, his honey curls falling foppishly forward.

"And from Geoffrey and myself." She handed him a

6

wrapped package and Gilbert took it warily, as if it might blow up. The gift was one of the gay colored knitted woolen scarfs which they had hastily bought for all their student friends this morning.

Before he could properly thank her, Lenore shoved a glass of cider into his hand and the door swung open to admit Michael—handsomely garbed in a new red velvet cloak—and his friend Lewis. Michael surprised Lenore by giving her a length of warm green wool, which she exclaimed over, saying it would match her cloak perfectly— and Lally told her that together they'd manage to make it up into a dress. Lewis shyly gave her a bit of Florentine lace, and Geoffrey raised amused eyebrows at these tokens of devotion from her ardent young admirers—and at their exuberant joy at being presented with colorful woolen scarves by young Mistress Daunt.

"You'd think Lenore wove them herself," Lally laughed, but her slate-blue eyes were sad.

Then Mistress Watts came hurrying up the stairs with a white linsey-woolsey petticoat for Lenore, so that she might face the rigors of Oxford weather rather better. Lenore was glad she had bought a bright shawl for the kind landlady. "And a tidbit for Puss," she added, handing Mistress Watts a small wrapped package containing salmon.

They all laughed at that, and Mistress Watts hastened to tell them that Puss expected Christmas presents "same as anyone," and confided that she always spiked his Christmas milk with a bit of spirits.

"Should Puss get too drunk, Mistress Watts, let him stagger on his paws over to my lodgings," Gilbert said. "I've a fondness for strays." He was looking at Lenore as he said that, and she flashed him an angry look. He was standing beside the window looking very rakish in bronze silks, his weight supported on one foot as he lounged against the wall. As she met his sardonic gaze, he shifted his weight so that his other hip was thrust forward and a lean bronze silk thigh was thrown into high relief in the bright winter light reflected off the snow. His easy smile was knowing, and raked over her as if he had stripped her

7

down to her chemise and already was tossing back her skirts. Before that cool, insolent look, remembrance flooded bitterly over Lenore, and she turned quickly away, to find Lally watching her with a penetrating gaze.

"Has Gilbert been bothering you lately?" Lally whispered.

"No, of course not," Lenore lied with an innocent look. "Why should he?" Her shrug said: *one rebuff should be enough*.

"Oh, I don't know—he's very persistent and I just thought he might. Well, I must be going."

"Don't go, Lally," urged Lenore. "Stay with us till time to dine—'twill not be long."

" 'Twill be very long," corrected Lally. "I remember last year 'twas late at night before all was ready! We were near to starving before the goose was carved. The Great Tom bell had already tolled curfew, so we'd no choice but to stay the night sleeping on the floor in Mistress Watts's common room!"

Last year . . . so Lally had been with Ned a year, at least. Lenore had not known it had been so long.

"I'll be back." Lally rose and pulled on her gloves. "Tonight is a festive occasion, and I mean to dress for it!"

What Lally meant became clear that evening when she made a sensational entrance on Gilbert's arm. He was resplendent in honey-colored velvets frosted with Mechlin, and she was every bit as spectacular in a deep red velvet gown cut shockingly low. Her ash-blond hair was magnificently done, every hair swept up in place. From her soft kid gloves to the tips of her velvet pattens she was a fashion plate, and she bore in her arms great sprays of holly for Mistress Watts's table decoration.

Lenore felt plain by comparison. She was wearing her usual russet wool, full-skirted, with a starched white linen collar and cuffs edged in point. For a moment she gazed wistfully at her flamboyant friend. And yet—she looked down at her dress; she remembered that Geoffrey had arranged with Mistress Watts to have this warm woolen dress made shortly after their arrival in Oxford and had

8

surprised her by its early completion on the first bitter cold day. "Of russet wool to complement your hair," he had said gravely as he presented it to her, but she had suspected him of choosing that color out of sentiment, because russet was the traditional color of country brides' dresses.

She looked up again, from fingering the russet material. Lally might be garbed in rich velvets, but her slate-blue eyes were unhappy, and the fashionably dressed man on her arm was not her lover. While she. . . ! Lenore gave Geoffrey a soft look. He was everything to her—and she to him.

Christmas dinner was a happy occasion, marred for Lenore only by Gilbert's presence. Although several times before dinner he had tried to corner her, she had managed to avoid him. True to Lally's prediction, the sun had waned before the meal was served, but Mistress Watts had been reckless in her use of tapers, and the beamed low-ceilinged common room downstairs blazed with light. Wide-topped polished boots scuffed over the clean-scoured stone floor and masculine voices made a low hum, for with the exception of Lenore and Lally, Mistress Watts's guests were exclusively male.

At one side of the room a Yule log burned brightly on a great hearth with an iron crane above it from which hung a great iron pot. The aproned cook was tasting the oyster stew from this pot with a long-handled iron spoon, and the goose was being turned on a spit by Jack, the stableboy. The warm hearth emitted a mouth-watering aroma. Potatoes were baking in their jackets in the ashes at the edge of the roaring fire and pitchers of cider sat in the deep windowsills waiting to be poured into pewter tankards.

Gwynneth, aided by her younger sister Dora, who had been hired for the occasion, were arranging pewter knives and trenchers and tankards and linen napkins atop the improvised "dining table." This was a number of long boards supported by carpenters' "horses" and covered with an assortment of odd-sized linen tablecloths—for Mistress Watts's linen chest was inadequate for the enter-

9

tainment of so many guests. The holly Lally had brought had been arranged into three handsome centerpieces spiked with candles and spaced down the long board. And although some of the students' cuffs were frayed and their boot soles worn almost through, Lenore thought she had never seen so glittering a company.

She was seated between Geoffrey and red-coated Michael (who had vied with Lewis in a friendly scuffle to sit beside her) and directly across the table from Lally— and unfortunately across from Gilbert also, for he was squiring Lally this evening.

The steaming oyster stew—served in wooden bowls and eaten with pewter spoons—was rapidly consumed, for by now the guests were ravenous. Then the Christmas goose was brought to table on a huge pewter charger and received a cheer from the company. Lenore smiled as she watched an elderly admirer of Mistress Watts carve the goose with obvious trepidation. He lived across the street, and had gallantly contributed the chestnut and oyster stuffing.

Seeing her suitor was nervous at carving before so many guests, Mistress Watts attracted their attention by saying loudly, "I've a rare sight for you, a trick I've taught Puss here." She ordered Gwynneth to bring up a low stool and place it beside her, and the big white cat obediently jumped atop it, his head and half his body now showing above the table. "I've trained Puss to eat at table," Mistress Watts announced in an important voice. "See? He'll eat every course, won't you, Puss?"

A round of exuberant applause greeted Puss's quick demolishing of a small bowl of oyster stew, but the noise frightened the cat, who jumped down from the stool and sought an empty windowsill where he licked his paws and gazed balefully at the company.

But Mistress Watts's elderly suitor gave her a grateful look for diverting attention from his clumsy efforts at carving and her kindly eyes twinkled back at him.

As the goose was served, Lenore leaned forward to speak to Lally, and saw that Lally was staring somberly

10

down at her hands, her fair head bent a little and reflecting the candlelight, while Gilbert argued with the student on his left.

Sensing Lenore's compassionate gaze upon her, Lally looked up and her slate-blue eyes hardened. "*You* have a muff for each hand," she said bitterly. "While I—!" She broke off, but Lenore knew it was not muffs Lally was talking about.

Except for one or two bad moments when Gilbert looked across the table at her with unadulterated lust in his gaze, Lenore found herself enjoying the occasion. Geoffrey was at her side and witty remarks flew back and forth as the guests stuffed themselves. The servants ran about, flush-faced and bright—they'd been nipping at Mistress Watts's French brandy in the pantry. That brandy had been smuggled into Oxford up the Thames and so had arrived duty free. Lenore was glad the servants were having a good time of it, even if the service was careless—glad, too, that she'd remembered to buy them baskets of red apples for Christmas.

The meal progressed. The goose and pease and hot baked potatoes, bursting in their brown jackets, were consumed along with a large amount of cider. Then the stableboy proudly brought forward the great plum pudding, flaming on Mistress Watts's treasured silver tray. They ate it with a thick wine sauce, drank wine and brandy, and uproariously toasted each other's health—and as they grew drunker and more reckless, the King's. Lally matched the gentlemen, glass for glass. Lenore watched her anxiously, for Lally in her daring red gown was too merry tonight, her forced laughter too shrill. Gilbert, too, was watching Lally with heavy-lidded eyes, watching her flushed face and the strand of ash-blond hair that had come loose from her intricate hairdo and which she irritably pushed back to lift her glass again and stridently toast "All of Royal England!"

Gilbert drank with the rest and looked across the table. "Took ye the white horse on your journey this time, Geoffrey?" he asked carelessly. But before Geoffrey could

11

answer, he added "Nay, I suppose not—a white horse shines like a beacon in the darkness, but a bay horse slides into the shadows well."

"What are ye saying, Gil?" Geoffrey's voice was lazy, but a pair of cold gray eyes challenged his cousin.

Gilbert shrugged. "Only that mayhap the bay does keep ye safer from . . . *highwaymen*." He emphasized the word and laughed discordantly; Lenore could see that he was getting very drunk.

Geoffrey studied his cousin, obviously making allowance for Gilbert's drunken state. "I've managed to hold my own with the gentlemen of the road thus far," he said in a level tone. "Perhaps my luck will hold a bit longer."

"Aye, 'tis luck we all need." Gilbert's gaze played mockingly over Lenore, and she flushed and turned pointedly away. He shrugged and turned back to Lally. When Michael said something that turned her attention that way again she saw that Gilbert's drunken gaze was bent fixedly on Lally's heaving red velet bodice. Lenore—though relieved at this respite from Gilbert's unwelcome attentions—could not help feeling angry with Ned. His Marston lady had expected him to spend Christmas Day with her, of course, but—his lonely daughter of the regiment needed him as well, and her heart might well break because of him.

When, after dinner, Gilbert and Lally slipped away early, Lally weaving on her feet and being supported by Gilbert, whose condition was almost as bad, Lenore's shoulders jerked spasmodically, and she made a convulsive gesture as if to stop them.

" 'Tis not our affair," Geoffrey murmured in her ear, seeing the direction of her lowering glance. "Each must make his own bed, Lenore, though sometimes 'tis thorny sleeping in it."

"But—can't she see him for what he is? Corrupt?"

"Women have always forgiven Gil his corruption," Geoffrey sighed. "He has a pretty face."

"*I* do not find him pretty," snapped Lenore.

Geoffrey laughed. "Then you're in the minority."

"I just don't want to see Lally hurt," she sulked.

12

"Nor do I. But Lally's a grown woman—yes, and a worldly one. She'd not appreciate your clucking over her like a mother hen."

Around them now the wine was being poured by unsteady hands, spilling over pewter tankards, drenching lace cuffs and splashing onto the clean-scoured floor as the young bloods clashed their tankards together and roared out forbidden Christmas carols. The very walls rocked with "God Rest Ye Merrie Gentlemen" until Mistress Watts's eyes rolled in her head in fright as she sought vainly to quiet the singers. Lenore was hard put to avoid several roguish youths who sought to kiss her beneath the mistletoe Mistress Watts had hung from the beams to snare the attentions of her elderly admirer.

When the guests had all departed—three of them were so drunk they had to be carted awkwardly through the snow to their lodgings in wheelbarrows, to Mistress Watts's distress (she muttered that the neighbors "would think she was running a bawdy house"), and Lenore was once more alone in her upstairs lodgings with Geoffrey, he went over to stir up the fire and Lenore came up behind him and wrapped her arms about him.

"Our first Christmas together, Geoffrey," she said in a soft voice.

He put down the poker and turned about, taking her shoulders in gentle hands. "Pray God the rest will be better ones," he said huskily. "And celebrated in a home of our own."

"Oh, do not say that!" She hugged him. "For a finer Christmas I have never known!"

"God's grace sent you to me, Lenore," he said simply, his lips brushing her bright hair which she had loosed to cascade down about her shoulders. "For surely I do not deserve you."

For the moment Lenore had forgotten Gilbert, and her laughter brimmed with confidence. Roguishly she cuffed his face. "Deserve me? Certainly you don't deserve me, but I'm a foolish woman and I love you as you are!"

"Come to bed and prove it!" His white teeth glinted in a wide smile and he pushed down the neck of her chemise

13

and pressed a warm kiss into the gleaming whiteness of her bared shoulder.

"Look, Geoffrey, it's snowing again," she murmured as he carried her to the big square bed. "The town will soon look like a wedding cake!"

For a moment she felt his muscles stiffen, and she rushed on to say something else. Marriage was a subject they avoided now, as if it were treacherous ground where they must never tread. Once they were abed and fondling, her foolish remark was forgotten as their love flamed on this cold, unforgettable Christmas night.

CHAPTER 2

During the Twelve Days of Christmas, winter tightened its icy grip on Oxford. All Christmas week Geoffrey did not leave her side and with Geoffrey home, Gilbert prudently avoided Lenore—for he had a healthy respect for Geoffrey's sword arm. She saw him once, when Geoffrey took her skating on the frozen Thames. He was skating arm in arm with Lally, and they made a handsome couple, scarves flying, their breath frosting the air and their noses red with cold. Seeing them together sobered Lenore because she knew that room had been made for Ned at Marston and he would be staying there till Twelfth Night, which left Lally to spend the holidays alone. Lenore knew she should have been grateful Ned was at Marston, for Gilbert's new fascination with Lally gave her a respite, but she could not help feeling sorry for her friend, whose sad face haunted her.

Lenore loved the icy crystal weather and Geoffrey affixed her pattens and together they explored the old walled city afoot. She found it to be a long narrow town built

15

upon a gravel bank, with a crossroads at the center. The Roman roads had passed Oxford by, a wind-whipped pink-cheeked scholar told them pleasantly when they stopped to rest in the shelter of an ivied wall—the Romans, from bitter past experience, mistrusted roads built on swamps.

Happy to be with Geoffrey on these walks, Lenore hurried along beside him, laughing at the cold, for she was muffled to the ears. Scrambled about her among the twisting streets were the big buildings of the university. But commerce as well as learning were important here, Geoffrey told her, for as soon as the ice broke, barges would ply up and down the Thames, carrying wool downriver from the Cotswolds for the looms of Oxford, and wines upriver to the old walled city from France—and sometimes, for the militant, arms. At taverns where they stopped to warm themselves on bitter days, they shared tankards of hot buttered rum and sometimes beef or mutton pies.

During the whole of that enchanted Christmas week they were gloriously happy.

Early in January, Geoffrey rode out. He would be gone a fortnight, he told her. He was not. He returned three nights later and limped up the stairs leaving a bloody trail. Lenore, who'd been prudently staying downstairs with Mistress Watts on the grounds of an indisposition—actually to avoid Gilbert in case he tried to pay her a call, heard the outer door open, heard limping footsteps ascending the stairs, seized a lighted candle and ran up after him in time to open the door to their rooms as he sagged against it.

"What happened?" she cried, frightened at the sight of his white face.

"I've been shot," he said grimly. " 'Tis only a leg wound, but it opened as I dismounted, and I fear that my blood stains the snow outside. 'Twill cause questions. Would you go down and scrape up the bloodstains from the snow and wipe them from the stairs, Lenore? And stable my horse?"

16

"But your wound——!" gasped Lenore. She set the candle on the table and ran to help him to a chair.

"Go now." Geoffrey waved her away. *"Now,* Lenore!" He staggered to the table and leaned heavily upon it for support.

Lenore hurried away to do his bidding, but from the landing she heard a heavy thud and rushed back to find he had slid to the floor unconscious.

Lenore had had practice binding up Meg's wounds when Tom Prattle had come home drunk and beaten her. Now she moved quickly and with dispatch. She brought Geoffrey to, weak from loss of blood. She removed and tossed aside the bloody scarf that bound his wound. Somehow she got his boot off and with water from the pitcher she washed the wound, bound and stanched it efficiently with clean linen napkins. Once that task was done she slipped down the stairs and out into the frozen moonlight and quickly removed all evidence of blood from the snow—and from the stairs. After that, she stabled and fed the bay horse.

When she came back in and closed the outside door, Mistress Watts had wakened and stuck her head out. "Is anything the matter, Mistress Daunt?" she inquired sleepily.

"Nothing at all," lied Lenore in an easy voice. "Geoffrey is back, so I'll spend the rest of the night upstairs."

"Back so soon? That's good." Mistress Watts yawned. "No, don't come out, Puss—I can't be chasing you!" Hastily she pushed back a furry white paw and closed the door, and Lenore fled up the stairs to Geoffrey.

He had got himself over to the bed when she got back. He was lying fully clothed and exhausted across it, his wounded leg stretched out and his other booted one dangling over the edge of the bed. Lenore pulled that boot off, too, slid a pillow under his head, threw the coverlets over him, and wrapped a warm brick for his feet.

"Ye're a good nurse," he gasped, beads of sweat frosting his forehead as he moved his injured leg to a more com-

17

fortable position. "One would think ye'd been battle-trained, Lenore."

She glowed with pride, held up his dark head and poured some brandy down his throat, took the glass and then sat down on the bed beside him, smoothed back his dark wavy hair and asked him how he'd come to be shot.

'Twas cursed bad luck, he told her. A friend of his father's had recognized him at an inn and—glad to see him—had blurted out his name in greeting. 'Twas too well-known a Royalist name not to cause remark. And his way out of the town had been barred by soldiers, hastily summoned by the Puritan innkeeper. He'd fought his way through—Lenore shuddered to hear—and lost them on well-trampled roads. None had followed him here, he was sure of it.

Lenore held that well-loved head to her breast and thanked God he had made it home to her.

All January Geoffrey convalesced, passing off his condition as a distemper of the lungs. Since Oxford was filled with distempers of the lungs at this season, his story was readily accepted. Lenore was glad to have him with her, but their funds were running perilously low. Mistress Watts did not press them for the rent, and once without Geoffrey's knowledge, Lenore even borrowed a small sum from Michael, who came over shivering, with his red cloak clutched around him and two woolen scarfs wrapped around his neck. Oxford had the worst weather in the world, he assured Lenore gloomily—July and August were the only frost-free months this miserable town had. There'd once even been a snowstorm right in the middle of summer term, and he for one found it unbearable! He had no plans to spend another winter here, but would return to his home near Coventry in June.

Lenore had to laugh at so much gloom, but even she found the weather irksome. Winter had indeed closed down on Oxford town. January was a gray month with fall after fall of snow. Snow perpetually covered the city wall with its high walk for sentries and its bastion. Snow drifted

18

down on ivied towers and warrens of medieval cottages, on shops and stables and taverns, iced the streets and made work shoveling for day laborers with red noses and patched clothes. Snow almost closed the cobbled alley called Magpie Lane, where in better weather footfalls echoed after dark, and hampered the efforts of young Mistress Daunt to get some exercise by walking about the city with Lally. Fast sleighs glided past them over the hard-packed snowy streets and sleigh bells tinkled in the frosty air. The Thames stayed hard-frozen—the Oxford students called these lovely upper reaches of the river, romantically, the "Isis"—a river goddess. Lenore would have gone skating there with Lally, but Geoffrey objected, lest she fall on the ice. Lenore gave him an impatient look—she was a good skater. The sound of sleigh bells, reaching them from Magpie Lane, made her yearn to ride out on Snowfire over the hard-packed snow, but Geoffrey sharply forbade that, lest it bring on a miscarriage. Lenore fretted at that, but she arranged with Lally to exercise Snowfire, and spent long hours petting and currying Snowfire in Mistress Watts's warm stable—and giving attention to the bay, too, who had brought Geoffrey home to her through the blizzard. The stable boy was fond of the bay, and exercised him for her, but he was afraid of prancing Snowfire, who had once inadvertently kicked him.

For Lenore this time of Geoffrey's recuperation was like a truce in a battle. Time seemed to hang suspended for her. Geoffrey's constant presence was a bastion against Gilbert—although as the month wore on and her pregnancy became more apparent, Gilbert gave her an angry, sulky look when he passed her trudging down the High Street with Lally. He seemed to take her pregnancy as a personal affront, for he pointedly eyed her stomach and after that brief encounter almost ceased to notice her altogether. Lenore had the uneasy feeling his attentiveness would return once the baby was born, and she was slender again, but that was a long time away, and she refused to think about it—their circumstances might be much changed by then.

19

Lally was amused by Gilbert's sullen manner. "Don't mind him," she blithely counseled Lenore. "Gilbert hates women who are increasing—can't stand the bulge. Last year he sent poor Millie Tippert away to the country to have hers, said he couldn't bear to look at her ungainly form—and *he* was the father!"

Lenore shuddered. "Where is she now?"

"She died in childbirth. There was a terrible storm, the farmhouse where she was staying was on the riverbank, and with the flooding it became an island—the midwife couldn't get through and the farmer's wife got hysterical, didn't know what to do. It must have been awful."

"I don't see how anybody could even *speak* to Gilbert after that!" cried Lenore. "It was all *his fault!*"

"Of course." A cynical smile curved Lally's mouth. "But Millie had her revenge posthumously. She was lonely in the farmhouse and she felt cut off, so the night before she died she sat down and wrote a long letter to Gilbert's mother complaining about the way Gilbert had treated her. The farmer saw that it was delivered, too—he'd felt sorry for Millie. Gilbert's mother read it and flew into a passion—Gilbert said she was positively *livid* with rage—he was supposed to come home, but she refused to let him—said he could jolly well stay in Oxford for another two years until he'd learned how to behave! That's why he spent Christmas here—he can't go home until she decides to forgive him."

"I hope that's never!" said Lenore with vicious emphasis, although in truth she'd have been glad to see Gilbert through the city gates at any time.

"It wasn't because of what he did to Millie." Lally gave her an amused look. "It was because of what she was. Millie was a laundress, and Gilbert's mother couldn't abide his taking up with a low-class doxie!" Her laughter pealed.

Lenore was appalled. She gave Lally an uncertain look, but Lally shook her head ruefully. "You're very innocent of the ways of the world, Lenore. Perhaps that's what Geoffrey saw in you—oh, I didn't mean that," she added hastily, for Lenore had broken stride and stiffened.

20

Lenore relaxed. Lally was, after all, her friend. But she knew it would be even harder for her to be civil to Gilbert after this.

They stopped at a coffee house for warmth and refreshment. It was forward of them to come in unattended, but Lally knew the proprietor's wife, who promptly whisked them back to a small private room where they enjoyed steaming coffee and little wheaten cakes. The proprietor's wife bustled away, leaving them sitting companionably at a small wooden table, beside them a window with small leaded panes that gave onto a stable with icicles dripping from the thatched roof.

Lally was watching her brightly, and Lenore cast about for a way to break the awkwardness that had arisen between them over the story of Millie. She could scarce say she had another reason, as well, for hating Gilbert! Her hand passed nervously over her white collar, smoothing it, and brushed a lump half-concealed by her bodice —she had her subject: eagle-stones!

This morning Mistress Watts seemingly had at last discerned that Lenore was pregnant. She had been remarkably slow to discover it—Lenore suspected her landlady guessed they were not married and thought Lenore might not wish to admit she was bearing Geoffrey's child. But this morning Mistress Watts had hurried upstairs with a silk bag of eagle-stones, which her wealthy cousin in Bath had brought home from abroad. This, she told Lenore importantly, her scanty curls bobbing for emphasis, was a very efficacious charm which had helped her cousin in Bath through two difficult pregnancies. The silk bag must be worn on a ribbon around Lenore's neck until two or three weeks before the baby was born—just to make sure all went well at the birth.

Lenore had accepted this well-meant gift with grave thanks, threaded a ribbon through the eyelets of the silk bag and put it around her neck immediately. She was uncertain as to the efficacy of charms, but one could not afford to take chances. Charms were popular with pregnant women. Women in the Cotswolds wore them, too— Meg had worn several supposed to give her an easy de-

21

livery, but whether they had helped her was debatable, for she had miscarried all the same.

Now Lenore eagerly pulled the silk bag from her bodice and displayed it to Lally. "Mistress Watts gave me these eagle-stones to make certain a good birth. Think you they will help?"

Lally, stirring her coffee, stared at them with a kind of fascination; then she shuddered and turned away. "Eagle-stones did not help *me*," she said shortly. "My baby died. In Stratford, the day he was born."

Lenore's violet eyes widened. She had not known Lally had gone so far with her Kevin. . . . It helped explain why Lally's strait-laced relatives had been unwilling to take her in after her father died.

"That surprises you, doesn't it?" challenged Lally grimly, swinging about to face Lenore. "You've wondered about Ned and me. The baby was Kevin's, but 'twas Ned saw me through it—though it ended badly all the same."

"No—I never wondered," said Lenore, hastily taking a swallow of near-scalding coffee.

"Of course you did. Everybody does. They can't understand why I stay with him, filling in the time until he marries. But—" she bit her lip and frowned. "I wanted *you* to understand, Lenore."

"You're very good to Ned," Lenore said soberly. "I've often felt he should wed you instead of some ninny in Marston."

"Ned likes small pretty brunette women," Lally informed her in a brittle, hopeless voice. "Not long, stringy ones like me. And her name is Lavinia."

Lenore felt called upon to protest. "I don't even like the name Lavinia," she said hotly. "And you have the carriage of a queen, Lally. Geoffrey often comments on your spirited walk."

Lally laughed bitterly. "But not on my pretty face, I'll wager." She looked out the window at the hanging icicles. " 'Tis unsettling, but I've grown fond of Ned these past months we've been together. When he marries—God's teeth, I'll miss him!" Her voice roughened.

Lenore gave her a sympathetic look. She had a very good idea of what blond, fashionable Lally was going through.

"Perhaps Ned will change his mind," she suggested hopefully.

Lally's harsh laugh stung her. "Not till after he's wed Lavinia and bedded her," she said bitterly. "*Then* when the thrill of the chase is gone, he may miss me—he may want someone to talk to. But I'll be gone, for I won't be able to sit by and wait in hopes he'll come back to me for an hour, a night. . . ."

"Where . . . will you go?" Lenore wondered.

"I'll find a new protector, as I once told you I would," Lally replied in a determined, hard voice.

Gilbert, thought Lenore with a pang. That caramel head was often bent over Lally's fair one these days. "I wish spring would come," she sighed.

"Ned will marry Lavinia in the spring," Lally reminded her, studying her hands.

"I'm sorry," said Lenore in a contrite voice. "It's just that I hate being cooped up indoors so much, and I suppose I'm impatient to hold my baby in my arms—" she stopped lamely, for Lally's face had twisted for a moment.

"It's all right," Lally told her softly, pressing a hand down over Lenore's on the table. "It hurt terribly at the time but—I'm over it now."

Lenore suspected no one ever got over it.

This conversation with Lally made Lenore all the more conscious of what she had—a strong man's arms to comfort her, a strong man to love her—and his baby on the way. Geoffrey mended fast, and at night their bodies responded vibrantly to each other in a perfect union. By day they found it easy to laugh off the gloom of others who found the continued cold depressing.

It was only lack of money that plagued them.

The next time she trudged with Lally through the snow, they met Gilbert coming out of an alehouse. He made them both a sweeping bow, but his smile was for Lally.

"If you make a leg so handsomely in this weather,"

23

Lally cautioned him lightheartedly, "you are apt to land on your backside in the snow!"

"You and Mistress Lenore seem to keep *your* footing," was Gilbert's cynical rejoinder. He was looking at Lally's muff—which was the one he had given Lenore for Christmas and which she had promptly presented to Lally on the pretext that "after all, you're exercising Snowfire for me." His lazy gaze passed over Lenore's plum velvet hat and muff—Geoffrey's Christmas gift—and his voice held an edge of spite. "I see from Mistress Lenore's fine clothes that Geoffrey must have found a way to live without working—certainly his father is not supporting him, has refused to see him, in fact. I heard through an aunt that Geoffrey traveled a great distance to see his father but was turned away at the door."

Lenore flushed and bit her lip. "Your aunt must have been misinformed," she said icily.

Gilbert's laugh was a trifle unpleasant. "You've no need to worry, Mistress Lenore," he told her smoothly. "Geoffrey's tough—he'll be back on the road soon enough. He's never let a wound hold him back for long," he added on a taunting note.

Lenore cared little that Gilbert was implying Geoffrey was a highwayman, for she doubted he could prove it—but it frightened her that Gilbert had guessed Geoffrey was wounded. "I don't know what you mean," she said carelessly, her hands gripping inside her velvet muff. "Geoffrey has an indisposition of the lungs—not a wound!"

Lally gave Gilbert an angry look. " 'Tis too cold to stand here talking nonsense," she said crisply. "We bid you good day, Gilbert."

When she returned home, Lenore taxed Geoffrey with it. She did not look at him as she pulled off her gloves and spread out her cloak before the fire. "Gilbert believes you've turned highwayman." When he said nothing she turned and faced him. "Tell me how you were wounded, Geoffrey—the truth."

"It was as I told you," said Geoffrey. "Be damned to Gilbert!"

24

She studied his face, that dark, loved face with the steady gray eyes. They were looking at her now, with tenderness. She sank down on a chair. "Oh, Geoffrey," she said in a hopeless voice. "What are we to do? We have no money, no—"

"Come here, Lenore." Very tenderly he enfolded her in his arms. "My leg is almost mended. Trust me. I will find a way for us."

He would need to, she thought sadly. Their situation was fast growing desperate.

In February rain fell soddenly and melted the snow and everyone—Town and Gown alike—caught cold. Candlemas was marked more by deep slush than revelry, and the city of towers became a dismal place of stuffy noses and hacking coughs and gloomy, wet, cobbled streets. On winter mornings vapor rose all around the city from the numerous rivulets about the river.

Geoffrey, up and mended, was now gone most of the time. He told her once gravely that he was trying to arrange a "living" for them. She wondered what he meant, and surmised he might be trying to arrange through relatives for a pardon and perhaps to borrow enough money to buy a commission in the army, for soldiering was the only trade he knew.

That he was unsuccessful in these attempts was apparent, for he came home through the gray winter mists looking grim and had little to say about where he had been or what he'd been doing. But he brought with him little trickles of money, enough to keep them alive, and now as she grew big with child, she was grateful. For with the baby coming, she no longer felt capable of riding the boggy winter roads and shivering through the nights in caverns and barns and chance hovels.

Now that her advancing pregnancy had—happily— made her repugnant to Gilbert, Lenore had lost her fear that he might try to repeat his performance of just before Christmas. She hated the sight of him and gave thanks that he no longer frequented her lodgings.

In the meager rooms off Magpie Lane, young Mistress Daunt held uneasy court, for she was always edgy these days, feeling that Geoffrey was off somewhere taking some great chance and instead of riding home might be brought back to her in a cart—for burial.

Michael was her most frequent visitor, for with her advancing pregnancy, the rash young men who had written her love sonnets drifted away to woo likely tavern maids, and Lenore, save for her visits from Lally and occasional dinners with Lally and Ned, on those infrequent occasions when he was not at Marston, was much alone. She spent long hours practicing her penmanship under Michael's guidance until even Geoffrey admitted her much improved, and she read borrowed books until her candle guttered out.

It was a pleasant respite from the miserable weather when Michael would come swinging over in the afternoon in his red cloak, bringing with him a bottle of wine and sweetmeats sent from his ancestral manor south of Coventry. He seemed bent on entertaining her, and would regale her by the hour with stories of bloody riots between Town and Gown which had been erupting since medieval times. Lenore didn't know whether to believe him or not when he told her that on one occasion hooded country folk had swarmed into Oxford bearing a black flag, killed sixty students, and scalped some of the chaplains. It was not, he conceded, chewing thoughtfully on a sweetmeat, the university's finest hour.

Sometimes Mistress Watts joined them, trudging upstairs with the big white cat purring in her arms, to tell them with sparkling eyes and a tremor in her voice of the wild days during the reign of Charles I when university courts had banished lewd women and arrested night-walking citizens. She recalled how Charles had made Oxford his headquarters during England's Civil War. Why, the town had been like a garrison, with New College turned into a magazine, and All Souls into an arsenal, New Inn Hall a mint, and the King himself at Christ Church, where the main quadrangle was turned into a cattle pen! How the town had rallied to his cause, then, with undergraduates throwing up great earthworks! Things were different now, she sighed. Lenore understood her longing to speak of these things, for they were memories of the days of her youth.

26

But being indoor so much chafed Lenore.

"Mistress Watts warns me I should not go out in this weather," she complained to Lally one day. "And in truth I grow so ungainly that I may pitch forward on my face on the cobbles—on wet days I fear to go out in my clogs for fear I will slip, and not to wear them would drench my shoes!"

"Stay indoors," advised Lally.

"That is very hard for me," sighed Lenore. "For I am a country girl and used to fresh air."

With the flowing green cloak to hide her condition, she continued to prowl the town on good days, sometimes walking all the way to Port Meadow, the pastureland which lay just to the northwest of Oxford. Now in the winter, damp mists lay over Port Meadow, which was owned by the Freemen of Oxford and was grazed by ponies and cows, frequented by flocks of ducks and geese and other birds. From its soggy ragwort and thistle-sprinkled grass the towers of Oxford rose in the distance in immense majesty, and Lenore would pause, shivering, to admire them.

Geoffrey heard of these prowlings and sternly ordered Lenore to stop going out alone—it wasn't safe. Did she not know there were footpads about?

"In daylight?" she asked wearily.

"Take Lally with you," he said.

Lenore gave him a resentful look. "Lally's busy enough exercising Snowfire—I can't take up all her time."

"Then get Michael to accompany you. He's a bright lad, and too cautious to let you get into trouble."

Lenore was over-surfeited with Michael's adoring company already, but when the weather moderated a bit, she relented and let him take her walking beneath the syca-mores and wych elms and mulberry trees. Honestly be-lieving Lenore would be interested in anything that interested him, Michael took her to the Ashmolean Museum to see the famous unicorn's horn, and Guy Fawkes's lantern and near it the bulletproof hat with its iron lining which had been worn by John Bradshaw when he presided over Charles I's trial. Lenore studied it and shivered.

The Lord Protector, men said, was an evil man, but . . . Michael had casually shown her the old gate where Cranmer, the Protestant Archbishop of Canterbury, had been burned to death by Bloody Mary's Catholic regime. The fires of burning Protestants had lit up the countryside then . . . no wonder sturdy Englishmen had brought the Lord Protector to power, they wanted an end to the burning. But now she looked at that bulletproof hat and thought of the beheaded King and shivered.

Michael's eyes had danced at that. He loved gruesome things and spoke of them with relish.

Lenore went home from that excursion sighing, wondering if all men were children at heart.

She found Lally waiting for her, sitting on the edge of the table, swinging one long leg and looking very depressed.

"I came over to show you my new blue velvet gown." Lally stood up and swung around so Lenore could view this new creation. Then, dispiritedly, "No, I didn't. Ned's gone to Marston again, and I had a falling out with Gilbert over that ridiculous barmaid, Dorothy. Oh, Lenore, I don't know what's wrong with me these days. I—"

Lenore poured her a glass of wine and handed it to her silently. "Perhaps Gilbert is what's wrong, Lally. Had you thought of that?"

Lally shot her a look. "You're wondering why I bother with Gilbert, aren't you?" she asked softly. "Ned isn't even married yet and . . . here I am, slipping around back streets with Gilbert."

Lenore's rising color was an admission that she had indeed wondered.

"I'm the kind of woman who has to have—someone," said Lally dispassionately. "Arms to hold me. If not Ned's—someone else's. Mind you, I love Ned—I never told anyone that before, not even Ned. But it's true, Lenore, I do love him. When Kevin was drowned and my father died, it snowed soon after and it was bitter cold, I thought on death. It seemed to me the answer was out there in the snow. I could just walk and walk until I froze to death and all my troubles would be over. I actually started out across the fields, trudging along through a white, faceless world. I remember growing sort of numb and sleepy and slowing down and finally I couldn't move any more and I thought, *This is death. Soon it will all be over.* Suddenly I felt someone slapping my face, and I came to and I was looking up into Ned's face. I'd never seen him before. He'd been riding across the fields, taking a shortcut to see some friends, and he found me lying there in the snow. He brought me back to his lodgings and warmed me—with rum and hot broth and with his own body, he made me want to live again. And when he learned my story, he helped me through with the baby—and then he brought me with him to Oxford. I've been very happy here, Lenore. But now that—that I'm losing Ned, I have to look around. Gilbert isn't the man I want, but he's witty and well-dressed—and he makes me feel like a woman. And sometimes I need that." Her smile was wistful. "I wanted you to understand, Lenore, because you're my friend and I care what you think."

Lenore felt a lump rise in her throat. Quickly she poured Lally a glass of wine.

Absently, Lally accepted the glass and toyed with it. "There have been times this winter," she said, her slate-blue eyes clouded with bitter reflection, "when it was bitter cold and Ned was in Marston and I have looked out through the frosted panes and yearned to go out and just keep walking, walking in the snow until the hurting stopped and I grew numb and dropped down and down and down. . . . Freezing's an easy death, they say."

Lenore stared at her. Worldly and witty, Lally had been through so much. "What stopped you?" she asked, her mouth dry.

Lally gave her a rueful smile. "At the last minute, I always found a shred of hope to cling to. That's what Ned's done for me, I suppose, given me hope. I'm a victim of my sometimes optimism. It's kept me going."

"Lally," Lenore's voice was husky and sincere, "I wish with all my heart that Ned would marry *you*."

29

"So do I," shrugged Lally. "But 'tis not like to happen."
She sighed. "It's growing late, I must go."

In the gathering dusk, Lenore watched her friend walk around the corner into Magpie Lane, a solitary figure hurrying home to a cold hearth—and a colder bed.

CHAPTER 3

With the spring, the wind off the Downs brought with it the scent of damp woodland, meadow wildflowers, and a promise of summer to come. With the spring, the face of Oxford, a city set amid the floodlands, changed. Hawkers came swinging into the town, selling the dead swans and moorhens they'd snared on baited eelhooks in the nearby Thames. Yeomen farmers walked about, gypsy caravans with bright painted carts lumbered through the streets, their horses jingling with fancy trappings. The market abounded with fish and fowl and venison, and from the swampy land the wonderful gardens overshadowed with huge oaks and sycamores and wych elms sprang to life, and a breath of warmth ruffled the ivy that clung to the honey-colored stone towers.

As Lally had gloomily predicted, Ned and Lavinia, his "Marston lady," were married—first a civil ceremony according to the law, and then another ceremony at home in Marston "to make Lavinia feel married," as Ned said happily. To this home ceremony Geoffrey and Lenore were invited.

"Are you going? To Marston?" a forlorn Lally asked Lenore.

"No," Lenore said moodily. "My excuse is that my delicate condition won't let me make the trip, but the truth is I couldn't stand it, seeing Ned marry somebody else when he should be marrying you."

"Oh, please go," Lally urged with a break in her voice. "Ned actually told me I could go if I wished, that he'd pass me off as a distant relative." She tried to laugh, but it didn't quite come off. "But I couldn't bring myself to. I couldn't bear to see it but I—I want someone to tell me about it. How—how it goes, and whether Ned seems happy." There were tears in her voice, and Lenore almost cried, too.

Though large with child by now, Lenore reluctantly assented to Lally's pleading and together with Geoffrey attended the wedding. She wore her russet wool gown and green cloak and the plum velvet hat and muff Geoffrey had given her for Christmas, for the weather was still unstable and the day dawned damp and cold. She and Geoffrey crossed the Cherwell by ferry with some of Ned's friends. On the opposite bank they were picked up by the bride's family coach and went on to Marston. The jolting coach made Lenore feel slightly ill, and she was not prepared to like Marston. She found it a swampy town, filled with fingers of the Thames, where white swans rode the placid waters like a bevy of brides.

The manor house they rode up to in the jolting coach was small but elegant, of red brick turned greenish by the damp climate, and approached by a flight of mossy stone steps. Geoffrey kept a firm grip on her arm as she negotiated those slippery steps, and Lenore gave him a grateful look.

The heavy oaken doors swung open and they found themselves inside a handsome wainscoted hall, stone-floored and sparsely furnished. At one end a bright fire crackled on a large stone hearth, moderating the spring dampness. Lenore would have headed at once for that fire, but Ned and his Lavinia came forward to greet them.

It was the first time Lenore had met Ned's Marston lady, and grudgingly she found she liked the small, buxom, bright-eyed brunette, who kissed her warmly and made her welcome.

"Ned, now that I've met Mistress Lavinia, I realize what a fortunate man ye are!" Geoffrey gave Ned a hearty slap on the back. Ned grinned idiotically, but Lenore, with a pang, thought of Lally and how disconsolate she must be today. Gilbert had stayed in Oxford with her, and for once Lenore was glad Lally had Gilbert—Lally would need arms around her this night.

"Cheer up," Geoffrey whispered as they followed their hostess into the big withdrawing room to the left of the hall, where the mullioned windows were heavily draped with handsome green damask. A number of guests milled about there, their bootheels grinding into the big Oriental carpet which had traveled half across the world and up the Thames and into the heart of England. "This is a wedding," he reminded her in a low voice, "not a wake. We owe it to Ned to be cheerful."

Lenore gave him a wan look. It was a wake to her. But she rallied a little as she drank warm wine and ate sweet cakes with the other guests. They drifted out into the hall and saw a group of new arrivals, the women wearing plumed hats. People flitted up and down the heavily carved acanthus scroll staircase. Many guests were to stay the night, but she and Geoffrey were not; along with others from nearby Oxford, the family coach would be taking them back to the ferry.

"I do not like weddings," muttered Geoffrey at a moment when no one was near. "Had I been in Ned's boots, I think I'd have come out on the Puritan side, for once, and said 'Let be' after the civil ceremony!"

Lenore gave him a scathing look. For once she lined up on the side of Lavinia, the Marston lady. "The poor girl wouldn't feel married!" she protested.

"She'll feel married enough when their first child comes along!" said Geoffrey. He looked abruptly sorry he'd said that, and Lenore sighed. There was always this awkward-

33

ness between them on the subject of marriage and—it wasn't right that it should be so. Their love for each other was as sturdy and sure as any marriage could be. She watched the little bridesmaids flit by with wistful eyes. They looked so young and fresh—so innocent and so happy.

She was still pensive when she went in on Geoffrey's arm to partake of a hearty meal of cold ham, haunch of venison, boiled leg of mutton and capers, flour pudding and sturgeon—all washed down with white and red wine, beer and cider—and so many tarts and pasties that Lenore felt stuffed as a Christmas goose.

Some of Ned's relatives were very late in arriving—among them his brother—so the ceremony was held up awaiting his arrival. Lenore, because of her condition, was given a cot in a corner of one of the upstairs bedrooms to rest in. She found herself unable to nap, for people came and went, greeting each other, hugging each other, eagerly giving news of friends. Many of the women's clothes were quite beautiful, with pastel silks and satins garnished with lace and plumed hats and pearl necklets. Lenore in her plain russet wool felt quite out of it.

After her rest she went back downstairs and found Geoffrey standing among a group of friends from Oxford, drinking wine.

"Ned's brother—still not here?" she asked him.

"They fear his coach may have lost a wheel—'tis known he was on his way, for there are those here who passed him on the road."

"How long will they wait?"

Geoffrey shrugged. "Faith, they seem in no hurry. The knot is already legally tied, and this ceremony is just a garnish on the cake." He turned and smiled as Lavinia came by and told them prettily that the ceremony was sure to be so late they'd never reach Oxford before curfew and of course they must spend the night here at Marston. At first Lenore demurred, but Lavinia insisted, smiling prettily with her small Cupid's bow mouth, her voice persuasive. "And you haven't seen my house linens—or my wedding gifts!" she told Lenore merrily, taking her by the arm.

34

"Every stitch of my linens is mine—I made them all myself, yes and embroidered them, too! Ned is so proud of me! The flax was spun here and the wool is from the Cotswolds—Ned tells me you're from the Cotswolds, Mistress Lenore."

Lenore admitted it.

"All those beautiful green hills and the flocks of white woolly sheep!" cried Lavinia ecstatically. "How could you bear to leave it?"

Lenore smiled and forbore to enlarge on her manner of leaving. She couldn't imagine Lally making that remark or looking at her in that lost, starry-eyed way. She wondered what Ned's married life was going to be like.

Then she found herself looking at the handsome collection of bridal gifts. The little silver cup she and Geoffrey had been able to afford was lost among massive candlesticks and handsome silver bowls, but Lavinia raved over it at length. She had never *seen* anything so beautiful! Lenore knew Lavinia meant well, but it all made her sad. She was glad when Lavinia rushed on to gush over somebody else.

At last Ned's brother arrived, covered with mud and with a wild tale of an overturned coach and some hastily procured help to drag it out of the mud—a large undertaking, as it turned out, for it was tightly wedged between a boulder and a tree and when righted was found to have lost a wheel. But at least now the ceremony could proceed.

Lavinia looked so joyful that she could now be "proper wed" that even Lenore had to smile. Lavinia retired to her room, waving to Lenore to come along with her. There her mother and sisters and female cousins helped get her into an elaborate costume, all of white. Sewn all over it were knots of colored ribbon—after the ceremony the young men would pull these off and wear them as bridefavors in their hats. Everyone gasped at Lavinia's gloves, which were of delicate lace-trimmed leather with tiny seed pearls sewn into rosettes. When Lavinia was ready—her mother having combed her long, dark hair down loose and set on it a circlet of myrtle—Lenore and the others went downstairs and waited for Lavinia to come floating down.

When she reached the bottom step, Lenore caught Geoffrey's eye from across the room. He raised a gauntleted glove to her (Ned had given all his friends fringed gauntlets as marriage tokens, as was the custom). Like the other guests, Lenore was now wearing a brightly colored scarf, and she adjusted it as she walked over to him.

This was a country wedding, and blithely free of the strictures of Puritanism save that the bride would wear a plain gold ring instead of a jeweled or enameled hoop. Beside Lenore, an elderly lady in a regal plumed hat and stiff brocades muttered, "*I* would have had Ned give me a jeweled hoop, had *I* been Lavinia."

"I think I would have been content with gold," sighed Lenore.

The woman gave her an odd look, and Geoffrey said in a vexed voice, "Mistress Lenore has lost her ring—when she pulled off her gloves as she came in from skating. But —I intend to buy her a better one, with jewels to match her eyes!" He squeezed Lenore's hand.

The plumed hat bobbed in approval—and then forgot her, for the bride was coming down the stairs.

A ring . . . Geoffrey meant to give her a ring. Wistfully Lenore remembered the gimmal rings used in the Cotswolds, rings that were separated into two parts—half given at betrothal to the man, half to the maid. Then both halves were united into one ring at the church. As a little girl she had been determined to wear such a ring. Now she knew she never would, but perhaps . . . one with blue stones to match her eyes. Her gloved fingers—which had felt no need of a ring in the wilds or Dartmoor—felt suddenly quite naked, and she twisted them together during the ceremony.

Ned looked so happy . . . not a thought of Lally in his merry gaze. To get her mind off Lally, Lenore studied the bride's crowning circlet of myrtle, which she wore so proudly over her long, dark hair. It reminded her of Meg's circlet of myrtle—though this wealthy bride wore white and Meg had worn russet, as became a village girl.

Lenore sighed. She should not attend weddings. They

reminded her of all that she had lost and all that would never be hers.

After Ned and his Lavinia were pronounced man and wife, all present drank wine with sops in it—and Lavinia shyly dipped in a sprig of rosemary "for everlasting love" before she drank. She giggled as the ribbons were stripped from her gown by eager hands and stuck rakishly into the gentlemen's hats.

Afterward the guests—hardly hungry, for they had already been well stuffed—were seated at long boards covered with linen and embellished by tall silver salts and with a centerpiece of holly and ate their way through a banquet of some fifteen courses. Lenore could hardly force herself to touch another scrap, but Geoffrey and the others seemed to enjoy the roast duck and roast piglet and bullock's heart and boiled fowl, and urged on her the roast beef and oysters and cheese and plum and apple tarts.

"Geoffrey," said Lenore, laughing, "if I eat any more, I will burst!"

He grinned. "Ned's in luck. His bride's family sets a good table!"

Wine flowed so lavishly that as they left the table many of the guests were already weaving, their tongues slurred. But the merriment continued, and that night they all drank the traditional sack posset which was made of spiced wine and milk and eggs and sugar. Voices rang as they toasted the bride's health, the groom's health, the health of all present. And at bedtime, as was the custom, the bridemen gaily pulled off the bride's garters. Lavinia had previously untied them, with much giggling, so that the dangling ribbons hung down and were easily grasped ("else they might grasp my knee instead!" she had cried merrily). Lenore fastened Geoffrey's to his hat, as did the others, and went with the bridesmaids to the bride's chamber, where they helped her undress. With a half-scared look, her eyes enormous, Lavinia climbed into the great feather-bed, sinking down into it as if in a white-capped ocean.

After that the bridesmaids retreated, passing with much giggling the groom, attired for bed with a nightcap hang-

37

ing down over one eye and being escorted to his marriage bed by unsteady-footed friends.

"Ned will ne'er survive it!" grinned Geoffrey. Lenore gave him a wan look. Lally was the one who might not survive this wedding—Ned and Lavinia would be fine, she thought sadly.

No sooner were the couple in bed together than the whole company poured into the room to wish them happiness and drink their health once again. Lenore, exhausted, was glad when the curtains around the great fourposter were finally drawn and the party withdrew below stairs for an evening of revelry. There would be no honeymoon, she knew, for Ned would stay here with the bride's family for a time, and then he would take her to the new house his father was building for them in Somerset on land he had purchased for Ned.

The wedding guests so overflowed the house, and so raucous was their merriment, that sleep was impossible and they made their way back to Oxford, yawning, via the family coach and the ferry at dawn. Lenore knew she looked haggard. Exhausted, she let Geoffrey undress her and put her to bed as if she were a child.

Tenderly he kissed her forehead and drew the coverlet up about her neck and offered her a glass of wine. Lenore shook her head and smiled at him through a daze of fatigue.

"Lenore," he sighed, taking her hand and looking down at her ringless fingers, caressing those fingers as he spoke. "There will be better times for us. When the child is born and you can travel distances again, what say ye to America? In the Colonies a man can indenture himself for, say, four years—and after that he's free again and can make a fortune if he's a mind to."

Lenore's eyes opened wide. For a moment fatigue left her and she felt excited, as she had in the Cotswolds on fair days. The American Colonies seemed far away and hospitable and beyond the law. Who would care there if Geoffrey's name was Wyndham or Daunt? Who would know that he had a French wife?

38

"I'd like that," she said honestly. "Oh, Geoffrey, I'd like that so much."

"I'm trying to arrange it, but 'tis devilish hard without money."

Lenore was smiling as she went to sleep.

Geoffrey had dressed and gone out before she awakened, but she opened her eyes to a loud banging on the door. "Lenore, open the door—Gwynneth had your tray ready and I've brought it up."

Lenore got up and opened the door. Lally brought in the tray and set it down, then straightened up to confront Lenore. Her face was white and drawn. "Is it done, then?" she asked tensely. "And is Ned happy? Oh, Lenore, do you think he will be happy with her?"

Sleepy and disoriented, Lenore stared at Lally. Her rose silk dress was so shimmery, her slate-blue eyes so sad. Lenore pulled up a chair for Lally and went back to sit on the bed. She ran a hand through her long hair.

"It is done," she said. "They are married and"—she studied Lally's mask-like white face—"I think he will be happy with her," she added hesitantly.

"Tell me about it—and eat your breakfast." Lally sank down on the bed studying her gloves; she did not look at Lenore.

"I'm not hungry," sighed Lenore. "Lavinia is pretty and . . . and rather silly. But I think she loves Ned; at least, she seemed very happy."

Lally winced.

"There was a great deal to eat and drink—far too much, and most of the guests were reeling or sleeping it off in corners when I left. Lavinia wore the handsomest bridal gown I have ever seen," Lenore continued. "It was white. All the guests wore beautiful scarves in bright colors, and Ned gave his friends gloves like these." She nodded at the fringed gauntlets Geoffrey had received, which were tossed carelessly on the table beside the tray.

Lally turned to regard them. "Ned always had good taste," she murmured.

"And a deep pocket," said Lenore on a note of

39

asperity. "His father has bought land for him and is building them a home in Somerset."

"So the wedding went well?"

"Yes. The bridesmaids carried rosemary branches—gilded. The ring was plain gold. There were beautiful wedding gifts, and a great deal of dancing and pledging the bride's health, and that night—"

"I think I have heard enough," said Lally in a thick voice. "I only wanted to—" her voice shook—"to know if you think Ned will be happy. And you have told me he will." Suddenly she turned a tormented face to Lenore. "Is—is Lavinia very pretty?" she asked hoarsely.

Lenore nodded, swallowing. "She is a little thing, with a great deal of dark hair and bright eyes and a tiny mouth. She seems lost in her rich gowns, they billow about her, and she smiles a great deal—and giggles. Yes, Lally, she is very pretty."

"I am glad for him," said Lally in a broken voice. She brushed her hand across her eyes and rose. "Ned wanted to provide for me, but I have already made my arrangements."

"You—you have?"

"Yes." Lally moved rapidly to the door. She almost blundered into it, and Lenore guessed her vision was blurred with tears. "I am moving in with Gilbert." She ran through the door with a swish of rose silk skirts and closed it quickly behind her. There was a sound of finality in the closing of that door.

Lenore's heart ached for her. She hoped Lally would find happiness with Gilbert, but she doubted that was possible.

Geoffrey came home, bringing her a pouch of apples—for just before arriving in Marston she had expressed a mad desire for apples. She was full of fitful fancies where food was concerned these days, suddenly dying for a potato or something more exotic at odd hours—and sometimes losing her taste for it, even before it could be procured for her.

She was pleased that Geoffrey had remembered her ardently expressed desire for apples—even though that desire had now departed. Carefully she arranged them in a bowl, polished one against her petticoat, and bit into it. Geoffrey sat down across the table facing her.

"Did you really mean what you said about going to the Colonies, Geoffrey?"

He flashed her a quick smile and polished an apple on his sleeve before he answered. "And would ye like that?"

She nodded.

"Then I must find a way to make it possible." He leaned back, rested a booted foot on a nearby bench, and frowned. "Money is an obstacle, even if one is not so nice in the way one comes by it."

She did not press him. To show too much eagerness might lead him recklessly into danger. Meanwhile there was to be an even more important event—the birth of their first child, conceived on their first, memorable night of loving.

CHAPTER 4

Lenore, who had felt so well during the bulk of her preg-
nancy, now found herself nervous and short-tempered and
full of aches and pains. She felt incensed that as her waist
thickened and she moved about with difficulty, the wild
young lads had all fallen away, leaving only young
Michael, with his cherubic face and dog-like devotion,
who came over and sat with her on the excuse of tutoring
her in penmanship. Even bookish Lewis now occupied
himself elsewhere.

Feeling ill much of the time, her fingers all thumbs as
she tried to work on the baby's layette, she was brusque
and quarrelsome with Geoffrey. He bore it well, blaming
it on her condition. But on gloomy days she fell to brooding about his wife in France and imagined Letiche sailing
for England and converging on Oxford to whisk Geoffrey
away. The unlikelihood of such an event comforted her,
but the thought that it *could* happen gave her world a
sour flavor. Sometimes the wine of youth was turned to
vinegar.

Lally—now living with Gilbert—stopped by some-times, but she was dispirited, not her former breezy self. Once she sported a purple bruise beneath her right eye and replied shortly to Lenore's query that she had fallen. Lenore was sure Gilbert had struck her, and she worried.

"Ned and Lavinia have left Marston—they have gone to Somerset," she told Lenore in a dispirited voice. "He was in Oxford today, and I saw him for a moment. He is very busy overseeing the building of their new home. He said he missed talking to me." She sounded wistful.

Lenore had thought Ned might miss talking to spirited Lally after scatter-brained Lavinia's giggles. "You should forget him," she counseled sternly.

"Easy to say," murmured Lally. "Lenore, the reason I came by today is there's a play being given this afternoon in a barn outside town."

"A play?" Lenore was fascinated. Although plays were strictly forbidden in Cromwell's England and the Puritans had closed the theatres, she had learned in Oxford that there were threadbare roving companies of strolling players who still wandered the back lanes when the weather was clement and held their plays in forest glades, in barns, even in caves. But these were of necessity furtive gatherings, for should the strict Puritan authorities descend on them, they well might fine the audience and whip the players out of town tied to a cart-tail. "I've never seen a play, Lally," Lenore admitted.

"I know 'tis near your time, and with Geoffrey away you hesitate to go out," said Lally. "But there'll be a cart to take a group of us there, and I'd take it as a favor if you'd accompany us, Lenore. You see . . ." she hesitated and her slate-blue eyes were clouded. "I'm not getting along well with Gilbert."

Lenore's gaze flew to Lally's black eye.

"And it's not the first time," Lally muttered. "Although 'tis the first time the bruise *showed*."

"*Leave him!*" cried Lenore fiercely.

"That's what I must decide," said Lally in a weary voice. "But in the meantime, it would help to have some-one . . . along with me today." Her voice faltered a little.

43

"You see, Lenore, it hurts Gilbert's pride that I still love Ned. He can sense it. I suppose that wounds a man."

"Certainly I'll go with you," said Lenore warmly, and Lally gave her hand a quick squeeze and left, promising they'd be back to pick her up.

In the big barn that warm afternoon Lenore sat on a pile of hay beside Lally and watched the play—her first. On her other side a pair of lovers whispered and giggled, never took their eyes off each other, and so missed the entire performance. On Lally's other side Gilbert sulked, rarely laughing even at the actors' best sallies. Lenore watched with rapt attention as the players—all men, though some were dressed in skirts portraying women's roles—wearing their ordinary clothes, presented Will Shakespeare's *A Midsummer Night's Dream*.

But the gaiety of the performance was spoiled for her when, in the general buzz of conversation between acts, a name jumped out at her from someone speaking just behind her: "Letiche d'Avigny," and someone else said, "You mean Letiche Wyndham?"

They were speaking of Geoffrey's French wife!

Lenore sat straighter and then hunched down as another voice muttered sharply, "Hush! Can't you see—?" Lenore scrounged down in the hay and tried to make herself smaller; not for worlds would she have looked behind her to see who was speaking. Lally, who'd been talking to Gilbert in a low tone, turned and asked anxiously, "You're so flushed, Lenore. Do you feel all right?"

She snapped resentfully, "I'm fine," and Lally looked surprised.

But for her the play was ruined. She hardly heard the rest of it and yearned for it to be over. She only nodded when, at the end of the performance, Gilbert seemed to have mellowed and Lally murmured a "thank you" in her ear as the returning party of playgoers let Lenore out at Mistress Watts's in the gathering dusk.

She walked cumbersomely upstairs and opened the door to her lodgings to find Geoffrey waiting for her, hands clasped behind his back, pacing the floor. He swung

44

toward her as she came in, looking exceedingly tall and with a grim expression on his dark face.

"Where've ye been?" he challenged. "Mistress Watts said ye rode off in a cart. I knew not where to seek you."

"I went to a play with Lally and some others," she defended.

"A play!" he exploded. "Lally must be mad! Faith, had the authorities got wind of it and taken actors and audience together in their net, think you they would not have questioned you? 'Tis your life would be forfeit! So Lally is carting you around to plays these days! Does she not know how often such performances are raided?"

"Well, nothing happened," said Lenore in a sulky voice, pulling off her gloves. Actually the jolting ride in the cart had made her feel a bit ill.

He was not to be put off. "Since I cannot always be here to protect you, promise me you'll do nothing rash when my back is turned."

"I do nothing rash whether your back is turned or not!" she flashed. "I wait, wait, wait to have your baby! I'm so awkward I can hardly get around. I'm *tired of waiting*, Geoffrey! And," she added accusingly, "someone in the crowd mentioned *your* French wife."

He looked taken aback, but Lenore, ill and irritable, put her hands to her throbbing temples. "Tell me of Letiche," she said in a hard voice, "for all seem to know more of her than I do!"

Geoffrey sighed. His face looked drawn. "I have told you about her, Lenore."

"Tell me again."

"Lenore, you flay yourself with these thoughts. 'Tis—"

She swung on him like a tigress, her face white, eyes blazing. *"Tell me*, Geoffrey! I have a right to know more about this woman whose very existence denies my child a name!"

"She does not concern you!" he shouted, flung out and was gone for three days.

Feeling desolate, as if Geoffrey might never return, Lenore struggled out and clumsily walked the cobbled streets. She had begun to think much on death. It could

45

be she would die when her baby was born . . . in this city where so many had died before her. Her thoughts were morbid. Oxford was a bloody place. Here in St. Frideswide's priory all the Danes in the city had once been collected and burned alive. Here the murdered Fair Rosamond, Henry II's beautiful mistress, lay buried, her epitaph calling her the Rose of the World . . . and in an unmarked grave somewhere lay Amy, wife to Robert Dudley, that favorite of Queen Elizabeth, who perhaps had had her hurled downstairs to her death in a fit of jealousy.

Mistress Watts sensed Lenore's despondency and had Gwynneth bring her up a hot posset, saying it would give her strength. Cooped up in her lodgings, Lenore fretted, for with her new unwieldy awkwardness, walking tired her. She wandered downstairs and fell into conversation with the cook. The cook had been married ten years and wanted a child. She dipped out a cup of soup from the kettle with a long iron dipper and sat down and told Lenore earnestly that she was drinking the waters—sold at a guinea a bottle—of the holy well behind the little church at Bimsey, said to make women fertile. 'Twas so expensive, she sighed, that if she did not become pregnant soon, they'd have no money to buy a christening gown! She looked at Lenore's girth enviously.

Lenore sipped her soup and listened. Mistress Watts came in and tried to entertain her, briskly maintaining that the house next door was haunted by the ghost of a Puritan housemaid who had been deserted by her Cavalier lover and had died of a broken heart. Lenore gave her a wan smile. She had no assurance at the moment that she too had not been deserted by her cavalier lover.

Lally came by, bearing a beautiful long gown for the baby made of fine linen trimmed in lace. Lally's bruise was fading, she sported a bright, brittle smile and walked with a challenging swagger. Lenore saw how happy she was and brooded about this change in her friend.

She slipped into a terrible despondency, feeling herself as much a prisoner in her upstairs lodgings as those unfortunate university prisoners lodged in the old prison of

46

Bocardo, from which everyone maintained there was no escape. She had seen them lowering collection boxes on long strings, hoping for alms, and had even sent up in compassion a few pennies she could ill afford to give away, when she had chanced to walk by. Even the time she spent in the stable with Snowfire did not cheer her very much.

And so passed the late days of her pregnancy, with the world outside bursting into blossom and Lenore's own heart heavy as she waited for her child to be born.

Though he had left her in anger, Geoffrey came back in a very different mood. She did not hear him ride up, did not even hear his footsteps on the stairs, for she was dozing, lying awkwardly on her back on the big square bed. His touch must have waked her, for she opened her eyes to find him looking down at her as he smoothed back the hair from her pale face, and the expression in his eyes was very tender. "Lenore," he said, "I was wrong to fling out and leave you. I realize that you do not feel well, that you are on edge, that this waiting—especially in our uncertain circumstances—is hard for you. If it is Letiche you wish to hear about, I will tell you of Letiche."

Repentant, now that she had got him back, she reached up and put her fingers against his mouth to silence him. "I have no need to hear, Geoffrey—I was angry."

"Nay, perhaps you do. I thought you understood, but if you do not—a friend of mine told me the d'Avignys were wealthy; I saw for myself how Letiche dressed, how she lived in Brussels. And the d'Avignys were said to have a finer house by far in their native France—in Paris. Little did I know that her parents had spent all their substance to launch Letiche into society in hopes of a rich marriage for her! My friends contrived that I would seem rich myself, with rumors of great estates in the West Indies. Her mother convinced me that little Letiche would inherit the d'Avigny estates near Boulogne, which I knew were extensive. We rushed to one another's arms, each believing the other to possess a great fortune. Came the reckoning, after we were wed. When I admitted I was penniless, Letiche's mother set up a great wailing. A doctor had to

47

be called. It all came out at her bedside then that they'd nothing, either—the great estates near Boulogne were indeed d'Avigny estates, but they belonged to a widowed uncle with two strong young sons of his own! So even though Letiche was an only child and his favorite niece, there was really no dowry, nor any chance of our making our way together."

"And you left her for that? Because she was not rich?" mumbled Lenore.

"Nay, I'd not have left her for that. 'Twas not Letiche's fault that her mother told lies, or that I hoodwinked them. Letiche berated me, 'tis true, but . . . I deserved it. I know not what would have happened had not her mother snatched her from the house and left me with the debts we'd incurred in our brief marriage. I left within the week, and I've neither seen Letiche nor heard from her since. I'm sure the d'Avignys pray daily for word of my death to reach them so Letiche can marry again and bring them the fortune they seek."

"She's—pretty?" This had been plaguing her, but the words came out with an effort.

"Letiche is small and dark and has a round face and a bubbly laugh. Some would not call her pretty, but she has a certain comeliness."

Like Ned's Lavinia, thought Lenore. *Small, dark, bubbly.* Not pretty like Lavinia, perhaps . . . but his wife. Lenore kept her head bowed as she thought about that.

"Have you ever written to her, Geoffrey?"

"No." His answer was emphatic. "Nor do I think she'd relish hearing from me. Lenore, you must know I consider you my wife—and you would be my legal wife, could I but arrange it. And I will guard you and the child you bear me as tenderly as if the words had been spoken over us in some vast cathedral."

"Oh, Geoffrey, I'm so ashamed that I doubted you!" Blinded by tears, she flung herself into his arms. "What more could I ask than that?"

"A great deal more," he said, holding her close, gently caressing her golden hair. "And I would that I could give it to you, Lenore."

48

" 'Tis only that I'm so tired of waiting to have the baby," she sighed. "It makes me irritable, it makes me say things I do not mean."

Geoffrey's arms tightened warmly about her. "Someday," he promised, "things will straighten out for us, Lenore. I've not led much of a life, but once our child is born"—his voice grew rich, telling her how much this baby meant to him— "I promise we'll mend our affairs. There are places where such as we can make a new start . . . The Daunts of Williamsburg, how does that sound to you?"

"The Colonies? Then you meant what you said about going there? 'Twas not just idle talk to cheer me?"

" 'Twas not idle talk. I've been scheming to arrange it. So far all has fallen through, but next week there's a man —a planter, Lenore, who's visiting relatives just three days' ride from here. 'Tis said he's in England looking for an overseer for his Virginia plantations and will pay a good price for the right man. He cares not for politics, but if I impress him well, he could arrange our passage."

Williamsburg . . . far from Letiche, far from France, far from the iron grip of the Lord Protector. "Williamsburg," she murmured, nestling into his arms.

"What troubles me," he admitted, "is that this is the last week of May. Next week will be June. The baby could come while I'm away, but—'tis my only chance to see this man, Lenore. He stays with his relatives but a week."

"I'll be all right," said Lenore staunchly. "Lally will come and stay with me. I'll send her word after you've gone."

He nodded, and held her in his arms for a long time. "You're so brave," he murmured half to himself. "If aught should happen to you . . ."

"Nothing will happen to me, Geoffrey," she insisted.

When Geoffrey rode off, Lenore sent a note to Lally at Gilbert's lodgings.

And received word that Lally had left Gilbert, left Oxford. She had taken only her clothes and her meager jewels. No one knew where she had gone.

To Lenore it was a crushing blow. Lally gone . . . she

had counted on having Lally around when her baby was born . . . she had gone without even saying goodbye. Gilbert must have done something awful to her to make her leave abruptly like that.

Now, for the first time, Lenore felt not merely gloomy, but frightened.

I will not have the baby until Geoffrey gets back, she promised herself nervously. *I will barely move around. I will sit very still and eat little and drink little, and Geoffrey will come back and I will have someone to cling to when the pains come.*

At other times she cursed herself roundly for a coward and deliberately got up and walked about, ate heartily, and told herself that she could do it all alone if necessary.

As it happened, she very nearly did.

She was sitting on a chair by the window, looking out at the rain pattering down from a gray sky, when she saw Michael in his red cloak swinging up the wet street. She sighed. She did not feel at all well, she did not feel like hearing horror stories of terrible times between Town and Gown, nor did she wish to practice her penmanship, which she was sure he would suggest, even though she had grown very passable at it by dogged effort and Michael had even bragged of her progress to Geoffrey. Moving cumbersomely, she went out onto the landing to call down to Mistress Watts that she was unwell today and was not receiving visitors.

Always alert for a meal, the white cat, who had been attentively crouching at a mousehole in the upstairs hall, turned to look at Lenore. The mouse saw its chance and ran out almost under Lenore's feet. She jumped aside with a little cry and collided with Puss, streaking forward intent on the chase.

Trying to dodge the running cat cost Lenore her balance. Her foot caught in the hem of her skirt as she teetered on the top step. She tried vainly to grasp the newel post as her weight, heavy to the front due to her pregnancy, toppled her. With a wild scream she tumbled down the stairs, arriving at the foot just as Michael opened the door.

His face turned white at the sight of her lying there in a crumpled heap, and Mistress Watts, who had heard Lenore scream, came running out. "What have you done to Mistress Daunt?" she cried fiercely.

Michael was taken aback. He gave Mistress Watts a wounded look. "I've done nothing to her. I was coming to call, and when I opened the door she was falling down the stairs." Anxiously he bent over Lenore. "Is she dead, do you think?" he asked fearfully, studying her unconscious form, afraid to touch her.

"Nay, 'tis her time has come, that's all. Let us hope she has broken no bones in her fall. There, you see, she's coming around now"—this as Lenore moved and groaned and opened her eyes—"can you get her upstairs by yourself, or shall I call the stable boy?"

"I can—do it—myself." Panting with effort, for he was not very strong, chunky Michael managed to pick up Lenore and stagger up the stairs with her in his arms. There, under Mistress Watts's clucking supervision, he laid her very carefully on the bed.

"Thank you, Michael," said Lenore weakly. She gasped as a sharp pain went through her.

"Don't talk," said Mistress Watts crisply. She adjusted the coverlet. "I'll send for Mistress Rue, the midwife."

"I'll go for her—'twill be quicker." Michael was obsessed with a need for action. He darted away.

"On Mount Street," Mistress Watts called after him.

Michael, just rushing out the front door, called back something unintelligible and kept going. But he had misheard. He hurried to Blount Street through a heavy shower that soaked him through and searched for Mistress Rue in vain. In rising panic, he blundered about the wet streets and finally ran back over the slippery cobbles to announce in an almost tearful voice that he could not find her. But Mistress Rue was already there, for Lenore's shrewd landlady had seen the state of upheaval Michael was in and had prudently sent her stable boy running to Mistress Rue's.

" 'Tis all right, all right," she assured Michael, for she

was quite pleased with herself that Mistress Rue had arrived so speedily.

"You mean she's here?" he asked incredulously, wondering how this miracle had come to pass.

"Indeed she is," Mistress Watts smiled as Michael slumped down exhausted. "Mister Daunt favored a doctor, you know. 'Twas I persuaded Mistress Daunt to insist on a midwife." In this she had been assisted by Lenore's experiences in Twainmere. "Midwives assisted at the birthings in Twainmere," Lenore had told Geoffrey stubbornly, "and 'tis after all up to me to have this child—neither doctor nor midwife can do it for me."

"And a woman will be more comforting than a man," Mistress Watts had chimed in to add, as she walked by the door and overheard their conversation.

She chose to forget that Geoffrey's dark brows had formed a straight line and he had gone over and closed the door rather hard, although at the time she'd sniffed and thought he should be grateful that she could provide such a good midwife.

And see how well Mistress Rue was doing! She had arrived, fat and bustling and energetic and wearing a large gray linen apron. "What, is Mistress Daunt already in labor?" she'd demanded, tossing her wet cloak to Gwynneth. "Then all the knots about the place must be loosened at once—in the kitchen, indeed in all the rooms!" The woman had foresight. Rushed as she was, she'd bethought her to snatch up an old garment—one that might have been new during the Old Queen's reign—"for luck" to wrap the newborn child in. Ah, this midwife was worth her salt indeed, and would never neglect any of the necessary childbirth charms!

Mistress Watts hurried upstairs. "Ye be lucky!" she beamed. "Mistress Rue is here."

"Where—is she?" gasped Lenore, pale and perspiring from her last bout with the fierce labor pains that had seized her.

"Down in the kitchen seeing that all the knots in the place are loosed."

52

Knots? What was this about knots? Another great pain struck Lenore, and she cried out. "I care not a whit for charms!" she gasped when she could speak again. "Only that my baby be born alive and healthy! Tell Mistress Rue to forget about knots and come upstairs at once!"

Mistress Watts sputtered. So shocked was she by this lack of proper feeling for time-tested charms that she withdrew from the room altogether in a huff and went back downstairs and slammed the door to her quarters.

"Your husband's very young," Mistress Rue observed to Lenore when she finally finished with the knots and went upstairs. For she'd glimpsed Michael sitting on the top step, looking tired and forlorn, and naturally assumed him to be the father.

Lenore gave the midwife a dazed look. She was just coming up out of a well of suffering.

"Never mind," said Mistress Rue, from out of her years of experience. "We'll get you through this, mistress."

But as the hours dragged by and Lenore's condition worsened, Mistress Rue began to look worried. She muttered that she had never placed great reliance in eaglestones herself. "But your husband might run to the church and demand the bells be rung," she suggested, brightening. "Indeed that often eases a difficult labor!"

Lenore, lying weak and pale between pains, said a little testily that the Daunts were of no consequence in Oxford and the bells would doubtless remain silent, no matter what they demanded.

At that declaration, Mistress Rue tore from the room and whispered something in Michael's ear. Michael, who had winced every time he'd heard Lenore groan, got up and went out looking dazed. He came back with a piece of frayed rope, which he silently handed to the midwife. She snatched it from him and went back into the bedchamber.

"We've had this from the bellringers." She waved the piece of rope at Lenore importantly. "It should do almost as well as having the bells rung." She tied the rope around Lenore's waist—rather tightly, for it was a bit too

53

short—and there it remained as a good luck charm until Lenore, screaming in agony, ripped her fingernails in tearing it off.

Mistress Rue clucked in dismay. "Now I must tie this back on," she insisted, moving to do so.

The pain had subsided for the moment, and Lenore gave Mistress Rue a baleful look. "If you even try it, I promise you I will claw your eyes out!"

Mistress Rue straightened up with a wounded look.

"Very well, Mistress Daunt, but if things go badly for you, I am not to be blamed!" She turned to Mistress Watts, whom curiosity had brought up the stairs again to see how matters were going. "She do be a bad patient," the midwife sighed. "I hope that she may not die, but I have attended at two birthings this past month where the ladies did die after they broke the rope—and they do say things happen in threes."

Mistress Watts clucked her tongue and gave Lenore a worried look. Michael, who had overheard this as the door opened to admit Mistress Watts, was slumped down on the stairs looking as if he too might expire. "Do you need more rope?" he croaked.

Mistress Watts turned to say impatiently, "Mistress Daunt refuses to use it."

"I do think he could do with a hot posset," Mistress Rue told the landlady, with an uneasy look at Michael. "Husbands do take on so at birthings!"

Mistress Watts forbore to tell the midwife that Michael was not the father, that the father was off on one of his many trips of which she so heartily disapproved—a man should be at his wife's side at a time like this! She brought Michael a hot posset herself; it was made of hot spiced milk curdled by ale, and he rallied as he drank it.

"Do you think she will live?" he asked in a tragic voice. "I heard what the midwife said."

"Keep your voice down," said Mistress Watts sharply. "And why would she not live, a fine strong girl like her? Mistress Rue is always looking on the dark side—but then, she sees so many as won't follow her instructions."

54

"But you heard her say Lenore broke the rope and tore it off!"

"Ah, but we've countered that with the knots we've loosened." She looked sharply at Michael. "Have ye any knots about ye?"

"I don't think so—yes, yes, I have!" Excitedly Michael scrabbled at his pursestring, a narrow leather thong, which he kept knotted for safety's sake.

"There, that may be what's been causing the trouble!" Mistress Watts told him triumphantly, when at last his awkward fingers had it untied, and Michael sank back, much relieved and feeling terribly guilty that the knot of his pursestring should have been holding back the birth.

It was a difficult birth. The hours dragged by, day slipped into night, and Lenore thought that terrible night would never end. She gripped the soaked bedding and fought down screams as her back arched in agony and her hand gripped Mistress Rue's with a pressure that numbed the midwife's fingers. She screamed for Geoffrey, and once for Meg, and could not understand the midwife's crooning answers. For a time the whole world seemed to turn to a hot blackness and there was only the pain, a livid leaping thing, knifing through her body as if to rend her apart. She came to, out of a long-drawn-out agony, in a red haze, dimly aware that the midwife was speaking to her.

"A fine lovely daughter ye have, mistress!" The fat puffing midwife was chortling. She held up the child as proudly as if she'd borne it herself. "I'll be calling the father to come in now—I do think he's gone to sleep out there on the steps. He'll be so pleased!"

"No—wait," murmured Lenore, reaching out for the baby, and the midwife handed the small precious bundle that was her daughter to her and went out to call Mistress Watts and Michael.

Weak and exhausted, with her face wet with perspiration and her hair plastered to her forehead, Lenore looked with wonderment at the small sweet creature she was holding so carefully.

She had done it! She had done it! She felt a thrill go

55

through her that was like none she had ever known. Her daughter! Out of that scalding night of pain, she held her daughter in her arms at last. Tears of joy trembled on her lashes as with a fierce sweet tenderness she cradled her baby.

She looked up in triumph, violet eyes aglow, as Mistress Watts entered the room. To the confusion of the midwife, Mistress Watts had just banished Michael sternly from the stairs and told him he could sleep in the common room downstairs, since curfew had long since sounded and the watch would get him if he left now. The midwife looked appalled at this, and turned to Michael as if expecting him to assert his rights.

"I'm not the father," Michael admitted sheepishly.

"Not the father?" Mistress Rue looked at Michael in bewilderment. "Then who's to pay me?" she demanded in a strident voice. "I'd not have come if—"

"Here, I'll pay you!" Hastily Michael pulled money out of his untied purse and counted out coins into the midwife's hand. "Is that enough?" he asked her doubtfully.

It was more than she'd expected. Mistress Rue closed her fingers on the coins and sniffed. An odd household, this! With a man who was not the father pacing the floor outside, and a woman giving birth who was so reckless of charms she'd near killed herself birthing! Determined to say as much, now that she'd been paid—and also that she doubted Lenore could have any more children—she followed Mistress Watts into the room.

There she found Mistress Watts almost in tears herself just to see the glorious expression in Lenore's violet eyes. With a rare instinct for a precious moment, kindly Mistress Watts hurried the protesting midwife away to let Lenore enjoy these first moments with her baby in private.

Raptly, by the light of a single taper, Lenore studied that small sweet face. What a great beauty she would grow up to be! she thought fondly. Already she was beautiful. *Her daughter!* It was hard to realize that she, Lenore Frankford, had a daughter! Although she had wanted a boy, had fully intended to name him Geoffrey, all thought of that was gone now, and the small pink child in her

56

arms seemed the most desirable thing on earth. Her daughter . . .

I will name her Lorena, she thought dreamily. *For my mother.*

She cradled the baby in the crook of her arm. "You must grow up beautiful—and strong, Lorena," she murmured, cuddling the child to her. "For your father cannot give you his name, and you will have to fight the world for your birthright. I will help you." Gently she hugged the baby. "But most of it will be up to you."

Then she laughed at herself for trying to counsel a newborn infant, and went deeply, peacefully to sleep with Lorena warm and pink beside her.

It was the third of June, 1652. Outside the midnight bells were chiming in the rain.

CHAPTER 5

Michael bustled in the next morning, chafing because Mistress Watts had sternly denied him entrance to Lenore's lodgings until she had been served her breakfast tray. Had he but known it, he had also waited until Mistress Daunt had completed her morning toilette. She had combed out her long, bright hair, let it fall loose around her shoulders as she fed the baby, and when she lay back it spread luxuriantly over the pillow. She had wound the long gown Lally had given her for this occasion round and round the baby to keep her feet and body toasty warm, arranged the baby in the crook of her arm for viewing, and smiled as Michael entered the room.

He tossed his red cloak onto a chair and came and gazed at Lenore as she lay in the big bed with a kind of reverent awe. Lenore was touched by the look of wonder in his eyes. Michael had been a devoted friend, and she was positive he must have had a very bad night because of her.

"Isn't she beautiful?" she asked him, gazing fondly at Lorena.

Michael looked at Lenore, with her red-gold hair tumbled in shimmering masses about the pillow, her skin—from the long winter and being indoors so much—pearly and sheer. He swallowed. " 'Tis you who are beautiful!" he declared intensely. "Ah, Lenore, Lenore." He sank down on his knees beside the bed. "Sometimes I think I will die of love of you!"

Lenore looked at him in trepidation. She had known Michael loved her in a young, unformed way; that he had cherished secret thoughts about her she had long since guessed. But now to look at that woebegone cherubic countenance, flushed and earnest, and to hear his boyish voice blurting out such things. . . !

"Michael," she said, distressed, "you must not say such things to me—not even if you think them. You must remember that I am a married woman."

Though he reddened still further at this soft rebuff, Michael sturdily held his ground, impelled by desperation and by last night's very real threat of losing her. "Gossip has it ye are not married to Geoffrey, that he leaves ye alone while he prowls the highroads with a scarf over his face, seeking coaches to plunder!" The abject pain in his voice took away the sting of his words.

" 'Tis true we are not legal wed in a church, Geoffrey and I," Lenore said carefully, "but we are wed in our hearts, Michael—'tis a bond I cannot break, nor would if I could."

He looked so crestfallen that she reached out and touched his hand. "You are very young," she said gently, "and when—"

"I am older than you!" he interrupted defiantly.

In years, perhaps, she thought, but women of his age were having babies, while he was still at his books. She sighed. "Someday you will understand. Perhaps by then you will have met a girl who means as much to you as I do to Geoffrey."

His voice roughened in despair. "I want no other girl!

59

And you mean more to *me* than you do to Geoffrey! Ah, but say the word, Lenore, and I will take you away and shelter you and the babe—"

She put gentle fingers to his lips to silence him. "These things may be thought, Michael, but they must not be said," she told him sternly. "Your mother has great plans for you. I know, for you have told me so."

"I would take you home to her," he sulked.

And she would throw me out! thought Lenore wryly. She could well imagine the scene if young Michael showed up with the Angel of Worcester in tow—and carrying a newborn babe! "Your mother would faint at such an alliance," she reproved him. "Michael, I am honored that you love me, but—"

"But—you will stay with Geoffrey?" he finished for her.

She nodded, smiling a little sadly.

Michael sighed, got up off his knees, and dusted them off. She had the faintly amused feeling that he had been delighted to unburden himself of his feelings, but that he was also faintly relieved that she had not taken him up on his rash proposal.

"Wouldst tell Mistress Watts that I have finished with my breakfast tray, Michael?" This small errand, she felt, would give him a chance to retire gracefully and collect himself.

He gave her a pensive look. "I'll tell her on my way out, Lenore."

"Come back soon, Michael—I don't know what I'd have done without you." She pressed his hand, and he stood looking down at her with big reproachful eyes in his youthful cherub face, then clattered downstairs and was gone.

Not till after he had left did she learn from Mistress Watts that he had paid the midwife. It embarrassed her that he had done so, and she was sorry she had not known so that she could thank him.

The rain that had begun on the day of Lorena's birth continued to drizzle down. But word reached Oxford from muddy farmers who struggled through mired roads into the city with their carts that the rains were worse to the south. There it rained steadily for days and washed out all the roads. Lenore was not surprised that Geoffrey was late in returning, for he must have found his way blocked by torrential rains that made the roads impassable.

Lenore, at first unable to walk, began to mend. Her natural youth and strength prevailed, and by the time Geoffrey returned—slogging in from the south through deep mud that made the bay's chest heave with exertion—she was up and about, dressed in the green dress she had been wearing when she met him—although she had made herself a new white cambric petticoat. And in her arms was clutched her small daughter, whose frosting of pale hair haloed a small head and framed a small face of surpassing beauty.

What matter that Lorena's hair was pale and Geoffrey's dark? She was so proud of Lorena! She could hardly wait to exhibit her to Geoffrey.

It was midafternoon when he came in. The drizzle that had greened up moss all over Oxford had stopped at last, but the skies were still sullen, gray clouds chased each other overhead, and the air was damp. Lenore heard him running up the stairs three at a time, and her heart thudded with joy. Geoffrey was back!

Quickly she snatched Lorena up from the bed and seated herself gracefully on a chair by the window where the light would glow on her red-gold hair and Lorena's moonlight frosting. She had planned for Geoffrey to see them thus—a lovely sight for a new father, she thought.

The door came open as if blown by a gust. Lenore started, and the motion tipped the blanket she was holding down around the top of baby Lorena's head. Geoffrey strode in, tall and energetic, on muddy boots. His cloak was flying, and he tossed his hat on a chair and came toward her pulling off his gauntlets. His gray eyes lit up to see her sitting there, slender and beautiful again, with her bright hair agleam and her eyes shining in greeting.

"Lenore!" His voice was deep-timbred as he bent to kiss her. "And who's this? Don't hide the baby under

61

a blanket—let me see his face!" He sounded so happy Lenore wanted to cry.

"*Her* face, Geoffrey," she corrected huskily. "We have a daughter."

Gently she drew back the blanket that had slid down almost obscuring the baby's eyes, and Lorena, who had been sleeping, opened her eyes—they were big and blue —and stared up in wonder at the dark, smiling visage that looked down into hers. The blanket slid back to show that small perfect head and the frosting of silky pale hair.

"A daughter!" Geoffrey stared down at the baby eagerly. Then his features stiffened, and his jaw seemed to harden into iron; it was a furious look he flung at Lenore.

"Her hair is white as hemp and her eyes are blue!" he accused her.

"All babies' eyes are blue," defended Lenore, encircling Lorena with protective arms.

" 'Tis not mine!" he cried, and she winced at the note of anguish in his harsh voice. " 'Tis the child of that fellow at Worcester!"

From the moment she'd seen the baby's coloring—so identical with Jamie's—Lenore had feared he would say that, but she had deliberately put the thought from her. "And is that so terrible?" she demanded. "You knew I was handfasted before you!"

"Yes," he said hoarsely, "I knew it—damn you! You've cheated me! Ye said the child was mine!"

Fury gave her strength. She leaped to her feet with the child clutched in her arms. Her body was rigid with rage and the agony of Geoffrey's betrayal. "How dare you accuse me!" she shouted. *"You with a wife in France!"* She fell to crying stormily.

He flung out, slamming the door so hard the house shook, and she heard his boots clatter loudly down the stairs.

Anger and disappointment and fright fought within her. She set Lorena down carefully, clawed at the casement, got it open, and stuck her head out. Geoffrey was just remounting the bay, who looked tired and woebegone.

"Where are you going?" she screamed.

62

"To France!" Geoffrey roared back at her and was off around the corner into Magpie Lane as if driven by devils.

Lenore slammed the casement—so hard the leaded panes nearly splintered—and fell back, covering her face with her hands, trying to control her sobs. Lorena, who until now had been quiet and bewildered, gave a sudden cry and Lenore picked her up. Wounded to the heart, Lenore grimly surveyed the tiny, perfect child in her arms through tear-wet eyes. What if Lorena did have Jamie's hemp-white hair and blue eyes? A beauty she was, so tiny and soft. Lenore held her and rocked her and wept afresh. This was *her* child, no matter who the father was! Hers to cherish, hers to love!

Never for an instant did she believe that Geoffrey meant his threat about going to France. But Mistress Watts, who had been just coming in from marketing when Geoffrey left, heard it and believed it and sent word on her own account to Gilbert. "For I know you are Mister Daunt's cousin," she wrote, "and that you would wish no harm to come to Mistress Daunt. Especially now that the baby has come."

Lounging in his cluttered lodgings, Gilbert read the note thoughtfully and crumpled it. Geoffrey gone to France, leaving the beauteous Lenore? He could hardly credit it! He got up and went on a tour of the taverns and found Geoffrey, lying drunk at a disreputable alehouse at Headington Quarry. Obviously Geoffrey had chosen a place where he would not be likely to encounter any of his friends. Gilbert went and stood over his tall cousin, stretched out on a bench and snoring lustily.

A very vicious smile lit Gilbert's handsome face. He fingered the jaw Geoffrey had struck, and thought of the delights of holding Lenore in his arms. There was a way to induce her to his bed, which Lally had so lately left and which was in dire need of warming these nights by someone better than drunken Dorothy, the tavern maid.

He turned about to go and speak to the tavernkeeper, a brawny giant of a man who watched him silently, great arms folded. As he did so his foot caught on a loose board. He tripped and was thrust against a wooden table before he could right himself. With a curse he got his footing again, never noting that the rough table edge had torn off one of his fancy enameled buttons. It had rolled unnoticed against Geoffrey's arm, which dangled to the floor from the bench.

Seeing the proprietor eyeing him, Gilbert thoughtfully dusted himself off and looked around him. Save for the snoring Geoffrey, he and the tavernkeeper were alone here.

"That long, tall fellow with the black hair." Gilbert's casual nod indicated Geoffrey's prone figure. "Do you think you could keep him drunk for a week?"

The tavernkeeper scratched his head with a stubby finger and studied this caramel creation with shrewd, practiced eyes. Gentlemen didn't often frequent his establishment, and here were two on the same day. The first had spun into the place in a fury and drunk alone, but this one with the hard caramel eyes—up to no good, he reasoned.

"Now that might be done for a price," he admitted. "But 'twould take an ocean of ale, for it took an ocean of ale to put him on his back there."

Deliberately Gilbert was counting out coins. They fell from his gloved hand with little tinkles onto a scarred wooden table top. At the sight of gold, the tavernkeeper's eyes glinted with greed.

"Here's the price," Gilbert said in a ruthless voice. "I care not how you do it, but keep him here for a week. He's not to know I ordered it, he's to see no one, talk to no one."

"I've a back room." The tavernkeeper's big hand swept up the coins. "Leastways, there's a curtain that separates it." He nodded toward some filthy hangings.

"Nay," said Gilbert thoughtfully. "That would make him suspicious when he wakes. Ye'd best leave him where he is—just keep pouring ale into him."

"Aye, that I will." The tavernkeeper winked. "A husband, I'll be bound? And you plan to frolic with the wife while he tarries here?"

Gilbert gave him a wintry look from flat caramel eyes.

64

"Just see that he stays where he is," he said with a thin smile. "And there'll be more coins for you."

As he left, the landlord—galvanized by this sudden wealth—was trying to pour ale down the unconscious Geoffrey's throat.

The first night Geoffrey was gone, Lenore frowned angrily and flounced off to bed. The next day she sought out Mistress Watts to ask if anyone had seen Geoffrey.

For once Mistress Watts's cheerful composure cracked. "Men!" she declared gloomily. "They'll be the death of us! If they're not off getting themselves killed in wars, they're home deserting us for other women! Though why any man would leave a face like yours is a puzzle."

"He already has a wife," said Lenore in a thick voice. She had a desperate need for someone to confide in.

"I knew that, my dear," said her landlady bluntly. "For all knew your lover's name to be Wyndham and not Daunt, as he claimed. But I presumed you knew and did not care."

"I—cared," said Lenore haltingly. "But I—I found out about her too late." Ah, was that the truth? she asked herself wildly. Would she not have succumbed to Geoffrey's charms in any event? And where had it led her?

"Did . . . everyone know I was not his wife?" she asked painfully.

"All within the range of Master Gilbert's voice," was the wry response. "For I think he sought to supplant Master Geoffrey in your affections and did not wish to be thought dangling after another man's wife."

Lenore was overwrought. "Tell Master Gilbert for me," she said with suppressed violence, "that I hope he sinks into the pit!"

Mistress Watts sighed and tried to reason with Lenore. "This is no time to be taking on this way. Now that Mistress Lally has departed, 'tis surely Master Gilbert you must turn to now."

Such blazing anger gripped Lenore that she felt her head must melt. "I would as soon bed a demon—tell him that, too!"

65

"Then . . . where will you go? What will become of you?"

Lenore guessed this was Mistress Watts's subtle way of telling her the lodgings must be paid for, and a woman with a small babe had scant chance of earning a living.

"Geoffrey cannot have left me," she said, taking a deep breath. "He would not do that."

"Fine gentlemen have a way of leaving."

There was so much bitterness in Mistress Watts's voice as she said that, that for all her misery, Lenore cast a startled look at her landlady. That hatchet-face had once been young and piquant. Those eyes, melting . . . That dumpy figure had once been ripe and supple. Mistress Watts, too, had loved and lost. For a moment Lenore, who felt bereft herself, pitied Mistress Watts, trying to make do with her elderly suitor across the street.

"I must go and look for Geoffrey," she said abruptly. "He may be lying hurt somewhere."

Mistress Watts shook her head as determined young Mistress Daunt climbed the wooden stairs and returned again carrying Lorena, wrapped in a shawl. "You're not taking the baby?" she cried, scandalized.

"I must," said Lenore simply. "I shall walk all over town and inquire about Geoffrey—and I cannot keep coming back here to feed Lorena. She'd best go with me."

Mistress Watts was still shaking her head as her determined young lodger went out the door.

Into the town went Lenore, asking all of Geoffrey's friends if they had seen him. Encountering Michael on the High Street, she hailed him and asked him to help her in her search. Michael assented eagerly, glad to be of service to his adored Lenore. He looked in all the wrong places, earnestly searching the halls of the university, the Ashmoleum Museum, the Magdalen Tower, the churches. He seemed to think Geoffrey might be hiding from Lenore with a good book. Crestfallen, he had to admit he'd come up with nothing.

Lenore did not give up easily. She made the rounds of likely taverns and asked all his friends again. None had

66

seen him for more than a fortnight, they swore—and all were telling the truth, for none of them frequented the disreputable alehouse at Headington Quarry, where Geoffrey was having more ale poured down his gullet every time he sat up. It did not occur to her to ask Gilbert, nor would she have gained the truth if she had.

Five days later, with all avenues of information exhausted, Lenore faced the bleak fact that Geoffrey was not going to return. And now the pain that went through her was of a different kind, but in its way as sharp and deep as the pain of Lorena's birth. Geoffrey was gone. He had deserted her in anger.

And without even a goodbye.

Her face must have reflected this terrible new certainty, for her landlady, when Lenore came downstairs asking as usual if Mistress Watts had heard anything, gave her a sharp look. "Your fine gentleman's really gone," she surmised. "Ach, that's the way they go—once the babe is born."

Lenore couldn't speak. She made her way unsteadily upstairs and sat down to think.

She couldn't stay here. That was plain. She had only a few coins left, not enough to pay for her lodgings—not enough to repay Michael for the midwife. Soon she'd be turned out. Mayhap she'd end up in debtors' prison. She had no trade, no way of earning a living except as a serving-woman—and even that would be difficult. For times were lean in England now, and soldiers, crippled in Cromwell's wars, limped about willing to work for a pittance, their wives reduced to slatterns who slaved for their keep, their children often begging on the streets for their very bread. Lenore shuddered. Her little Lorena must not come to that!

She could ask Mistress Watts for work—but that would mean supplanting poor Gwynneth, who so badly needed her job. And Gwynneth's meager salary would not furnish housing for herself and Lorena and stabling for Snowfire. And—and anyway, it would be very hard staying in Oxford and serving ale in some tavern—though she guessed she might find a job in one, for men liked to look at her

67

as they sipped their ale. But in Oxford she would constantly run into friends of Geoffrey's, who would be embarrassed for her and pity her, and Gilbert could come and lord it over her. She ran a distraught hand through her hair. No, she would not stay in Oxford.

It did not occur to her to sell herself on the street, or to try to move in with Michael, who would have been glad to have her. Her mind didn't work that way. Instead, she pondered the possible alternatives of making her own way.

Her hands were clenched white in her lap. *I will not let him wreck me,* she told herself fiercely. *I will make my way alone.*

But how to do that? That was the problem.

At last she thought she had the answer. She would have to leave here, of course. But there were things to do first.

She sat down and penned a note to Michael, sending it by Jack, the stable boy. In it she thanked him again for all he had done and asked him for his family's address, since she knew he was soon to leave the university, and she wished to repay him the money he had laid out for her to Mistress Rue as soon as she was able.

Then she went downstairs and sought out her landlady, who was occupied with counting the spoons and looked up with a frown at Lenore's approach. "Two spoons missing," she muttered. "That careless Gwynneth! Probably thrown out with the slops!"

"I have not the money to pay what I owe you." Lenore came to the point at once. "And since Geoffrey has left me, I am not like to get any money here."

"Ye can stay without money," interrupted Mistress Watts with an expansive gesture that knocked the spoons to the floor. "Oh, dear—see what I've done! There's plenty of room, Mistress Daunt, and ye'll find a way, ye'll find a way." She was thinking that Gilbert, whose mother sent him money from time to time, would be glad to pay the bill for Lenore's lodgings—if not, some other young buck. And she would come to it, given time!

Lenore, helping her pick up the spoons, took her meaning and frowned. "No, I cannot do that," she said soberly.

"I know that you rent lodgings for your livelihood and cannot afford to have beggars such as myself occupying them. Do you chance to know where there's a fair being held, Mistress Watts?"

Mistress Watts straightened up and took the spoons Lenore held out. "A fair? Well, I did hear there was to be one at Banbury. Next week, I think—no, perhaps it is going on now."

"Then I'm to Banbury. I'll send you the money I owe you—if not from Banbury, from another fair."

Mistress Watts was aghast. Surely young Mistress Daunt did not propose to sell herself to the fair-goers—'twas known fairs were the haunts of prostitutes, who had rich pickings there of farmers and drovers on holiday!

"And now if I could ask cook to provision me for my journey to Banbury?" Mistress Watts looked taken aback, but Lenore reached in her purse. "I have enough money left for that."

"I'll tell her," said Mistress Watts, taking the money. "But I do think ye are making a mistake, Mistress Daunt."

Cook liked young Mistress Daunt for her spirited ways. She packed a big square of linen with brown bread and Cheshire cheese and apples and plum tarts and left it hanging over the newel post.

Puzzled by the urgent tone of Lenore's note, Michael hurried over and knocked at Lenore's door.

"Come in," she called over her shoulder, and glanced up as he entered. "Oh—hello, Michael." She hoped he wasn't going to try to persuade her to stay.

"Why, where are you going?" he burst out, seeing that Lenore was busy packing her belongings.

"Can ye not see?" asked Lenore irritably, without raising her eyes from folding a petticoat. "I'm taking my leave of Oxford before I pile up mountains of debts I can't pay and they send me off to debtors' prison."

"I could lend ye a little," he ventured, frowning.

Lenore straightened up and smiled into his eyes—albeit it was a wan smile. She was touched by Michael's offer, knowing how straitened were his circumstances. For all his fine clothes, Michael's parents kept him on a paltry

69

allowance that allowed him few luxuries, and she felt deep in his debt already. "I couldn't do that," she said gently.

"Lenore," he said earnestly, his cheeks pink with emotion, "come home with me. I would be *so glad* to take care of you."

She patted his shoulder, looking ruefully into his flushed face. "I know you would, Michael, but . . . I couldn't."

"I know." He flinched a little. "I would promise not to touch you. I would remember that you belong to Geoffrey —wherever he may be."

She gave him a long, sad look. "No." Her mouth twisted bitterly. "Never again will I belong to Geoffrey. I belong to myself alone. As to where Geoffrey is, he's gone to France. He shouted that was where he was going as he left. I didn't believe him—then. But now I do."

Michael digested this. "Perhaps you might change your mind about me later?" he ventured. "Since you're a free woman at last."

Lenore turned away lest he see the agonized look in her violet eyes. Free? Would she ever be free of Geoffrey? Would a night ever pass with the wind sighing in the trees that she would not remember his lips, his burning touch, the strong masculine feel of him in her arms? She'd be alone . . . but not free.

Her lips denied it. "Yes," she said woodenly. "I'm a free woman at last. But"—from shadowed lashes she considered him, feeling compassion for his youth, his hopeless love for her—"I am not apt to change my mind about you, Michael," she added sadly.

"I see." He spoke hurriedly. "Can I help you pack, then?"

She shook her head. "I've little to pack, just what I can take in my saddlebags. Mainly I'm trying to clean up these rooms so they'll be no trouble to Mistress Watts and Gwynneth after I'm gone—she'll be wanting to show them to let." She was polishing the leaded windowpanes with a scrap of woolen cloth as she spoke.

"Where will ye go, Lenore?" Michael asked soberly.

70

"First, to Banbury, where Mistress Watts tells me a fair is being held."

"A—a fair?" he faltered, waiting for an explanation.

"Yes. I plan to race Snowfire there. That's how I'm going to support myself, Michael—by racing Snowfire at the fairs, wherever they are held."

"You—you mean to ride the length and breadth of England with a suckling babe in your arms . . . *racing at the fairs?*" He looked at her incredulously. "But the prizes are usually only a turkey or a small purse at best!"

Lenore nodded grimly. "I've had a taste of it. 'Tis not so much the purse or the fat turkey—'tis the wagers. I'll goad men into wagering good money because they cannot admit that a woman can beat them!" Her jaw hardened, remembering big Hobbs, who had tried to run her off the track at Wells.

"But—but ye've no money to wager!" he gasped.

"Pebbles will make a purse heavy," said Lenore. "And if I should lose, why then—why then, I will indenture myself to pay the debt!"

Michael was beyond speech. He looked at Lenore as if she had taken leave of her senses—a woman racing at the fairs, indeed! And wagering without money!

"At least, let me accompany you to Banbury," he pleaded. "For I'm quitting Oxford, as you know. I was going next week, but no matter, I might as well leave now."

"No," said Lenore absently. "Your mother will expect you home speedily, Michael. You must not linger at Banbury."

"But Coventry lies to the north of Banbury, Lenore. Banbury is on my way—I always stop there to eat cakes, Banbury's famous for its cakes!"

Lenore wasn't sure whether she believed him, but she knew she'd be very glad of his company as far as Banbury. Michael, at least, had stood by her. In the uncertain new life on which she was about to venture, it would be good—at least for a little while—to have a friend. Her smile was sad. "You are too good to me, Michael. I

71

would I could pay you for what you laid out to the midwife, Michael."

" 'Tis no matter." His voice was rough. "I was glad to do it, Lenore. I—I kept wishing the child was mine."

Lenore swallowed. His devotion was foolish but overwhelming.

"Michael," she said, "I will win enough at the fairs, I promise, to repay you all that you have spent on me."

"Win enough you may," he declared fiercely, "but you cannot make me take it!"

She smiled and leaned over and gave him a light kiss. His face flamed up as her lips brushed his. Later she was to remember that moment, and be so glad she had kissed him.

"I'll take you to a good dinner at the Crown and tomorrow we'll start out," he told her energetically.

Lenore shook her head. "I owe Mistress Watts too much already, and I mean to leave today. Cook has provisioned me. I am almost ready."

"But you cannot be in such a rush as that to be out of town," cried Michael, upset. "I'll rush home now and pack my saddlebags—the boxes can follow me later!"

"All right," Lenore assented. "I'll wait for you here, but do hurry, Michael. I like not the idea of spending a night on the road."

"There's a good inn," he began, but she waved him away.

"Hurry." She gave him a small push.

Michael had barely sprinted around the corner of Magpie Lane when Gilbert turned into it from a different direction. He has estimated his timing to be exactly right. With Geoffrey five days gone, Lenore should be at her wits' end, a ripe plum for the picking. Briskly he headed for Mistress Watts's establishment, slapped on his plumed hat, and opened the door.

"Not back yet?" he asked Mistress Watts, brows lifted in interested query, when he encountered the landlady in the downstairs hall.

"If ye mean Mister Daunt, that he's not," said Mistress Watts with tightly compressed lips. "And it's as well, I say, to be rid of him—a man who would leave his poor lady thus right after she's borne him a child!"

"True, true," agreed Gilbert piously. "And how does she take it—Mistress Daunt?"

"She has been very upset," confided Mistress Watts. "But now she packs, poor lady."

"Packs?" Gilbert was startled; this was one contingency that had not occurred to him. "Faith, I should dissuade her!" He hurried by the landlady, mounted the stairs on his high yellow heels, and knocked on Lenore's door.

Lenore had been burning her used parchment and trash on the hearth, preparatory to leaving. Now she was bent over, impatiently stirring the fire with a poker to make it burn faster. "Come in," she called over her shoulder, thinking it was Mistress Watts.

"Lenore, what is this foolishness I hear about your packing?" Gilbert came in and closed the door behind him, a foppish and elegant figure in honey-colored satins.

At the sound of that voice, Lenore straightened up, the red-hot poker still in her hand. She turned a malevolent face toward Gilbert, unaware that she looked very wild and beautiful as she stood there with her face flushed by the June heat and the roaring flames. "I am leaving," she said in a cold voice. "Kindly get out." Since he did not move to go, she walked toward him and seized the door handle as if to usher him through it.

"Lenore, Lenore." Gilbert's voice was indulgent. He moved toward the door and took her shoulder in a light grip. She flinched and jerked away. "Ye could move in with me. I'd accept the babe——"

Lenore seemed to grow taller. Her voice quivered with fury.

"At least I am spared that," she said grimly. "Now that Geoffrey is gone, I've no longer need to protect him from you! Let me not see your face again!"

"Lenore, you don't mean that." The caramel curls bent forward as he seized her shoulder again, insistently. "Think how it was with us," he urged. "Remember! I'd treat ye better than Geoffrey. Ah, Lenore, ye must re-

73

member the night ye spent in my arms—the joys we shared!"

In a wave of revulsion Lenore twisted away from him and drew back the poker. A moment later its red-hot tip had snaked through the air and landed with force on Gilbert's cheek. With a howl he fell back against the door-jamb, eyes wild as he regarded her, clutching his face with his hands.

"I have *longed* to do that!" she choked. "Get you gone, or I'll mark your other cheek as well!"

Gilbert turned and lunged through the open door. "I'll see ye hanged for this!" he cried, almost sobbing with rage and pain. "Think not ye can mark me and go scot-free! I'll tell the authorities who you are!"

"Tell them!" screamed Lenore, following him to the stair landing, poker raised threateningly. "Tell them who marked you! *Tell them why!*" Her angry voice followed him as he plunged down the stairs and into the alley, blundering around the corner into Magpie Lane.

When he had gone, she flung the poker away from her in revulsion. Pale and shaken, she swept up her baby in her arms and ran down the stairs, picking up the linen square of food the cook had left draped over the newel post as she went. There was no time to lose; she must take Lorena and make her run for it. Before Gilbert could make good his threat, before the authorities came.

"Tell Michael when he comes that I've ridden on ahead," she called to the open-mouthed Mistress Watts, who had witnessed Gilbert's headlong descent down the stairs with Lenore at the top brandishing the poker. "Tell him to ride hard and catch up with me—if he doesn't, I'll wait for him at the first crossroads. I'll remember to send you the money. Thank you for everything—and goodbye."

Running away with Michael! Mistress Watts was caught speechless. She stood and watched the beauty who'd been the toast of Oxford hurry to the stables and come back riding Snowfire. At that point she recollected herself and ran forward. "Mistress Daunt, Mistress Daunt!"

Lenore paused impatiently as Mistress Watts hurried

74

up and clutched her skirt. "I did not like to tell you before when you were so upset, but now that you're going, I'll not have another chance. I ran across Mistress Rue and she said she thought you'd been hurt somehow in your fall down the stairs and that ye were not like to have any more children."

"My fall? Or perhaps 'twas Mistress Rue's bungling," said Lenore bitterly. "Tying a rope around me while I was in labor!"

Mistress Watts looked shocked. "A good midwife she is," she protested, bridling. "The best in Oxford!"

Lenore gave her a sardonic look. "Mistress Watts, if you marry your suitor across the street and decide to present him with a child, I suggest you lock Mistress Rue out of your house—you'll do much better!"

"Well! Well!" Mistress Watts hardly knew what to say.

Lenore's face softened. "You've been very good to me, Mistress Watts, lending me your eagle-stones, and letting us make so much noise you might have landed in the stocks!" She leaned down and planted a quick kiss of gratitude on Mistress Watts's cheek, and the older woman beamed with pleasure and sniffled.

"Do you take care now, Mistress Daunt," she admonished Lenore.

Lenore took a deep breath. "Not Mistress Daunt—Lenore Frankford!" Her voice rang.

Mistress Watts looked nonplussed at this public declaration, delivered in the street. "Fine gentlemen do let us down," she said weakly.

"Don't they?" agreed Lenore in a hard voice. "Goodbye, Mistress Watts! Tell all my friends goodbye for me." She started to ride away, but Mistress Watts still clung insistently to her skirt.

"Suppose—suppose Mister Daunt comes back, after all?" she faltered.

"From France?" Lenore gave a short, scornful laugh. "Not likely! But if he does, tell him to go to the devil!"

She brushed off Mistress Watts's restraining hand, wheeled her horse and galloped away down the street, for tears were springing to her eyes and she did not want

75

Mistress Watts to see them—she did not want anyone to see them.

From the corner, Lenore turned and waved a hand at Mistress Watts, who still stood in the street bemused. For a moment her gaze lingered on the plain Tudor exterior of the lodgings that had meant so much to her. She was saying goodbye to her first home of her own where so much, both good and bad, had happened to her . . . the place where her little Lorena had been born.

Squaring her slender shoulders, she turned down Magpie Lane, keeping her gaze straight ahead. It was all behind her now: Oxford . . . all of it. She had a new life to make, and make it she must—not for herself, but for that small pink bundle sleeping in her arms. She must make a life for little golden Lorena.

She was galloping past Michael's lodgings—which lay directly on her way out of the city heading north—when a shout hailed her, and she turned to see Michael himself leaning out of an upstairs window. "Lenore, where are you going?" he cried. "Lenore!"

Reluctantly she reined in. "Catch up with me!" she called. "I must go!"

"I'm coming!" he cried desperately. "Wait!" He turned from the window and collided with Barney Claypoole, who had the rooms upstairs and who had come down to help him pack.

"What, won't she wait for you?" Barney's brown eyes were laughing at him.

Michael regarded Barney steadily from a cherubic face. Barney was always laughing at him. And now Barney had seen Lenore about to race by and would view his mad dash to catch up as ridiculous. He grasped his packed saddlebags and swung two more big bags over his shoulder. The weight made him gasp. "Ye'll send my boxes after me, Barney?"

"Aye," promised Barney. "But your boxes are like to catch up with you, so slow must ye go—a cart will catch ye, Michael, ye're so heavy-laden. I pity the horse!"

Weighted down, Michael dropped one of the big bags. "That one can come later," he groaned. "I told ye I'd

76

no time to procure a packhorse, my nag will have to carry these as best he can. Goodbye, Barney. 'Tis been fine sharing lodgings with ye, and I hope ye'll visit me in Coventry."

Barney wrung his hand, but his expression was still mirthful. "Think ye the lady will wait?" he jibed. "Mayhap ye'd best look to see if she's vanished!"

Michael never meant to return to Oxford, and Barney's home was almost at Land's End—'twas very doubtful their paths would ever cross again. How he'd longed to wipe that amused, lofty look off Barney's face! And now at last he had the chance to do it—with one bold lie. He took a deep breath. "'Tis only because ye're my friend that I tell ye this, Barney," he confided, throwing out his chest. "But Mistress Lenore is only displaying her impatience." He paused impressively. "We are running away together."

"What!" For once Barney was startled out of his supercilious attitude, Michael noted with relish. "Wait till Geoffrey hears of it! He'll crush you like a maggot!"

Geoffrey! Always Geoffrey coming between him and his precious Lenore! Michael felt jealousy pricking at him as it had so often in the past when he'd guided Lenore's quill pen across the parchment, feeling her barely concealed impatience for Geoffrey to be home. "Geoffrey can hear and be damned to him—in France or wherever he's gone!" cried Michael, coloring up. "Because by the time he hears of it, Lenore and I will be wed!"

"Ye're taking her home to your family?" demanded his friend incredulously. "A woman with another man's bastard clutched to her bosom?"

"If my family won't accept her, I'll take her beyond their reach!" Michael declared fervently. He staggered to the door with his bags.

"Here, let me help you with that!" cried Barney. "Where will you go?"

"That I must keep a secret," gasped Michael, spurning aid and bumping his way through the door.

Barney followed him downstairs with a respectful look. You could never tell what stuff a man was made of! Who'd have thought pink-cheeked Michael, who had mooned around Lenore like a lovesick calf until he was the laughingstock of Oxford, would have the courage to run away with her? What a story he'd have to tell at the tavern tonight! Fascinated, and hoping for more revelations, Barney pursued him out the front door. "Faith, I envy you, Michael!" he cried, overcome by admiration of this unsuspected boldness in his previously insipid lodging-mate. "Mistress Lenore's a rare beauty!"

"Aye, that she is!" agreed Michael, now adjusting his saddlebags with the help of a stable boy. "Wait, wait, Lenore!" he called despairingly, for she was already cantering up the street. Panting, he got himself aboard the horse, cursing as one more of his bags fell off. "Send it along with the boxes!" he bellowed. He tossed a coin to the grinning stable boy, who caught it dexterously, and careened off over the cobbles after Lenore.

Lenore heard his wail and turned her head. Seeing him in the saddle at last, she slackened her pace until his overburdened mount could catch up.

"Why are ye in such a hurry?" he gasped.

"Because I attacked Gilbert with a poker and burned his face for him—and he's threatened to call the authorities and prevent my leaving!" she told him tersely.

"Burned his face with a poker?" Michael was amazed. "Aye, Gil would take that amiss! Whatever possessed ye to do such a thing?"

Lenore had no intention of telling Michael that Gilbert had raped her. "He tried to force his attentions on me. 'Twas the only way I could think of to beat him off, for he is stronger than I am."

"Oh." Michael gave her a round-eyed look of great respect. He had half convinced himself as he caught up with her that they really were eloping, and now he had new proof of what a fiery woman she was. "Then we'd best hurry along," he said inadequately.

"Indeed we had," agreed Lenore, "if ye think that poor beast can hurry, weighted down like that!"

Michael looked unhappy, and she sighed and slowed her pace.

78

But as they walked their horses along the rutted road that led along the River Cherwell north to Banbury, she stopped and looked back for a last glimpse of Oxford. Like Lot's wife, she could not resist looking back at what she had lost. Under scudding clouds the river valley seemed dismal, gray—but suddenly a fleeting shaft of sunlight illuminated the honey-colored spires, and she caught her breath.

A fairylike place it seemed from here—beautiful, insubstantial, and unreal. Her expression hardened. As unreal and as insubstantial as Geoffrey's love for her had been! With a defiant toss of her head, she turned her face resolutely toward the north. Let all the gentlemen of England sail for France if they chose—*she'd* make her way at the fairs!

She touched Snowfire with her knee. Fit and rested and eager to run, he leaped ahead—and behind her Michael groaned. "Lenore," he cried, "my horse can't keep up with the pace you set!"

Vexed, Lenore slowed her pace to one that Michael's mount could match. Slowly they wended their way beneath the tall old trees that lined the lovely riverbank. Lorena was clasped lightly, firmly in her arm, and sometimes she crooned to her, or rocked her a little, or dropped a quick kiss upon the baby forehead or tiny reaching fingers. She looked soft at those moments.

But when she lifted her head and surveyed the road ahead, her expression changed. There was a hard new light in her violet eyes as she headed north on an eager, prancing Snowfire—a light that boded ill for any man who dared to love her.

CHAPTER 6

At the alehouse at Headington Quarry, the proprietor stooped over a tall man who lay in a corner, half on a bench, half off. He stirred the recumbent figure with his foot. "Time to go, sir," he said cheerily. And then when that prone figure didn't move, more loudly, "Time to go, ye beggar!" He had begun to suspect that the elegant gentleman with the toffee-colored hair who had given him money to keep this long, lean fellow drunk would never be back. Certainly there was no profit in continuing to waste good ale on a man who was too drunk to know what was going on. Best get rid of him, in case the authorities came snooping around, as they sometimes did.

Encouraged by the toe of a boot, Geoffrey came slowly back to life and bestirred himself from his drunken condition. He opened one bloodshot eye and saw the corner of a battered table near his head, and beyond that and above a low-slung ceiling. As he struggled to rise, a pain shot through his head like a hammer blow, and he groaned and sank back, resting one palm upon the floor to ease his descent upon the bench. Something hard and round bit into his palm and his fingers closed around it automatically. A coin, perhaps, dropped from his pocket? No, too sharp. Almost as a reflex, he stuck it in his pocket. Any motion hurt. With a groan he clasped his head, which seemed to have a steel band around it biting into his brain—but his questing fingers could feel nothing but his own flesh. Where was he? What day was this? Gradually he collected his wits, assessed the fact that he had a full complement of arms and legs, and sat up.

"How long have I been here?" he mumbled.

"Well nigh on a week," said his host grimly. "And I'd be glad to be shut of ye, as the sayin' goes."

A week! Geoffrey shook his head to clear it, and winced. His throat was dry, his condition filthy, and his head ached abominably. "What do I owe ye?" he asked, struggling up.

"Naught," said the tavernkeeper laconically (he had already gone through Geoffrey's pockets and removed all the coins). "A friend paid for ye."

Geoffrey looked surprised, but he shrugged and left the alehouse. The strong breeze, carrying with it a tang of salt, rippled his thick, dark hair. It was good to be out of that dark, foul-smelling place. He stood a moment stretching in the bright June sunlight, breathing in deep draughts of that bracing air, then reached into his pocket. He'd been very giddy in there, but was it possible that he had actually come out of the place with a coin?

He studied it in the sunlight as it lay in his palm. Not a coin, but a button—handsomely enameled and of a very distinctive design: a stag on a gold ground. One of Gilbert's. But . . . how had it come there? He had no memory of seeing Gilbert at the alehouse—though to be truthful, he had precious little memory of anything there. Still it was not such a place as his foppish cousin would visit. So how had it got there, lying so near his hand?

Vaguely disturbed by the discovery, he found his horse in the stable behind the alehouse (the proprietor had been afraid to steal his horse) and mounted. He forgot the button as more disturbing thoughts plagued him. The child . . . the child was not his. His face grew bleak as the memory of that bitter disappointment assailed him. In his rage he had blasted out at Lenore—he winced at the things he had said—and yet . . . now he asked himself, honestly could she have known? He had taken her that first night by force, in full knowledge that she was handfasted. How could he blame her?

By heaven, he was lucky that she had come to love him! He would go back, he would admit he was wrong, he would beg her forgiveness, he would make amends. Aye, he would even take the child and dandle it on his knee. For it was hers . . . as she was his. By heaven, he would protect them both!

And he had been gone a week since he had flung out! What must she think, hearing that he was drunk in an alehouse all this time?

His brow creased with worry, he rode rapidly back to his lodgings off Magpie Lane to right his grievous wrongs with the woman he truly loved.

He found those lodgings empty of Lenore's things, though his own were still in evidence, piled neatly on a table. She and the baby were gone. He whirled at a sound at the door.

It was Mistress Watts, her wig askew, her furbelows looking shabbier than ever. As Geoffrey's tall figure advanced on her, she fell back, looking scared.

"Where's Mistress Daunt?" he demanded.

"She's fled. Yesterday." And at his thunderous expression, "The authorities were here," she bleated. "For what she did to Master Gilbert's face."

"To Master Gilbert's face?" Brought up short by that odd remark, Geoffrey waited for illumination.

"Aye. Pinked him with a hot poker, she did. He ran down these stairs bawlin' and hollerin' what he'd do to her. He shouted he'd tell the authorities who she was! But all they told *me* was that she was wanted for assault."

Geoffrey's face hardened. He could well imagine what provocation would cause Lenore to do such a thing. And she just out of childbed! There was a sword and baldric lying on the table, and now he buckled the strap of the baldric over his right shoulder so that his sword hung down under his left arm—convenient to his strong right hand.

Mistress Watts quaked as he swept by her. "A veritable demon he looked!" she told Gwynneth later, her hand on her palpitating heart. "I was afraid to tell him she'd left with Master Michael—I was afraid he'd cut my head off! And the way he slammed the door—'twas like to come off its hinges!"

Directly to Gilbert's quarters Geoffrey strode. Taking the stairs at three bounds, he kicked open the door with a booted foot and leaped inside. He seized the surprised Gilbert by the lace at his throat, twisting it cruelly.

When Geoffrey barged into the room, Gilbert had been sitting at his ease amid his usual clutter, leaning back in a chair propped against the wall. His long legs were stretched out indolently, booted feet resting on the edge of the table as he drank a glass of malmsey and brooded about the deviltry of a woman who would mark a man's face. He did not even have time to rearrange his legs before Geoffrey seized him. A screech rose in his throat, but that screech ended in a gurgle as he felt the chair knocked out from under him and the lace at his throat—it was strong and new and expensive—become a gallows knot cutting off his breathing.

A dark face that might have been the devil's own thrust itself juttingly into his, and he found himself gazing with terror into a pair of wild, bloodshot eyes. The voice that rang in his ears might have risen from the depths of hell. "Tell me what ye've done to Lenore!"

Choking, clutching at his throat, Gilbert, made an effort to rise and was forced to his knees. "Ye're mad," he gasped hoarsely, as the grip on his throat lightened enough for him to speak. "I've done nothing to her!"

He made an effort to twist free and was suddenly released. Geoffrey flung Gilbert from him so hard he bounced off the wall. As he staggered forward, Gilbert saw Geoffrey reach down into a pile of articles that had been

83

carelessly swept off the table. From the clutter he found one of the collection of swords of which Gilbert was so fond. "Defend yourself," he said crisply, flinging it to Gilbert and almost simultaneously snaking out his naked blade and advancing upon his cowering cousin.

Gilbert picked up the sword in haste and leaped aside in a frantic attempt to ward off this new menace. He was no match for Geoffrey's sword arm, and he knew it. "She's fled you!" he cried in a voice that cracked. "Faith, none could blame her—look at you, already thirsting for my blood!"

"Fled where?" demanded Geoffrey inexorably, bringing his blade down with such mighty force that Gilbert's sword, which he had swiftly raised in an attempt to parry the blow, was immediately torn from his grasp and went clattering across the floor. For a moment Gilbert stood riveted and livid—and Geoffrey, his face entirely satanic, gave him a mocking smile and presented the point of his blade to his cousin's throat. Gilbert fell back and came up against the wall—that deadly point followed him.

"Before I dispose of you . . . speak!" growled Geoffrey.

Faint with terror, Gilbert looked into the devil lights that flashed at him like summer lightning out of Geoffrey's gray eyes. "She has fled with Michael!" he cried.

"With Michael?" Geoffrey's incredulous look turned into a contemptuous laugh. He pressed the point in a little deeper so that it drew a drop of blood.

Gilbert's face grew a shade whiter, and he gasped. "'Tis true!" he yelped. "I had it straight from Barney Claypoole, who has rooms above him. She came over to Michael's lodgings yesterday, Michael was all packed, and they rode away together." He felt the point leave his skin and relaxed a little. "Had you eyes to see," he added in an injured tone, stroking his bruised throat and wiping away the blood, "ye'd have readily seen Michael's in love with her. Why else spend so much time teaching Lenore to better her penmanship? Why else work with her over all those dull books?"

"Why indeed? echoed Geoffrey thoughtfully. "And which way did they go?"

"Michael told Barney he was for Coventry," said Gilbert sulkily. "I gather he's taking Lenore home with him."

Geoffrey looked startled. "I see you are wounded," he said grimly, sheathing his sword. He was staring at the court plaster on Gilbert's cheek.

"'Tis a boil," said Gilbert instantly. "I had to have it lanced. The surgeon has bound it up."

Geoffrey's gaze was ironic. "I know how it came to be lanced," he said in a low deadly tone. "I would like to hear your version."

Gilbert was sweating profusely now and looking from side to side for some means of escape. "Have done, Geoffrey!" he cried in desperation. "I but offered Lenore shelter for herself and the child when she told me you'd left her and gone to France! She took offense and gave me this!" Sulkily he indicated his cheek.

Geoffrey turned red-rimmed eyes of hell on his cousin Gilbert. Before that look Gilbert flinched. He tried to retreat and once again found himself backed against the wall.

"You of all people knew I had not gone to France," said Geoffrey in a steely voice. "Yet you did not tell her? You let her go away believing that?"

"I did not know!" gasped Gilbert. "I thought you were gone! She told me you were!"

With his left hand Geoffrey drew out the unusual enameled button with the distinctive stag design. "Have you lost a button from your coat?" he demanded.

"No—yes!" Paralyzed with fright, Gilbert looked from the button to that glowering face. "What does that signify? Where did you get it?"

"On the floor of an alehouse at Headington Quarry!" roared Geoffrey, flinging the button into Gilbert's face with force. "'Tis plain to me, cousin, that you had me drugged in some way—"

"I did not! Geoffrey, I swear—"

"So that ye could make a try for Lenore, believing she'd turn to you in my absence!"

"I did not! Michael has bilked us both, Geoffrey. He . . ." Gilbert was babbling now, his words almost in-

85

coherent, and they faded into gasping silence. He seemed to shrink before the towering menace above him.

Geoffrey smiled down at his crouching cousin, a terrible smile. "What's clear to me is that ye did something to Lenore bad enough that she struck you with a poker. Ye need fresh air, Gilbert—ye look to be choking!"

He pounced on Gilbert, seized him by the shoulders in a grip of iron. Words were bubbling out of Gilbert now. "Remember, Geoffrey—we are cousins!" he gibbered.

Cousins! In violent revulsion, Geoffrey hoisted him into the air and with all his force hurled him through the window, shattering the wood and leaded panes. Gilbert shrieked as his bones broke the panes and the casement, and there was a long-drawn-out howl as he catapulted through the air to the alley below.

Hoping sincerely he had broken Gilbert's neck, Geoffrey strode out of the place. He did not bother to look out the broken window into the alley where he had pitched Gilbert, and from which now rose a number of high-pitched screams and the sound of running feet. His mind was seething. It was ridiculous to think that Lenore had eloped with Michael. She would not! Still . . . he'd best ask Mistress Watts about it. One could put no credence in anything a liar like Gilbert said.

With fear in his heart that he had lost his woman —nay more than that she was, his life—he made his way back to his lodgings at an even faster gait.

"It must be true," Mistress Watts sighed, when Geoffrey confronted her with Gilbert's allegations. "For Mistress Daunt did leave word with me that Master Michael was to catch up with her, that if he did not, she'd wait for him at the first crossroads." She gave him an accusing look. "She believed you gone to France."

Geoffrey winced. Indeed it must have seemed like it when he'd been gone almost a week! "Should she come back, Mistress Watts, tell her I have gone seeking her." He paused, studying the landlady keenly, for he sensed she was holding something back. "Have you any knowledge of where she may have gone, Mistress Watts?"

"Ye'll not . . . harm her?" Mistress Watts asked in an altered voice.

"Nay," Geoffrey sighed. "I wish only to make amends."

"She did ask cook to provision her to Banbury—and told me she would send me the lodging-money from the fair there, or from some other fair."

Geoffrey frowned, and then his face cleared. Snowfire! Of course!

"But after Master Michael came over, she may have changed her mind." She bit her lip. "And when she left, I asked her what to tell you if you came back—and she said you could go to the devil."

So she had consigned him to the devil, had she? Geoffrey's expression was wry.

"Ye'll not—ye'll not harm her because I told ye that?"

He shook his head. "I deserved it. And as to the lodging money, I'll see ye receive it, Mistress Watts."

She watched him mount up, her faith in fine gentlemen somewhat restored.

But it was a grim face Geoffrey turned toward the north as he rode out of Oxford. He liked not the idea that Lenore might have changed her mind after speaking with Michael. She was proud, and if his apparent desertion of her had caused her to fall into Michael's arms, she well might turn him away when he found her.

That he would find her had no doubt. Gilbert had said Michael was bound for Coventry, and Mistress Watts had said Lenore planned to take in the Banbury fair. In either case, they'd have taken the Banbury road that led north along the Cherwell. They were only a day ahead of him, and Michael was no kind of rider. If he moved swiftly, he might even catch up with them, lying over at an inn on the way.

North along the Cherwell's beautiful riverbank he rode, making inquiries at all the inns along the way. Had they seen a young fellow garbed in red accompanied by a beautiful woman riding a white horse and carrying a small baby? A pair worthy of remark surely, yet none had seen them.

87

He passed tall haycarts pulled by sleepy-eyed lumbering oxen, and trudging farmers carrying pitchforks, moving sturdily along the roadside, big muscles rippling. He passed apple-cheeked country girls who looked at him with bright interest, and an occasional painted coach drawn by four or six horses. At one point, he rode down a green tunnel of overhanging branches where the trees pressed in upon the road. And midway down that tunnel he almost had to jump his horse over a deep depression some turned-over wagon must have dug in the mired earth. He looked at it grimly. A bad overturn, that. Someone could have been hurt, and it must have blocked the road in a place as narrow as this. He was distracted by a flock of sheep that poured like foaming water from a sheep track on the left and overflowed the road in all directions. They were being driven in from the Cotswolds and their baaing filled the leafy countryside with sound. They flowed around him like white-capped rapids, their woolly sides brushing his horse's legs, and the shepherd smiled at him for sitting his mount so still and letting the flock stream by. In desperation, Geoffrey even asked the shepherd if he'd seen a beautiful woman on a white horse, but he got a regretful shake of the head. Plainly the young shepherd would have liked a glimpse of the woman Geoffrey described in terse, vivid terms.

It was easy for Geoffrey to paint Lenore's picture in words. And his gray eyes betrayed his longing. He parted company with the shepherd, brooding about her. By heaven, how she had fitted into his arms! With a twisting pain in his heart, he remembered the silken feel of her slender body, her soft murmurings as he held her close, the agonizing sweetness as he took her. For a moment the summer air was filled with the fragrance of her hair, the sunlight blazing on a gilded coach ahead no brighter than its sheen.

But although he combed the road as thoroughly as he could and asked all likely travelers, though he stopped to inquire at inns and taverns and searched for her at Banbury where the fair was being held, no trace did he find of

Lenore. She seemed to have vanished from the face of the earth.

Haggard now—and with fear eating at him—he rode on to Coventry, dismounting at Michael's ancestral home, Maltby Manor, just south of the town. He found it to be a crumbling stone manor house, pleasantly situated on a little knoll amid a grove of beeches. The rotting outbuildings and air of general decay—no less than the ancient farthingale in which Michael's mother, the mistress of Maltby, was attired—attested to the fact that all their substance had been spent on their adored only son, Michael. On learning that he was a friend of Michael's, they ushered him in as if he were a prince and promptly supplied him with partridge and wine while the whole family gathered round to question him eagerly. Michael was not expected until next week—what, had he taken the road already?

Geoffrey assured them Michael had left Oxford.

"But we have not heard from him!" Michael's mother interrupted anxiously. "Are you sure he left Oxford before you and came up the Banbury road?"

"I am not sure he came by the Banbury road," said Geoffrey thoughtfully. "But that he left Oxford the day before me—of that I am sure, and I set no great pace, for all the way I stopped and inquired if any had seen him."

"And why?" This penetratingly from Michael's grandmother, a sharp old lady who sat bolt upright wearing stiff brocades and a yellowed ruff—obviously one she had worn as a girl, from its present state of dilapidation. "Why do you seek Michael in such haste, young man?"

They seemed so impoverished that Geoffrey was almost ashamed to eat the food they urged on him. " 'Tis not Michael I seek." He chose his words carefully. "But the lady Lenore who travels with him."

Michael's mother blanched. "T-travels with him?" she asked faintly.

"Aye," he said gravely. "She is my wife. She was under the mistaken impression that I had left her, and I think Michael gives her his protection on the way to . . . some safe place."

89

"And where would that be?" demanded the grandmother testily.

Geoffrey gave her a sad look. "If I knew, I would not be here."

"Oh," said Geoffrey's mother. "Oh, I see. But surely word will reach her through friends that you have not deserted her and—oh, I see, you believe it will not?"

Geoffrey inclined his head in assent.

"Perhaps he has taken another road this time," suggested Michael's aunt placidly, her cherubic face reminding Geoffrey sharply of young Michael.

Michael's worried mother threw her sister an impatient look. "It is not like him not to let us know," she said sharply. "And he should be here by now, if he left Oxford when this gentleman says he did."

"You see, Michael has always come straight home to us from Oxford—no dallying along the way," explained the wispy gentleman who was Michael's father, suddenly entering the conversation. He studied Geoffrey's worried face. "If Michael brings this lady here, we will promptly apprise her that you have been here seeking her," he said earnestly. "Where can we reach you?"

Geoffrey had been thinking about that, although he now had little hope that Michael would return to Maltby Manor anytime soon. Michael had always had with him a little money, provided by this poverty-stricken crew. It would be enough to provide a brief wedding trip, Geoffrey realized bitterly, should Michael's intentions be honorable. The thought gnawed at his insides. "Tell her I'll to Oxford," he told Michael's father. "And if she finds me not there, she can reach me through Ned—she will know where to find him. I will be in touch with Ned."

He thanked them for their hospitality, rose and escaped the bare, run-down surroundings that had spawned a cheerful young popinjay who—he drew his gauntlets on his hands with unnecessary force—had made off with his mistress.

He was about to ride away when he saw Michael's mother hurrying after him, impeded by her awkward

90

farthingale. He halted and waited for her to catch up.

"You are not—you are not saying that Michael is—is enamored of this wife of yours?" she blurted, when she could catch her breath.

Geoffrey gave her a wintry look. "Such is Mistress Lenore's beauty that all men are enamored of her," he said savagely. "Michael no more than others, perhaps."

"But—but—"

"I believe him to be protecting her," he said shortly. "Perhaps from me."

He cantered rapidly away, leaving her staring after him, her face white and drawn.

Geoffrey's mind was working furiously as he rode away. Where could they have gone? Twainmere he discounted as impractical—Lenore would be afraid to return there with her lover. It was doubtful any of Michael's relatives would take him in. They might have gone to London, pretending to ride away as a feint, but actually slipping into a boat and floating down the Thames. If so, someone in Oxford might have seen them leave—Lenore with her bright hair and Michael in his red cloak would have made a memorable pair.

It occurred to him suddenly that Mistress Watts might know more than she had told him, that Gwynneth the serving-girl, with whom Lenore had been on friendly terms, might have heard her say something about her destination before she left—and he cursed his stupidity that he had not wrung them dry of information before he galloped off to the north. And that fellow who lodged upstairs from Michael, Barney—he'd seen them ride off together, according to Gilbert. Perhaps he'd have a clue as to where they might have gone.

Fast he rode back to Oxford. On his way back from Banbury he passed a crossroads marker. Above it some vultures were circling. A dead sheep, he thought, or perhaps a fox. He was impatient to get to Oxford and put those dark, circling wings from his mind.

Had he stopped to investigate, it would have changed the course of his life.

As it was, he went on to Oxford, riding in openly, impatient for news. He headed directly for Barney's lodgings.

But he had reckoned without Gilbert.

CHAPTER 7

When Lenore had branded Gilbert, he had rushed to a surgeon to have his face attended to. It would leave a scar, he was told calmly.

A scar on his handsome countenance! Gilbert had leaped up and staggered from the surgeon's house and gone running to the authorities intending to denounce her. But on the way a crafty thought had entered his head. He wanted to punish Lenore himself, and perhaps there was a way. . . .

Seething with rage and pain, he had charged her with assault upon his person. Once imprisoned, he told himself with demonic glee, she'd do anything to gain her release. His price for dropping the charge would be that she move in with him—and he'd keep her docile by threatening to denounce her as the Angel of Worcester. His caramel eyes glittered with anticipation. He'd stripe that pretty back of hers! Mayhap he'd even tie her up and brand . . . the sole of her foot, perhaps? For he'd no wish to destroy the beauty he intended to enjoy. Half his pleasure would be making her beg!

With a ferocious smile on his injured face, Gilbert accompanied the authorities to Lenore's lodgings. There a pale and shaken Mistress Watts stuttered that Mistress Daunt had ridden off, she knew not where.

Gilbert had given her a black look. He did not believe that—a woman with a small babe and no money! Lenore was in hiding. Well, he would find her himself!

On his way back to his lodgings, he ran into Barney. Barney, intrigued by the court plaster that adorned Gilbert's face as much as by the angry scowl that brought those caramel brows together, hailed him.

"Ye look like ye've been in a duel," he observed.

"An accident," said Gilbert shortly. It would hurt his pride to have Barney know he'd been branded by a woman. "What news?" he asked, to change the subject.

Barney laughed. He was full of news today. "Michael has run off with Mistress Lenore."

Rage broke over Gilbert like an onrushing wave. She had escaped him! Almost he rushed back to the authorities he had so recently left and denounced Lenore as the Angel of Worcester. But as the mist cleared from his eyes, he pulled himself together. He muttered something incoherent, flung away from Barney, and went back to his lodgings with murder in his heart.

There he quickly downed a brandy and sat down to plan. Perhaps she had not escaped him after all, this woman who had marked his face forever.

He touched the court plaster and winced. Barney had assumed he'd been pinked in a duel. He poured himself another brandy, and his eyes narrowed. He bethought him that he could indeed brag to strangers that it was an old dueling scar—even, in the right circumstances, that he had been wounded at Worcester; none would know the difference, and it would enhance his reputation. His mother had contemptuously called him "too pretty" more than once—this scar would give his narrow face character. On thinking it over, he could almost be glad it had happened because he could turn it to good account.

94

Lenore, of course, must not go unpunished. He thought about that, too, as the brandy burned his throat, and his lazy countenance was evil. He'd a mind to get her back and . . . there was a way.

Michael was a weak reed, he reasoned. He knew something of Michael's circumstances, enough to know that Michael always wore red because by having clothes of the same color, he could distract attention from a frayed cuff, a worn sleeve, by wearing some other garment that was dazzlingly *new*. Although Michael had pocket money, Gilbert was fairly certain the lad had no source of income other than his doting family.

Lenore was obviously without resources; if she'd had a place to go, she'd have taken Geoffrey there and had her baby. So she must go where Michael took her.

Even should Michael marry Lenore—and Gilbert thought him mad enough to do that—it would be beyond belief that Michael's mother would take in as a daughter-in-law, this cast-off doxie dragging another man's bastard.

So, Gilbert reasoned, times would become hard for Michael, his money would be quickly exhausted, he would abandon Lenore and scuttle back to the safety of his home near Coventry.

And at that point, Gilbert thought with a cruel smile, Lenore would be ripe for the taking.

He sharpened a quill, dipped it in the inkwell, and dashed off a letter to Michael at Maltby Manor, Warwickshire, in which he said:

"I know that you have run off with Geoffrey's doxie, Lenore, and knowing her fickle ways, must believe that you have now tired of her and returned home. Having lain with her myself—" he paused with the quill in the air; he wanted to say "on numerous occasions," but young Michael might not believe that; he sighed and began to write again—"I would account it a favor if you would apprise me of her whereabouts—and would send you my new 'jackanapes' coat which you so admired as a token of regard, upon receipt of such information.

Your obedient servant,
Gilbert Marnock."

He posted the letter and sat back with satisfaction to await developments.

Geoffrey's attack had come as a complete surprise. He had been so sure the doings at the alehouse at Headington Quarry would never be traced to him. And for Geoffrey to know that Lenore had branded him! In the agony of his burn and the horror that his handsome face might be marred for life, he had not even noticed Mistress Watts, her eyes popping, gaping at him from the downstairs hallway as he rushed out. Never had he thought that *she* might tattle to Geoffrey!

But Gilbert, for all that he had been found out, had in the end been born under a lucky star, and when Geoffrey threw him through the window of his lodgings, his luck had held. He had landed, not in the alley below, but in a tall-sided haycart parked beneath his window. The farmer who owned the cart had gone inside to collect for his hay in advance, for Geoffrey's landlord was careless with his hay payments for the stable he kept behind the house.

It was in this hay that Gilbert had landed—undoubtedly saving his life, for he arrived head first.

Hearing the crash of broken wood and glass and Gilbert's high-pitched shriek, the farmer, the landlord, and the cook all came running out to see in amazement Gilbert's flailing boots protruding from the mound of hay and weird inhuman noises issuing from its soft depths.

Sure he was dead and groaning loudly, Gilbert was pulled out. They brushed the hay off his handsome clothes —he struck one of them in a petulant rage as this was done—and stood him on his wobbly legs. There was nothing broken, but he presented a bloody sight, bruised and cut as he was from breaking through the stout casements with his body. That they were all minor wounds save one—a gouge in his other cheek where he had grazed a hidden pitchfork in the depths of the hay— attested to his luck.

"Geoffrey will pay for this!" he sobbed, putting shaking fingers to this new marring of his handsome face. "Geoffrey will pay!"

The landlord, secretly pleased at Gilbert's mishap, for he was an unruly tenant and slow to pay, was solicitous in helping Gilbert up to bed. There as the afternoon progressed his friends crowded around, clucking their tongues, for it was a self-serving tale Gilbert told them. Lenore had been bent on fleeing Oxford with Michael, he said—adding spitefully his own invention: Lenore's scheme was not to elope with Michael, as the lad believed, but to bilk him of what money he had, to steal his purse as he slept at the first inn they put up in, and make her way to London, where a woman of her endowments would have greater scope—she had bragged to him of this.

Amazed faces greeted this revelation, for they had all liked Lenore and loath to believe evil of her.

"'Tis true!" cried Gilbert, rising up in a passion at sight of those unbelieving faces. "When I remonstrated with her and tried to stop her—as indeed I should have done, being Geoffrey's cousin and Michael's friend—she flew into a rage and burned me with a hot poker and took off on the run with poor Michael!" He sank back upon his pillow and laid a listless hand upon his forehead. "When Geoffrey came back, he would not listen—he was sure I must have done her some injury that she had burned me! He threw me out the window and near killed me!"

His friends eyed each other thoughtfully. Gilbert did indeed seem to have reason for complaint—and the burn and cuts and bruises were there as vivid proof of his story. Though doubts lingered, young Oxford subsided before Gilbert's accusations. Geoffrey would turn up, some muttered, and they'd hear *his* version.

Sulking—and furious that both cheeks were wounded, for the pitchfork point had been dirty and the gouge festered—Gilbert convalesced with the aid of wine and Dorothy the tavern maid, who tended him faithfully. But when Dorothy brought word excitedly that Geoffrey had returned to Oxford, she had seen him riding toward Michael's old lodgings, Gilbert leaped out of bed, flung on his clothes in haste, and rushed past her. "I'll be back," he cried. "Wait for me!"

Gilbert raced for the authorities. His eyes took on a

wicked gleam as he ran—and a scared gleam, too, for he feared Geoffrey might hear that he had survived the fall and come back to finish him off! He composed his features as he explained to the authorities that he had recently learned, through family letters, that Geoffrey Wyndham, who in Oxford went by the name of Daunt, had fought for the king at Worcester. He sank down as if overcome as he said that, muttering that he had thought Geoffrey merely a rogue, but now it seemed he was also a traitor—and he had leaped up from his bed of pain to apprise them that Geoffrey was back and heading for Michael's old lodgings.

So it was that Geoffrey, when he clattered down the stairs after an unsatisfactory interview with Barney, found himself surrounded by a ring of steel.

Backed into the house by weight of their numbers, he fought them—up and down the wooden stairs he fought them, his sword blade flashing through the air to parry several blades that snaked at him. Wild-eyed, Barney watched the battle from above ("I've never seen a man fight like that!" he swore later in admiration) until a bullet fired at close range creased Geoffrey's forehead and he went down like a felled ox and woke up lying on a filthy pallet in the jail.

Lying in jail, slapping at spiders and fleas, kicking at rats, he had time to consider. For time was nothing here, as men waited in stinking cells to die or be transported.

But to the lean prisoner with the haggard face and the dirty rag bound about his wounded head, who lay in a room high up in the jail where desperate prisoners were kept, the days were haunted with memories of a winsome smile, the nights made restless as he tossed on his pallet longing to hold a certain fair body in his arms again.

Reluctantly now in the prison dimness, which cast a clear, hard light on his musings, he accepted what he had refused to believe before: Michael and Lenore had not headed up the Banbury road for Coventry, Lenore's story about provisioning for the fair was but a screen to hide the truth. Lenore had believed him gone to France and had eloped with Michael. She was lost to him!

Bitterly he speculated on where they might have gone. Most likely they had traded their horses for passage downriver to London and Michael had indentured himself to pay for ship's passage—as indeed Geoffrey had planned to do. For since Michael's disappearance had showed unexpected initiative, Michael might have other unsuspected resources—he and Lenore might even now be embarking on some tall white ship bound for the American Colonies, where his irate family would never find him.

He imagined her there, standing at the rail beside Michael, beneath billowing sails, while the wind rippled her hair, bravely embarking on a new life.

And the truth, he told himself painfully, though he had flinched to face it, was that Lenore was better off with Michael. He could offer his name—a good name and an old one—and blind devotion. Eventually, since Michael was an only son, he would inherit decaying Maltby Manor. The sale of it should ensure him a good position in the Colonies, and the bright-haired girl from Twainmere would be at last what she had longed to be—a respected wife.

If only he could have given her that . . .

He stood at the small barred window—so high that only a tall man might see out—and gazed out at Oxford's ancient spires, softened to tan by the haze. Somewhere in that jumble of buildings was Magpie Lane, and off of it an alley and a tumbledown Tudor building where he had passed some of the happiest days of his life. His hard gaze softened and grew wistful as he tried to locate the house where he had dwelt with Lenore.

They told him charges were being readied against him. Not only of being a Royalist and therefore a traitor to the Commonwealth, but they were also investigating a rumor that he'd prowled the roads as a highwayman these past months. Geoffrey gave them a ribald look when they told him that. On either count, his life was forfeit; this multiplicity of charges only amused him.

He gave little thought to the way he would die. All men died sometime, and it might be he'd escape the gallows

99

yet. Instead his mind dwelt lingeringly on Lenore, and at night he dreamed that they were on the run again, camped beneath the high tors, and in the dying glow of their campfire he looked deep into her violet eyes and she moved silently into his arms—a lustrous woman, his alone. By day there was a whole treasure chest of memories to illumine his drab cell: the fire, the passion, the oneness that had consumed them both. Ruefully his waking mind traced every little inch of her sweet body. In the silence of his cell he could almost hear her sigh, and the little breeze that reached him through the bars reminded him of her gentle, delighted quiver as he entered her. His hard body ached with longing for the tremulous response he had always felt in her, and he groaned as he recalled too vividly an incurving waist, an outcurving hip, the maddening pressure of her firm young breasts against his hard chest.

How gallantly she had ridden beside him when they were hunted! How valiantly she had thundered to the finish on the makeshift race course at Wells—and returned flushed and triumphant that she had bested big Hobbs. He was proud of her, he loved her, and—a dry sob formed in his throat—though he deserved to lose her, dear God, he missed her so.

Now he would dance out his life on a gibbet and she would never know he had not meant the ugly words he'd hurled at her in pain and disappointment. That was what hurt most—she would never know.

Gilbert, resplendent in fawn satins, came to crow over him in the jail. Gilbert's bruises had turned from purple to yellow, his cuts—save for the festered one from the pitchfork—were healing fast, but the burn Lenore had given him with the hot poker was livid even in the little light afforded by the cell's small window on a cloudy day. Geoffrey took some satisfaction in the sight of that weal.

Though the jailer would have obligingly locked Gilbert in the cell with Geoffrey for a private interview, Gilbert hastily declined that and chose instead to speak to Geoffrey through the small grating of the iron door that held the prisoner secure inside.

100

"Ye made a mistake, Geoffrey," he taunted through the grating.

"Aye," Geoffrey agreed with a sigh. "I should have pitched ye through the front window onto the cobbles instead of through the side window into the muddy alley!"

Gilbert paled, and his teeth clenched. "Ye are about to die!" he stormed. "For no court will clear ye of both charges! Either ye'll hang as a Royalist or ye'll hang as a highwayman!"

"How can ye be so sure?" mocked Geoffrey. "Neither charge is yet proved."

Gilbert took a ragged breath and fought to compose his features. "I did not come here to quarrel with ye, Geoffrey."

Geoffrey laughed. "No? Then why did you come?"

"Because we are cousins and—"

"Faith, ye should have thought of it sooner!"

Gilbert edged nearer the grating. Seen through that square in the iron door, his face was crafty. "I am willing to forget that ye tried to kill me, Geoffrey, and do ye a last good turn."

Geoffrey eyed his cousin. "A draught of poison to speed me, perhaps?"

"Nay, do not jest." Gilbert lowered his voice confidentially. "I do not believe that ye know not where Lenore is. If ye will tell me her whereabouts, Geoffrey, I promise ye faithfully that I will go to her and tell her of your trouble so that she may slip into the jail and see you before the end."

Geoffrey gave a short laugh. "So that she may die with me? Is that what ye offer? Or perchance save her life by becoming your doxie?"

Gilbert empurpled. He smote the iron door, with the hilt of his sword until it rang. "Guard! Guard!" he cried in fury. "I am finished with my interview with this prisoner! Sirrah!"

Lounging against the wall, Geoffrey favored that square of grating that showed his cousin's baleful face with a genial smile. "I am sorry, Gil," he began softly, and Gilbert turned an interested look toward him, hoping his

101

cause was not lost, after all. "Sorry that I did not mark ye so well as Lenore," Geoffrey fetched a deep sigh. " 'Tis an error I'll correct one day—if I live."

Gilbert almost ran over the turnkey in his blind wrath as he charged out of the jail.

Geoffrey heard his departure and gave thanks for one thing—at least Lenore was clear of Gilbert's wrath. That Michael had taken her beyond Gil's reach was the one ray of sunshine in the eternal night that would soon descend on him.

His next visitor was more welcome.

Geoffrey had been resting in a corner of his cell, leaning against the stone wall and contemplating the spiderwebs that hung down from the ceiling. He looked up as a key turned in the lock and Ned's familiar form—plumper than he remembered—hurried through. In a bound he was on his feet and met Ned in the center of the room, clapping him on the shoulder in delight. Behind Ned the iron door clanged shut, and the turnkey's voice reached them. "I'll be within call—let me know when ye've done."

"Ned, I thought ye were in Somerset! Faith, ye've a paunch these days! I hope your lady's well."

Ned wrung his hand. "She's very well. I came when I heard ye'd been taken, Geoffrey. And as to the paunch—marriage is good to me; I'm well fed." He grinned at Geoffrey.

"I'll not ask ye to sit down, Ned—'twould ruin your clothes. But the air is better by the window. Ye'll have heard Lenore has left me."

"Aye."

"Is there any news of her?" Geoffrey eyed him anxiously.

"Nay, I've had none. She seems to have vanished—as Lally has." Ned's voice was melancholy.

Geoffrey was startled. "Lally? I did not know."

"Aye. I'm told she left Gilbert and none know where she has gone."

A tiny hope sprang up in Geoffrey—that Lenore might have sought out Lally, they might be hiding somewhere

102

together—and was immediately quenched. Lenore had left with Michael, and he had not turned up, either.

"I think you must face it, Geoffrey," Ned said soberly. "Lenore has left you. Ye must look to yourself."

"That would be easier were I not in jail," said Geoffrey wryly.

Ned lowered his voice. "That can be remedied. I've a plan." Even as he spoke, he was disrobing. "Keep a sharp eye out for the jailer, Geoffrey. I've so much rope tied around me I can hardly move!"

"Faith, ye're a practical man, Ned!" Geoffrey's eyes lit up as Ned handed him a file and a short dagger. He kept his eyes pressed to the grating as Ned, panting, unburdened himself of a great length of rope. "I've yet another file in my other boot," he muttered, and Geoffrey chuckled.

"Ye're a walking arsenal, Ned! I'm surprised ye did not bring black powder to blow up the jail!"

"I've a better plan," Ned told him grimly, getting back into his clothes while Geoffrey stowed the rope and files and dagger beneath his pallet. " 'Tis dangerous, but—it should work."

He outlined his plan, and Geoffrey nodded. Then he frowned. "Gilbert was here to plague me, Ned. He'll try to stop us if he hears."

"Aye—I've heard the stories he spreads about Lenore."

Geoffrey said sharply, "What stories?"

Ned told him, and Geoffrey smote his palm with a hard fist and cursed softly. "I should have broken Gil's neck *before* I tossed him through the window!"

"I heard about that." Ned was amused. He began to pack some of the straw bedding into his clothes so that he would again have a paunch.

"Ye'll get fleas, Ned."

Ned shrugged. "Be easy about Gilbert, Geoffrey. He's had a falling out with Dorothy—you remember that tavern maid who used to be his doxie? He beat her black and blue, and she's swearing vengeance to all who will listen. For a few coins she'll manage to get him drunk for us."

103

Geoffrey nodded alertly. Except in matters of the heart, Ned always managed well.

"Ye're a good friend, Ned." Geoffrey's voice was deep. "I'll not forget this."

"I've not forgotten how you climbed a rotting tower to get me out of Wilby Hall that night when the place caught fire and I was trapped inside with a great cupboard toppled on top of me that I could not budge. All were against your climb, which they said was impossible —including the long leap you made from the tower to my window."

It was Geoffrey's turn to shrug. " 'Twas not so big a thing, Ned."

"No? Well, I thought it was. I was lying there half crushed with clouds of black smoke billowing around me —and you came through it with your eyes bloodshot and dragged me out and let me down the building with a rope. I had already consigned myself to the devil, and when I saw your face—"

"You thought 'twas he come to collect you," chuckled Geoffrey.

Ned slapped him on the back. "Take care, Geoffrey. We'll have but the one chance."

"Aye," Geoffrey wrung his hand. "We'll make it a good one."

"Let's hope no one bumps into me," muttered Ned, already scratching as fleas bit into him. "For my paunch will have an interesting crunch! I'll leave you now, Geoffrey. Jailer! Jailer! I'm ready to take my leave of the prisoner!"

When the iron door was unlocked, Geoffrey was seen to be reclining upon his pallet, looking melancholy. The iron door clanged shut.

Ned rounded up those Oxford students whose Royalist leanings he could count on, and they assaulted the jail— not with weapons but with music and song. The town-folk muttered about their unruliness—but then they were often unruly. They made enough noise that the rasp and occasional shriek of Geoffrey's file, sawing at the iron bars, went unnoticed.

When at last enough of the tough bars were sawed partway through—so that a good kick would finish them off—Geoffrey tied his scarf to the window of his cell and it floated out bravely on the afternoon breeze.

It was the signal. That evening a raucous crowd of students, inspired by Ned, appeared in the street at the other side of the jail. They seemed very drunk and carried with them a kettledrum and an assortment of iron pots on which they dinned and thumped with iron spoons and pokers. The attention of jailers and guards was thus attracted to that side of the jail. By five minutes past nine o'clock when the Great Tom bell began its hundred and one peals that announced curfew, the din was so great that Geoffrey was able to kick out the bars—they rattled down to the cobbles completely unnoticed—affix his rope, and start his dangerous climb down the stone side of the building.

In the dim alley below, a horseman had appeared with another horse on a lead. He jogged along slowly, as if on his way home at the sound of curfew. It was Ned—painfully conscious of Geoffrey's necessarily slow descent. He watched anxiously as Geoffrey came down the rope —and winced as fifteen feet from the ground the rope broke and Geoffrey fell rolling to the alley below, to end up almost under the hooves of Ned's horse.

The horse shied nervously, and Ned leaned forward tensely. "Are ye hurt?" he whispered, alarmed.

Geoffrey was already up and seizing the bridle Ned handed him. "Naught but a bruise or two," he said grimly. "I thank ye, Ned, for all ye've done. Now get ye gone so that ye are not caught in the net if I be taken!" He took the pistol Ned gave him, stuck it in his belt, and buckled on the baldric and sword.

"Wait, ye'll need this." Ned tossed him a purse, which Geoffrey caught. "There's gold in it." He gave his friend a troubled look in the dimness. "Where do ye go, Geoffrey?"

"God knows," Geoffrey flung back over his shoulder and galloped away. Ned had done enough for him, he thought—aye, more than enough; he would not endanger

Ned further with involvement in his plans. With luck he'd get out of Oxford and head southeast. It might be safer for him in the West Country, in Somerset or Cornwall or Devon. But—he wanted no reminders of Lenore. She was better without him, of that he was convinced—aye, being with him had held her back from the life she might have had: good wife to a good man. Not the life of a fugitive, which was all, God knows, he had to give her.

There'd been a thin chance for them there for a while; he'd hurried to Oxford over mired roads to tell Lenore he'd made the arrangements for them to go to America —but he had never told her, he'd seen the child and flung out . . . he deserved what had befallen him. And by now the ship that was to have carried them across the waters would have sailed without him—which mattered not, he'd no heart now to emigrate and work long, hard years of indenture overseeing the work on another man's plantation. For Lenore he'd have done it, and gladly, but for himself—he shrugged, he'd see what a man could do on the highroads.

Ned went back to Somerset, and though he was suspected of aiding in Geoffrey's escape—especially by Gilbert, who was loud in denouncing him—nobody was ever able to prove anything against him. Ned might indeed have been the source of the rumor that circulated around the taverns of Oxford: that the Angel of Worcester had flown to the windowsill of Geoffrey's cell and left him a rope and a file. It was just one of the many miraculous things now attributed to the woman who had "ridden in like Godiva to save the King at Worcester, and finding him fled had taken a dead man from the battlefield instead, breathed life into him, and vanished!"

Geoffrey made it out of town that night, using a ruse he had used before, and headed southwest, leaving behind him Oxford's stone spires, tall and pale in the light of a rising moon.

He never looked back—except once when he thought he heard sounds of pursuit. His memories of those months in Oxford were not concerned with the towers or their lodgings . . . they were memories of a woman, soft and sweet in his arms, a splendrous woman who had melded into his arms and into his heart. He would carry the memory of her with him all his tormented days.

For a while he turned highwayman, ruthlessly taking what he wanted where he found it, for life had been none so good to him of late and he was haunted by what he had lost. With a black scarf wound around his face and a steady pistol cocked and ready, it was a wintry pair of eyes indeed that he turned toward the scared coach travelers who had the misfortune to cross his path by night. There was a price on his head now, but he shrugged that off. Doubless he would die as he had lived—violently, in his blood on the highroad, with none to mourn.

And when he rode recklessly into market towns on fair days seeking a bawdy respite from the rigors of the road, and lost himself in the packed humanity that surged between the stalls, it was at the girls with red-gold hair that he turned his somber gaze, seeing in the flash of their bright hair in the sun a brief glimpse of the alluring woman he had lost. His face grew grim as he remembered. All that a man could want he had had—and thrown away. He cursed himself for his folly, and drowned his memories in wine.

It was a reckless face Geoffrey turned to the world now. He took ever more chances, for he cared little whether he lived or died. But a ball in the arm from an alert coach driver temporarily ended his career on the highroads. Mending, he drifted toward the coast.

At Dover, wise in the ways of the hunted, he fell in with a smuggler named Rice who brought French laces and French brandy across the channel duty free and pocketed a neat profit. On Rice's next trip across the channel—a dark, moonless night was chosen for the run—Geoffrey accompanied him. They were not lucky; midway across the channel the moon came out bright, and they were chased by a British revenue cutter. Almost in sight of the French coast, the cutter launched a nine-pound shot into their side. The next shot broke the mast —and when it fell, the heavy wooden mast caught Rice across the head and broke his neck.

107

Geoffrey did not wait for the cutter to come alongside. He went over the side and into the longboat. Fortunately clouds once again obscured the moon, and his going was unobserved. He rowed mightily toward the distant coast. A few cold stars were breaking through the murk when he pulled the longboat ashore in the surf and raked the empty coast with a keen, hard look. Without money, without friends, cast up on a foreign shore, something dogged in him refused to give up. He was determined to survive, and his first thought was how to get back to England. But what held England for him, indeed, what held any place for him—now that Lenore was gone? He might as well stay here!

But he knew a moment's sadness as he thought how, had things gone differently, he and Lenore might this day be landing on another coast—the American coast, ready to start a new life. He looked at the cold stars and hoped —with a pain like the twist of a knife in an old wound— that Lenore was happy with Michael, that he would make her a good busband and give her the kind of home she deserved.

Then he started a long walk toward a distant winking light that might be a candle in a cottage window, or might signify a town. As he strode along in the salt air, his mouth twisted into a grim smile at the irony of this landing on the French coast—he had made good the threat he never intended; he had gone to France.

PART TWO

THE FORSAKEN

CHAPTER 8

On her sad journey north, away from the town that had become, in her heart and mind, her home, Lenore kept her head high, but her gaze upon the sweet summer countryside around her was bereft.

The long wild road she had ridden with Geoffrey was behind her now, the trauma of Wells, the sharp, brief glory she had known as "Mistress Daunt" in Oxford— and the bitterness, the lies. Love was behind her, too, lost somewhere in the ruins of her life. Lenore felt she would never again know the wild, fierce sweetness that had drenched her as she clung to Geoffrey, the wonderful fulfillment as a woman that had been hers as she rode beside him.

But . . . though she had lost so much, she had not lost all. Fiercely she clutched Lorena to her breast, soothing the pretty child with a swift kiss or a soft caress if she cried. "You will be good," she whispered brokenly to the baby, her lips brushing that small pink cheek. "Yes, and you will be beautiful—and your beauty will bring you good things, not harm as mine has done."

For that it was her beauty that had brought her to this cruel pass, she was certain. It was beauty that had made Geoffrey desire her, that had made Gilbert scheme to win her and finally to take her so savagely by force . . . beauty, too, that had made Jamie the Scot seek her for his handfast bride.

Like a quicksand made of pearls, her beauty had dragged her down—and now it had finished her. She was on the run again, this time alone, for Michael would leave her at Banbury. And although she had faced up to her future bravely, in her heart she knew the chances of a woman making a living racing and betting at the fairs was not good.

Lost, lost Lenore . . . sadly she watched her reflection float by in a still, shallow pool as they rode along the riverbank. A vivid shadow—Lenore, young and lovely as she rode erect and proud on her white horse, her fair face reflecting nothing of what she had suffered. Snowfire, after his long, tiresome winter and spring spent mainly in the stable, was undaunted and ready to run. It was difficult to hold him back to match the sedate pace of Michael's mount. So glad was he to have her on his back again that he danced and arched his white neck, tossed his silky mane, and whinnied to her in small, soft sounds. Lenore patted him ruefully and sighed. This was to have been such a wonderful time for her, these first weeks with the wonder of her firstborn in her arms and lean, sardonic Geoffrey by her side.

Michael was fretting because he had left with his baggage to be sent the clothes he wanted to wear to-morrow—and because he was grimly afraid the garter that held up his hose on his left leg was coming loose. His frenzied mind was checking over what was in his saddle-bags and bundles that flopped about his horse's back—no garters, he was sure of it. He would doubtless arrive in Banbury a figure of fun. Though he loved Lenore and would have followed her anywhere, he was already having

112

second thoughts about this wild flight from Oxford and had little to say.

In her suffering, Lenore was almost oblivious to Michael's silence. She was used to Michael's doglike devotion and found it comforting. When she thought about him at all, she hoped vaguely that he would find some smiling girl with enough income to keep him in the red raiment he so loved and forget all about his infatuation for her.

As they rode along and Michael observed the beauty of the woman who sat her saddle so easily beside him—or more often just ahead, for it was difficult to hold back her prancing mount—his spirits lifted. He was secretly glad that Geoffrey had treated Lenore so shabbily, leaving her and going to France, for it had given him this chance to woo her and perhaps to win her. Any guilt he felt when she turned her head and he saw the shadowed pain in her violet eyes he dispelled with the airy thought that he would be *much* better for Lenore than Geoffrey. He daydreamed that she would give up this wild scheme of racing at the fairs and ride with him to Coventry, where his mother would see at once how beautiful she was and how he had to have her and immediately consent to their marriage. His father would mention bitterly the inroads Michael's Oxford education had made on their finances, how he had hoped to recoup through a rich marriage arranged for his handsome son, but he would come around if Mother did. Michael's father always came around to whatever his mother decided was best—like spending all this money on an Oxford education for Michael and dressing him like a peacock all in red so that people would notice him.

Lenore scarcely noticed Michael's wistful smile, his covert admiring glances. Immersed in bittersweet memories of Geoffrey, she swallowed painfully and said, "Yes, yes," to something Michael said, unaware of what his words were. Around her bees and cicadas hummed and songbirds flitted through the summer meadows, and great trees dipped leafy green branches into the reflecting water

113

at the river's edge. She had left Oxford as she had arrived, she thought wryly—unnoticed.

In that she was mistaken. Their departure from Oxford had not gone unnoticed. Hardly had they cleared the city gates when they passed a pair of riders, headed south. The road was well populated at that point. Produce-laden farm carts streamed into the city, and along the edges of the dusty road strode sturdy country lads, and occasionally broad-hipped, deep-breasted country wenches swung by carrying baskets of eggs and herbs and sometimes live chickens with their feet tied together, into town for sale. In the bustle of all this coming and going, Lenore, preoccupied with her sad thoughts, did not notice the two riders—the big, coarse, black-bearded man and the small, sandy, weathered one—who reined in their horses and turned to stare speculatively after her and Michael.

This pair, whose names were Tubbs and Swan, had ridden in from Banbury, where—after a bad knife fight in which wiry little Swan had carved up a local drayman— the constable had warned them to leave before the fair started; drifters like them could give Banbury a bad name. So Tubbs and Swan had mounted up and were now headed into Oxford to see what pocket might be picked or what purse cut. A pair of cutthroats who'd long ago left all their scruples behind them, they were used to leaving places in a hurry. They'd been harried out of London, out of half a dozen towns since, so it was no novelty to be turned out of Banbury with their fair coming on. It had, however, put them in an ugly mood, and Swan, a wizened little fellow with coarse, sandy-red hair, a broken nose, and a slight limp, who was as quick with a dagger as any in Shoreditch, had been casting about him for easy prey on the road south.

As Michael and Lenore passed, he reined up. "Did ye see that?" he asked Tubbs in a low voice. "The wench and the stripling?"

"Aye," rumbled Tubbs, rubbing his matted black beard. He was a huge man with small, mean eyes and a voice that rasped almost painfully in his throat—souvenir of a barroom brawl in which he'd caught a flying bottle

114

in the Adam's apple. His gaze followed Michael's heavy baggage and Lenore's supple body thoughtfully. It was a tempting combination.

"A sight like that do heat the blood, don't it?" Swan was almost licking his chops as he looked after Lenore. "Now, there's a piece I'd like to get my hands on." He moved aside to avoid a passing farm cart. "The lad travels heavy—think you there could be something of value in those bags?"

Tubbs, who had been thinking the same thing, grunted. "The lad's armed with a pistol—I could see it."

"I doubt yon pink-cheeked lad can use it," sneered Swan. "Anyway, the girl's to my liking. How say you we turn about and ride north?"

The farm cart had now gone its creaking way, and there was a momentary lull in the traffic headed into Oxford.

"Not so far north as Banbury," Tubbs reminded him. "Or we'll land in jail."

"Nay, not so far as that. I say we take them somewhere twixt here and there—some likely spot. The wench reminded me of a tavern maid I knew in London—same color hair. She were a hot one. Not so pretty as this wench, though."

"I have eyes for the girl, too," rumbled Tubbs. "So if ye're thinkin' not to share her—"

"We'll share her," agreed Swan quickly, fingering his dirk as Tubbs's mean little eyes fixed on him. He had seen friendlier eyes on a charging boar. "But 'tis not to be like last time when ye was too rough and killed the girl afore I got my chance at 'er!" he warned in an aggrieved voice.

"Agreed," said Tubbs laconically. "We'll take care of the lad first and split up his belongings."

"And then we'll split up the girl!" finished Swan with an evil cackle and a flash of broken yellow teeth.

Heavy-handed Tubbs gave his companion a long, slow look from those little eyes. He'd been thinking of parting company with Swan before he got a dirk stuck through his ribs some night for some imagined grievance. The girl Swan spoke of had been but a young thing spitting

115

curses. She'd given him a sharp kick—but he'd not meant to break her ribs when he'd crushed her to him angrily and thrown her young body to the ground beneath him. That she had died of it—well, that was the luck of the road, wasn't it? They'd got away clean, even though there'd been a great to-do about it, for the girl had turned out to be the daughter of the local magistrate. Now this bonny wench on the white horse, he'd be more careful with her, for she looked a rare piece, and it might be good for a wanted man to travel with a "wife" to draw suspicion away from him—at least for a while. Should he get in trouble, he might use her favors to get him out of it —and if he grew tried of her, he could always take her into London and sell her to a brothel. "Mother" Moseley or "Lady" Bennett could always use a pretty piece like her in their establishments, or any of the brothels in Southwark. Meanwhile he'd humor Swan. "Ye can have her first," he shrugged in an offhand way, spitting in the dirt at the side of the road.

Swan brightened. "Now, that's more like it," he beamed, bobbing his sandy head until his unkempt hair fell over his face. "And right handsome of ye!" He pushed back his hair with dirty fingers and slapped his huge friend on the back, noting again how ironlike were those great knotted muscles beneath the soiled jerkin. Idly he considered just where a dirk would best slip in—in case they had a falling out—for treachery came easily to him, and he'd a mind to have this hot-looking wench all to himself.

Up ahead Michael had decided to try his luck. " 'Twould be better if ye forgot Banbury and came to Coventry," he insisted. "The baby's so small—suppose it rains at the fair?"

"Then I'll find shelter," sighed Lenore.

"We have a big house just south of Coventry—you could stay in a spare bedroom. My mother would see there were clean rushes on the floor, and you'd like the view."

Lenore smiled at him. His next question was obvious;

116

she hoped to forestall it. "Thank you, Michael, but I—I couldn't. I must make my own way."

"If ye married me, there'd be no need to leave—ye could stay forever. 'Twill all be mine one day."

"Michael, you know your parents would never countenance your marrying me. What would your mother say?"

" 'Tis not what my mother would say that worries you," he discerned shrewdly. " 'Tis Geoffrey who stands in my way."

He was right about that, she thought wryly, and looked away that he might not see the answer so plain on her face. In her arms Lorena gave a little sleepy cry, and she busied herself with comforting the child.

"Am I not as good a man as Geoffrey?" Michael shot at her in an aggrieved voice.

How to answer that? "Michael," she groaned, "please do not talk so much about Geoffrey. How can I forget him if I am constantly reminded of him?"

Michael saw the sense of that, but for the moment it left him with nothing to say. He had been priming himself with arguments concerning Geoffrey, thinking up ways to disparage him, to convince Lenore how much better he could take care of her. It was slowly coming to him that she did not expect anyone to take care of her—that she meant to take care of herself. Now he bounced along with a frown on his pink-cheeked countenance—for he had never had a very good seat on a horse—and tried to think up new arguments to convince Lenore that she should marry him.

Lenore was glad of the respite. She would need her wits about her when she got to Banbury, and she did not want to arrive tired out from arguing with Michael. But unbidden her thoughts slipped back to Geoffrey, and she found herself brooding as she rode, only half seeing the road which Snowfire danced along.

Weighed down by her unhappy thoughts, it was some time before Lenore realized they were being followed. Michael, concentrating on what seemed to him the more important problem of pressing his suit, had become

117

accustomed to the pair of riders whose horses jogged along behind them just too far for a good view of them to be had, but Lenore's sense of danger—sharpened by her wild flight with Geoffrey through southwest England—had awakened.

Now that the traffic had thinned out and the road had become lonelier, for the twentieth time Lenore looked back. "Think you that pair mean us harm?" she asked, squinting at them in the distance. She looked restively about her, wishing for a farm cart—even one that would block the road and make passing difficult. " 'Tis unnatural that whether we speed up or slow down, they keep that same distance between us."

Michael frowned as he looked behind him. A vague unease plagued him. "We'll lie the night at an inn—we won't wait till dark, there's one up ahead that we'll reach well before sundown." It occurred to him that the remark made him sound timid—he doubted that would have been Geoffrey's reaction to the situation. "But ye've naught to fear," he added hastily. "Can ye not see I've a large pistol to deal with knaves who might try to harm us?"

"I see it, Michael, but—have ye ever fired it?"

He bristled. "Of course I've fired it! At target. And hit what I aimed at."

Lenore sighed. Like the two cutthroats who followed them in the middle distance, she very much doubted if Michael could hit anything he aimed at. She gave his overladen mount an impatient look—it was plain they could make no better time, and if the pair following chose to overtake them, they could do so at will.

Still, if they stopped at an inn before dark, all should be well.

"Ye'll be at the mercy of every robber and highwayman in the countryside—not to mention country rogues who might do you harm—if ye go from town to town with the fairs, whilst if ye married me—"

"Oh, Michael," wailed Lenore, "please *stop*. I do not love you, Michael," she added more gently. "And I have told you that before."

118

"But I love *you* enough for both of us," he said with ingenuous enthusiasm. "And in time——"

"We'll part at Banbury," said Lenore. "And in time you will forget me—soon, I hope. I would bring you no luck. What is that up ahead, can you see?"

They had been riding through meadowlands along the river, but now they had come to a heavily wooded area, overgrown with brush, and the track had narrowed so that sometimes they were scraped by branches even riding single file. It was as if a green foliage tunnel had closed around them.

"I think it's a cart," said Michael.

"I *hope* it's a cart," muttered Lenore, for squinting back, she had come to the panicky conclusion that the pair were gaining on them. Now she could see that the road ahead was solidly blocked; directly across it a huge wagon lay overturned and the six big draft horses that had drawn it stood disconsolately tangled in their reins before the wreck. Spilled from the wagon were several enormous pieces of oaken furniture and the driver, a big rough fellow in a worn leather jerkin, was standing on one edge of the deep rut that had broken his wheel, roundly cursing his luck.

Perforce they came to a halt before the wreck. Lenore looked at the broken wheel, the upended load, and felt sorry for the driver—the roads around Twainmere had been rutted sheep trails and she had seen many a broken wheel and helped to right many an overturned cart.

"Can ye move your horses so that we can go around?" asked Michael in a peremptory tone that reminded Lenore that Michael came from a manor house and was an only son.

The beleaguered driver did not relish that tone. He turned about, running a hand through his thick hair, and fixed Michael with a stern gaze. "I've got to take this load all the way to Southampton," he growled. "Furniture it is for my master, who's taking ship there for the Colonies—and me with it, if I can but get there. If ye'll help me move these chests and this cupboard, young sir,

119

perhaps I can get my wagon righted and out of your way."

Michael looked down at his clean red clothing, bethought himself of his left garter hanging by a mere thread, and then eyed with distaste the fallen furniture, now covered with road dirt. These draymen were a careless lot; could not this oxlike fellow have seen that rut plain before him? "I have a weak back," he said testily. " 'Twas injured some years ago in a fall—I can pick up nothing heavy."

Lenore turned to gaze at Michael with some interest. This was the first she had heard of a bad back—and the load with which he had staggered out of his lodgings in Oxford was sadly tiring his horse.

The wagon driver understood perfectly. His jaw hardened.

"Then, young sir and mistress, I'm afraid ye must take the track off to your left," he said curtly. "For ye cannot get past me—not with that great tree and the thorn bushes pressing in at the side of the road." He peered down the green tunnel behind them. "There look to be two sturdy travelers coming up who might help a man reload his wagon. Should they choose to help me," he added with a sour look at Michael, "they'll get through speedily."

Lenore, who did not wish to wait until the two sinister travelers, who paced them in the distance, caught up, turned and looked in the direction he indicated. She saw a faint trail that wandered off between the trees—a sheep trail, she took it to be, leading down from the Cotswolds. She looked back restively at the oncoming riders and her voice sharpened.

"Let's not wait, Michael. Let's take the track."

"Where does the track lead?" asked Michael, a little crestfallen at this detour.

"If you look sharp and keep turning right, 'twill lead you back to this road," said the driver. "It comes out at a crossroads that lies ahead."

"Come on, Michael," said Lenore crisply, for those dark silhouettes she could see behind them down that

120

long, leafy tunnel were fast closing the distance. "We can find a quiet place to rest the horses and have a bite to eat before continuing on."

Sulkily Michael followed her as she turned Snowfire down the almost indiscernible lane that led into the forest. She lost the feeling of fear that had nagged at her as they rode along to the sound of birdsong and the fragrance of wildflowers, for this was the kind of country she understood—sheep country on the edge of the Cotswolds.

"I think we're lost," said Michael unhappily.

"No. I've been watching the track. There's been no turnoff, and now the trail is veering to the right. Your horse is near to falling from all that weight, Michael, and I must feed Lorena. I can hear a brook tinkling over there to the left. Listen, can't you hear it? What say we find it and stop for a bite of bread and cheese?"

"All right," said Michael glumly. "But I still say we're lost. We'll end up spending the night in this forest."

"Nonsense." Lenore dismounted and located the brook. A tiny rivulet it was, clear and cold. It was fed, she guessed, by a spring. From it, they and the horses drank. On the shady leaf mould of its bank she spread a linen square and laid Lorena down upon it. The baby slept on. As she busied herself getting out the food that Mistress Watt's cook had packed for her journey, Lenore said over her shoulder, "You should take all those heavy bags off your poor horse, Michael—he needs rest more than we do."

Michael, bent over the brook dashing water on his hot face, muttered something unintelligible.

Lenore turned to fix him with a level gaze. "If your back is too weak to lift them off," she said evenly, "*I* will do it."

Michael reddened. He got up at once and fell to unloading his horse. Lenore smiled grimly as she heard him mumbling to himself.

"Now," she said with puckish humor, as he flung himself down panting beside her and she offered him some brown bread and cheese, "you can count yourself lucky to have escaped me! Suppose I had said yes to your offer

121

of marriage! What would your life have been like then?"

"In truth you do drive a man hard," Michael admitted, taking the bread and Cheshire cheese she offered him. "But"—he looked wistfully into her beautiful face—"I'd hope that once wed, you'd lighten your grip on the reins."

"Never," she told him, biting into the brown bread. "You should have helped that man with his overturned load, Michael. 'Twas unkind to leave him there in the road."

"You heard him say those two travelers would help him. Besides, it was his own fault that he ran his wheel into that great rut. 'Twas plain before him to see!"

"Some would say 'tis my own fault I'm where I am today," mused Lenore. "But I could still use a bit of sympathy for my plight!"

"Ah, I *do* sympathize with you, Lenore—"

"Only because you love me."

"What better reason?" he asked simply.

Lenore sighed. What better reason indeed? Who was she to criticize Michael, who was so childishly, so ardently in love with her? She fell silent, watching the horses graze as best they could, and she and Michael finished munching their bread and cheese and shared a plum tart.

She was suddenly aware that Michael was staring at her very wistfully.

"Lenore," he said in a husky voice, "we will part when we reach Banbury and—and I have never kissed you. I love you with all my heart, and I have never once kissed you."

His plea was so genuine, his face so earnest and sad that Lenore felt pity for him. She leaned over and gently pressed her lips to his.

Michael gave a great shuddering sigh and pulled her to him. He was awkward as he kissed her—and kissed her again.

Achingly she was reminded of all the nights Geoffrey had held her in his arms and she had thrilled to his touch. Remembering was a kind of sweet anguish that grew unbearable. She pulled away from Michael.

"I must feed my baby, Michael."

122

"Oh, Lenore, couldn't we . . . ?" His voice shook and his hand trembled as he touched her breast.

She flinched. "No, Michael, no."

"All right," he sighed, and hunched his shoulders away from her, a picture of abject misery. She gave him a hopeless look, wondering if this sort of behavior had got him his way at home. She supposed it had.

Briskly she moved over to where the baby lay, sat down beside her, picked her up very tenderly, and kissed her awake. Big blue eyes considered her gravely.

Then, deftly tossing a napkin over her breast to hide it modestly from Michael's view, Lenore fed Lorena. She was able to forget Michael, to forget Geoffrey, to forget the world for a little while as she rocked her baby in her arms, tickled her under the chin, and was rewarded by a small gurgling laugh. One by one she took up Lorena's tiny fingers and counted them in tune to a singsong nursery rhyme.

A bit sulky that there were no more kisses forthcoming, Michael stretched out by the brook with his hat over his eyes to shade his face from the summer sun slanting through the overhanging trees and rested as Lenore, leaning against a dark tree bole, sang her child a sad, sweet lullaby.

It was peaceful there in the woods with the birds singing overhead, but the slanting sun reminded Lenore that it was growing late. She got up and put the food away, and Michael again loaded up his weary horse. They mounted up—Lenore with Lorena sleeping peacefully in the crook of her arm—and rode on. For all that she'd told Michael they weren't lost, Lenore was beginning to be uneasy about finding the road again when just ahead through the heavy brush they saw the stone crossroads marker.

CHAPTER 9

Lenore frowned. Something wasn't right—the birds had stopped singing. Around them the air seemed still and heavy, somnolent and waiting.

Michael had no sense of danger; he brightened. " 'Tis the road at last," he sighed, urging his horse forward. "The inn should be—"

He never finished his sentence.

From behind the bushes at the roadside leaped two men. Lenore screamed. The big one—Tubbs—lunged at Michael, whose horse reared up and gave him time to drag out his pistol and cock it and fire it. The ball struck Tubbs in the chest. He gave a curse as he toppled, but his hamlike hand had latched onto the hem of Michael's short red cloak and he pulled the slender youth from the saddle as he went down. Michael's horse snorted and darted away, heading back down the road to Oxford, and the two men fell to the ground, locked in unequal struggle.

Swan meanwhile had leaped for Lenore's bridle, and

she had lifted her foot and given him a solid kick in the jaw that numbed her toes but sent him sprawling backward to stretch his wiry length by the roadside. As he toppled she heard Tubbs give a howl—Michael had kneed him. Now Lenore saw Tubbs bring his hamlike fist down with such ferocity on Michael's head that she could hear the crack when Michael's neck snapped and his head tilted at a crazy angle as he slumped over, dead.

Paralyzed by this turn of events, Lenore had no time to react to them, for Snowfire, rearing and terrified at this sudden attack, wheeled and bolted, almost unseating her. Back down the track they had come he ran wildly, and over Lorena's thin, frightened wail she heard big Tubbs howl, "Get the wench, Swan—I'm bleedin' half to death!"

Swan, on his feet again and cursing, ran for his horse and streaked off after Lenore.

Lenore, with the white stallion charging down the narrow track she had so recently traversed, looked back through whipping branches to see Swan thundering after her in wild pursuit. Snowfire was faster, but the track was treacherous at this pace. Lorena was wailing at the top of her voice, but Lenore was thinking fast now. She dared not return to Oxford, nor could she now take the road to Banbury with that great hulking brute waiting to cut her off at the crossroads. Just past the place where they had stopped for lunch, she had noticed a tiny track leading off to the left—another faint sheep track leading into the Cotswolds. It lay just ahead around a turn. She would have a chance to dart into that wall of greenery and lose her pursuer there—and if she did not lose him, she would be no worse off, for she dared not seek the main road.

She managed to turn Snowfire's head, and without hesitation careened off down an unknown trail.

It was a mistake.

Twenty feet down the track Snowfire caught his foot in a hole covered up with leaves and stumbled to his knees, throwing Lenore over his head.

My baby, my baby! she thought in panic as she sailed through the air toward a wall of green. Head bent and arms locked protectively around the bundled-up Lorena

125

as if they had been a cage, she landed rolling in a bush. Thorns tore at her, she felt her head jerked violently as some of her hair was pulled out by clutching twigs, there was a sharp pain in her shoulder as a branch gouged her, caught and ripped the material of her sleeve—and then skidded harmlessly by as the material tore free.

She came up with a sickening jolt against a big tree trunk and for a moment lay there, gasping for breath. In terror she sat up, lifted her head to toss back the tangled hair that hung like a shawl over her locked arms, and unlocked those scratched, bruised arms to assure herself that Lorena—still squalling lustily—was all right.

"Hush, hush," she murmured in anguish, for those pounding hoofbeats were coming closer.

Behind her Snowfire scrambled to his feet and Lenore, on her feet now and prepared to remount, realized sickeningly that he could hardly bear his weight on his right forefoot. She'd never outdistance her pursuer now—and already he must be rounding the turn.

They could not run—they must hide!

She grasped Snowfire's reins, and putting gentle fingers over her baby's mouth to silence those strident wails, she led the limping white horse through a stand of poplars into a deep thicket. On she struggled through the heavy undergrowth, wincing at the pain that shot through her left shoulder, but managing to reach out bravely to protect both the baby and the horses's head from whipping needled branches.

After several minutes of this she paused to rest—and listen. No sound of hooves came to her through the patch of thorns behind her.

The silence worried her. Her pursuer could not have passed on—surely she'd have heard him thundering on up the track. But she'd best be still now, for the slapping branches she'd had to part to let them through had made some noise even though her shoes and Snowfire's hooves had padded almost silently over the soft, damp leaf mould underfoot.

In the oppressive stillness where even the birds had

126

ceased to sing, she cast an anxious look around her—and screamed.

From behind a tree Swan leaped, grinning, and plunged toward her. She could see his yellow teeth flashing past an intervening thorn branch. Dropping Snowfire's reins, her only concern now to save her baby, she ducked and slid through an opening in the green wall to her left, heard Swan's howl as he plunged full tilt into the thorn branch and the long needles tore into him.

Weaving through the heavy underbrush, she could hear his crashing progress behind her, his muttered curses, as she fought her way through the thicket, bending this way and that as she squeezed between tree boles, tore free of rope-like vines whose tendrils threatened to twine about her and hold her fast. Her breath was rasping in her throat as she broke free of the thicket into a tiny clearing. Her foot caught on an exposed tree root and she stumbled and went down heavily on her knees—once again breaking Lorena's fall with her bruised, scratched arms.

Before she could rise, Swan had crashed through the thicket into the clearing behind her, seized her by the collar of her dress, and was hoisting her, half-choked, to her feet. His arms were wiry and hard, and as if she were a puppet on a string he swung her around to face him with a triumphant laugh.

"Thought ye'd got away, didn't ye?"

"Please," gasped Lenore, "I've no money—"

"Money?" He laughed again. "Did ye think it was money I was chasin' ye for?"

Lenore swallowed. "I know people who live on this road," she told him fiercely. "They're due to come by any minute—and they have dogs and guns. You'd do well to let me go!"

"So-o-o . . . ye still have fight in ye." He leered down into her face. "I like a wench with fight."

Lenore flinched away from him, but her mien was defiant. His fingers were digging into her shoulders so hard she was sure there'd be a blue mark where each one pressed. The pain in her left shoulder sickened her, but she stood her ground.

127

"The people I know will pay you well if you let me go unharmed!" she cried, trying to buy time.

"Ye're a good liar, too," he approved. "Course that cart driver told us which way he'd directed you when Tubbs and I helped him move his cart so's we could get through. So we both know ye're a stranger to these woods."

Lenore felt she might faint.

Swan's jaw jutted closer. His voice grew surly and held a threat more terrible than any she had heard before. "Now ye'll give me no more trouble," he told her heavily, keeping a viselike grip on the arm with the torn sleeve and running a stubby finger down her flinching throat and between her breasts. "Ye might escape me, mistress, but yer baby won't. I could make do with *it*—if *you* get away."

Lenore's face turned so ashen that her violet eyes stood out as dark, horrified spots. With all that was left of her ebbing strength she edged her baby further from that yellow-toothed evil face thrust down into hers.

"Let me put the baby down," she said hopelessly. "Don't hurt her and—and I'll do what you want. Just so you don't hurt my baby."

"Thought you might." He grinned, but he kept his painful grasp on her arm as she turned and carefully placed Lorena in the bole of a hollow tree—he didn't trust her.

Lenore straightened up and faced him. Her gaze was steady, her jaw clenched. She might have been a woman going to the stake.

His greedy eyes roved over her as if she were a juicy roast he was about to devour. He licked his lips and studied her.

"I'll take ye here out of sight of the road," he decided. "And if ye're nice to me—*real* nice—I won't turn ye over to big Tubbs back there. He'll be meaner'n a bear 'cause he's been shot, so he'd rough ye up—kill ye, maybe. Me—I won't do nothin' ye won't enjoy!" An uncontrollable shiver went over Lenore. She kept her head high. "Course," he added on a note of warning, "do ye fight me, I'll remember how ye give me a kick in the face back there and maybe break yer legs so ye won't go nowhere and I can take my time with ye."

Lenore's knees went weak at this threat.

"Do what you want," she said dully. "Just so you don't hurt my baby."

"Aye, now that's what I like to see—a docile wench," he said with satisfaction. "Lay ye down where ye are. Them leaves'll make a nice nest for us."

Slowly, wincing as her weight fell on her hurt shoulder, Lenore stretched herself out on the ground. The leaves beneath her were wet and smelled of leaf mould. They wet the back of her dress clean through, and she could feel moisture crawl along her spine. To her wide-staring eyes, it seemed that the devil himself stood above her, tearing open his dirty trousers.

"Ain't never seen nothin' like this, have ye?" he crowed. "Nothin' but weak nubbins of the gentry, I'll be bound!"

Lenore looked quickly away, and he snickered. At the sound her taut nerves made her muscles jerk and her breasts quivered. She looked back to see him staring at them, beads of perspiration forming on his forehead.

"You don't have to take your clothes off—now," he said thickly. "We can do that tonight. We'll have to run from Tubbs—he's hard to kill."

So he meant to take her with him! Her eyes dilated and her lashes were a dark fringe against her chalky skin. Her hair—full of leaves and twigs—had come down and was spread in a tangled shawl over the wet leaves. In the nearby tree-bole Lorena was wailing. The sound made Lenore feel sick. What would happen to her baby, once this monster had had his fill of her?

Desperation gave her strength. This man whose eyes goggled down at her had a dagger—it was stuck in his belt. She forced herself not to look at it, but to stare up into that lust-filled countenance. If she could but reach that dagger . . . !

She closed her eyes with an involuntary shudder as Swan lowered himself, chuckling, onto her and clawed up her skirts over her shrinking legs. "Ye're the prettiest

129

wench I ever had!" he declared in a husky voice, slobbering over her cheek as she turned her head sharply away from him. "Ain't no need to be afraid," he cooed ingratiatingly, clutching her hurt shoulder in a grip that made her cry out and left red weals where each finger pressed. Nearly paralyzed with pain, she slumped as he released his grip. "There, that's better," he said in a cruel tone. *"Relax!"* He slid one of his arms under her back, the other beneath her head, and his knee jabbed viciously at her locked legs in an attempt to wrest them apart.

"Lie still, damn ye!" he commanded fiercely—but Lenore, writhing beneath him, had got her right arm free. Now as he ripped at her bodice, exposing her breasts, she craftily worked that hand toward the hilt of his dagger. She cried out again as his lips closed suckingly over her right breast and both his hands violently clasped her bare buttocks, jerking her hips upward toward him. Lenore twisted in his grasp, but her hand was firmly on the dagger's hilt now. She moaned loudly to distract him—and pulled it out.

"Ye like that, aye?" he chuckled.

Lenore kept her eyes firmly closed that he might not read their murderous expression. By now his knee had wrested her legs apart and as he made to consummate their union she pressed suddenly toward him in simulated passion—to give her arm a better swing. Drawing the dagger back as far as she could, she plunged it hilt deep into his back.

Swan made a sudden strangled sound in his throat and rose up from her, clawing behind him. "Tubbs— damn you!" He staggered to his knees and Lenore managed to jerk her legs free as Swan looked wildly about for his erstwhile companion. His incredulous gaze turned to Lenore, who rolled away from him and gained her feet. *"You* done it," he gasped. *"You* done me in!" He seemed to wilt before her eyes, slipping down into the wet leaf mould. "You got to help me," he whispered. "If you don't, I'm done for."

How long she stood there gazing down at him, she did not know. He was a terrible sight, lying on his stomach

130

with the knife stuck into his back and blood oozing out. Worse, his head was twisted to the side so that he could look up at her out of the corner of one eye. "Help—me!" he gasped.

She stared down at him in revulsion. This monster had been about to violate her and do God knew what to her little Lorena. The memory of big Tubbs's hamlike fist smashing down on Michael's unprotected head swam up before her eyes. Once again she heard the snap as his neck broke. And Lorena's baby skull was so thin and soft.

She had not known her voice could be so cold. "You will live if God wills it," she said. "But not with *my* help!"

Swan groaned as she found his horse tethered to a tree and led it past him. Ignoring his cries, she picked up Lorena from the hollow tree where she had deposited her. Soft and warm in her arms, Lorena's wails subsided to hiccups as Lenore cuddled and petted her. Lorena had never seemed more precious to her than she did at that moment. Closing her eyes, she gave thanks to a merciful heaven that she had been spared to see her through to safety.

Lorena had quieted by the time she found Snowfire and led him back to where the gray mare stood. Carefully she mounted the unfamiliar animal—she could not afford to be bucked off with a baby in her arms.

"Ye can't take her!" cried Swan piteously. "Ye can't take my horse! I'll bleed to death!" He lapsed into a storm of curses.

She did not even give him a backward look. All the pity she had left she gave to Snowfire. His leg was swelling now. "Come along, Snowfire," she said gently. "We must away from here before the big one comes looking for us." As if he understood, the white horse—who had begun the day so gaily—limped after her as she set off on the gray mare along the unfamiliar trail that must, she guessed, lead into the Cotswolds.

Twice she changed direction, taking off on stony trails where she'd be hard to track. Sometimes she looked back to give Snowfire a compassionate look and murmur an occasional word of encouragement. His leg must be very

131

painful by now, she knew, but he kept plodding along after her valiantly.

After riding a long while, she felt safer and sat for a moment, silent and listening. Lorena was asleep again. No sound but the wild birds and humming insects of the dusky summer forest broke the stillness. Nearby she could hear a little stream tinkling, and the last of the light gilded the tree branches to gold.

She drew a deep sighing breath. She must have lost any pursuit by now. Indeed big Tubbs might still be waiting at the crossroads for his confederate to return. She remembered how he had struck Michael, and a sob went through her.

Behind her Snowfire looked very woebegone. His leg was badly swollen now, and she dismounted and found the stream and led both horses over the softest earth she could to its bank. There she laid Lorena down gently and watched Snowfire and the gray mare drink their fill. She tore strips from her petticoat and gently bathed Snowfire's swollen foreleg and wrapped it carefully. Then she took off her clothes and washed her whole body in ice-cold water, wincing as her scratches hurt with renewed fury and her left shoulder ached.

It was not much, but the bath made her feel as if she'd washed Swan's filthy touch from her skin.

And then, half-dressed, she sank down and wept for a boy who had loved her and would never drain a tankard with his friends or wear a stylish red cloak again. Michael might be alive had he not dashed madly out of Oxford to follow her.

But she could not afford the luxury of a long weep. There was more to be done. She finished dressing, combed the twigs from her long hair, made a pillow of her saddle-bag, ate a little, and fed her baby, crooning as she did so and holding her with a terrible tenderness, for she had been so very close to losing her . . . so close.

That night in the tiny copse she slept beneath a tree with Lorena cradled in her arms—at least, she tried to sleep. Her shoulder throbbed dully. Once she dozed and the wild cry of a loon startled her awake. The night

132

sounds of hunting owls, small screeches, and slip-slaps in the water of the gurgling brook brought her to instant alertness. Was big Tubbs nearby? Had he found her? She clutched Lorena to her more than once and muttered a prayer.

Though Lenore did not know it, she had nothing to fear from big Tubbs. The letting of his own blood by Michael's pistol ball had cleared his angry head, and he quickly realized that he must get rid of Michael's body. He stuffed a dirty handkerchief into his bleeding wound, which he judged none too bad since the buckle of his baldric had deflected the ball. Systematically he went through Michael's pockets, pocketed his coins, and finding them too few for his liking, gave Michael's inert body a kick. Michael did not feel it; he'd been dead for some time. Tubbs yearned to leave him where he was, but this was a crossroads and someone might happen along at any time and raise a hue and cry. Unceremoniously he dragged Michael into a thick clump of bushes nearby and threw a couple of tree branches over him—animals, he thought grimly, would take care of the rest.

From this chore, Tubbs straightened and peered down the road. Michael's horse and baggage were nowhere in sight—probably halfway back to Oxford by now. Torn with a desire to follow the horse—at least the beast would have value, even if the baggage proved worthless —Tubbs began to curse. He dared not follow the horse, for he half expected Swan to run away with the girl— and she was worth more than the few coins he'd garnered from the dead lad in the red cloak.

Grimly, he mounted and set off down the track in the direction Swan had disappeared.

"Swan," he called cautiously as he rode along. And again, "Swan?"

At last he heard a weak voice answer.

"Here. Over here."

Following the voice, he blundered through the thicket into the little clearing where Lenore had left her attacker. Tubbs came to a surprised halt at the sight of Swan's body sprawled out with the dagger sticking in his back.

133

"Help me, Tubbs," cried Swan desperately. "The wench done me in!"

Tubbs gave a low whistle as he dismounted. "Did a good job on ye, didn't she?" he marveled admiringly. "Clean to the hilt! How d'ye feel, Swan?"

"Bad," muttered Swan. "Real bad. Draw the knife out careful, Tubbs. Mind you staunch the wound."

"Aye." Tubbs was imperturbable.

He leaned forward and Swan gave a banshee screech as the knife was drawn out of his back. "Staunch it!" he sobbed, seeing Tubbs sit back, wipe off the blade on the leaf mould, and stick the knife in his belt.

"Staunch it!" wailed Swan.

Tubbs pulled out a handkerchief and stuffed it casually into the wound. "Ye'll be all right," he said. Squatting on the ground, Tubbs rocked back and forth on his feet and surveyed his injured friend. "Where's your horse, Swan?"

She took it," said Swan vengefully. "Wait'll I find that wench! Just wait!" He tried to move and gasped with pain. "Here, help me up, Tubbs."

Tubbs rose. "I can't take ye up on my horse, Swan. We'd break his bloody back."

Perspiring with the effort, Swan had managed to rise to a sitting position. "But ye can't leave me here!" he panted.

"Nay, I can't—ye'd talk if they found ye," muttered Tubbs. "Well, I guess ye'll have to go, Swan."

Swan was shaking with relief. He'd thought big Tubbs meant to leave him to die in these woods.

"Maybe this stick will help ye—something to lean on." Idly big Tubbs picked up a heavy tree branch.

Swan saw this primitive cudgel cudgel poised above his head, screeched, and tried vainly to duck. The branch caught him in the temple and he plunged forward with a rattle in his throat. After a moment, he stopped twitching and lay inert.

Tubbs went thoroughly through his friend's pockets, took everything of value, and was about to depart when a frown crossed his heavy features. He and Swan had been seen together at Banbury—indeed the constable there had warned them both to depart before the fair. If Swan were found dead here, he'd no doubt be held accountable for his murder. He sighed. A man couldn't be too careful. Reluctantly he dragged Swan's body back a ways into the woods. Finding a soft spot of earth, he used Swan's knife to dig him a shallow grave, rolled him in, and covered him up with earth and leaves. Some animal might find him there, 'twasn't likely people would—at least not until he, John Tubbs, was well out of this part of the country.

He remounted then, headed back to the crossroads, and hurried back along the road to Oxford. On the way he caught up with Michael's horse, took what he wanted from Michael's baggage, and sold the horse in Oxford. He laid up there at a brothel until his wound was healed and started out again, for he was uneasy that one or both of the bodies might be found and there'd be questions he'd not care to answer.

He made his way without incident to Bristol—save for cutting a purse or two on the road—and there he was "pressed" into the navy and died from a blow with a marlinspike when he got into a fight with the second mate.

There were none to mourn him, and sullen Tubbs died without confessing any of his crimes. Swan's grave was never found.

Tubbs had got away with both murders, for he died without being suspected of either. But he'd left Lenore with a sticky problem, although she didn't know it for some time.

CHAPTER 10

Morning dawned bright and beautiful. A soft stillness enveloped the countryside, and the birds' songs were muted and sweet. A sky of brilliant blue with soft, floating white clouds could be glimpsed through the canopy of branches overhead. Around her was the chirp and hum of tiny living things going to work with the new day. Lorena gurgled up at her and reached up a tiny hand. Lenore kissed those tiny fingers and got up and washed her face in the ice-cold stream.

In the purity and beauty of the morning she found it hard to believe in the reality of yesterday's events. Surely they were all a nightmare and would be forgotten soon, melted away by the bright sunshine.

But a limping Snowfire and the gray mare were both grim reminders. As was her shoulder whenever she moved. And she knew that back at the crossroads lay Michael's body and along that wooded track behind her a wounded man. . . . It was a somber-faced woman who nursed her child and soothed it. Afterward she ate an apple and sat and stroked Lorena pale, downy hair and tried to plan for the future.

Racing at the Banbury fair was impossible now, of course. Snowfire's leg was hurt, how badly she could not tell, but it would be a long time before he could run again. The gray was a passable riding horse but not built for speed. Mentally assessing her assets, her eyes fell on the gray mare's saddlebags. She had not thought to look in those; automatically she had thought of them as belonging to somebody else. Now ruthlessly she checked through them, finding several pins—which she promptly used to pin her torn dress together—a dirty pack of cards, a bottle of rum, a dirty shirt, and—something hard. Her heart leaped, hoping it was money. But it was not. The object was wrapped in a small linen cloth, and when she unwrapped it an amethyst ring fell into her hand. Amethysts were highly regarded, and Lenore looked at it speculatively. Stolen, of course, but there was no way she could return it. Perhaps she'd be able to sell it. . . . With a sigh she put the ring in her pocket, kept the bottle of rum, and threw away the rest. It was a thoughtful woman who made ready to begin her journey once more.

The horses were hungry, so as noon approached and she saw a hayfield with only the rooftop of a cottage visible over the rise beyond, she dismounted and walked Snowfire and the gray carefully toward it, keeping a wary eye out for the farmer. Snowfire's limp was a little better today, but she hated to make him use that leg at all. At the edge of the little field she stopped and let the horses graze on the hay. It was stealing, she knew, and some farmer would no doubt curse her for it—unless he believed a wandering deer had done it—but she was at least careful to keep the horses on the edge of the field so their hooves did not trample down the upstanding hay. Snowfire nuzzled her gently, as if in appreciation of a good meal, as she remounted the docile gray. When she rode away he limped after her.

She no longer feared pursuit by Tubbs, for the crossroads grew farther away all the time, she had changed

137

course several times, and Tubbs was, after all, wounded. Bolder now, following first one sheep trail and then another, she moved deeper into the Cotswolds, and when she sighted a shepherd seated on a hill watching his flock graze, she waved to him and rode up boldly.

The shepherd's dog came running to meet her and circled her warily, but the shepherd called to him in a low voice and the dog went back to his master. As Lenore rode up, she saw that the shepherd was an old man, stooped, with pale eyes used to studying far distances.

Glad of the company in his lonely vigil, he offered her a bit of stew and as she ate, gratefully, he studied her with those shrewd pale eyes.

"Where are ye bound, mistress?"

"To Twainmere," said Lenore before she thought. And suddenly she knew that was where she would go, for it was the only place that, without money, she was sure of a roof. Flora would take her in. When Snowfire was well again, she'd take him out on the road and race him at the fairs for a living, just as she'd planned. "I am a widow," she improvised, "and must return to my people."

"Twainmere," he murmured. " 'Tis a long way off."

"I know," she said. "I think I'm lost."

He smiled and pointed out directions and told her what landmarks to watch out for. She thanked him warmly for the stew and rode away, and he followed her with his pale eyes as long as she was in sight. Widowed she might be, he thought, but not for long. Such a woman as that would have another husband soon. Somehow seeing her had increased his loneliness, for once he'd had a young wife . . . once long ago. Now he recalled too vividly what it had been like to hold her in his arms, to sleep with her, to wake up with her beside him in the pink dawn and turn over and lay a sleepy arm across her breast. He sighed and got up to move his sheep to a new pasture.

Feeling easier now that she was sure of her directions, Lenore pressed on, following the sheep trails, which

138

indeed were almost the only roads of these Cotswold Hills. She moved by easy stages because of Snowfire's leg, riding by daylight, hiding by night in sheltered copses where she was beset by nightmares that left her white and shaken in the moonlight. She prayed that there would not be a summer thunderstorm to bog down the track and make the going more difficult for Snowfire—and she was fortunate, the weather held.

Her shoulder no longer hurt her much, and her scratches were well on their way to healing, but her food had run out and she was very hungry when in the fading light of a red sunset she reached Twainmere. People were at supper, she guessed, as she rode down the deserted street of the familiar village.

The honey-colored stone of the cottages was turned deep pink by the rosy light. But the smithy was empty, the cottage behind boarded up and deserted, the garden that had been Flora's pride overgrown with weeds. Lenore dismounted and with a sinking heart peered in through a broken shutter. The dimness showed her an empty room with a rat scurrying about. Flora's cat must have left, too. Somehow she felt the cottage had been empty for a long time.

Lenore, usually so resolute, for once was daunted. Could Flora, disheartened by Jamie's death, have packed up and gone back to Scotland? If Flora had left, Twainmere might not be safe for her. Tom Prattle would be quick to denounce her, and there'd be none who'd care to take in the town flirt, come back with a babe in her arms. Doubt twinged at her. No one had seen her yet— perhaps she should leave quietly the way she had come.

She remounted, feeling a sudden rush of homesickness for a village that no longer had a place for her. She remembered then that Robert Medlow, the young vicar —one of the few men in Twainmere who had seemed immune to Lenore's wiles—had been very fond of Flora. If anyone would know Flora's whereabouts, Robert Medlow would. She wheeled her mount and headed down the deserted street, past the churchyard where Meg slept beneath a fresh-hewn stone, and dismounted at the vicarage.

It had not changed—just as nothing in Twainmere seemed to have changed. She hesitated, then carefully placed the sleeping Lorena in one of Snowfire's saddlebags—she did not want to answer questions about the baby just now, and the young vicar was sure to ask. Lorena continued to sleep peacefully. Lenore flexed her arm, which had gone nearly numb from holding Lorena for so long, and stood studying the pleasant ivy-covered building with its yew hedge and low stone wall overrun with red roses. She had been careful to tie Snowfire to the hitching post, as well as the gray mare. For these were familiar surroundings to Snowfire, and she wouldn't want him limping down to Tom Prattle's lean-to stable, expecting hay and currying and a comfortable bed of straw!

She had rapped but once on the oaken door of the vicarage before it was flung open and Flora herself stood before her in the rosy evening light. Each was as startled as the other.

"Flora!" gasped Lenore.

Flora, her blue eyes filling with tears, held out her arms and Lenore went into them with a sob. They stood there rocking and laughing and crying. Lenore hadn't realized until this moment how much she'd missed Flora; somehow gaunt Flora had taken in Lenore's heart the place of Meg who was gone, and now here she was at the vicarage and somehow she couldn't stop crying.

"There, there," said Flora, moved. Surreptitiously she wiped the tears from her eyes as if it were shameful to cry. "We thought you'd died at Worcester, Lenore. We got word you'd been seen going into the town—at least, some wild tale; we thought it must be you from the description—but none had seen you leave. We thought you might have been buried along with—with the others."

With Jamie, she meant.

Lenore stood back, smiling through her tear-blurred eyes and catching her breath. "I wanted to stay, Flora —I wanted to bury Jamie myself. But a cavalier wouldn't

140

let me—he said I'd be taken if I stayed. 'Twas he who saved me from the Ironsides, Flora; he got me through Cromwell's lines outside the city. We ran half across England together. How is it you're not at the cottage, Flora?"

"I married Robbie—the vicar," said Flora simply.

Lenore's eyes widened. The vicar, no less! "I'm glad for you," she said sincerely.

Flora sighed. "I would have married Robbie long before this," she admitted, "but for Jamie. I felt Jamie needed me, for he wouldna settle down—and you were but a young thing. But come and sit yourself down, Lenore. Robbie's out visitin' the sick and I'm waitin' supper for him. We can have us a talk. You'll be stayin', of course?"

Lenore hugged her. "Indeed I will. And just wait till you see my baby!"

"Baby!" Flora trailed her out. "And I see you've still got Snowfire!"

Lenore nodded proudly. "But he's gone lame and needs resting." She drew Lorena out of Snowfire's saddlebag. "Flora, this is my little Lorena."

She held Lorena up for Flora's inspection, and the older woman bent down and smiled at the child—then she peered closer and her eyes widened in shock.

" 'Tis Jamie's," she whispered. "That hair, those eyes . . ."

"Yes," said Lenore in a tight voice. "That hair, those eyes—that's why my cavalier left me. He said the baby wasn't his, but belonged to the Scot."

"And he was right," cried Flora in an excited voice, bending over the baby. She looked up sharply at some inflection in Lenore's voice. "This cavalier was your lover, then?"

Lenore nodded gravely. "I'll not keep it from you, Flora. I lived with him when we were on the run, and later in Oxford where I went to bear the child. I would have married him, Flora, but—I learned he already had a wife. He left me after Lorena was born."

Pity shone in Flora's eyes. She looked at Lenore, so beautiful in the rosy copper light from the dying sun.

141

"You are young," she murmured. " 'Tis no more than I would expect. Young blood runs wild. But ye're scratched and bruised, Lenore. Did you take a fall?"

"Yes—a fall." Lenore did not feel she could tell Flora about all the recent things that had happened to her just now; that must wait till later. "I'd nowhere to go after he left me, and I thought of you and hoped you'd take me in."

"And you were right to come here," said Flora warmly. "Come into the house. My, it's getting dark—I'll light a candle. You must be hungry, Lenore."

"Yes, but—Flora, could I take Snowfire and the gray mare back to the stable? Snowfire's exhausted, and I'd like to feed him and water him and bed him down in the straw. I've been bathing his ankle in the streams and springs every chance I got, but 'tis badly swollen still."

"Of course. Put the bairn down on my bed—ah, she's a sweet child with a fair face!"

"She may wet your bed," Lenore objected.

"Let her," said Flora crisply. " 'Tis good to have a bairn in the house—and this one Jamie's." Her eyes sparkled, and in the candlelight dusk she looked suddenly years younger. "She's my niece, you know," she added proudly.

Together they fed and bedded down Snowfire and the gray, and Lenore tended Snowfire's hurt foreleg.

"Your gray mare looks to be a valuable horse," commented Flora.

Lenore nodded. She did not explain how she came to have the mare, who was probably stolen like the amethyst ring. She could not bear to speak of the crossroads attack, which still haunted her dreams. For now she would let Flora think this gray riding horse was a gift from her lost lover.

"You can have the small room at the back," decided Flora. " 'Tis an extra room we don't need and 'twill be a great help to me to have you about again, Lenore."

It was all Lenore could do not to cry again. She gripped Flora's hand thankfully.

Robert Medlow, the vicar, was a pleasant, vacant-faced,

unassuming young man of medium build who always seemed a bit absent-minded. In a way he seemed a strange match for tall, gaunt Flora, but when Lenore saw the way they looked at each other, she knew they were in love. There was something shy and humble in the way Robert Medlow treated Flora. He greeted Lenore with courtesy and much less surprise than Flora had, saying it must have been God's will that had spared her at Worcester—and see, here was the fruit of it!—indicating Lorena.

Lenore, remembering the horror of Worcester, thought grimly that it had indeed been God's will—and Geoffrey's will, too, for had his hard fist not rendered her senseless at Barbour's Bridge, she would have stubbornly stayed and doubtless gone to her death for it, like other hapless souls.

They made her comfortable and fed her a good supper of cold mutton and cider and berry tart. Afterward Flora led her into a little room that was better than anything she had ever had except at Oxford. That night she slept dreamlessly, even able to forget the nightmares of the road.

The next day, walking with Flora in the scented old garden with its moss roses and musk roses, surrounded by hedges of clipped yew, she paused in the shade of a May-flowering beech. "I don't deserve you, Flora," she said simply.

"Ah, that's foolishness," said Flora, flushing with pleasure. "Robbie is as glad to have you as I am."

"But to take in not only myself, but the baby, too—it's very good of him, Flora." She brushed away a lazy bumblebee that wanted to light in her hair.

"Robbie's glad to have a bairn around the house," said Flora, carefully smoothing her full linen skirt. "Since there's not likely to be one of our own." She reached down, plucked a musk rose, and cupped it in her bony hand. "The bees are all at work gathering honey. Our hives should do well this year."

Lenore blinked. "Do you not plan a family of your own, Flora?" She would not be put off by talk of bees.

143

Flora looked away, through the beech branches toward the north. She might have been looking at Scotland, so distant was the look in her shadowed blue eyes. "That is denied me," she said in a low voice. "God's will or man's will, it is all one—I'll bear no child."

Lenore was puzzled. "I don't understand."

Flora sighed, looking down into the musk rose as if she might somehow find the answer there. "Robbie's been very good to me," she said carefully. "He'd offered for my hand before you and Jamie were handfasted, Lenore, and I'd always said no, I must look after my wild young brother. But when Jamie died, Robbie hurried over and offered for my hand again. I said no, 'twas not proper—there should be a period of mourning—but he told me roughly we must be married right away. He was right, Lenore. Marrying Robbie was all that saved me from the wrath of the village. For there were those who claimed Jamie was a traitor who'd rebelled against the Lord Protector, and they might have whipped me through the village tied to the tail of a cart. But once I married Robbie, all was forgotten, for the people here love Robbie."

"I know that, Flora, but what has all that to do with your raising a family?"

Flora turned and gave her a level look. Her voice was wistful. "I've no child of my own, nor like to have any, since Robbie comes not to my bed."

"Never?" gasped Lenore.

"Not once." Flora sighed. "Robbie is an humble man, a man of God, and—he had a strange childhood. Robbie holds me in high esteem that will not allow a sinner such as himself to touch me."

"Robbie a sinner?" Lenore stifled a laugh. "Get him drunk," she advised. "Maybe he'll forget he's a sinner and remember that he has a wife!"

"Robbie touches not spirits," declared Flora gloomily.

"Nor women?" Lenore asked hesitantly.

"Nor women," said Flora firmly. " 'Twas hard getting used to, for my first marriage was—was not like that. My Kenneth strove with me every night and thrice got

144

me with child—though each time I miscarried. I had not thought that Robbie . . ." She tossed the moss rose away. "But now I manage to turn my mind to other things." She held out her arms and took baby Lorena and rocked the child in her arms and began to croon to her.

Lenore looked pityingly at Flora, a stiff but kindly woman, so eager to give affection, yet balked at every turn. " 'Tis something I'd never get used to," she told Flora frankly. "I've need of a man's arms about me." *Geoffrey's arms,* she thought sadly. *No one else's will do. Not now, not ever.* Since those arms would never hold her again, her bed would be as cold as Flora's. Her eyes flew to the baby. Lorena would get her through it. Bringing up her child would fill her days, her nights. . . .

"Robbie's a good man," said Flora absently, smiling as the baby began to laugh and coo. "Mayhap one day . . ." She shrugged. "Meanwhile it will be almost like having my own child to have Jamie's bairn in the house!"

"Do people here still feel so savage toward those who fought for the King?" Lenore asked, troubled. "It could be they'll think that I aided—

"Robbie will tell them better, and they'll believe him. 'Twas bad here at first with neighbor suspecting neighbor and treason in the air everywhere. 'Twas worse at other villages than our own. We had no hangings here."

Lenore shivered. How often she and Geoffrey had come upon gallows erected at the crossroads and looked up and seen their grim burdens swinging aloft. "Those were bad times," she murmured soberly. Even as she acknowledged how bad those times were, she realized now they had brought her the best thing in her life—her love.

"Bad times are still with us," Flora told her in a crisp voice. "These vengeful Puritans," she said in a cautious, lowered voice, "would take the starch out of everyone. Why, a laddie can scarce make eyes at a lassie without courting the stocks! But my Robbie's a godly man, and his cloth will shield us from troubles others might have. But ye'll wear no red dresses here at the vicarage, Lenore," she added sharply. "Nor red heels, either!"

145

Wistfully Lenore remembered those notched red heels . . . notches for would-be lovers . . . How long ago it seemed! She followed Flora into the house, pensive.

"First ye must change your hair," Flora decided. "It may have been proper in Oxford, but 'tis outlandish here. If ye want the town to accept ye, Lenore, ye must quieten down your wild looks."

Meekly Lenore arranged her hair in as severe a style as she could. It gave her dignity but only made her more striking.

Flora peered at her and frowned. "Ye're still too beautiful, Lenore. Ye'll incite envy. Your dress, now— we'll take the lace off those cuffs. It's torn anyway." Lenore winced as the delicate point lace was ripped free and tossed aside. "And we'll replace that collar with a new one that hides you better." Flora shook her head and sighed. "Anyone would think that having a baby would have made ye heavier, steadier, but ye look like a girl still!"

Lenore was proud that should be so, whatever Twainmere felt about it, but she made no comment.

"On second thought," said Flora, studying her with her head on one side, "ye still look like a flirt. I'd best cut down this gray dress of mine for you." She pulled a dress out of a chest and showed it to Lenore. "The material is old—which will show ye're not rich. And plain—which will show the old women ye've repented."

Lenore quirked an eyebrow at Flora.

"Whether ye have or not's another matter," said Flora grimly. " 'Tis the *appearance* of repentance that counts!"

"I never made a very good impression on the village, if you'll remember!" Lenore reminded her wryly.

"We'll change all that." Flora was confident.

"Will we?" Lenore gave her a troubled look.

"Yes. Ye were a flirt then, out to make all the men want ye, out to make all the other girls jealous. Now..."

Now I'm a woman with a child, a deserted woman. . . . Lenore finished the sentence silently. *No longer a woman to be feared, but one to be pitied.* It was a galling thought.

146

She bent her head over Lorena so that Flora would not guess what she was thinking.

Lenore settled in at the vicarage, although Twainmere's reaction was mixed. None raised the question of her possibly traitorous acts at Worcester, for she was now a member of their well-loved vicar's household. Tom Prattle glowered and muttered whenever he saw her—but that minor irritation Lenore could ignore. The lads who had been so hot to wed her had thinned out. Two had moved to distant towns, three had married village girls, one had drowned in the river while fishing. Dick Fall and Stephen Moffat, who had fought over her by St. John's bonfire Midsummer's Day before last—how long ago that seemed to Lenore!—looked startled when they saw her. Dick Fall was now betrothed to honey-haired Mollie Paxton, of whom Lenore had once been so jealous. And big Stephen had wed a girl from the next town and gone to live with her people; it was said they had a baby on the way—he was seldom in Twainmere.

Not that Lenore would have lacked for suitors, had she shown any interest in the matter. Young Bob Sonners had lost his wife to a distemper in May—she'd been cupped and bled to no avail—and he was looking for someone to share his bed and care for their three children. Cart Moffat, Stephen's older brother, whose health had long been so poorly none had expected him to live, though he'd been treated with all manner of herbs and even conserve of violets, had finally rejected all treatment—and had magically recovered from his mysterious ailment. Now, though still thin and pale, he was casting sly sheep's eyes at village maids. And old Dunster, who had made life so miserable for his milkmaids when he was in his cups, had hiccupped and said loudly after church that if no one else wanted Lenore, he'd have her—aye, and her babe, too!

But Lenore's heart was filled forever with memories of Geoffrey. The pain of his defection was deep and searing. These were good offers, by Twainmere's standards, that she was receiving, she knew, for she was

147

dowryless, no longer a virgin, and saddled with a small baby—but good offers or not, they were not for her. She supposed she should have been grateful for them, but she was not. These offers made her feel vaguely guilty, as if her stormy heart should have been willing to settle for something less.

Michael's fate haunted her. At times it seemed that he could not have perished at the crossroads, that she would look up and see his round, smiling face, his lively red cloak. Then she would look down at Lorena and realize that had not Michael slowed down big Tubbs—and died doing it—neither she nor Lorena might be alive today. Her world seemed ringed round with guilt and heartbreak. Some nights she woke screaming from her sleep thinking of the cutthroats who had pounced upon them at the crossroads. Sometimes she woke from bright shining dreams of Geoffrey . . . and remembered he was gone and thrust her face into her pillow, soaking it with her longing tears.

Outwardly she remained calm. She walked the cobbles and the dusty paths in her plain gray dress with eyes cast down. She was like a penitent, doing penance for sins she could scarcely remember . . . for Twainmere knew naught of Geoffrey; it was wild, golden Jamie they remembered.

She did not seek company, but walked alone . . . sometimes to the churchyard to stroll among the graves. It was redolent with the sweetness of wild honeysuckle that in summer made a riotous growth over the grave-stones. Her lovely young mother she had hardly known lay buried there, her stern carpenter father who had never loved her—and Meg.

It was Meg's grave she wept over, touching the cold stone—so new among so many mossy ones—with quest-ing fingers as if to bring Meg back. Vividly she re-membered the young Meg who had been so sure life would be good to her. She shivered. She wouldn't want Lorena to end up as Meg had.

It did not occur to her that she, too, might end up as badly.

On lazy summer afternoons she sat on the churchyard's low ivy-covered wall and looked at the blue and yellow wildflowers that had burst into bloom over Meg's grave, and past it she saw the simple stone that Flora had erected for Jamie, her handfast lover, even though his body lay at Worcester in some unmarked grave. And sometimes she pondered over how different her life would have been had Jamie not belatedly remembered he was a Scot and fallen beneath Worcester's south wall. . . .

That Lorena was Jamie's she did not doubt. Her coloring was too perfect a match for Jamie's. She sighed. Geoffrey had been right about that, although it still puzzled her, for by her count Lorena should belong to Geoffrey. . . .

One day she saw the black-haired girl, Lizzie, who had giggled with Jamie in the marketplace. Lizzie was trudging past the vicarage on her way to market, carrying a huge basket of fruit. And in her browned left arm was clutched a small baby just a little older than Lorena and already with a mop of hemp-white hair and blue eyes. When she saw Lenore, Lizzie came to a sudden halt, and her dark eyes flashed.

"What a pretty baby," said Lenore in an attempt at friendliness. "Can I hold him?"

"No," said Lizzie sullenly, backing away. "And it's a her, not a him." She hurried away dragging the baby and the heavy basket of fruit.

Flora came round the corner of the house.

"Have you seen Lizzie's baby?" asked Lenore.

Flora gave her a keen look. "I have. 'Tis Jamie's." Flora's voice was gruff. "I knew he was seein' her," she said. "Slippin' over to her house in the afternoons. But ye must not feel bad about it, Lenore—'twas not in Jamie's heart to be faithful to a woman. Lizzie married Silas Tilson right after—after Jamie was killed at Worcester."

"Silas Tilson? But he must be past ninety!" gasped Lenore.

"Aye. And glad our Lizzie was to get him—so she'd have a name for her brat! I think he knew about Jamie, when he offered for her. He's not like to have any children

149

of his own at his age, and now he has a young wife and a child he claims as his." She shrugged.

"Poor Lizzie . . ." murmured Lenore, for Lizzie had had a light dancing foot.

She noticed that after that day Lizzie avoided the vicarage and reached the market by some other path.

Lenore looked about her more keenly after that. After Jamie's death, there had been a rash of marriages in Twainmere, it seemed. Lighthearted Jamie on his visits to village maids had enjoyed more than honey-cakes . . .

Mollie Paxton alone had held out—and she was being married on Thursday.

When Mollie's wedding procession filed past the vicarage on a path strewn with wildflowers and rushes, Lenore stood with her baby in her arms at the low wall watching them go by. She thought Mollie looked radiant in her russet dress, with a circlet of myrtle crowning her honey-colored hair. Mollie tossed her head and gave Lenore a triumphant look as she passed, a look that said plainly she had taken Jamie from Lenore—if only for a while—and now she was taking permanent possession of another of Lenore's erstwhile suitors, Dick Fall.

Flora came up behind her. "Find a good man and wed him," she advised, seeing Lenore's wistful gaze follow the procession. "Although 'tis true I'd miss the bairn"—her voice roughened, for she now loved little Lorena almost as much as Lenore did—"but 'twould be best for ye."

Lenore, the flirt who had gaily notched her red heels—a notch for every offer, and from all the best catches in the village—gave her a shadowed look. Was that the way to forget Geoffrey, for whose arms she longed every night?

All that first week after her arrival she had had wild nightmares when she had cried out for Geoffrey. Sometimes in those black dreams she was running lost and barefoot through endless dark forests, being stalked by terrible pursuers—Swan, Tubbs, and dark faceless demons that boiled up out of a hell that seemed near and close—behind that next tree, past that clump of thorn

150

bushes. As she fought her way through brush and vines and low-hanging branches with her breath sobbing in her throat, she would see before her a clearing and know in her heart that all would be well could she but reach it. And just as she broke through the last of the tangled foliage, Swan would leap out to bar her way, grinning hideously. At those times she screamed for Geoffrey and woke up in a cold sweat, shaking.

" 'Tis—'tis the nightmares," she'd gasp, when Flora would burst in.

"I know." Flora was a grim figure in her nightcap, but her voice was gentle. "I've had them."

Lenore remembered Flora's nightmares, how she had seen a blood-soaked countryside before the Battle of Worcester. On one of these occasions she turned a frightened face toward Flora.

"What do you see for me, Flora?" she asked. "You have The Sight. We all know it."

Flora gave her a troubled look. "I see nothing," she mumbled. "Sometimes The Sight is given me and I can foretell a thing as clearly as if it were happening before me—but for you I do not see the future."

To Lenore as well as Flora her future was impenetrable.

At first she had planned to write to Michael's mother, had even chosen the words: "Your son died bravely. . . ." But a letter could be traced, and she had to remember that Gilbert waited vengefully in Oxford and would like nothing better than to see her on the gibbet. How could she be sure Michael's moher would not be in touch with Michael's Oxford friends, who would casually pass on to Gilbert what they had heard? She waited, telling herself that Michael's mother already knew of her son's death, for he had been felled at a crossroads marker and his body would have been found by the first passing traveler. It never occurred to her that Tubbs might have hidden Michael's body.

She had not even told Flora of her terrible experience in the woods, or of Michael's death . . . for her explanations of why she had not written Michael's mother her condolences would have brought out other painful recollections of Gilbert . . . and of Geoffrey, who never ceased to haunt her dreams.

Resolutely she tried not to think of Geoffrey, filling her days with caring for baby Lorena. She launched into the housework at the vicarage with a vengeance. She'd have loved to go to market, swinging a basket over her arm, but Flora said wisely that the people of Twainmere would have to get used to her gradually again—going to church was all right, but she must not appear to flaunt herself, Flora would do the marketing. Sometimes, left alone at the vicarage, she was plunged into sadness, remembering Geoffrey, who was—God alone knew where; he'd made it to France, she supposed, back to his French wife . . . The thought made her cry, and she cursed the day she'd met him, for she doubted her sad heart would ever be her own again.

Oh, why could he not have believed the child's coloring an accident of fate, gift of some remote ancestor? Why could he not have accepted Lorena as his? She realized, of course, how much he had counted on the baby, how he had looked forward to Lorena's birth—and what a shock it must have been to see that blond hair, those blue eyes staring up at him from her small piquant face. Well, it had been a shock to Lenore, too. She had counted up the days so carefully, and she had been so sure, so sure. . . . She smiled down at baby Lorena through her tears and the child cooed back at her. She sighed. It was all over now. Her girlhood had changed into womanhood, and her womanhood into motherhood, and she would never see her lover again.

"Don't grieve so," said Flora abruptly one day as she carried in a basket of fresh sun-dried laundry.

"I—I'm not grieving," protested Lenore guiltily.

"Yes, you are. Any fool could see it. Your life isn't over, you know. I thought my life was over when my Kenneth went a-hunting in Scotland and fell and twisted his leg and froze to death and never came back to the glen. I was sure I'd go to my death a miserable, weeping woman. But then Jamie was having so much trouble with the kirk—he being young and only wanting to be

152

a natural man and have good times—and I found myself thinking about him instead of my own troubles. You've got Lorena—you should think about her."

"Oh, I do." Lenore gave a wan nod.

"The hurt will stop," stated Flora, so firmly that it must be a fact.

The hurt did not stop, but it abated from time to time. The community, which had been aloof at first, was beginning to accept her again. Sedately Lenore now accompanied Flora to church on Sundays. A new and different Lenore, garbed in a plain gray dress with a white linen collar—and with her flaming hair bound up tightly beneath a coif. People who had frowned when they first saw her on the street began to unbend and nod to her pleasantly. Men who at first had looked at her warily, eyeing the child in her arms, began to give her long, lingering glances again. It would not be long, Flora warned her, before suitors would come banging on the vicarage door, and Lenore would be well advised to take one of them.

But this lull in Lenore's stormy existence was not to last. Before the month was out, Flora came flying into the house on a sultry day with her face a thundercloud and grabbed Lenore, who was making a pie on the kitchen table, her linen apron dusted with flour. She grasped Lenore by the shoulder and spun her around so fiercely she knocked over the flour crock.

"Why did ye not tell me ye'd killed a man?" she cried, shaking Lenore. *"Why?"*

"But I didn't!" gasped Lenore, choking on the white cloud of flour that had arisen and borne almost back to the kitchen wall by this onslaught.

Flora, too, choked on the dust that filled the kitchen. Her face encrimsoned and she was temporarily unable to speak. Lenore beat her on the back and then ran and opened the kitchen door to let out the white cloud. She tore off her linen apron and flailed the air with it.

"I was—almost to Lizzie Tilson's, bringing her a poultice for her sick child," gasped Flora, and stopped to cough. "On the other side of the hedge I heard two men

153

questioning Old Ben, the mute. They were angry because he wouldn't answer their questions, and I was about to call through the hedge to them when I realized they were asking about *you!* Some student was found dead at the crossroads north of Oxford. He'd told a friend you were running away together, and the friend swears you left Oxford with him. His mother says he had money on him—she believes *you* killed him for it! They traced you through a shepherd who directed you to Twainmere when you left the road and got lost. They're here to arrest you, Lenore!"

Her face almost as paper-white as the flour dust that covered it, Lenore laid down the apron. "I did not kill him, Flora," she said. "And we weren't running away together. He was on his way home to Coventry and I was to Banbury to race Snowfire at the fair. We were attacked by robbers at a crossroads. They killed Michael and—and I may have killed one of them, for I plunged a dagger into his back rather than let him harm by baby."

Flora stared at her, blue eyes blazing from her floury face. "I believe you," she said shortly. "But others will not, for no robbers were reported seen about, and the student's was the only body found. They'll ask why ye did not report it, why ye fled."

Slowly the force of that sank in on Lenore. She was trapped. Everyone would believe she'd killed Michael—lured him away from Oxford and killed him for the money in his pockets! The very fact that she'd not reported his death was a black mark against her. She could hardly explain she'd not reported it because she was fleeing treason and assault charges in Oxford!

"Oh, Flora," she whispered, appalled, "what am I going to do?"

"You must run for it," said Flora grimly. "For they'll be here soon, and I'll have no way to keep them from taking you."

The two women looked at each other.

"Lorena . . ." whispered Lenore, brushing the flour from her white face.

"Ye must leave her with me. Snowfire's leg hasn't healed well enough for a long ride and—'twas a daft idea, anyway!

Whoever heard of a woman making her living racing at fairs? Lorena will stay with me—till you can come for her. . . ." She let that trail off. "I'll find a wet nurse for Lorena and take care of her as if she were my own child. Come, Lenore, ye must pack!"

But Lenore was hardly listening. She was looking instead out the kitchen door, past the bee-haunted musk roses, past the clipped yew hedge, out at the low hills of the Cotswolds. She had hoped to lose herself at the fairs when Snowfire was well enough again to race, for the hunt for "traitors" was dying down and it was unlikely assault charges would be pressed beyond the walls of Oxford. But murder! For that they would hound her the length of England—and to deliver herself from the one trap would be to fall into the other.

She dusted the flour off her hands and swallowed. Never had she meant to give Lorena up. But—what chance would Lorena have, if her mother was on the run? It would be hard enough to make it alone, impossible with a small baby. Here Lorena would be raised with all the care and trappings of a vicar's daughter, she would learn to read and write and to cipher—arts Lenore had so recently slaved over herself at Oxford and in which she was hardly proficient. Her beloved daughter would be well-dressed and housed, for Flora would see to that.

A sob escaped her.

"There's no sense crying," Flora flung over her shoulder. Already she was throwing together meat and cheese and bread and honey-cakes into a linen tablecloth which she knotted at the corners. "You'll take the gray horse," she said. "I'll tell them you rode away on Snowfire so they'll be looking for a woman on a white horse. Tuck your hair under a coif, for it's conspicuous. I'll hide Snowfire in the woods and 'find' him later. You can be sure I'll be good to him." She turned. "Where are you, Lenore?"

Lenore was in the next room bent over Lorena, hugging the child's small body to her own and crying. She pressed a last kiss on Lorena's sweet, smiling face. Her baby . . . she was leaving her baby! Lorena gurgled and lifted a tiny hand toward her, and Lenore's will nearly turned to water.

155

"Lorena well may die if you take her with you," Flora warned from the doorway. "A baby cannot stand the hardships we can. Here." She thrust a purse into Lenore's hand. "This will get you gone. Seek the back ways. I'll say you went west. If ye're careful," she added gruffly, "it should be enough to take you all the way to London."

Lenore shook her head and put the purse down on the bed. "I've taken too much from you already," she said wearily, "and you will need that money for Lorena's keep. I'll take nothing with me, Flora—that way they can search the house and you'll have proof you expected me back shortly."

Flora's eyes glinted with a kind of fierce admiration. "I will insist they search," she promised. " 'Twill slow them down."

"I'd best go." Lenore fled from the room back into the kitchen. Already her arms felt empty. She had need to place distance between them. For if she stayed another minute, she'd snatch Lorena up and run away with her . . . and then Lorena might end up like those other children she'd seen in a dozen towns, children who'd once had secure homes and were orphans of the war and were now small tragic beggars on the highways.

"I'll write to you," she mumbled.

"Letters can be traced," warned Flora. "The townsfolk will not take this lightly. They'll expect you to write, and some will doubtless keep a sharp eye out. I wouldna write were I you."

Lenore expelled a ragged breath. "Very well, then I will send you money. In pincushions. Expect them—for somehow I will get it. I mean to pay for Lorena's keep."

She took the food Flora thrust upon her and hurried out the back door before her decision could crumble.

Flora followed her to the stable and offered to help her saddle the gray mare, but Lenore was traveling light. "Sell the saddle and saddlebags and buy Lorena things she needs—I'll ride bareback, I've done so before. And in my room there's a linen handkerchief beneath the mattress and in it an amethyst ring. 'Twas in the saddlebag of the gray mare that I took from the robber that I stabbed after I'd

156

lamed Snowfire trying to escape him—'tis his horse and his ring, and I've no doubt he stole both. But I do not want the crime of stealing the amethyst ring charged against me, too, so keep the ring against a time Lorena needs the money."

Flora's eyes misted over. "You take too little for yourself, Lenore."

Lenore's delicate jaw tightened. "I have made my own troubles, Flora. I will not visit them on my daughter. She deserves more good things than I can give her."

She threw her arms about Snowfire's white neck, buried her face in his silky mane, and whispered a goodbye. He nuzzled her lovingly and whinnied as she led the gray mare from the stable.

"Take care of Snowfire for me." Lenore's voice broke as tears streamed like rain from her tormented violet eyes, "I want Lorena to have him—she'll love him as I do. And—thank you for everything, Flora."

Flora gave her a rough hug. "All will be taken care of," she said huskily. "You need have no fears for what you leave behind, Lenore."

Lenore did not answer. She couldn't just then. She swung up on the gray mare's back and skirted the garden and plunged into the trees. She did not look back at the vicarage, for she could not have seen it—the world before her, green and leafy, shimmered with her tears.

Flora watched her ride away to the east with troubled eyes. She was sure she would never see Lenore again, and her heart ached for the valiant girl to whom beauty had been such a dangerous and deadly gift. At least the bairn would be safe, for she'd care for Lorena tenderly—that much she could do for Jamie and his wild young handfast bride. Sighing, she led Snowfire deep into the trees and left him tethered by a little spring where none would find him. She gave him an encouraging pat as she left—he'd have water here, and she'd come back for him tomorrow.

When she returned to the vicarage the men who had come for Lenore were waiting for her. She pretended shock at their news, asked endless questions to slow them down, insisted they search the house, and at last told them that Lenore had said she was going to take some cakes to old Mother Greer, who'd been ailing lately—which was strange, now that she came to think of it, for old Mother Greer lived to the south of town and Lenore had ridden her white horse away to the west.

The two men exchanged significant glances and left quickly, asking her to let them know if Lenore came back. Flora watched grimly as they rode away to the west on the wild-goose chase on which she'd sent them.

The vicar had come in just in time to hear her last revelation, and he frowned as they disappeared from view. "I doubt me that Mistress Lenore was on her way to see Mother Greer, Flora. They were not on friendly terms."

Flora sighed. "She'll not be back, Robbie. The bairn is ours. 'Twill be up to us to bring her up."

The hills and vales around Twainmere were thoroughly searched, but no trace of Lenore was found. When Flora reported next day that Snowfire had limped in from the west, a new furor erupted, for it was assumed Lenore had been thrown. After a while it was believed she might have fallen into Watson's Gorge, which lay to the west, and that the dangerous whirlpool just before the river disappeared into the mountain might have sucked her body down to whirl forever in dark endless depths.

It was a fate some of the village women had once wished upon Lenore.

With Jamie dead and buried and Lenore gone under such evil circumstances—for her flight was considered an admission of guilt—her reputation was any man's game. Wild were the tales they told of her at the local tavern. Half the men in the village bragged they'd bedded her. Boys so young they'd barely have reached up to her shoulder insisted they'd spent long, wild nights with her; older men winked and muttered stories to each other and guffawed.

Mollie Paxton came to believe she'd been done out of her sometime lover—Jamie the Scot—by a veritable demon, a murderess at the least and perhaps a witch to boot, who had by sorcery lured Jamie to Worcester to his doom. Married now to Dick Fall and of a garrulous nature, she fanned the gossip to flame.

Around Twainmere hearths at night they talked of Lenore, enlarging, expanding the tale with each retelling. Children listened round-eyed and then stared surreptitiously at Flora as she walked by carrying baby Lorena.

Wild young Lenore Frankford with her red dancing shoes and flame-colored hair had become a village legend.

CHAPTER 11

Her departure from Twainmere marked a time of terror for Lenore. She felt hunted as a fox is hunted, and at first was afraid to break cover lest some farmer or wandering shepherd report seeing a bright-haired woman and her pursuers start off with a fresh scent. That first day she rode as far as she dared, and when the gray horse was exhausted, spent that first night hiding in a deep copse and weeping for Lorena.

The next day was uneventful, but toward evening she heard mounted men moving about and sometimes she could hear shouted orders and curses. Hastily she retreated to a grove of beech heavily laced with thorn, where she hid the night. She had no way of knowing whether the men were hunting her (indeed they were not, but sought a rogue who had escaped the gallows in Cirencester), but she dared not take chances. So as soon as it was light she kept the gray mare floundering down the rocks of a narrow winding stream and over rocky places—in case of pursuit by dogs, though she'd heard no hounds baying—until the mare gave her such a reproachful look that Lenore felt pity for her and guided her out upon a soft green hillside, doubtless soon to be used by sheep, and dismounted to let her graze the waving green grass.

She'd avoided hamlets and taken the twisting sheep trails, and by the next afternoon, when she rode deep into a forest, she was thoroughly lost. On she blundered, seeking a high place that would give her a view of the countryside where she could find her bearings—and came to an abrupt halt at the sound of clashing swords.

She might have turned and ridden away in panic, but the sound of swordplay was promptly followed by loud laughter and a ribald masculine voice crying, "Nigel, ye do be awkward today—ye're supposed to run me through! Try again."

This startling statement was too much for Lenore's curiosity. She slid off the mare's back, slipped her bridle over a dead tree branch, and tiptoed forward to peer between some low-hanging limbs into a small woodland clearing.

There, ringed about by a small ragged company, who sat or lay at their ease as they watched, two men flailed cheerfully away at each other with swords that flashed bright in the sun. As she watched in amazement, the shorter one cried, "Aha!" and plunged his sword into the chest of the taller.

With a hoarse cry the taller one fell backward, clutching his chest while the smaller fellow withdrew his sword— amazingly bloodless—and strode away. A moment later the tall one scrambled up.

"Is that better, Monty?" he asked anxiously, addressing a man whose back was to Lenore.

"Aye," was the cool reply. "And 'twill be realistic enough when you have a bladder of sheep's blood tied beneath your jerkin to soak through and confound the audience!"

"Nigel had best not strike me too hard," objected the tall fellow, "for 'tis only a part of that sword that slides into the hilt—slippery with goose grease or no!"

161

"I'll be careful of your timid hide!" roared short Nigel. "Was it not well done, Monty? Was it not?"

Amid general laughter Lenore relaxed and took a deep, sighing breath, remembering the play she'd attended back in Oxford. These men must be strolling players, rehearsing their lines. And like herself, actors were outside the Lord Protector's stern law, so she need not fear them.

"Well done!" she cried and began to applaud.

All heads turned alertly toward the leafy foliage that concealed her from their view.

"It seems we have an audience!" cried the man called Monty. "And an appreciative one! Come, show yourself."

Lenore stepped boldly forward into the clearing and for a moment their voices were stilled at the sight of a beautiful woman, come apparently from nowhere into their midst.

"By the Lord Harry—a maid!" muttered Monty. He came over to her, limping a little, but a courtly figure nonetheless. Tall and thin with a shock of thick white hair that waved to his shoulders, his white beard trimmed to a point, he wore a threadbare red velvet coat with a handful of dirty lace at his throat, flowing knee breeches of tattered olive silk, and a pair of boots that seemed about to depart his legs. But his stride was vigorous, his step firm, and his stance and the look he gave Lenore marked him as one of authority—and admiration. Although he must be more than twice her age, before that admiring gaze Lenore found herself wishing she were not clothed so unattractively in Flora's made-over gray dress.

He made her a handsome leg, this old-young man, his wavy hair almost sweeping the grass as he bowed low.

"Montmorency Hogue at your service, mistress."

"Lenore Frankford," said Lenore and bit her lip. She should not have given him her right name.

"How did you find us, mistress? For we thought ourselves well hidden in this glade."

"I was not seeking you," Lenore told him frankly. "I was but passing by when I heard your voices and peered through the branches in time to see that mock duel."

"Ah, don't call it a mock duel," Montmorency Hogue

162

chided her humorously. "For Alan and Nigel take it as
seriously as any real life contest. As you could see, they're
very desperate about it! We are but a company of strolling
players and have not much to offer a lady, but would you
share a tankard of cider with me?" He shook his head to
warn away those who would have crowded around Lenore
and led her a little apart from the others. There he poured
a tankard of cider for her and one for himself and set back
the keg.

Lenore accepted hers gratefully. She had had only water
to drink since she had left Twainmere, and she was fond
of cider.

Montmorency Hogue dusted off a fallen tree trunk with
an elegant gesture—and a threadbare glove—and bade her
sit.

"Whence came you, Mistress Frankford?" he asked with
studied casualness that belied the alert look in his green
eyes. "And . . . did you chance upon anybody on the way
here?"

That, thought Lenore shrewdly, was what he really
wanted to know. She took a sip of cider. "Last night I
heard mounted men riding by shouting to one another,"
she admitted cautiously.

Hogue frowned.

"But I have heard no one today," she added hastily.

It was his turn to be shrewd. "These mounted men—did
you ask them what they sought?"

Lenore sat a little straighter. "No. They—they seemed
to be going in a different direction."

"A different direction . . . I see." He studied her and
then he laughed. "I believe it possible they were seeking
you, mistress."

"Or possibly *you,*" countered Lenore, her eyes glinting.

He gave a courtly nod. "Either one. We are wanted for
giving an unlawful performance of one of Will Shakespeare's plays outside Coventry, and we've been harried
ever since. I know not why a theatrical performance
should be counted so great a crime!" He sighed, downed
his cider, and rested the tankard on the tree trunk. "And
you, mistress?"

163

Lenore liked this white-haired man with the young face and keen eyes and genial smile. She took a deep draught of the cider and decided to take him into her confidence. "On the road north from Oxford, robbers attacked us. My friend was killed, the robbers got clean away—and now the law seeks me, for 'tis the general belief that I killed my friend for the money in his pockets."

Montmorency Hogue drew in his breath in a long, low whistle. "Methinks, mistress, ye are in worse case than we!"

Lenore nodded. "I am not sure I can prove my innocence, so I am in flight. Could it be"—she gave him a look of entreaty—"that I could travel with your troupe?"

His heavy eyebrows elevated. "A woman? But as you can see, we are all men in our troupe. If you have seen any plays, mistress, then you must know that young boys perform the female roles."

Lenore looked about her. "I see no one here under thirty."

He laughed. "Yes, we are all growing old. 'Tis unfortunate, but there are few new recruits for a poorly paid profession that these days must be performed on the run. There were brave days for us in the old king's time—I myself have performed at Blackfriars and at the Hope—but the Lord Protector has closed the theaters. Our clothes grow tattered and hardly keep out the winter cold, we can scarce afford feed for the horses that draw our cart, and the men of our company can afford to keep neither wives nor doxies!"

Lenore flushed. "I am not a doxie," she said tartly.

"Nor did I mean to imply it," said Montmorency Hogue hastily. "But what could you do to earn your keep, mistress? Stitch a fine seam on our worn costumes? For all here must work."

"I do not stitch so fine a seam," admitted Lenore in a rueful voice. " 'Tis not one of my accomplishments. But I could do your laundry—and there must be a great deal of it, for you are so many."

He sighed. " 'Tis another service we perform for our-

164

selves when we camp along convenient streams and rivers. Poverty makes a man master of many callings."

Lenore felt crestfallen, but she comforted herself that she had not really hoped to join them. She rose.

"I thank you for the cider," she said. "And I will be on my way."

"No, stay a moment." Montmorency Hogue was considering her thoughtfully. "Could it be you know the way to Cirencester, mistress?"

"I have been to Cirencester," admitted Lenore. "Once. To a fair. But now I am quite lost. If I could but climb to the top of a hill and perhaps see where I am—"

"No matter, I will point out the way. You see, we have been waiting for our advance man all week."

"Advance man?"

"Aye. We have a man who goes ahead of us and prepares the way. He arranges for our lodgings, he finds a place for us to hold the performance, he feels out the land to see if the authorities keep too fierce control and we should shun the place and seek another—and he makes arrangements with one or two good men in the community to let out the word in the right quarters that a theatrical performance is to be held."

Lenore gave him a look of surprise, and he said grimly, "Did ye think plays were impromptu affairs, mistress? Much careful planning do they take in advance—and now with the law stalking us, even more so. Will Summers is our advance man, and he has been gone these two weeks to Cirencester, where we are to perform *Twelfth Night* . . . we hope. Will should have been back a week ago, but we have heard naught from him. Our faces are too well known in Cirencester for any of us to go and seek him there, in case aught is amiss. But we would give you money for your food and night's lodging in Cirencester, and shelter and protection to the next town we visit after Cirencester, if you would go in and see what is keeping Will."

"It could be that my face would be known in Cirencester also," murmured Lenore. "Yet I would do it if—do you perhaps have a costume I could wear? Those who

165

seek me will have a description of what I wear and know the color of my hair."

Montmorency Hogue rose. "That I can." He led her to a high-sided cart. "We cannot afford costumes for the male parts," he admitted frankly. "We wear our own clothes, whether we play *Julius Caesar* or *King Lear* or *Hamlet*. But for the female parts the men don dresses. We have needle and thread—you can baste one up to fit you. And I think we could find you a black wig."

He was pawing through a large wooden chest as he spoke, spilling out laces and tinsel, an orange-plumed hat and a broken fan. He straightened up holding a gown of yellow satin garnished in copper lace. It was stained at the hem, but Lenore looked at it wistfully—how beautiful it must have been when new!

He watched her finger it lovingly. "It would not be wise to wear so bright a gown to Cirencester, mistress," he chided gently, taking it from her. "This would do better." He pulled out a costume of widow's weeds complete with a heavy black veil. "This veil will hide your features well. And this wig—though it may sit a trifle askew until you have gentled it a bit—is yours as well." He handed her a tousled black wig and a coarse wooden comb. "And when ye return from Cirencester with word of Will Summers, we'll have a brown wig for ye, and ye can wear the yellow satin then."

Lenore knew that was subtle bait to ensure her return, for he could not know that she would keep her promise; with lodging-money in her pocket, she might well continue her journey in the opposite direction. She smiled her thanks, knowing no way to reassure him—but something in her steady eyes managed that very well. He found her a needle and black thread, dug into his pocket, and gave her some coins—she suspected his store of them was meager—and waved his arm at the trees. "Your dressing room!"

Lenore retired into cover of the foliage. And when a little later she paraded out before the company in her somber mourning garb—the black gown basted with big stitches so that it outlined her delightful figure—and tossed

166

back the black curls that now fell down over her ears, there was a general round of applause.

"None would know you, mistress," approved Montmorency Hogue. "And Will Summers will be easy to remark. He will be laying over at the Ox and Bow, for he was once on friendly terms with the innkeeper's sister—before she married a man with a less chancy profession. Will is of medium height and very florid—his nose is as red as a cherry. He will be wearing an orange coat, for 'tis the only one he possesses, and he has long stringy hair the color of butter. You might pretend to be his niece seeking him. Will professes to be from Torquay and has many nieces." He grinned.

"I will find him," promised Lenore. Indeed, how could she miss him, she wondered—a man who looked like that? "Is it your wish that I should start out now?" She cast a longing look at the cookfire at the edge of the clearing where two of the company were roasting venison.

"Nay, tomorrow is soon enough, for we want no mishaps on the road. It could be that Will is taken, and the law must not be led back to us. You understand?"

Lenore nodded her black curls soberly, for his admonition had reminded her that her present assignment was not without its dangers.

That night, ringed around a campfire, the company feasted on venison, and Monty and the others told her stories of the great days when they had worked at Blackfriars Theatre, built on the ruins of an old monastery—or the Swan or the Globe or other open-air theatres. Monty bragged of knowing Will Shakespeare, dead more than thirty years, and the others chimed in. For most of these men had spent their lives on the boards; they had been boy actors or had come of acting families.

In their company for a little while she was able to tear her mind from Lorena—was she happy, was she smiling, did she—and this very humbly—did she miss her mother? Lenore knew such thoughts were useless, for the die was well cast, but they tormented her just the same.

Monty fixed her a bed in the wagon and promised kindly that she would not be disturbed. She took his meaning and gave him a rather trusting smile. She slept well, not feeling a need to stay alert lest something pounce on her in the night.

She waked once at the cry of an owl, night-hunting.

A white moon cast its frosty light upon the forest, silvering the little clearing. All were sleeping but one; hands clasped behind his back, head bowed, Montmorency Hogue walked back and forth. She had learned enough this night to know that the responsibility for this company lay on his shoulders and that times were indeed hard for them. She liked him and thought that no matter how many summers lay behind him, he would never truly grow old.

The sun and sounds of stirring around the campfire's ashes woke her the next morning. Automatically she reached out to make sure Lorena was all right—and pain struck through her that her baby would not soon lie in the crook of her arm again. By the time she could come for her, the first bloom of babyhood would be gone, and Lorena would look to Flora, perhaps, for mothering—not Lenore.

Lenore lay there in the morning sunlight with her eyes squeezed shut, willing tears not to trickle down her face. And that morning she swore a great oath to herself: she would not look back. As soon as she could, she would go back for Lorena, but she must not waste her energy in grief, she would need all the strength she had to make her way in the world so that she could have her daughter with her again. She refused to let Geoffrey enter her mind—but he was there, always, in her soul, in her broken heart.

She ate a companionable breakfast, with the company, of cold venison and cider. Before she had finished, some were already hard at work learning their lines, practicing their swordplay—or the jigs the whole company performed between acts. They looked very merry as they pranced about the green, and they gave her a rousing cheer as she mounted up.

Feeling well fed and with her horse fed and refreshed, she set out for Cirencester along the path to which they directed her—a black-haired woman well disguised in her widow's weeds. Many roads since time immemorial had

168

led through the Wold to Cirencester: the White Way which led to Winchcombe, and the great Salt Way—and when she had lived in Twainmere, Lenore had ridden both of them. But now Lenore caught the Fosse Way, which had been built by the Romans on an ancient Celtic track, and which led from Exeter to Lincoln and passed Cirencester en route. So deserted was this stretched of blue-stone road as it wound through what Will Shakespeare had called the "high wild hills" that she passed but one village before she rode out of the leafy green woodlands, predominantly of ash and elm and beech that would flame to red and yellow come September, and saw ahead the towering perpendicular spire of Cirencester's beautiful cathedral-like church with its famous peal of twelve bells.

Though she had been there but once, to a fair with Meg, Lenore remembered Cirencester well. Lenore could not have told you that this had once been the lavish Roman city of Corinthium, wrecked by the Saxons at the end of the sixth century—but she knew where the Ox and Bow was. The ruins of the great abbey she could see—and regretted its state of disrepair—and she had once been told that the city had been taken during England's Civil War by Prince Rupert. But Cirencester's rich past was far from her thoughts as she rode in; what interested her was the tall-hatted Puritans who walked or rode by, studying the woman on the gray horse with interest. Lenore looked down, intently studying the road, for any of them, she feared, might remember having seen her at some time—in fact, there might be among them someone from Twainmere.

Deciding it was best to take a bold course, she rode directly up to the Ox and Bow—thankful, at least, that this was one place she was not known. She dismounted, strode into the common room, drank a tankard of cider, and inquired of the innkeeper about her "uncle," Will Summers, who had arrived here some two weeks past. Her own husband, she declared with a deep sigh, had recently passed away, and she was seeking her uncle, who would "know what she should do."

The innkeeper's sympathy was aroused at once. He was

more than helpful to the lissome young widow who asked his aid so prettily. Regretfully he informed her that Will Summers had indeed stopped here. He had seemed of good health, he had drunk deep of the claret, eaten generously of the leg of lamb, and more than generously of the plum pudding—and that night had complained of great pains in his stomach and chest. Though the doctor had been hastily summoned, Will had died—and since none knew where his relatives might be that they could notify them, he had been hastily buried in an unmarked grave as a pauper. Will had once said he lived in Torquay; did he still have people there?

Lenore murmured that she would let them know.

Will's clothes and the few coins on him had not fetched enough to pay for his burial, the landlord promptly explained but Will had had a watch he always carried, and the landlord had saved it in case any relatives showed up looking for Will.

Dabbing at her eyes—for she pretended to be much affected by the news of her "uncle's" death—Lenore suggested that the landlord's sister might like to have it as a keepsake; "Uncle Will" had been very fond of her.

The landlord brightened and refused to take any coin for the cider and urged on her a pasty and a joint of meat. Regretfully Lenore refused this offer. She had managed to down the cider gracefully, holding the veil so that it concealed her eyes, but she would have to throw aside her veil to eat, and this would expose her face to the curious view of the inn's patrons. She was, she choked, too upset to eat a bite, but she thanked him deeply.

As she remounted the gray mare, her mind was racing ahead.

Will Summers's death in Cirencester would indeed be a blow to Monty. With their advance man gone, the troupe would be in desperate trouble. Will had apparently had no time to make any arrangements, had died, in fact, the very night he arrived. She could turn about, of course, and ride back the way she had come and bring the disappointing news to Montmorency Hogue.

Or she could make the arrangements herself! With

mounting excitement she rode the gray mare to a public horse trough and let her drink. Why should she return with bad tidings? Why should she not make the arrangements for the performance herself? There was an old stone barn outside town where illegal cockfights were held. She and Meg had stopped by there once for a dipper of water from the farmer's well on the road to the fair. The farmer—a pleasant round-faced man in his forties—had been enchanted by the two pretty girls from Twainmere and had leaned upon his pitchfork and engaged them in conversation in the midday heat. He had even unbent so far as to bring them a tall pitcher of milk which had been cooling in his springhouse, and Meg had twitted Lenore all day about her "conquest."

That barn, which was easily reached by a good road, yet was isolated, would make an excellent theatre—far better than the barn where she had attended a play in Oxford. Its stone walls gave coolness against the muggy summer heat, and—she would do it! If the arrangements were successful and Monty approved them, he might let her take over Will's job—she would be able to earn her keep, she could even in time look forward to having Lorena with her again!

Seething with excitement, she guided the gray mare out of Cirencester on the road to Twainmere. It made her uneasy to be heading so directly for Twainmere, for anyone from Twainmere might well recognize her gray horse— even if they did not immediately identify the rider—and she was glad when, without incident, she saw over the next rise the roof of the big stone barn she remembered so well. That the farmer would recognize her, she had no fear, for her widow's weeds and black wig were a good disguise. She could tell him her late husband had frequented his cockfights and so feel him out about holding a play there. He must be well acquainted, he could circulate the word and so procure the audience!

As she approached, she slowed her pace to a demure jog, mindful that in her widow's weeds it would seem odd to dash up at a great speed. In the distance she could see the farmer's wife washing goose feathers to stuff a featherbed, and a couple of bright-eyed little girls who seemed to

171

be leaching wood ashes for lye to make soap. She was growing anxious, for she did not wish to speak to the woman and children about this, and she could not remember the farmer's name. But just then arround the corner of the barn walked the farmer, a bit plumper than she remembered him, and she greeted him.

He came politely over to the side of the road, and she told him she was riding out "for the air" since her "good uncle" had died as well as her young husband, and the black hangings of her room made her mournful. The farmer nodded and asked her who her "good uncle" and young husband might be, would he perchance know them?

When she replied hesitantly that her young husband was from Bath and had died there, but that her uncle was named Will Summers and had been staying at the Ox and Bow, the farmer looked surprised. "Aye, I knew Will," he replied. "And I am sorry indeed to hear of his death."

"Then—then you knew how he earned his livelihood?"

"Aye—he did arrange for plays to be held."

"I—I knew you used to hold cockfights here," she ventured, hoping the little breeze that had sprung up would not blow back her veil, for he well might remember her, might have heard indeed that the law was looking for her. And if a reward had indeed been offered, she would not care to put any man to the test—he might seize her and haul her to the nearest authorities, even though some of his own doings would not bear looking into.

"Aye, I held them. Until last year. Then the authorities closed down on me and did put me in the pillory. See this eye?" She peered at a long, jagged scar that ran from his eyebrow past the corner of his eye and down his cheek. "Someone did throw a rock at me while I was in the pillory and I near lost my eye!" He went on vengefully denouncing the Puritan authorities, and Lenore felt the time was ripe.

"Would you let our players hold a performance here in your barn?" she asked him bluntly. "For now that Will Summers is dead, we have no one to take his place. I rode in for news of him."

"You are not Will's niece, then?"

172

"No, I never knew him. I come from Montmorency Hogue."

The farmer reached down and pulled up a grass blade, bit into it, and spat. He appeared to be thinking.

"Aye—I might," he said at last. "For you see yon feathers my wife washes? Two geese run down by coaches within a week! My barley crop ruined by blight. No cock-fights in more than a year—I'm hard put to rub two coins together! Yes, I could give ye shelter for the players, a place to perform—and I could arrange for the audience, too, for I've but to pass the word around!"

She had chosen the right man! Lenore was congratulating herself when he gave her a sudden sly look. "Of course, I'd need some money now to get me started. . . ."

She hadn't expected that. She hesitated. "Monty never expected anything like this to happen. All I have with me is lodging-money for the night. I could give you that, if you'd let me sleep in your barn and have a bite of bread and cheese for supper."

"Ye can sleep in the barn," he said shortly, "and ye can eat with us. But the money's not enough."

Desperate, Lenore promised him a share of the profits and told him they'd be ready to perform three days hence —she hoped it was true the troupe would be ready and prayed Monty would find the deal reasonable. If not, she was out the lodging-money and would have spent the night in a barn for nothing.

The farmer seemed so mollified by the share she had mentioned that she wondered fearfully whether it was too large.

"Come in and sup," he said.

Lenore bethought her that he might remember her face if she took off her veil; a careless word that she'd been seen in Cirencester and they'd be after her again, hound her to her death.

"I—I have a rash on my face and do not wish to be seen," she objected.

" 'Tis not a pox, is it?" he cried. "We want no pox here, mistress!"

Lenore sighed. "Actually 'tis bruises from a cuffing my

173

husband gave me when I wanted to join up with Monty's troupe. I am ashamed—I will have no one staring at me."

The farmer peered at her suspiciously. Muttering to himself, he went back to the farmhouse and she noticed that he brought out her food himself—his wife and daughters stayed within the farmhouse. She breathed a sigh of relief and ate hungrily the thick clotted country cream, the fresh berries, the wholesome brown bread and thick slab of cold mutton that he brought her. After eating she climbed into the loft and slept while below her the gray mare bedded down contentedly, having eaten her fill.

When morning came, she downed a hasty breakfast of barley-cakes and a big tankard of milk and departed with a bag full of apples to eat on the way. She'd slept later than she meant to, and she had to ride hard to reach the woodland glade, where the troupe waited, before sundown.

Monty strode to meet her when she rode in. She threw back her veil and slid from the gray mare's back.

"What news?" he demanded.

"Bad news, I'm afraid," said Lenore, and told him of Will Summers's death.

Monty was stunned by the news, and around him the others gathered, muttering. There was a general air of consternation.

"We'll miss Will," said Monty slowly. "We've known him for a long time."

"What will you do now?" asked Lenore.

"Will's death means we must have a new advance man," he said, running a hand through his thick white hair. "And there are none of us who do that well." His green eyes looked sad. "I would hate to disband the troupe."

"You've no need to," Lenore told him. Amethyst lights flickered in her violet eyes, and her voice held an undertone of suppressed excitement as she outlined the arrangements she had made.

An amazed smile broke over Monty's face. "I cannot believe it," he said. "We have found our new advance man —and she is a woman!" He turned to the others. "I think Will himself could not have done better. Are we not agreed that Mistress Lenore should be our new advance man?"

174

There was surprise on every face as they looked at Lenore. Then heads began to nod.

"It is agreed!" cried Monty. "And if there's enough money from the performance in Cirencester, we'll erect a stone to Will!"

There was a murmur of approval, and Lenore smiled at Monty—she approved of erecting a stone to Will, too.

So a strange new occupation opened up for Lenore. As "advance man" for a troupe of strolling players, putting on clandestine Shakespearean plays in stern Puritan England, she had need to use her wits. The varied disguises their wigs and costumes gave her helped considerably. Sometimes she rode into a town in the guise of a tavern maid, seeking employment; sometimes as a lady with a plumed hat and lace—albeit a bit mended—at throat and cuffs; sometimes—as at Cirencester—as a widow in deep mourning garb. Although her activities were known, none could really identify her.

The beauty from Twainmere had found a new profession.

And it was well she had, for with Geoffrey's loss and the stunning additional blow of having to desert Lorena— and no matter how good the home where she had left her, Lenore considered that she had indeed deserted her daughter—ice had locked around her heart. The bitterness she had felt as a girl toward men—and which had made her a shameless flirt—now hardened into a cold inner hostility. For Lenore, Geoffrey's abandonment was the first bitter blizzard in a long, cold winter of the heart.

She did not take a lover. If the troupe found that odd, they kept their silence about it because Lenore was so valuable to them. And, too, she was seldom with them, because as soon as a performance in one town was arranged, she must be off to another town to arrange the next one.

She journeyed openly into towns, always with a new story and differently garbed. Sometimes her wig was red, sometimes brown or black or even pale as honey. Her beauty quickly gained her the confidence of men, and she made arrangements for the players' performances to be

175

held swiftly and well. As time went by, the troupe came to consider her their lucky charm.

Her share of the profits was not so much as she had hoped. Although she often wore fine clothes and even stayed at good inns, the troupe was always beset by money problems, and Lenore always remembered that she—and they—were outside the law. She must not attract too much attention lest she be too well remembered. She must not form lasting attachments . . . the rules of the road were harsh.

Still she earned enough that sometimes she could send pincushions with a few gold coins stuck inside, to Twain-mere by way of travelers crossing the Wolds. It was dangerous, and she was careful never to send letters, but Flora knew whence these coins came and bought Lorena pretty clothes and bright ribbons for her hair.

Monty would gladly have taken Lenore to his bed. She knew that from the way his green eyes glinted as they followed her, from the timbered resonance of his voice when he spoke to her, from something indefinably protective in his manner—more than from anything he said. But Monty, too, was interested in keeping the services of a superb "advance man." He made occasional overtures—a gift of a pair of sheer silk stockings or beribboned garters, the offer to share a bottle of sack with him when they were in funds. Lenore talked to him companionably as an equal, but she did not share his bed.

Sometimes when she rode into camp after a long, hard, dusty ride, and heard his pleasant melodic laugh ring out, she asked herself why. Why could she not love him? She liked him, she admitted honestly to herself that he attracted her, that she might even be happy living with him, but . . . Monty's way of life was precarious and she knew she could never have Lorena with her if she became his mistress.

There was another reason, too—Geoffrey. Her love for him, so deep and real, acted as a barrier between her and other men, a high wall that she could not climb over even if she wanted to. Bitterly she reminded herself that Geoffrey was the past, which was over, but something young and stubborn in her heart would not have it so. She

176

was being true to Geoffrey—but she would never have admitted it.

Nights when she longed for Geoffrey's arms, and to hold little Lorena to her breast again, Lenore tossed on her pillow at strange inns and fought back the urge to write to Flora, to send for her child, or even to ride boldly into Twainmere and take Lorena and Snowfire away with her. But in the sleepless gray light of dawn she always realized her folly. Her life on the road was dangerous and impermanent. She could provide no proper home, no proper friends for a growing child. Perhaps it would not always be so; she could pray and hope for a better day. A day when she would be reunited with her golden daughter; hoping that love could one day reclaim her heart . . .

BOOK
II

THE
LONDON
WENCH

PART
ONE

THE
KING'S
DOXIE

CHAPTER 12

It was the last of May, and a great day for England. For on Friday just after dawn King Charles II—who had fled from Worcester in defeat nine years ago—returned in triumph to his homeland. In beautiful clear weather he landed at Dover and knelt on the beach to give thanks. His journey to London was a triumphal march. Cheering crowds lined streets hung with garlands of ribbons, and scarves and spoons, and even silver plate.

Having banqueted at noon on Tuesday with the Lord Mayor, the scarlet-robed aldermen, and numerous notables whose gold chains glimmered against the black velvet of their clothing, the young King was at last ready to enter his capital. And at half-past four the mighty procession poured over London Bridge and into the City, where costly tapestries festooned the streets and the conduits ran with claret.

In the jostling crowd along the Strand, Lenore Frankford waited for the procession to pass. Her thick, red-gold hair had been carefully combed into a shining coil at the back, while fashionable long side curls reached down to her shoulders. She was dressed in the best she owned—an amber silk gown with a low wide neckline which showed her gleaming white shoulders to great advantage. Her tight bodice hugged her round breasts and tapered to her narrow waist, and her billowing skirt was slit down the front and tucked up at both sides to reveal a full petticoat of rippling russet satin. From beneath her full skirts peeped a pair of dainty square-toed shoes with high yellow heels.

The effect was so striking that of the many admiring glances she'd received as she hurried to join the crush along the Strand, few had noticed that her dress had been cleverly mended in several places, that her petticoat was threadbare, or that her high-heeled shoes were badly worn. Who would guess that she wore one glove and carried the other because it was too badly stained to wear? For the woman in the amber silk gown would always command attention. When a tall man with a cane elbowed her with a curt, "Sorry, mistress," in an attempt to get a better position, Lenore turned and looked at him. Looking down into her lovely face, he had said softly, "Sorry, indeed!"

Lenore was used to these tributes to her beauty, for she was as slim and as lovely as the day she had ridden out of Twainmere, seven years ago. Her complexion was as sheer and fair, her glorious violet eyes had the same heart-stopping quality, and her swift, blinding smile still dazzled the viewer.

But the years had given Lenore other things—a sense of style which she had not had in Twainmere, and a certain hardness of viewpoint. She had not made her way easily, and often she'd endured hard times, but she had never once given up. Now she stood on the Strand in the full flower of her beauty, looking a woman of molten gold in the sunlight.

Nearby hawkers cried their wares—little cakes and pies and other sweetmeats. People shouted to one another and leaned out the windows from above. In the distance now came the sound of trumpets and hooves. The procession was approaching, and the crowd strained forward.

Beside Lenore, a stout little woman pulled her small

184

daughter back from the street. "Look where those pikemen are standing, Sallie," she told the child. "That was where Charing Cross stood until the Ironsides tore it down! Well, the new King will put it back, you'll see!"

Lenore's gaze flew to the company of six hundred pikemen who waited to parade before the new King. All London, she knew, had mourned the loss of Charing Cross, erected in 1290 by Edward I as a memorial to his dead Queen. A lovely monument to love, destroyed in the struggle between the Ironsides and the King. Just as in another way that struggle had destroyed *her,* she thought with a fine sense of detachment . . . first Jamie, then Geoffrey, and finally Lorena had been wrested from her. And now the bachelor Charles was returning to London to ascend his throne—bloodlessly, by invitation!

Shouts and applause dinned in her ears, for the procession was in sight now. Three hundred horsemen flashing drawn swords in the sun and wearing scintillating cloth-of-silver doublets led the way. They were greeted by a mighty roar. Many other companies followed, and Lenore was pushed this way and that as people shoved each other and craned to see better. Now came the trumpeters, adding to the din, and eighty red-garbed sheriff's men, the silver lacing of their cloaks aglitter. And now the City Companies rode by, with liveried footmen attending them. From the windows ladies richly gowned leaned out waving scarves, their eyes bright. For England was to have a King again, a tall, handsome King—*and* he was a bachelor!

Buffeted and pummeled by the exuberant crowd, her pretty shoes trod on painfully more than once, and with several black and blue marks where she'd been elbowed, Lenore watched the great Companies ride by almost in a blur. So much . . . so very much had happened to bring her to this day. Now, with the crowd around her going wild, her own life seemed to pass before her in review.

After her first triumph at Cirencester, she had settled into her job as if she had been born to it. Montmorency Hogue had bragged that she was the best "advance man" in England! She had bethought herself always of the safety of the troupe of strolling players who depended upon her

—indeed, one mistake on her part could bring them to ruin. Early on, she had learned to be crafty in her choice of men to deal with in strange towns; she had learned to study men across a tankard of cider, or from beside the public horse trough in the village square—and to assess them for what they were. Her beauty—impossible to disguise—had been a mixed blessing. Often she had found it necessary to fight off unwelcome advances—once or twice with the aid of a large pistol. She had done her work unstintingly, making sure the towns she chose were "safe"—if anywhere was safe for such as they. She had even managed to save a little money and had dreamed of emigrating to the Colonies and taking Lorena with her— the old dream she had shared with Geoffrey.

When in September of 1658 Oliver Cromwell had died, her heart had leaped in hopes that the King would be restored—and she would be cleared of at least one charge they could raise against her; she could no longer be called a traitor to the Puritan regime. But Cromwell's thirty-one-year-old son Richard had succeeded him, and nothing was really changed. Dancing was still forbidden, alehouses were still closed on Sundays—and constables could still forcibly enter people's houses and search them for evidence of breaking Sabbatarian laws. Celebrating Christmas was still forbidden. . . .

But not only Lenore, all of merrie England was heartily sick of grim Puritan ways. Morris dancing and May Day games—even archery and cockfighting—had never been stamped out entirely in the villages, and although there was now a death penalty of adultery, juries all over England were refusing to convict accused adulterers. Nationwide there was a rising revulsion to stern Puritan repression.

In 1659 rumors were rife. The King was living in the Spanish Netherlands, holding his impoverished court at Brussels. Tall, athletic, good-looking and cynical, at twenty-eight he was more popular with the English people absent than was Richard Cromwell present. Monty ran his fingers through his white hair and his young-old face showed pent-up excitement as he told Lenore enthusiastically that it was just a matter of time—England would turn the fierce Puritans out and there'd be plays again, and dancing, and general merriment. She'd see!

What Lenore saw was something quite different.

On a quiet Thursday she rode into Winchester, casting about for the most likely sporting inn that would furnish information of the kind she needed. And scarce had her arrangements been made before she received word that somewhere on the road Montmorency Hogue had been recognized by a magistrate who passed by in a funeral procession—and he and his entire troupe had been taken. Lenore rode back at a gallop to try to help, pretending to be a bereaved sister of Monty's. He muttered in his jail cell that she should save herself—he and the others were like to be transported, if not worse.

Lenore, who had come to feel indeed that she was Monty's sister, had taken an emotional farewell of him. But she had taken his advice and ridden for London. She had arrived there on a bitter winter day—and found the city torn by riots. Strife had broken out all over England; the country was fast sinking into anarchy.

Monty's troupe of strolling players had avoided the larger towns through fear of arrest, and Lenore was amazed at the size of London. A city of some four hundred thousand souls, it was a warren of narrow streets and winding unpaved alleys, muddy, filthy, with no proper drains and continually weeping waterspouts and roof drips which drenched the hurrying passersby long after the rain had ended. Smoke from the "sea coal" and fog from the river combined to make the air a dirty soup, and coughing and consumption were rampant. Overcrowded and noisy, rat-infested, whole families were crammed into single rooms, and the poor and the wretched overflowed damp, dark cellars.

But it was an exciting place, for careening coaches and hurrying horsemen and people afoot filled the streets and, weaving between them, sedan chairs carrying great ladies and bewigged gentlemen who took snuff.

Lenore was enthralled by it. Like any visitor from the country, she took in the sights, staring in amazement at the great hulk of St. Paul's Cathedral and the mighty Guildhall, so huge they dominated the City's other buildings. Wistfully she studied the great Banqueting Hall at Whitehall, before whose handsome windows a great scaffold had been erected and Charles I beheaded there. It seemed to her an unnecessary indignity that the King should have been forced to climb a scaffold looking into the windows where he had so often dined, but she was even more shocked to learn that the lovely Tudor palace at Greenwich had been converted by the irreverent Commonwealth into a biscuit factory. The inns of London were still jolly places—if one had money to buy food and drink —but sometimes at night Lenore dreamed of the gaiety that must have been here before the Puritans came.

Lenore, who had saved a little money but had no real vocation, had decided to take lodgings and see which way the wind blew—commonwealth or monarchy. For surely, she told herself, the issue must be decided soon—England could not hang poised on the brink forever. She settled in at the George in Southwark near London Bridge, where another lodger, a Mistress Potts, took an immediate liking to the lovely young newcomer with the dazzling smile. Mistress Potts was a fat, garrulous woman in her midfifties who spoke in stage whispers and nodded her head significantly at her own remarks. She'd been widowed in Brighton and had sold out and taken her "widow's mite" and come to London to live out her days. She had no deep convictions about king or commonwealth, and since she received letters from friends scattered all about England— people she had met while they vacationed in Bath— Lenore found her a good source of news.

The weather was so cold that December that the Thames, its flow slowed by the great piers that supported London Bridge and the houses that lined it on both sides —froze bank to bank, and a great Frost Fair was held. Stalls were set up on the ice selling food and souvenirs and fancies. Lenore bought for Mistress Potts a slip from a printer's booth bearing her name and the imprint "The Thames," which Mistress Potts—temporarily bedridden

188

by a cold—exclaimed over and hung on the wall of her room.

By the end of January there was open talk of a Restoration. General Monk, at the head of a large force, had crossed the Tweed—word reached London that his troops had waded knee-deep through snow and icy water in Northumberland, but he had reached York and then Nottingham. Lenore chafed at the delay. If England was going to become a kingdom again, she wanted them to get on with it.

Although several men at the George showed an immediate interest in her, Lenore gave their advances her habitual cold shoulder. Coolly she returned the stares of hot-eyed men and admiring youths who stripped her with their eyes and brushed on by them, intent on her own affairs. This was Geoffrey's legacy to her . . . she still, in her heart, considered herself his wife. It would have galled her to realize that she was a one-man woman and was being faithful to him all this time, but it was so.

Mistress Potts leavened Lenore's time of waiting with gossip. She was one of those women who were certain every man she met intended to rape her. The stable boy, she whispered hoarsely to Lenore, had patted her bottom as she passed by him in the stable! Imagine! She had not told on him, for if the innkeeper knew, it well might cost the stable boy his job. Indeed, what were young men coming to?

Since Mistress Potts was nearly as broad as she was tall, and panted as she waddled about, Lenore thought it more likely that Mistress Potts's posterior had been caressed by a saddle hung from a beam or some other likely dangling implement as she lumbered by, but she forbore to say so. Mistress Potts was always so happy with her near-brushes with lascivious disaster.

"You should not go out on the public streets without a mask," she reproved Lenore. " 'Tis dangerous to do so! There are footpads about—and worse!"

Lenore sighed. Although it was true that many ladies wore masks at popular public gatherings—such as executions—she had always been quite happy to go about bare-faced. But when in late January Mistress Potts presented her with a face-mask like her own, Lenore took it—and accepted Mistress Potts's invitation to sup with her at the Swan in Fish Street. Since it was a fine, sunny winter day, marred only by the smoke from the sea coal pouring out of the chimneys, they walked there by a circuitous route. Along the way Mistress Potts kept nudging Lenore and loudly whispering that this fellow in the broad hat, or that one with the great beard, was attempting to attract their notice—and wasn't Lenore glad she'd worn her mask for this public outing "as proper ladies do"? Lenore was glad for quite another reason: Mistress Potts's stage whispers of imagined advances was attracting amused attention. With her face red above and below the mask—which left most of her forehead and her lower face below the eyes exposed—Lenore quickly interrupted to point out buildings of no possible interest, children playing with wooden swords—anything to distract Mistress Potts from her favorite subject.

At Cheapside Mistress Potts was distracted by something else, for there the rioting apprentices had set up a gibbet. She paused to exclaim over it, but Lenore seized her arm and forcibly hurried her on.

"But 'twas interesting!" Mistress Potts kept wailing. And later over their feast of marrowbones and loin of veal at the Swan, her round face grew avid, and she whispered loudly, "Think you there will be a hanging in Cheapside?"

Lenore gave her a quelling look. She had seen enough of gibbets, of bodies dangling at the crossroads, when she had ridden with Geoffrey after the King's defeat at Worcester.

"Oh, well!" said Mistress Potts in a huff. "If you don't *care* to know what's going on!" But a moment later her interest had shifted. "See that gentleman in the purple coat with gold buttons over there?" she hissed. "He is making eyes at me!"

"Is he?" murmured Lenore absently.

"Indeed he is! Well—I suppose he has given up, since I have not condescended to notice him," she said, as the gentleman rose and left. "Do try the tart, my dear—and these prawns and cheese are delicious!"

But memories were eating at Lenore. Memories of a dark sardonic face and arms that had held her close, memories of long languorous nights spent on the lonely wilds of Dartmoor, and an interval at Oxford when she had thought nothing could separate them, nothing mar or damage their love for each other. Her heart wept, and she shook her head at the great tart and hardly touched the prawns and cheese.

"I've been meaning to tell you," confided Mistress Potts. "You know that man in the blue coat who sits in the common room at the George every night smoking a pipe?"

Lenore, roused from her reverie, gave her a puzzled look.

"The man with the sharp-pointed nose and the very strange boots," elaborated Mistress Potts. "I think he comes to the George to watch you, Lenore."

"I think he comes there because he has nowhere else to go," said Lenore flatly. "He seems lonely and speaks to no one."

"But that's the worst kind! Mark me, he'll bear watching. I've seen him turn his head and look at you when you weren't looking!"

"Mistress Potts," said Lenore whimsically—for she refused to call her friend by her first name out of deference to her age—"you do me too much credit. Not all the men I meet are interested in me—some have very satisfactory wives or mistresses at home!"

Mistress Potts bridled. "Those that won't heed timely warnings may end up badly!" she said in a tart voice.

Lenore sighed. She had already ended up badly, by her way of thinking: deserted by her lover, out of touch with her child because charges of being a Royalist and a murderess hung over her head . . . she really did not fear the man in the blue coat, or anyone, for that matter.

Mistress Potts's concern for Lenore's threatened virtue became so obsessive that Lenore was almost relieved when, on the last day of January, the tense city's—and Mistress Potts's—attention was diverted by a public hanging at Tyburn.

191

The culprit was a woman who had disposed of her unwanted child by placing it in a large covered pot and taking it to a nearby bakehouse to be baked. When the horrified baker discovered the child, there was a public outcry. Mistress Potts had talked of little else for days. Her *child!* Imagine doing that to her little baby!

When Lenore heard about it, she felt physically ill and promptly turned down Mistress Potts's eager suggestion that they watch the convicted murderess "dance" at the end of a rope at Tyburn. But shy Mistress Potts outwitted Lenore, and asked Lenore to accompany her on an errand to High Holborn, where they stood with a large goggling crowd watching the hanging cart go by. Lenore stared at the dazed, terrified woman and clenched her hands and thought of Lorena. Thank God Lorena was safe with Flora, who would love her and keep her—both because Lorena was Jamie's and because Flora was Flora. And because Lorena was *hers*.

" 'Tis not too late to reach Tyburn and see her swing if we hire a chair!" cried Mistress Potts, fired by the sight of the condemned woman standing in the cart. "And there'll be seats for ladies for hire at Tyburn, I'm sure—though the lucky ones will watch from their coaches!"

"Perhaps she is not guilty," said Lenore coldly.

"Nonsense! Who else would place her child in a pot?"

"Her enemies," Lenore said soberly. The searing thought had come to her that people believed *her* a murderess, too! Perhaps this poor woman . . . she could not bear to look at the cart any more and turned away abruptly. "I do not feel well," she told Mistress Potts. "You go on to Tyburn— I think I will go back to the George."

By the first of February the City seemed calm again— until suddenly the next day the unpaid soldiery quartered near Whitehall blazed into mutiny and stormed Somerset House. There they mounted seven guns and threatened to blow up Parliament. Joined by a mob of seven hundred angry apprentices, they marched through Cheapside until dispersed by cavalry, with some forty jailed.

On the third of February General Monk's troops, five

192

thousand strong, marched down Gray's Inn Road into London.

Mistress Potts said admiringly that a general who would march his men three hundred miles through snow and ice water could handle anything—even London.

Her assessment seemed true. Amid a wave of mutinies which seemed to break out spontaneously everywhere, General Monk calmly took possession of the Tower of London. He ordered the handsome city gates and portcullises destroyed and took up headquarters at the Three Tuns in Guildhall Yard. When he decreed that the present Rump Parliament should not sit later than May 6, the City went wild—for this meant the young King far away in Brussels would soon be restored to his throne. Bonfires lit the streets, all the bells were rung, and amid the clangor and smoke everyone choked and slapped one another on the back and drank the King's health. Amid a wave of public whippings and executions, General Monk moved into Whitehall, and Tuesday, February 28, was celebrated as a day of public thanksgiving.

Mistress Potts was jubilant. From a seesawing middle-of-the-roader she had become overnight an ardent Royalist. Wasn't it wonderful? she beamed. The King would be on his rightful throne again, he'd be coming home—all the way from Brussels!

Lenore gave her a somber look. That meant Geoffrey would be coming home, too, for she had no doubt he was with the King in Brussels. She knew she should bestir herself to find employment but a strange lethargy possessed her, a feeling of waiting. . . .

March was a month of heavy rains, and on March 20 the swollen Thames overflowed its banks. Lenore fought her way home to the George against a strong east wind. They were rowing boats down King Street, she noted. She came in wet and shivering, to find Mistress Potts leaning back in the common room, filling the whole of a chair with her girth and toasting her square-toed shoes at the hearth. She waved a letter at Lenore and told her in an excited whisper that the soldiers in Dunkirk were drinking the King's health openly in the streets!

Glumly, Lenore tossed off her wet cloak and warmed herself by the fire. She hoped the King would come soon, for her money was running low. When she had arrived in London, she had had nearly enough for passage money for herself and Lorena, but now she would have to find a way to earn more. Somehow she had expected this change from commonwealth to monarchy to come overnight—with Cromwell dead, the King would immediately be restored to his throne. But the political machinations had dragged on for a long time.

It was some comfort that elections were at last being held and amnesty discussed. The two official newspapers had hastily changed their names; then there were rumors of a riot in York. But just when things finally seemed to be settling down, Lambert—who everyone felt was capable of raising a revolt—escaped from the Tower. Lenore had it from Mistress Potts that a lady had smuggled a silk ladder into Lambert's cell and he had made it down the wall into a waiting barge—while the girl, who'd received a hundred pounds for her efforts, had crawled into the prisoner's bed attired in his nightcap—and so they had found her in the morning! Mistress Potts tittered at this, but Lenore wondered uneasily what would happen to the audacious girl, who was now in custody.

The City was tense now. Chains had been set up, and three regiments stood guard. By Good Friday it was learned that Lambert had been cornered in a house in Westminster and escaped in a coach wearing a woman's dress and a mask. But on Easter Sunday he and the troops who had risen with him were defeated, and Lambert was once again a prisoner.

Lenore's interest quickened when late in April there was an attempt to reopen London's closed theatres—but this move was quickly stopped by the Council of State as being premature. Lenore, thinking sadly of Monty and his dedicated troupe of players, agreed with Mistress Potts that it was too bad—and joined her in watching Lambert brought by in a coach with two of his officers on his way again to

194

the Tower. Lenore shivered as she watched them pass; it was sad to be a prisoner.

The new Parliament assembled, and on May 1 England was again declared a monarchy. That night was bright as day, for London was lit by bonfires end to end. Maypoles (which had been forbidden under Puritan rule) were set up everywhere—even the King's flag was hoisted atop a maypole at Deal, where the fleet lay at anchor, and the castle guns fired a lusty salute.

Not till May 4 at Breda did the young King hear the news. He was champing at the bit when the following Tuesday he was again proclaimed at Whitehall. Amid much pageantry, with the sheriffs in scarlet and the Lord Mayor in crimson velvet gown and hood, a joyful procession wended through the streets to the Old Exchange. Everywhere was the King proclaimed. The fourth time was in Cheapside, where Lenore and Mistress Potts stood in a great crush of people. All the bells in the city began to ring, and the shouting around them grew so loud that they could not even hear Bow bells rung. Mistress Potts lost her heel and limped home with Lenore as the proclamation was read at the Old Exchange. They reached the George as the guns from the Tower fired a salute. That night was lit with bonfires and no one could sleep for the merry clanging of bells.

It has happened, thought Lenore. *It has really happened. The King will set sail at last. And . . . Geoffrey will accompany him.* Her violet eyes grew dark at the thought, and an involuntary shiver went through her. *Geoffrey would be coming home . . . she would see him again. She knew it.*

It seemed almost anticlimactic when Mistress Potts received a letter saying her stepsister had died in Oxford and left her a fustian blanket and a down bolster. She read the letter aloud dramatically, standing in the common room of the George.

"Will you go to Oxford to the funeral?" asked Lenore soberly.

Mistress Potts looked up and shook her head. "Nay, we've not seen each other for years—but the fustian blanket and bolster were my mother's, and we made a pact that she could use them whilst she lived, but I was to have them on her death. Besides, I wouldn't want to miss the King's return to London—oh!" She sounded disappointed. "I missed this part! It says here that when the King was proclaimed at Oxford on Thursday, the conduit ran claret for *hours!* The Mayor gave away hundreds of bottles of wine, and barrels of beer were set up in the streets—and a hundred dozen loaves were given to the poor!"

Lenore thought sardonically that Mistress Potts was wishing her stepsister had died last week so she could have attended both the funeral and the festivities in Oxford at the same time. Oxford . . . she had tried to keep that town of honey-colored spires and wrenching memories from her thoughts.

Channel gales postponed the King's embarkation, but at last on May 22 the sun burst through, and at four o'clock the following day the fleet set sail and anchored at Dover two days later at dawn. The young King went down on his knees on the beach and while the shore guns fired in salute, he thanked God for bringing him safely home again.

And then began the triumphant march to London—from Dover Castle to Canterbury, from Rochester to St. George's Fields, where the Lord Mayor of London waited, and on across London Bridge through cheering, tapestry-hung streets, toward Whitehall.

Lenore, standing in her threadbare mended finery in the crush of the Strand, watched them pass and thought of Worcester, of those who had gone and those who would return.

The kettledrum and five trumpets were passing now, the noise deafening. And now the Lifeguards, and more trumpets. Lenore had eluded Mistress Potts, who had intended to view the procession near London Bridge. If she should see Geoffrey ride by, she thought she might burst into tears and . . . that would require explanations.

Now the City Marshal, the City Waits, and all the City officers were filing by, splendidly garbed, now the red-robed sheriffs and the aldermen—complete with liveried footmen, heralds, maces. Now the Lord Mayor with sword upraised—and with him General Monk and the Duke of Buckingham.

Lenore took a deep, ragged breath and felt her heart must

stop. Geoffrey should be somewhere among the group about the King. She stood on tiptoe and clawed her way forward to get a better view, for the crowd had gone wild, waving scarves and cheering and screaming. That sudden outburst had to mean the King had come into view.

Ah, now she could see him. It was the King, flanked by the Duke of York and the Duke of Gloucester. The King, his trim, athletic figure clothed in a dark suit of cloth, his hat waving with scarlet plumes. Lenore studied him somberly as he passed. She had seen him once before, charging across the field at Worcester, his black curls flying, a flash of diamonds at his chest. Frantically her eyes searched among the King's close friends, riding by. That tall man in the wide-brimmed hat, could that be Geoffrey? The light was shining in her eyes. No—he was blond. Perhaps the .man in rich blue velvet riding between a cavalier in scarlet and one in gold-emboidered satin, she could not see him—ah, there he was looking around; it was a handsome face, but it was not Geoffrey's.

One by one she watched them ride by, until there were no more to see. For seven long hours she had stood on her high heels in the Strand watching the procession. Now at last she settled back from tiptoe to stand flat upon the sidewalk. Many cavaliers had returned with the King but—Geoffrey was not among them.

She turned away with an ache in her throat, not waiting to see the six hundred men of the City Companies ride by with their footmen. She had seen enough.

He must be dead, then, she thought sadly. For if he were alive, Geoffrey would have returned to London with the King. Perhaps he had never made it to France after all. . . .

Through tapestry-hung streets, past people giddy with joy and staggering from wine, a sad Lenore made her way back to the George. She found Mistress Potts waiting for her.

"Where've ye been?" she demanded of Lenore. "I've been afraid ye'd miss the party!"

"Party?"

"All London will have a party this night!" declared Mistress Potts. " 'Twill be a sight to see!"

And London did have a party. It went on for three days and three nights. Mistress Potts urged a mask on Lenore and they went out into the streets together, trailing by innumerable bonfires, seeing innumerable effigies of Cromwell burned. Everywhere, there were barrels of beer and wine, wine, wine—one foreign envoy kept a fountain of wine spurting before his very door.

Numbed, Lenore allowed herself to be dragged through these revels by energetic Mistress Potts. But when the festivities dragged to an end—mainly through the exhaustion of the participants—she sat in her lonely room with her head in her hands and at last admitted to herself how much she had been counting on seeing Geoffrey again, that it was the real reason she had lingered in London all this time.

Mistress Potts did not know the reason for Lenore's despondency, but she tried to cheer her. She brought daily bulletins of the athletic young King's doings. On Sunday he had played his favorite game—tennis; now he had taken up river bathing and every evening went with the Duke of York as far as Battersea or Barn Elms to swim.

When she learned that on a Saturday the King had touched six hundred people for "the Evil," Mistress Potts hurried to the Banqueting House on Monday to be touched. She returned with a white ribbon bearing an angel in gold which the King himself had placed around her neck. There'd been two hundred and fifty people there, and she urged Lenore to procure a ticket from the Royal Surgeon in Covent Garden—though, she added regretfully, there'd been such a crush that 'twould only be done on Fridays now.

Lenore was roused to hysterical laughter. As if a King's touch could excise the evil which had so long beset her! But she listened to the gossip that garrulous Mistress Potts had brought back from the Banqueting House—that not only the King but his brothers were hot in pursuit of beautiful Barbara Villiers—and she a married woman, wed to Roger Palmer! Mistress Potts was thrilled. Lenore said dryly that royalty was seldom *not* in hot pursuit, and Mistress Potts tittered inordinately.

But Mistress Potts's talk of the King's touch alleviating

evil had set Lenore thinking. It was said that all those who had helped the King during the days of his defeat and exile were hastening to London to claim rewards—and that he was giving them rewards with a lavish hand. Of course, she had never really *done* anything for the King, but . . . was she not known as the Angel of Worcester? And had she not suffered for it?

She took a walk to think about that, and as she passed the Queen's Head Inn she was hard put to avoid a limping man who stumbled on the cobbles and nearly plummeted into her. Instinctively she put out a hand to help him and as he regained his footing and turned to thank her, she realized that she was looking into the face of Montmorency Hogue, the head of the company of strolling players for whom for so long she had been the "advance man."

"Monty!" she gasped, and hugged him.

Monty Hogue, who was older and thinner than she remembered him, his face lined and weathered, was almost knocked off balance again by this onslaught.

"Mistress Lenore!" he cried. "I'd ne'er thought to see your face again!"

"Nor I yours, Monty! Word had it you'd been transported, that all the troupe had been. How come you to London?"

" 'Tis a long story," he said, and she saw that his cheeks were sunken and sallow; whatever his experiences, they had aged him. "We might have been let off with a light sentence, but I've a sharp tongue in my head, and I flayed the magistrate with it. We were transported right enough. The rest were sent to Barbados, but I was shipped to Virginia, where I was indentured to an elderly planter. He'd a mind for frivolity, and at supper I would entertain his guests with recitations. He was so pleased with me that when he decided to return to England he brought me with him. He died of bad food on the journey, but when his will was read, he had freed me of my indenture and left me fifty pounds to boot!"

"Then you're staying in London, Monty?"

"Nay, I was even now on my way to take a stage westward. I'm for Stratford, where I hope to assemble a troupe of strolling players again. And you, mistress, how do you fare?"

Ah, how she wished he would ask her to go with him. "I fare well enough, Monty," she said soberly. And then, with hesitation she asked, "Will you be needing an advance man, Monty?"

He gave her a look of sympathy, but he shook his head emphatically. "Nay, Mistress Lenore, that I will not. England is changing for the better, now that the King is restored to his throne. There'll be no need of advance men making clandestine arrangements to hold a play. We'll wander about the country with our cart and hold our plays in any likely place. 'Twill be like the old days when the old King reigned!"

She felt rebuffed. And yet—why should Monty go to the expense of using an advance man if he did not need one? "I wish you well, Monty." She smiled at him.

"I know that." He wrung her hand, his own thin and bony. It somehow hurt her heart to see how old he had become. Transportation had changed him, it had erased the youth from that buoyant young-old face, and now—like a dry leaf—he was blowing to the west. If she had thought he would rally her as he had once done, his twinkling eyes and merry manner urging her to his bed, she was mistaken. Wryly she asked herself if she had hoped to be asked to go along as his mistress, mending the costumes for the troupe—and perchance mending her own heart as well.

But . . . Monty was a part of her past, the only part she still dared cling to. "Will there not be plays in London, Monty?" she asked wistfully. "Could you not stay here?"

He shook his head. His voice was bitter. "The Puritans have ruined the theatre in London—at least for now. There's no good place to hold a play! They pulled down the Globe, and sent soldiery to wreck the Salisbury Court and the Fortune and the Cockpit—and five years ago they even pulled down the Blackfriars, saying they needed the space for tenements!" He gave a short laugh that was more like a bark. "No, I'd like to take you with me, Mistress Lenore, but acting is a man's profession in England—though if you could get to the Continent, women play the female roles there."

"I'd not thought to become an actress," Lenore told him ruefully. "Nor have I the funds to reach the Continent if I had!"

Monty took out a large gold watch. "My patron left this to me, as well," he said. "And it tells me that I must hurry if I'm to catch my stage. Good health to you, Mistress Lenore."

"Good health, Monty."

He limped rapidly away, and Lenore stood looking after him a little sadly.

The encounter had taught her one thing: a road which she had thought still open to her—not with Monty's disbanded troupe, but with some other troupe of strolling players—was now closed. She felt caught in a vise of despair that would never release her.

CHAPTER 13

The next day she applied for a job in a baker's shop—
and got it. It paid little, but offered lodgings above the shop
and meals with the baker's family. She was able to give
up her room at the George, which she could no longer
afford.

But Mistress Potts did not desert her. She huffed and
puffed from the George down to the hot, low-ceilinged room
where Lenore, a big white apron almost enveloping her
dress, her arms sometimes white with flour, sold heavenly
smelling loaves of bread.

Mistress Potts deplored Lenore's leaving the George, and
her visits were always sprightly. Did Lenore know there'd
been so many duels in London the King had had to pro-
claim against dueling? Lenore dusted off her floury arms
on her white apron and said with amusement that she hadn't
known it—very few duels had been fought over her of late.

Mistress Potts missed the irony of that and rushed on.
Did she know Mister Milton's books had been declared
treasonable—and Mister Goodwin's, too? They were both

in hiding! And had she heard of the capture of the cleric Hugh Peters? He'd hidden in a certain Mistress Peach's bed —and she with a child born just two days before! The searching officers hadn't wanted to search the woman's bed, of course—and Peters had got clean away! But the next day, she added regretfully, they'd caught him, and now he was in the Tower. Had Lenore any news, or was she so buried under this mountain of loaves she never heard anything?

Lenore smiled and received payment for a big loaf of bread. She turned to Mistress Potts. "I did hear that peace had been proclaimed with Spain."

"Peace? Oh, yes, peace." Mistress Potts made a gesture shrugging off war and peace as trivialities. "But did you hear the Duke of Gloucester died? Of the smallpox, they do say! Well"—as Lenore was once again busy selling loaves—"I suppose I must go if I'm to be home before dark. The traffic in London is terrible these days—hackney coaches everywhere, they'll run right over a body! You must come and see me when you've a day off, Lenore."

"I will." Lenore smiled and watched her go.

That fall London buzzed, for the men responsible for beheading the new King's father were rounded up and tried —most of them were executed at Charing Cross. Mistress Potts hurried over to tell her that Anne Hyde had given birth to the Duke of York's baby! And in Parliament a great debate took place on a bill that would prevent married women from leaving their husbands. A Mister Walpole stood up and said that if the bill were passed all the women in England would surely leave!

Lenore felt downcast. With all the wild revelry of Restoration London about her, she was in as bad case as ever—worse even, for she was busy at her job from morn to dark and eked out a bare living. Though no one could charge her now with being a Royalist, she could still be brought to trial for murder, and she was no closer than ever to sending for her daughter.

She, who had always been so buoyant, now found herself pensive as she worked, ignoring the bright-eyed overtures of the elderly gentleman from across the street who bought

203

enough bread for a household of eight, though he lived alone. He bought it a loaf at a time, lingering over his purchase. The jaunty married man from the next block she ignored, too, for since Lenore had come to the bakery, he had taken over his wife's duty of buying bread and never failed to try to rally the bright-haired woman who sold him the fresh loaves. The only man she talked to much was the soldier who had lost a leg at Worcester—no matter he'd been fighting on Cromwell's side, Lenore felt a kinship with him, for he'd been but a green boy dragged into the battle—and when he left to join his relatives in Nottingham she missed him.

In November Mistress Potts showed her a new book she had purchased called *The Horn Exalted: Or, Room for Cuckolds*. Mistress Potts tittered that it was very bad indeed—she had promised to send it to all her friends. London was uneasy now; even the carpenter who'd built the old King's scaffold had been arrested, and Oliver Cromwell's body had been disinterred from Westminster Abbey, where he'd been buried with such ceremony, and he'd been hanged in his coffin at Tyburn and reburied beneath the gallows.

The weather, in tune with the times, was wild; the Thames had overflowed its banks again, and Mistress Potts complained she had had to be rowed in a boat through the streets of Westminster when she went to visit a friend. A plot against the King was suspected, and forty men were imprisoned, and the Commons was rewarding many of those who had aided King Charles in his escape from Worcester (several had received a thousand pounds).

Anne Hyde, now Duchess of York, was holding court at Worcester Court, but Mistress Potts whispered the King's mother still refused to accept her! Lenore wondered how she felt about the King's mistress, Barbara Palmer.

On Christmas Eve the King's sister died of the same disease that had killed her brother—just when all believed her out of danger. But not even a royal death could stop the merriment of Christmas celebrations in England—so long forbidden by law. And although it looked to Lenore as if she was going to have floury arms and handle fresh-baked loaves for a long time, that Christmas was a bright spot for her.

That winter of 1660–1661 was a snowy one, and Lenore, now that the baker's wife had had another child and needed quarters for a wet nurse, was forced to give up her lodgings above the shop—although the baker granted her a small increase in wages to compensate. She moved into cheap, tiny lodgings with a grim view of the walls of Bridewell Prison—a workhouse and prison for women. Sad, pale-faced women entered those gates—and sometimes left in carts for burial. Every day it was a grim reminder to Lenore of where she could sink if her past was uncovered, and a reminder that she must take care not to entangle Lorena in her life— even though she never ceased to yearn to hold her child in her arms again—lest those grim walls enclose them both . . . and then Lorena could be torn from her to spend her young days in an orphanage, many of which were only slightly less harsh than Bridewell Prison.

But spring came at last. At Whitehall new earls and barons were being created right and left for the forthcoming coronation. And on St. George's Day in April, King Charles strode through Palace Yard over cloth of blue to the throne in Westminster Abbey and was crowned with St. Edward's crown by the archbishop. Salvoes from the Tower guns proclaimed him throughout London.

From the bakeshop where she was preparing hugh crocks of dough for the next baking, Lenore looked up as those guns sounded. Her face was flushed, and she looked tired. Crowds had come to London for the coronation, business was booming, and the baker and his wife had left her with only a small boy to help her and gone to stand outside the Abbey and view the notables. They came back talking excitedly of all they had seen, "so many fine gentlemen in great plumed hats riding prancing steeds," but Lenore turned away sadly and finished her backbreaking work. Out of all of Charles II's train, there was only one fine gentleman she had hoped to see—and she had waited for him in vain for seven hours at Charing Cross.

"The King will marry that Portuguese Princess—you'll see!" The baker's wife wagged her head at her husband and critically sampled a roll. "Not that she's a beauty or will bear him children!" Her voice was contemptuous. "But for the dowry!"

Hardly listening to the baker's mumbled answer, Lenore stumbled as she finished carrying the last of the great crocks of dough.

"Here, let me take that." The baker stepped forward. "Ye must be tired."

"A little," admitted Lenore, wearily brushing back a lock of damp red-gold hair. "I've been at it for sixteen hours!"

Too tired to go home, she fell asleep at once on the pallet the baker's wife graciously provided on the floor of the bakeshop. And dreamed of Portugal and princesses and of Geoffrey, who was never coming home.

The baker's wife proved right, for in June a wedding treaty was signed with Portugal—King Charles would marry the Infanta, Catherine of Braganza. Vast sums were said to have changed hands.

Lenore had lost her job at the bakery, for the baker's wife had angrily accused her of seducing the baker when she had found the two of them crouched by the oven. That they had only been picking up pieces of a broken crock made no difference—she had flared up and discharged Lenore. Lenore might have argued the point and got the baker to keep her, but she knew it was only a matter of time till the sturdy baker did indeed bear her to the earthen floor, for he'd been harder to handle of late, slipping up behind her for a sly pinch or a quick bear hug. The baker's wife had near caught him at that more than once—indeed, it was a sudden ill-timed pinch that had made Lenore drop the crock of dough!

But honest jobs were hard to come by, even for a beauty like Lenore. She worked briefly at several jobs, and for a short, terrible time was even reduced to being a laundress at Moorfields, scrubbing all day and spreading out the clothes to dry on the ground! If only she could have unlocked her heart to one of the many men who wanted to care for her, but Lenore was like a widow in permanent mourning. She wanted only one man—the one she'd never again have.

From this work the pretty laundress rebelled and in the fall found a situation as housekeeper in the home of a widowed mercer. The elderly widower was enchanted with Lenore and twice proposed marriage. She might even have considered it, for it would have meant she could have Lorena with her, and in a prosperous household where she would be well brought up—but the mercer's two elderly sisters were forever stabbing questions at Lenore about her background which made her fear the past would be all raked up again if she sent for Lorena. She managed to hold the mercer off, for—except that London had a heavy smog compounded of fog and sea coal smoke which coated the furnishings with grime—the job was an easy one, and she liked his younger children. But at Christmas his two elder daughters came home from school, were briefed by their aunts, and promptly schemed to be rid of Lenore, for they feared she might become their stepmother and—as the aunts had whispered—when their father died, turn them out.

Lenore, feeling herself secure in the mercer's regard, ignored their enmity in the rush of preparations for the holidays. On Christmas Day, Lenore—who felt the mercer's family would be happier celebrating Christmas alone—accepted an invitation to share Christmas dinner with Mistress Potts, whose health had been poorly of late. As she left, wrapping her warm brown shawl around the russet linsey-woolsey dress she had managed to procure with her earnings, the mercer's eldest daughter slid up to her in the hallway.

"Where did you say you came from, mistress?" she asked Lenore in her high-pitched treble.

Looking into that sly face, framed on both side by dangling corkscrew curls that flapped about like a spaniel's ears, Lenore came instantly alert. "I said I came from Winchester," she said lightly. "Where I worked for the Wynants on Candle Street just off the High."

"That is strange," said the girl, cocking her head so that her curls wagged and eyeing Lenore with bright inquisitive eyes. "For I asked Gwen Custer, who lives in Winchester, and *she* never heard of the Wynants."

"Perhaps," sighed Lenore, "they did not move in the

207

same circles. Or perhaps they have moved away. *I* never heard of Gwen Custer."

The mercer's daughter looked confused, and Lenore walked briskly out of the house before she could be asked any more questions. But the incident had sobered her. It had reminded her that—favored servant though she might be here, she was still a wanted woman, with a murder charge hanging over her head. Her past could still catch up to her.

She hardly heard the sleigh bells that rang in the cold snow-washed air as she headed for the Hart and dinner with Mistress Potts. Around her children munched sugarplums and hot roasted chestnuts and played at snow forts and threw snowballs—other people's children. Was she never to have her own beside her?

To be free of the charges against her, she knew she would need a royal pardon—for she did not feel she could trust the courts. She had fled—and that would be counted against her. She might well end up on the gibbet. Lenore was determined she should have that royal pardon.

Thrice she had attempted to gain an audience with the king—though she was not sure exactly what she would have to tell him. Thrice she had been turned away from Whitehall—indeed, there had been several snickers when the good-looking baker's girl had told them she was the Angel of Worcester.

"Claims to be a phantom!" someone had said in a hollow, sepulchral tone as she left, red-faced, the last time. And someone else said, "A fine, juicy piece she looks to me, and no phantom! Someone should bed her down and she'd forget to pretend she's an Angel and be content with earthly delights!"

Grimly, Lenore had decided she would see the King in spite of his minions. Although she tried at Hyde Park— and was nearly knocked off her feet by a prancing horse and then by some footracers for her pains, and though she haunted Whitehall for a while, she did not see the King.

When she reached the Hart, she found Mistress Potts waiting—and ready to chide Lenore for not wearing her face-mask through the streets. Lenore warmed herself at the hearth of the common room, smiling at Mistress Potts's

208

running summary of London gossip, and then sat down to share with her a hearty supper of roast stuffed goose and plum pudding. Afterward she hurried home to the mercer's through falling snow, listening to the merry sound of bells and Christmas carols from jolly groups of carolers.

But for all the merriment and idle gossip and drinking of toasts, Lenore had learned something useful from Mistress Potts.

"You're trying to see His Majesty in the wrong places," shrewd Mistress Potts had chided her, for she knew of Lenore's futile attempts to get into Whitehall. "The play's the thing! The King's always there at one theatre or the other—and usually with his mistress, Barbara Villiers!"

"Barbara Palmer," corrected Lenore dryly. "She's married, even though she may not be working very hard at it."

Mistress Potts ignored that. "Rumor has it the King's going to make her husband an earl!" she declared vivaciously, and immediately launched into a long-winded tale of how the gentleman in the blue coat—did Lenore remember him, the one who smoked the clay pipe by the fire?—had tried to seduce her to his lodgings, doubtless for immoral purposes, but she had fended him off!

Lenore smiled politely—Mistress Potts must indeed have recovered her health to be so exercised about her virtue! But her mind was racing ahead. At a play . . . of course! Why hadn't she thought of it? She'd heard, of course, that the new King had given Royal Patents to Thomas Killigrew and William Davenant, both of whom had been playwrights in the old King's time, in the hope of getting London's theatres started again. These two companies were known respectively as the King's and the Duke's; the King's Company was performing at the old Red Bull while building their great new Theatre Royal near Drury Lane; the Duke's Company performed in the Salisbury Court Theatre while they remodeled Lisle's Tennis Court in Lincoln's Inn Fields. If she merely waited outside the theatre, she would be able to see the King as he entered—and somehow manage to speak to him.

All the way home that night she planned how she would

go about it, and the mercer's daughters were surprised to see how preoccupied she was, hardly responding to their best-directed barbs.

On the next day that a play was to be given, Lenore dressed in the amber silk gown in which she had watched the King's procession enter London. It was shabbier than ever, but the fit was just as snug, and if one did not look too close, the effect was dazzling. Studying her reflection remorselessly in the mirror, Lenore decided the neckline should be lower—this was, after all, a King noted for his appreciation of womanflesh. Frowning, she managed to lower the neckline a bit so that it showed an even more extravagant sweep of milky neck and shoulder and the pearly tops of her round breasts. The mercer had objected to her taking the afternoon off, for he had declared his gout was most painful today. He sat stiffly in a high-backed Spanish chair with his gouty leg propped up on velvet cushions, flanked by his two elder daughters, clad in rustling taffety. Both girls—so glad to be rid of Lenore on Christmas Day—now glared their disapproval of this "desertion" of their father in his hour of need.

But Lenore was used to these bouts with gout. She was aware that the mercer was already bored with his children home-for-the-holidays and was merely being pettish about her leaving.

"I am sorry," she said with decision, "but I must not be late for my appointment." She did not say with whom, but she stopped and studied the mercer, who might be suffering more than she thought. "On my way home, would you like me to ask the barber-surgeon to call?"

"No need," replied her employer testily, adjusting his leg with a groan. "I'll probably have lost the leg afore that!"

Lenore gave him a look of mild amusement. He'd been irritable when she went anywhere of late; it occurred to her that his sisters might be inventing tales about where she went—and with whom. No matter, that could not be helped —she must be at the theatre well before the opening hour.

"Anyone could tell she has a lover, Father," she heard one of the mercer's daughters whisper as she left.

Lenore paused, wondering if she should take the time to

refute that, decided against it, and hurried out into a strong biting wind. She wrapped her heavy shawl around her and hoped she would not break her neck on her high wooden pattens on the icy streets. Her breath frosted the air as she made her way to the Red Bull in St. John's Street where the newly organized King's Company was giving a play. There she waited, standing in the cold outside the theatre.

When the King's coach arrived, Lenore tensed. Courtiers and great ladies brushed by her, carelessly shunting her aside. But when the King—tall and wearing his preferred black, with a sable-lined cloak—stepped from his coach, Lenore stepped forward, too. As he approached the entrance, she darted swiftly between the courtiers to reach him, tripped over a dress sword worn by a courtier in silver-embroidered velvets, and sprawled at the surprised monarch's feet.

"Here, wench! What are you doing?" Rough hands assisted her to her feet.

"Your Majesty," panted Lenore, her shawl at her feet, her bright hair tumbled from her fall, and one shoulder of her dress pulled down even further by the jerk to her feet one of the courtiers had given her. "I have been trying for months to gain an audience with you!"

The King paused and his cynical dark gaze studied that impudently bare white shoulder, the sheer lovely skin of her pulsing throat, the large pleading violet eyes under their fringe of dark lashes, the saucy figure and general look of dishabille. "Such diligence should be rewarded," he murmured flippantly, and turned to the courtier in silver-embroidered velvets over whose sword Lenore had tripped. "Tomorrow at two. See to it, Ramsay."

Lenore curtsied deeply and managed to retrieve her shawl. Beside the King a richly gowned woman gave Lenore an irritable look and then swept on beside His Majesty. The courtier, Ramsay, remained. "Your name, girl," he demanded curtly.

"Lenore Frankford."

"Be at Whitehall tomorrow at one o'clock. You will be admitted."

"But the King said two," pointed out Lenore.

Ramsay gave her an angry look. His great periwig

211

trembled with disdain. "Do you think His Majesty will wait for you? 'Tis you must wait for him! One o'clock, I say—and mind you be not late!" he finished testily and hurried on in an attempt to catch up with the King's party.

"*I'll* not keep ye waiting, pretty wench!" cried a drunken voice, and Lenore turned to see a beaming young apprentice, reeling from too much beer and carrying a shilling for a cheap seat. "Ye can sit on my knee and watch the play!"

She laughed and shook her head. Jubilant, with her shawl clutched around her against the cold, she hurried back to the mercer's through a lightly falling snow. He looked up sourly as she entered. "And what tale will we have now?" he demanded in a vinegary voice.

Lenore was too happy to be upset by his heckling tone —or by his daughters, giving her malicious looks from their chairs beside him.

"I am to have an audience with the King," she announced. "At Whitehall. Tomorrow at two."

The mercer's jaw dropped. One of his daughters dropped her embroidery, and the other stuck her finger with her needle and cried out sharply.

Lenore would have turned to go, but the mercer's stern voice called her back. "I have been too lenient with you, mistress," he declared, and Lenore thought bitterly that his daughters must have rehearsed him in this speech. "And these wild tales must cease."

"But it is true," she explained patiently. "I do indeed have an audience with the King."

One of the taffety-clad girls laughed contemptuously. "Audience with the King, indeed! More like a stroll in the park with some likely apprentice with a strong back and a soft head!" she scoffed.

Lenore swung about to give her a crushing response, but the old man was trying to struggle up. His eyes were flashing with rage and suspicion. " 'Tis easy to see ye're deceiving me, taking advantage of my good nature!" he rasped. "So now 'tis an audience with the King, is it? I think not, mistress. And I think that ye will be at your duties tomorrow at two—yes and after, at your duties till well after sundown!"

212

Lenore sighed. She had really liked the old man and was saddened that his daughters had managed to place this wedge between them.

"Then I will be leaving you tomorrow," she said soberly. "For the King I must see."

His face suffused with color and he fell back into his chair looking so disconsolate that she felt real pity for him.

"Please try to understand," she cried, moving forward. But one of his daughters blocked her way.

"You have said enough to upset my father," shouted the young girl, her face almost as empurpled as his. "Have the goodness to pack your things and get out!"

Lenore turned to the mercer for a stay of execution, but saw his jawline harden. He refused to look at her.

"Is it your desire that I leave at once, or in the morning?" she asked coldly.

"In the morning will be sufficient time," he said in a strangled voice, and Lenore stalked up the stairs to pack her few belongings.

No one saw her leave the next day. The door of the mercer's study, where he sat by a warm fire at this time of day, was firmly closed. Lenore guessed his daughters had closed it, and doubtless were patrolling it, as well, to keep their father from weakening and asking her to stay. But . . . even if he did, it would be but for a short time, for they would soon be leaving school and coming home for good, and then life would become impossible for the pretty housekeeper.

Lenore went to the George and left her few possessions with Mistress Potts, who clucked over Lenore's being dismissed. But Mistress Potts's eyes grew round when Lenore told her she was to have an audience at Whitehall, and she insisted on taking Lenore there in a hackney coach.

"After all, ye cannot arrive there looking winded or blue with cold!" she cried as they bounced and skidded over the icy cobbles.

"I looked blue with cold yesterday when I tripped and tumbled to his feet," Lenore said ruefully.

"Ah, but you'll not trip today! Today you'll be graceful

213

as a gazelle," Mistress Potts said romantically, snuggling into her fur muff.

Lenore laughed, but she was becoming edgy as they approached Whitehall. The royal palace had never looked so imposing to Lenore as it looked this day.

"Driver, we will wait," ordered Mistress Potts, leaning back in the coach with a languid wave of her muff as if she were herself royalty.

Very nervous now, Lenore alighted and gave her name to the first lackey who looked her way. He was a liveried footman with a fresh country face and merry eyes, who escorted her into a large handsome room alive with bustling courtiers. There she was handed from one bewigged and satin-clad personage to another, always in an ascending scale of importance. Some of these fine gentlemen regarded her thoughtfully, some were merely contemptuous, and one kept her waiting for a long time, then took snuff and looked down his nose at her in an insulting fashion. Lenore was sure they thought her a new doxie brought in for the King's entertainment and—from her threadbare garb—wondered at his low tastes. Though her color rose at this condescending treatment, she kept her head high. At last she was ushered into a small private antechamber and the door closed discreetly behind her. Obviously the King would see her . . . alone.

She saw that the room was devoid of furniture, though the walls and ceiling were sumptuously decorated. Lenore stared at them, twisting her gloved hands together—Mistress Potts had lent her a pair of hers and they did not fit. Her gaze wandered across the polished floor to the several pairs of double doors—all shut—which led she knew not where. There were two tall windows, both heavily draped, and impulsively she stepped behind those drapes and looked out into sumptuous gardens glittering wtih ice. It was cold here but her blood racing in her veins kept her feverishly warm.

She heard a small sound as the door opened, and turned to see through a slit in the heavy damask drapes that the King had entered the room. She had a good view of him from where she stood. He was of an athletic build and exceptionally tall—a height accentuated by the rather narrow

214

effect of his rich black velvet clothing, and he seemed quite oblivious of the cold. A single gold chain accented by a huge ruby hung around his neck and his whole stance was that of a man born to command—and enjoying it.

Surprised at seeing no one in the room, his swarthy face swung round irritably—and Lenore stepped forth from the damask curtains and made him a deep curtsy with a rustle of amber silk.

He stepped forward gracefully and took her hand. "You may rise, mistress," he said imperturbably and Lenore looked up into a pair of smiling dark eyes above a wide sensuous mouth. "What do they call you?"

"Lenore Frankford, Your Majesty."

He gave her a keen look that took in the too-daring cut of her gown, the ripe beautiful figure beneath it. "And why d'ye seek this audience with me?"

Lenore lifted her head. "Your Majesty," she said, taking a deep breath, "although you are doubtless unaware of it, I too had a small part in your return to your rightful throne."

King Charles regarded her cynically. He was used to false claims and over-inflated "services" rendered in the past in his cause. But . . . this wench was very pretty. "And how is that?" he murmured, studying her rapidly rising and falling breasts.

Lenore hesitated, fearful of appearing ridiculous. "Men called me for a while the Angel of Worcester," she blurted.

As she had feared, a smile curved that wide sensuous mouth, and his dark eyes glinted with amusement. "The naked wench on the white horse who rode with a flaming sword toward the town? And I had thought it all lies! But now you're telling me *you* were this Godiva?"

Lenore flushed. "There was no flaming sword, and I was certainly fully clothed. But I did ride my white horse into Worcester on the day of the battle. 'Twas to find my handfast husband who had ridden out of the Cotswolds with his claymore in hand to enlist in your cause."

The lively interest in that dark face continued. She could almost feel those cynical dark eyes stripping the clothes from her body, feel a lazy royal hand pushing down

215

her chemise to caress her naked back, her naked breasts.
... "And did you find him?"

She nodded.

"What was his name? I trust he seeks some reward from
me?"

"He seeks no reward," Lenore replied shortly. "And find
him I did—his body lay cold and dead by Barbour's Bridge
after the battle."

King Charles had seen many men die—in his cause and
others', but a wench was a wench. He took a step closer.
"But surely you seek something?" he challenged.

Lenore drew a long, ragged breath. This tall, dark man
who leaned so close was dangerously attractive. "I was
falsely accused of murdering a student named Michael
Maltby whom I knew in Oxford. He was giving me his
protection upon the road north to Banbury in the summer
of 1652 when robbers attacked us, killed him, and—and
fled." No need to mention that she might have killed one!
"His mother refused to believe I did not kill Michael for
the money in his pockets and brought charges against me.
I—I am a fugitive, Sire."

He reached out and carelessly toyed with a shining red-
gold curl that fell silkily down beside her ear. Involuntarily,
as his hand brushed her neck, she flinched. "And are these
all the charges against you?" he asked gravely.

"There—there is also a charge of asault against the
person of one Gilbert Marnock in Oxford in that same
month and year," she said hurriedly.

Was that laughter she saw glimmering behind those dark
worldly eyes in the dark face that bent over her own? His
voice was sober enough. "And how did you assault this
Gilbert Marnock?"

"With a hot poker. I marked his face because—because
he had raped me and then tried to blackmail me into becoming his doxie!"

His dark brows lifted, but he nodded thoughtfully. "A
just punishment surely. Have you any more crimes against
you?"

She thought he looked fascinated and mumbled, "No,
Sire," with her face crimson.

His dark face came closer, closer.

"Ye'll have my pardon," he murmured thickly. "No matter who ye've killed!"

For a feverish moment their eyes met, locked. His brown eyes had lost their cynicism, they were fierce, intense, brown liquid pools, too deep, too dark—a woman could drown there. Lenore was trembling. And yet . . . his lips brushed hers and involuntarily she turned her head away, she did not know why.

He stepped back, chilled of his ardor.

"As the Angel of Worcester, I may owe ye a debt," he said dryly. "for your name was a rallying point for the people . . . they believed in you, as a legend, something to hold onto when hope was gone. So for both these offenses, I will give ye a royal pardon, Mistress Lenore. Through that door on your way out, stop and tell that huge booted man at the desk about it. 'Twill be done, I promise you."

Lenore's face was flushed, for she was still shaken. She had been sorely tempted there for a moment. "Thank you, Your Majesty." She made him a deep curtsy that bared her décolletage for his interested gaze and turned to go.

His sharp eyes, watching her retreat, noted the hole in her stocking as her skirts swung round. His rich voice arrested her; it sounded speculative. "Could it be that ye seek employment, Mistress Lenore?"

She turned, saw the direction of his gaze at her ankles, and winced. He had seen that hole in her stocking! She lifted her dainty chin and gave him back a challenging look. "Employment—yes, Sire."

A ghost of a smile trembled on his cynical mouth at her slight emphasis on the word "employment." Lenore's color deepened. Tempted or not, she would not be a doxie, she thought rebelliously—no, not even a royal one! Her heart was hers for the giving, but it was neither for sale nor for rent!

"I've a thought where ye might find employment that would please ye. Ye have a certain flair. Have ye thought of the theatre?"

"I—I thought men played all the women's roles."

"No longer. Now, as on the Continent, we shall have

217

beauty in the theatre. Half the singing and dancing students of London have already been recruited!" he said jokingly. "The theatre will soon be bursting with young ladies of . . . virtue that will perhaps not equal your own." His voice was whimsical. "Your face is fair. I could well imagine you in a breeches part—if ye've the legs for it. Could one see your legs, Mistress Lenore?"

At this impudent royal request, Lenore, as if hypnotized, lifted her skirts just above her pretty knees.

"Turn around," he said, bemused.

A breeches part—and not in some barn or forest glade, but here in the London theatre! She would be part of the theatre again! Enthusiasm made her whirl about too fast so that her amber skirts and russet satin petticoat whipped up about her lissome hips and her lovely long legs were appealingly bared to the royal view.

"Do that again," he said, stepping toward her, his dark eyes becoming intense again.

Lenore stared at him, her breath coming fast, her violet gaze beneath her sweeping dark lashes defiant, wild. If she raised her skirts for him again, she knew what would happen. A long arm would snake out and grasp her. He would lead her swiftly through one of those tall double doors to a handsomely appointed chamber dominated by a great soft canopied bed, perhaps with the royal arms emblazoned in gold. There he would seize her and crush her naked body in his arms and discover all her secrets. She would move luxuriantly beneath him, moaning as she responded to his masculinity and . . . and she would become a royal mistress. She would compete with all the other women he slept with casually—and with his premiere mistress, the beauteous Barbara Villiers. She had heard as she moved through the crowd in that large room outside today that the King had made Barbara's husband, Roger Palmer, Earl of Castlemaine —just to send him off to Ireland so he could have his wife. 'Twas said the lovely willful Barbara held the King in the palm of her hand, that he feared to cross her, that she held him in thrall. But . . . something silky and devious in her mind murmured as she basked in that hard, hot royal stare . . . *she could take the King away from Barbara—if she tried.*

She felt mesmerized by his gaze—a rabbit paralyzed before the owl. Their eyes locked and held, and an unspoken challenge passed between them. So intent were they that they heard nothing, saw nothing but each other.

"I said . . . do that again, Mistress Lenore." He smiled lazily but she could feel the tension building up in him—just as it was building up in her.

He was a King . . . he had commanded her. Yet when his lips were brushing her own, she had turned away. Why? Why had she done that? For a man who had left her? For a man who was dead? A wild revulsion of feeling came over her. This was the life she wanted! She would make up to him for her coldness—the life of a King's mistress must indeed be eventful and wonderful!

She gave him her flashing magical smile and swirled her skirts alluringly again—and ended with a shriek as a whip flicked over her legs, and a voice at once husky and exciting and vividly angry cried, "Strumpet! Out! Out!"

Lenore whirled to see a beautiful woman attired in a green satin riding habit and a hat atremble with green plumes advancing upon her, whip upraised for another slash. With the quick grace of the athlete he was, the King leaped forward and clenched a bronzed hand down upon the dainty wrist that bore the whip. The woman's beautiful eyes flashed, and she tried angrily to twist away from him, to strike with her other hand at the royal countenance.

Lenore stood rooted as they grappled there.

No one had to tell her who this wild beauty was. She was looking at the celebrated Barbara Villiers—Lady Castlemaine.

The King's eyes were alight as he subdued his enraged lady, whose breasts heaved with effort and fury. She writhed in his arms, and now the deep intensity of his gaze, all his absorbed concentration was focused—as she had meant it to be—upon his fiery mistress, Lady Castlemaine. He wrested the whip from her and let her go free. In the struggle her plumed hat had fallen off and skittered across the polished floor, and now she swung away from him with a billow of green satin skirts and ruffled silk petticoats, paused with her dainty boots planted wide apart, and considered Lenore vengefully. Up and down two pairs of bold feminine eyes raked each other, while the King watched in amused silence.

"Who is this wench?" Barbara demanded icily.

King Charles gave her a wary look. Lady Castlemaine was a spirited mistress and not given to taking second place —not even to royalty.

"She is the Angel of Worcester, my dear," he said wryly.

Barbara looked startled. Then she shrugged. "She looks like a serving wench," she observed, her sweet voice dripping insult. "Faith, they get homelier every day!"

Lenore paled with anger, and her fists clenched. This richly garbed woman might call herself "Lady Castlemaine" because the King had bestowed an earldom upon her husband to get him gone from their sight, but in what other way were they different? Both of them—mistresses!

"Your ladyship would do well to hold her tongue," Lenore advised her with an insolent smile. "For a trollop on her way up meets the same faces on her way down."

The King laughed hugely, but Barbara's beautiful face whitened in fury. Her gloved hands were clenched at her sides, and Lenore guessed they itched for the whip. "Get you gone, wench!" she cried hoarsely. "From my sight!"

"As His Majesty commands," said Lenore in a brittle voice, making no move to go. *"He* will decide which of us leaves this room."

Barbara made a swooping dive for the whip, which the King had pitched aside, but he caught her easily. She trembled with fury in his grasp. "Are you going to let this street girl insult me?" she panted.

The King shrugged. Everyone knew how he felt about his dashing mistress—he would give her anything. Suddenly, before Barbara knew what he was about, he stripped a ruby ring from her finger and flung it to Lenore over Barbara's shriek of anger. "Take this to Killigrew of the King's Company—you'll find him at Gibbons's Tennis Court in Vere Street; they've moved from the Red Bull since yesterday. Killigrew will recognize the ring. Tell him I said you were to be given a breeches part, Mistress Lenore."

Lenore caught the ring in midair, this small token of a King's passing favor, and as their eyes met, a small smile crossed her face. Kings were like other men, she realized suddenly. Afraid of their wives, afraid of their mistresses. Whoever wrested Charles from the dashing Barbara would fight a hard battle.

"I thank Your Majesty." Her legs still burning from the whiplash, Lenore swept into her lowest curtsy, her bright hair almost touching the floor.

When she rose they were walking away from her, the King a tall elegant figure in black velvet with his vast black periwig of shining curls—and swaggering a bit; Lady Castlemaine with her haughty head in the air, her green satin skirts billowing. That was the last Lenore saw of them—the sight of their backs as they moved through the tall double doors and into a long handsome corridor, a pair of thoroughbreds indeed.

After they had gone she stared down at the ruby ring he had tossed to her. Just one of many, doubtless, that he had bestowed on his favorite, Lady Castlemaine. She looked after that tall figure thoughtfully, just disappearing down the corridor. If she had followed through and not wavered, she might have had him in spite of vivacious Barbara—for she had seen the quick interest burn in his dark eyes. If she had made her move at the right time . . . but she had thrown away her chance. Deliberately.

Why? Why? Why? She passed a weary hand over her face. Had Geoffrey so marked her that she would never find happiness in any other arms but his? Or . . . was it her stupid, stiff-necked pride that insisted she must *want* her mate, indeed must choose him? Was she unable to give herself for mere ambition?

Perhaps that was so. . . . If it was, she told herself, she had come to a sad pass indeed, for romance as she had known it with Geoffrey was not apt to come to her in lascivious Restoration London, which men now called the wickedest city in the world.

221

CHAPTER 14

The King had promised Lenore a royal pardon, and though she was slow in getting it, it came at last. Her job in the theatre came much quicker. She had left Whitehall and hastened over to Vere Street to speak to Thomas Killigrew, holder of one of the two Royal Patents given by the King in the theatre monopoly. She had found him very busy, almost inundated by young ladies who filled his outer chamber and overflowed into the hall. He was a bit testy with her. When she explained she was from the King, he muttered, "Another one!" And when she added that the King wished her placed in a "breeches part," he exclaimed that half the young ladies in the other room were from the King or the Duke of York or some other highly placed personage—all of whom wanted some special favor! Lenore who had thought them all candidates for acting careers from schools of singing and dancing, opened her violet eyes wider.

She explained—in a burst of honesty with this harassed gentleman—about the royal pardon she was to receive.

Killigrew stared at her, his brows drawn together.

"Pardon? Bah! You do not need a royal pardon to be an actress in London, mistress!"

Lenore gave him a startled look.

"There is a theatrical monopoly here now," he told her. "Two companies patented by the King—mine and William Davenant's. 'Tis but a revival of the old days. But no player in either company can be arrested or sued without the Lord Chamberlain's permission. Think you this will be given?" He gave a short laugh. "All apprentice players must work their first three months without compensation. Agreed, mistress?"

Lenore bit her lip. How would she live those three months?

"I see you are puzzled. Perchance you are not so well off as some of the young ladies outside?" Lenore had indeed noted many rich garments adorning the chattering females in the adjoining chamber. Killigrew sighed. "There are many gallants available to a winsome smile—such a smile as I see you have. And . . . you said you were sent by the King." A significant pause.

Color stained Lenore's cheeks. "I am not his doxie!" she flared. " 'Tis because he felt I had aided his cause at Worcester that he sends me to you!"

A skeptical glance greeted this. She was too beautiful to be believed. A face such as hers? Kings would vie for her, Killigrew thought with a wry smile. He doubted his new apprentice player would starve before she could reach the boards.

"Should you become disorderly or join others in riotous behavior," he warned her sternly, "a King's Messenger will arrest you. You could be whipped or imprisoned in the Gatehouse at Whitehall. Remember that you are here on sufferance and can be discharged at will. *Then* you would need a royal pardon for any crimes you may have committed!" He gave her a fierce look to emphasize his words.

Lenore nodded. She got up to leave with a rustle of amber silk skirts, but at the door she turned, suddenly curious. "Why did you decide to hire actresses? I thought young boys usually played the female parts."

223

Killigrew gave her a sharp look. "There were no trained young boys available for the work. Acting suffered a decline during the King's exile and as you'll observe, most of our actors are in their thirties and forties. Also the King and his court enjoyed the actresses of France and Italy." Lenore noted that he did not say "enjoyed their performances" but "enjoyed the actresses." She frowned. Killigrew saw her rebellious expression and added waspishly, "These young women onstage have proved a difficult lot to handle. To control them we now swear them in as royal 'comedians.' You also must be sworn in, mistress!"

Lenore nodded again, made her escape into the next room, and forced her way through a tittering crowd of young women. She gave them a harder look this time, seeing among them many obvious prostitues as well as arch ripe young things schooled in music and the dance.

Someone touched her arm. "Please, is he—is he very fearsome?" whispered an angelic-looking young girl with rich brown hair and large blue eyes.

Lenore paused and turned to look at the speaker. Barely fifteen, if she was a judge, with skin like Devon cream, and a dress that marked her as fresh from the country. "He'll eat you for supper," she grinned. And then, because the girl's lips trembled she added more kindly, "Killigrew is a busy man. He's brusque—at least, he was brusque with me, but he might be more gentle with you."

The girl swallowed; she looked about to turn and run.

"Have you acted on stage before?" asked Lenore. She knew what the answer would be, but it seemed a safe subject.

"Nay." The girl shook her brown curls vigorously. "But I daresay nobody else here has, either—I heard one say so."

"But all do wish to act . . ." murmured Lenore humorously, turning to survey the glittering group of females who milled about chattering glibly to each other.

"Oh, I am sure they do," agreed that eager young voice. "But I think all were sent here by various nobles, to hear them talk—all but myself."

"And what brought you here?" asked Lenore, whose

224

heart was light, in spite of the obstacles she faced. She had found employment that would support her—after the first three months were lived through. She was going to be a London actress!

The girl's answer surprised her. "Oh, I do not not really wish to act," she quavered. "On the stage—before so many people!"

"Then why"— Lenore looked with amazement into those wide, innocent blue eyes—"would you apply for a position as an apprentice player?" she wondered.

The girl clasped her hands; she might almost have been praying. " 'Tis because I do so wish for a noble protector," she breathed. "I came to London thinking to better myself, but in the butcher shop where I work, all the men have greasy hands. But the theatre will be filled with great cavaliers and—and one of them might fancy me!"

Indeed they might, thought Lenore, eyeing that dainty waist, that silken skin, that ingenuous expression. *More than one might fancy this pastry from the country! So the girl wished for a noble protector. . . .*

"What is your name?" asked Lenore.

"Emma. Emma Lyddle."

Lenore's witching smile played over young Emma. "When you speak to Thomas Killigrew," she counseled, "hold up your head. Your eyes are good, so stare at him directly. And" —she reached out a hand and gave the girl's bodice a tug—"see if you cannot pull your neckline down a little lower. Tell him you are seventeen. He'll not believe you, but 'twill ease his conscience nonetheless. Tell him—tell him you have watched performances given illegally in barns near your native village and that your great ambition is to excel in comedy. Blink your eyelashes—so—as you say it." Here Lenore batted her lashes fetchingly and gave Emma a demure look upward through their thick, dark fringe.

Emma tried it. The effect was heartrending.

"Yes, that's the way," Lenore encouraged her, "I think Thomas Killigrew will be enchanted!"

"I saw you go into his private chamber," breathed Emma. "But you spent such a short time with him—how did you learn so much about what he would like?" Her childish face was very appealing.

Lenore burst into laughter. "I was born a flirt—for me the part needs no rehearsing!" She was still laughing as she left and Emma Lyddle's breathless voice followed her. "Oh, thank you, mistress . . ."

"Frankford," called Lenore lightly over her shoulder as she breezed out. "Lenore Frankford." She was not afraid to use her own name again, and the sound of it was good to her ears. So many last names she had used, but now she was come into her own again—as soon as she received the King's pardon!

Mistress Potts, who had missed Lenore's company whilst she worked long hours at the bakeshop, and later while she was immersed in the mercer's affairs, insisted she move in with her for the months of her apprenticeship. Gratefully, Lenore accepted this kindly offer and moved back into the George, where men who had formerly regarded her as a circumspect young woman now made bawdy remarks within her hearing—for word had got out through Mistress Potts's ill-timed loud whispers that Lenore was now an apprentice actress. Had she been an apprentice strumpet, she could not have received more undesirable attention.

Lenore was able to ignore it, for she found her work in the theatre hard but exciting. It would be some time before she actually appeared in a play, but sometimes when an actress fell ill or for other reasons failed to appear at rehearsal, she was allowed to rehearse the part as an "understudy." These rehearsals were noisy affairs, and sometimes the players had to shout their lines to be heard above the noise of singers learning new songs, dancers stamping and whirling about, men practicing fight scenes —either fisticuffs or dueling. Under these crowded conditions, wherever they could find room, the tirewomen patched and mended and altered the costumes—which were mostly cast-off finery from the Court.

Lenore was first put in the charge of a raffish young actor named Blakelock, who wore tremendous unkempt wigs, and had melting eyes. He considered himself a divine gift to women and assumed outrageous postures that they might better admire him. Lenore detested Blakelock on sight, and when, in teaching her stage business, he casually ran a hand up under her skirts and gave her bare bottom a playful pinch, she turned and struck him such a blow as caused him to lose his balance and pitch backward upon the boards, to the delight of several older actors who had witnessed the incident.

Lenore left him there, lifted her head, turned on her heel, and went over to watch some players practicing a jig. Behind her she could hear Blakelock swearing testily that he'd have no part in teaching "that awkward piece" how to move about gracefully onstage! Lenore turned back angrily and was about to confront Blakelock again when Ralph Ainsley, a long-faced Shakespearean actor in his mid-forties, seized her arm.

"Mistress, we owe ye a debt," he declared merrily, still chuckling over Blakelock's discomfiture. " 'Tis good to see Blakelock cuffed by so dainty a hand!"

"Yes," sighed Lenore, "but now I have lost my teacher."

"*I* will be your teacher," he declared gallantly. "I was reading parts before Blakelock was born! Come, mistress, we will see if you can make a graceful entrance!"

Lenore liked Ainsley. Perhaps because of his deep-sunk eyes and melancholy face, he was mainly used in tragedies, where he played victims or villains with equal aplomb. But beneath his long face was a lively wit, and he spent long hours instructing his new protégée in swooning, gamboling, and good stage manners.

"Ye need no instruction in making '*doux yeux*,' " he observed. Lenore turned, puzzled, and asked, "Do what?"

"Languishing eyes," he grinned. "The last aspiring actress put in my charge had to be taught to coquet, to flourish a fan gracefully—even how to walk across a stage without lumbering. You, mistress"—he swept her a graceful bow—"are already beyond my teaching in these things."

"But I am not a very good actress," Lenore gravely acknowledged.

227

"Perhaps not," he shrugged. "But in a 'breeches part,' none are likely to notice your acting—they will be too busy admiring your silken legs! Tell me, hast found a protector yet?"

"I am not looking for a protector."

"Be of good heart," he said lightly. "You'll find one yet."

Lenore laughed ruefully, for Ainsley had but expressed the general feeling that actresses were promiscuous creatures, they were all looking for wealthy admirers. Occasionally one was so fortunate as to make a good marriage —most of them, Lenore suspected, would wind up in brothels such as "Mother" Moseley's or "Lady" Bennett's. Both were famous madams, and "Lady" Bennett had noticed Lenore when she visited the rehearsal one morning and had even asked her if she would care for an evening of well-paid frivolity. Lenore had politely declined this offer, and several of the young rakehell actors listening in delight nearby broke into chuckles.

"Mistress Chastity will have none of you, 'Lady' Bennett," sighed one of them—and Lenore recognized the voice as Blakelock's. "Mistress Chastity seeks to clasp a King to her bosom!"

"Mistress Chastity? Indeed, is that what they call you?" "Lady" Bennett turned an astonished face under her plumed hat to Lenore. "But you surely cannot be the one Blakelock calls The Iron Virgin?" Her laughter pealed.

Lenore glowered at Blakelock, who had so christened her in retribution for her well-timed blow. He grinned back at her and swaggered away. "Lady" Bennett, still laughing, followed him, and Lenore swept away angrily.

But the name stuck. Lenore had become "Mistress Chastity," the Iron Virgin of the London stage.

Not long after that, during a pause in one of the endless rehearsals, Lenore saw Emma Lyddle again. She had almost forgotten her encounter with starry-eyed young Emma, assuming since she had not seen her at the theatre that Killigrew must have turned her down. On this particular morning, during the rehearsal of an energetic scene in which she struggled with the villain, one of Lenore's garters had burst and she had hurried up to the tiring-room to see if one of the tirewomen could mend it quickly. There in the large room, its walls hung with green baize, she saw a short young woman standing before one of the big looking glasses the room afforded. She was pulling a voluminous dress of blue taffety over her head, and as Lenore approached, passing almost all the twenty chairs and stools provided for the use of the female comedians, she saw that the flushed young woman who had just struggled into a costume several sizes too big for her was Emma.

"Mistress Frankford!" cried Emma rapturously. "They have accepted me at last!"

Lenore stood and smiled at her. "I am glad to hear it. Is this your first day?"

Emma nodded blissfully. "But my costume," she added with a sad shake of her head, "is far too large."

"Indeed you're right." Lenore seized a handful of blue taffety that billowed around Emma's slender young waist. "We must have the tirewoman stitch it up to fit you."

"I was afraid to ask," admitted Emma in her soft voice. "They all seemed so busy and they turned their heads as I approached. Yet—I was told I must appear in it in half an hour!"

Irritably Lenore looked about for a tirewoman—they all seemed to have disappeared.

"They ignore the newcomers," she told Emma grimly, "for the regular players do reward them well."

Emma's eyes widened. "I—I did not know," she faltered. "And I'm afraid I—I have no money."

"You should not need money. 'Tis their job to see your clothes do not fall off of you onstage!" Lenore marched to the green baize hanging that separated the men's dressing room from the women's. "Tirewoman!" she called in a voice that carried. "In here, quickly!"

A woman's head poked through the curtains. "I am busy," she whined.

Lenore sighed. "This will not take long," she said, "but at least the waist must be tucked in and the hem basted up. As you can see, poor Emma will trip if she tries to walk across the stage in a dress so long."

The tirewoman came through the green baize curtains reluctantly. She was carrying with her a voluminous dress of mulberry satin. "But I'm already promised to shorten the hems on this costume for Mistress Gwyn!" she cried, aggrieved.

"And who is Mistress Gwyn?"

"A new apprentice player—like this one." The tirewoman bobbed her head at Emma. "I'm told they were both sent over by Master Killigrew this morning."

Lenore sighed. Actresses came and went in this place as if blown by on a strong wind—and most of them were prostitutes who'd walk out on the arm of any likely patron and return to the theatre when their patrons grew tired of them or—and more frequently—when their patrons' money ran out! She thought young Emma deserved her chance.

The tirewoman came forward muttering, thumped herself down upon a stool, and made to continue her work on the mulberry satin.

"Mistress Gwyn must wait," insisted Lenore, "for Emma here is supposed to wear this blue dress onstage in half an hour."

"Mistress Gwyn does not choose to wait!" rang out an imperious new voice that had in it the tang of the London streets. Lenore turned to face a shapely chestnut-haired girl in a red dress who flounced into the room. She judged the girl to be even younger than Emma, though the hazel eyes that challenged her were infinitely worldlier.

Lenore sighed. "Are you then to appear in this costume onstage?" She indicated the mulberry satin lying on the tirewoman's lap.

"Certainly—tomorrow!" snapped the girl in the red dress.

"Then it can certainly wait," said Lenore, and snatched the mulberry satin from the tirewoman's lap and thrust it upon the newcomer. "For Emma must appear immediately —and she cannot do so attired in a dress big enough for all of us!"

The chestnut-haired girl made a threatening gesture

230

toward Lenore but was distracted by Emma's eager voice. "'Tis too large because it belonged to a Duchess!"

The new girl looked down at the mulberry satin. "Belonged to—?"

"You heard her," said Lenore. "A Duchess. Some of them are fat. This one obviously was!"

"We're fortunate the gentry do give cast-off clothes to the theatre for the players," chuckled the tirewoman, already at work with her swift needle on the bodice of the blue dress.

"Cast-off!" said the chestnut-haired girl with an affronted look at the mulberry satin she now held in her arms. "And is this gown cast-off, too, pray?"

"They all are," said Lenore more kindly. Obviously this girl was unused to the ways of the theatre. "Else we'd have no alternative but to wear our own clothes onstage!"

The girl cast the mulberry satin gown from her angrily. "Well, *I* will not wear cast-offs!" she cried with a curse. "I mean to wear beautiful clothes—all made for *me!*"

The tirewoman was chuckling as the angry girl flung away. Lenore watched her go—good face, good figure, and fiery—good theatre. "What did you say her name was?" she asked.

"Nell Gwyn," said the tirewoman, looking up and biting off the thread with her teeth. "And she came to Killigrew well recommended," she added with a laugh. "By three Baronets and an Earl!"

"*Three* Baronets!" Emma sighed in envy.

"And an Earl," Lenore added crisply. "Don't forget him."

"She's a saucy one, is Mistress Nell," said the tirewoman. "Her mother kept a bawdyhouse in Covent Garden, and Nell was brought up there. Her sister Rose is one of the orange girls. But I think me Mistress Nell may surpass them both!"

Lenore cast a speculative eye after the saucy street wench just flouncing out through the green baize curtains. She was inclined to agree with the tirewoman. Young Mistress Gwyn might make her theatrical debut in new clothes after all!

But the next day she was told Nell Gwyn had demanded new clothing from Thomas Killigrew and had been dismissed even before she could begin her new career—everyone was chuckling over it. Lenore looked down wryly at the shabby creation she was wearing—of much-mended watered taffety. Not that it mattered, she was only wearing it at a rehearsal. For young women were almost fighting to get their chance in the theatre, and Lenore had not yet had a chance to act onstage.

Emma had. She had appeared briefly as a water nymph—once again in a dress too large—and just as she made her entrance the entire dress fell down over one shoulder, showing a great deal of pink and white skin. The audience had roared with laughter, but the incident had served Emma well, for a young Baronet had noticed her and asked her to a coffee house after the performance.

Emma had been so excited that Lenore had felt it necessary to see that she had sufficient coins in her purse to take a hackney coach home in case of need, and that she had not put her right shoe on her left foot or vice versa.

"It is my chance!" cried Emma, enraptured. "A Baronet! And so handsome! Oh, Lenore, do you think—do you think he will like me?"

Lenore surveyed that round, innocent face, the silky young skin, the big sparkling blue eyes turned so appealingly upward. How different was Emma from Mistress Gwyn! "There's little doubt he will like you," she said dryly. "The important thing is to be sure *you* like *him*."

"But how could I not? Have you not seen him? So tall and commanding—and such gorgeous clothes!" She touched Lenore's arm impulsively. "Oh, Lenore, won't you come with me? I am sure he must know other Baronets!"

Lenore shook her head. "Don't you know they call me the Iron Virgin?" she quipped. "It is because I do not frequent coffee houses with strange Baronets!"

Emma looked mystified. She took a last look in the mirror, was jostled away from it by another actress, one Lenore recognized as a notorious prostitute, and hurried away. Lenore smiled as she watched her go, and the prostitute, whose name was Floss, turned and gave Lenore a curious look.

"You're a fool—you know that," Floss said bluntly. "You could have a Duke with your looks. Is it true you're saving yourself for the King?"

Lenore laughed and shook her head, but her smile had turned rueful by the time she reached the room she still shared with Mistress Potts at the George. Perhaps she *was* a fool not to go to coffee houses with the glittering gentlemen who frequented the theatre. Perhaps silly young Emma had the right idea—to go out and find herself a man.

"You work too hard," said Mistress Potts, observing Lenore's strained expression.

"No," sighed Lenore. "I think too much. 'Tis a bad habit that I must somehow learn to break."

The next day Emma left the theatre for good. She came by at rehearsal time to tell Lenore breathlessly that she had found at last "a noble protector"—her Baronet! And the next week to twirl about displaying the new pink silk dress he had bought for her—it had been stitched up by a seamstress who had at one time worked for *the Queen!* Emma was breathless. She did not return to the theatre again. Once Lenore saw her riding down Drury Lane in a coach; she was handsomely dressed in rose sarsenet and waved gaily.

Then grimmer news reached her. Emma's Baronet had passed her along—to the notorious Lord Wilsingame. Lenore frowned at the news. One of the more vicious young peers who had come to London to seek the new King's favor, Wilsingame had rented a handsome house perched in the mid-section of London Bridge and had gathered around him wild young men of like kidney. There he gave roistering parties and there he was said to have installed his mad sister, whose screams rent the night. It was said she had several times attacked her serving-women, for often their screams were blended with hers. Lenore thought grimly of Emma, so young, so childlike, with her wide, believing blue eyes . . . Emma, who had

233

yearned not for honest marriage but for "a noble protector."

She determined to learn how Emma fared. Twice she made her way onto the narrow dangerous coachway that threaded between the tall houses that rose up on both sides of the bridge itself. The buildings overhung the street and leaned out precipitately over the River Thames, and several times Lenore walked through short dark tunnels on the bridge where the buildings met above her head. There were shops here, too, on London Bridge, and twice Lenore fell back hurriedly from the narrow street into an open shop doorway to dodge onrushing horses, for a coach going by filled the street—the bridge was so crowded with houses it was not wide enough for two coaches to pass!

This narrow press of houses and shops spanning the Thames seemed to her somehow menacing—to Emma, so full of young dreams. It was with foreboding that she banged the great boar's head knocker of Lord Wilsingame's tall, narrow house. A surly manservant stuck out his head and told her that Emma was not at home.

Lenore came back a week later and was told by the same servant that Emma had departed London for the country. *Used by Wilsingame and thrown away,* thought Lenore bitterly. She regretted that she had not seen Emma before she left, but she hoped poor foolish Emma had gone back to the pleasant country town from which she had come and would find herself there some stout country lad and forget her brief unfortunate venture in sinful London. She thought back to her friend Lally, who had been used, discarded, and she too had disappeared without a goodbye.

It was spring before Lenore got her first part in a play— and then because both the leading man and leading lady were sick (having drunk too deeply of the royal malmsey the night before), the play was cancelled and another put in its place. It was scheduled again—and once more postponed because Killigrew had promised Lady Castlemaine that its first performance would be played before the King, and the King had gone to Sandwich to join Catherine of

Braganza, the Portuguese Infanta. Twice did he marry his Portuguese Princess—once by Roman Catholic rites, and once by the English service—and great wealth did she bring with her: Bombay and Tangier, and two million cruzados. But in London the players tittered when they learned that Lady Castlemaine had been appointed one of the young Queen's ladies in waiting!

Since being sworn in as a royal piayer, Lenore had glimpsed the King only in the middle distance, from backstage, on those occasions when he attended a play. She'd seen his dark, saturnine countenance often split into a wolfish smile at some particularly broad remark onstage. Nor had it escaped her that there were always bewigged, besatined, and beauteous ladies about him—and most often next to him she glimpsed beautiful imperious Lady Castlemaine, to whom all deferred. Lenore found herself rather sorry for the young Queen, pitted against such a determined beauty.

Although it had been promised speedily, Lenore's royal pardon had not yet come through and she debated trying to gain another audience with the King, but reluctantly put the thought from her. If she saw him again at close quarters, dark, aggressive, virile . . . she might well become one of that perfumed, handsomely dressed group of doxies, patrician and otherwise, who swarmed about him. It was something she wished to avoid. Not because of conscience or fear that such an alliance might endanger her reputation—indeed in lascivious London being bedded by the King would only enhance her reputation! But because something strong and deep within her rebelled at the thought.

She had been Geoffrey's mistress without a qualm, but . . . she had loved Geoffrey. She did not love the King, she only found him physically attractive. If she became his mistress, she would be no better than that high-born strumpet, Lady Castlemaine!

But the slowness of her royal pardon bothered her, and when the play that had been deferred was finally rescheduled for private showing at Whitehall before King

235

and Court, she determined to find a way to speak to the King again about her pardon.

Playing Whitehall was very popular with the players, who were poorly paid and almost always in debt. Low in the social scale (for the players were listed even below the royal rat-killers) they often sneaked their handsome stage costumes out of the theatre's tiring rooms and wore them about the City. Though the actors wore swords, considering that the mark of a gentleman, they were never accepted as equals by the gentry. Lenore, as an actress, felt this less than the men, for a pretty woman could command her own respect. But she knew that at the King's private theatre at Whitehall, the players supped well and drank deep of sack and claret and beer. This was to be an important performance, and there would be understudies for all the parts, for the show must indeed go on.

Lenore was as excited as the rest by the prospect of opening in a new play at Whitehall—perhaps more so, for this royal performance would mark her debut on the boards. Her part, though small, was a good one—that of a girl who disguised herself as a boy to spy on her unfaithful lover, and Ainsley had said that if she succeeded in this part (which meant, she knew, if the King was pleased with her performance), it could mean advancement for her. She had two costumes for the role: a full-skirted peach satin in which she would appear in the last act, and an olive-green doublet and tight trunk hose and peaked hat for her masquerade as a man in the second act.

Opening night came at last. The players were all assembled in a chattering fluid group at Whitehall, and backstage Lenore repeated her lines to herself over and over— she must not forget them, this was her chance to impress the King and perhaps gain another audience to press for her royal pardon!

Through the curtains, from backstage, she watched the play proceed, the actors warmed with malmsey and delivering their lines in ringing tones, the actresses bowing so low their bare breasts almost slipped from their low-cut bodices, their skin creamy and golden in the light of the huge chandeliers with their hundreds of candles.

Past the players she could see King Charles in a huge black periwig, his glossy black curls spilling over onto the froth of Alençon lace at his throat, frosty against his purple velvets. He was leaning back at his ease, knees crossed nonchalantly. Beside him, a sultry beauty in mauve satin, lounged Lady Castlemaine, waving a delicate ivory fan. Around them were grouped the courtiers, wearing black patches on their faces and taking snuff from enamelled boxes, and the ladies-in-waiting, dressed elegantly in the French fashion which Charles admired. But nowhere was the young Queen to be seen. Lenore had heard backstage that the Queen had pleaded a "headache" and gone to her chambers—it was rumored that she and Lady Castlemaine were waging a pitched battle for the King and that Lady Castlemaine was winning.

Lenore gave the reckless beauty beside the King a sardonic look; it was her opinion that Lady Castlemaine would stop at nothing to hold her place on the royal lap. She smiled dangerously to herself, a smile that boded ill for the lady in mauve satin. That hot look in the King's eyes when he had looked at her that day when he had promised her a royal pardon could be summoned up again! Perhaps the young Queen could not take him from Lady Castlemaine, but the self-assured flirt from Twainmere had no doubt that *she* could do it if she put her mind to it!

And perhaps she would have a try for him, after all! It was something she would decide as she played her part before him tonight.

"Are you ready?" hissed Blakelock. "Hurry, you'll miss your cue!" He gave her a solid push that propelled her through the curtains and onto the stage.

Lenore, who'd hardly been following the dialogue as she toyed with dreams of becoming a royal courtesan, realized belatedly that her cue had indeed been given. She rushed onstage, propelled by Blakelock's push, wearing the long tight stockings and bright smile her part required—a smile she flashed directly at the King.

But Lenore got no chance to play her "breeches part" that night at Whitehall, for as she rushed onstage her foot slipped on a greasy spot on the floor and she fell headlong, almost knocking over the leading man and sliding half across the stage. Everybody laughed at such clumsiness, and Lenore's face was red as she tried to spring up—only to sink wincing to the floor again, for her painful ankle would not support her weight. The play was held up as Ainsley and several others hurried out to help her offstage.

Biting her lips to keep from crying out as she limped away on Ainsley's arm, Lenore met the mocking gaze of Lady Castlemaine above her lazily wielded ivory fan. Behind the fan she thought Lady Castlemaine might be laughing. The King looked thoughtfully at the greasy spot at the edge of the stage where Lenore had slipped, and his dark gaze narrowed as he turned to consider his beautiful, amused mistress; then he shrugged. He was after all accustomed to having women fight over him.

Backstage Ainsley eased Lenore onto a bench and lifted her ankle, red and beginning to swell, onto a red silken cushion which somebody had placed on a low marble-topped stool. He gave her a sympathetic look and handed her a glass of malmsey which Lenore took with shaking fingers. Lenore knew that her understudy—some new girl who had rehearsed the part this morning while Lenore was undergoing last-minute fittings of her costume —would be already dressed and waiting somewhere in the company. She looked around, wondering who her understudy was. In a moment she would come forward and the play would continue. She took a sip of the malmsey. "How did that slick spot get on the floor, Ainsley?" she groaned. "I didn't even see it!"

Ainsley shrugged. "Perhaps 'twas drippings from the great chargers that were carried across it for the King and Court to sup on dainties before the play began. You should have looked where you were going, Mistress Lenore." His voice was blunt.

Lenore gave him an angry look. She had, she was sure, studied every inch of the floor she was to walk over. But that was during the first act. Something must have been spilled on it since then, while she was daydreaming. Who had made his entrance from that particular spot during the second act? None but Blakelock, for a brief appearance—

238

and 'twas Blakelock who had given her that sudden push which had sent her plunging onto the stage. She studied the malmsey and thought about Blakelock. True, she had struck him for impudently reaching up under her skirts to pinch her bare bottom—and he had fallen from the blow and others had laughed, but . . . she could not think he would be so vengeful as to spoil her entrance for that.

Who had most enjoyed her discomfiture? Lady Castlemaine, surely, laughing behind her fan. And Lady Castlemaine could well have known the action of the play, for it was one of her protégés who had written this one—which was why it had been so long postponed; she wanted the King to be among the first to view it and give it the stamp of royal approval.

Hot with fury, Lenore decided it must have been Lady Castlemaine who had caused that spot to be oiled so that she would fall and make a ridiculous entrance.

After a brief pause, the play was now about to resume, and Lenore saw her understudy hurry forward. She could not see who it was, for people kept stepping between, but it must be her understudy, for the girl was wearing trunk hose. Lenore swallowed her malmsey at a gulp and promised herself that she would indeed play for the King's favor when next she appeared—if only to infuriate Lady Castlemaine!

But she was not to have that chance. For the young actress who hurried forward to replace Lenore in her "breeches part" was small and shapely and chestnut-haired—and back in Killigrew's company once again. As she swept past Lenore, her hazel eyes sparkled with malice and her lips, as she threw the curtains aside to make her dramatic entrance, were curved in a winsome, secret smile. She cast a quick covert look at the oily spot on which Lenore had so ignominiously slipped—and just before she disappeared onstage she gave a laughing nod to Blakelock, who stared innocently at the ceiling. Lenore seethed as she stared at the ripple of curtains through which her understudy had gone.

On the other side of those curtains, they were staring at her, too. For she wore a splendid costume of cream and

239

gold satin, did Lenore's replacement, with creamy silk trunk hose to outline her pretty legs. The costume was rumored to have been provided at great expense by the elderly Earl of Wytton—as was the gold chain around her slender neck. She wore her luxuriant chestnut hair in ringlets, and she swept onto the London stage with flashing eyes and made it her own. The King noticed her, too, and he straightened a bit from his lounging position. Beside him Lady Castlemaine moved restively. The King's cynical eyes darkened and grew fixed as they stared at the cream and gold "youth" who moved with such a graceful feminine walk up and down the stage. For the moment, he had lost all interest in Lenore, who had been ignominiously carted away—and even in the dark beauty, Lady Castlemaine, who sulked beside him.

The fiery young actress's name was Nell Gwyn.

An instant success, Nell was promptly invited to sup with the King—to the indignation of Lady Castlemaine, who was reputed to have smashed her wineglass and later to have attacked her hairdresser in rage. She was right to be angry, for before the evening was over, everyone knew that a new royal mistress would enjoy the delights of Whitehall.

By the time Lenore's ankle was healed enough so that she could walk gracefully again, London was baking in the summer heat. The King left for the country to escape it, taking with him the Queen, the Court—and Lady Castlemaine. Nell he had left behind, and she was sulking. Theatregoing customers fell off so badly the theatres closed down for the summer. It was a bad time for the players, for they were supposed to work forty weeks out of the year, with Sundays off, and they received no "sharing dividends" when the theatres were closed.

But Lenore received her royal pardon that summer and came home to the George shining-eyed. Not just immune from arrest while she worked as a royal player, she was a free woman at last! No longer wanted anywhere for any crime!

Now at last she broke her long silence. She sat down and wrote a long letter to Lorena.

PART
TWO

THE
ORANGE
GIRL

CHAPTER 15

September found Lenore a regular member of Killigrew's company, taking part in the onstage dances and masques that were held between acts and playing occasional small parts. The glittering gentlemen who frequented the theatre were quick to notice her blazing beauty onstage, and Lenore was besieged by offers to parties and little suppers in private rooms. Although her heart was still frozen in her chest where men were concerned, some of the teasing ways of the Twainmere flirt had returned, and one day, with a light laugh, she began notching her heels again—each time for an offer, whether it seemed honorable or no.

In time she might have slipped into the ways of the other actresses, some of whom were married but nearly all of whom had a succession of lovers. Many were little better than prostitutes—some indeed were famous prostitutes and were hooted at by a ribald audience whenever they played virtuous parts onstage. Or she might have married one of the lesser gentry who thronged the play-

243

houses and eagerly sought the company of young and pretty actresses.

But Lenore had made enemies—and they were her undoing.

One of her enemies was Nell Gwyn, who was by now a favored mistress of the King and never forgot that it was Lenore who had snatched her costume from the tirewoman in favor of Emma. Although Lenore was certain Nell had caused her downfall at Whitehall, there was no way to tax her with it, and Nell eyed her vengefully, perhaps sensing in Lenore a rival who could sweep both her and Lady Castlemaine out of the way.

Another of Lenore's enemies was Lord Wilsingame of evil reputation, into whose home young Emma Lyddle had disappeared without a trace. Lord Wilsingame was relentless in his pursuit of actresses and a steady patron of both those famous madams "Mother" Moseley and "Lady" Bennett—from whom he bought kidnapped virgins, young girls fresh from the country who had come to London seeking domestic employment.

Wilsingame was on hand when Lenore made her debut in a small part—on a night when the King was elsewhere. Lenore was to note that somehow whenever she played any part the King was engaged elsewhere, and she wondered if this was Nell's doing—for Nell and Killigrew had become very close. But Wilsingame, like the other jaded London rakes lounging in the pit, straightened up and leaned forward to watch the startling beauty of this new adornment to the London stage. When Lenore had finished her first speaking part, he sent a messenger to her backstage to inform her peremptorily that my Lord Wilsingame's coach would be waiting for her outside.

In the madhouse of the tiring room, where the messenger had found her, Lenore—who had unpleasant memories of being turned away from Wilsingame's house on London Bridge when she went there in quest of Emma—raised her high-arched brows and concentrated her calm attention on Lord Wilsingame's sallow-faced young messenger, whom she rightly guessed to be his groom.

"Tell my Lord Wilsingame I am otherwise engaged," she said in a clear, carrying voice.

Wilsingame was well known among theatregoers. At the sound of his name some of the buzzing of voices stopped and several backstage visitors turned curiously to look at Lenore.

"And tell my Lord Wilsingame," added Lenore with deliberate emphasis, "that I will also be engaged tomorrow—and the day after that." Calmly she turned back to considering her reflection in the mirror, and several dandies who'd been urging two young actresses to accompany them to a coffee house and had stopped to listen began to laugh.

"That should set Wilsingame back on his heels!" cried one, and Lenore gave him a cool smile and hurried out to brush by Wilsingame's coach and climb into a hackney cab.

"The Spur," she told the driver in a ringing tone, glancing back to see Wilsingame's gaze follow her in astonishment as he listened to the report of his sallow-faced messenger. Lenore smiled to herself all the way to the Spur—for she had changed lodgings when Mistress Potts had begun to sleep late and had objected to Lenore's rising early for rehearsals at the theatre in Vere Street.

The next night the same play was repeated, and Lord Wilsingame, his appetite for this insolent flame-haired beauty whetted by her refusal to notice him, sent backstage by his sallow-faced messenger a large nosegay and a pretty pair of glass earrings—and another summons to his coach.

This time in the tiring room there was a group of dandies clustered about Lenore, urging her to a party to be held at Dunster House. She was laughingly turning them down when the nosegay and the earrings were thrust toward her and the sallow-faced groom bleated out Lord Wilsingame's invitation. Nearby a dandy in rosy silk nudged another clad in russet velvet. From the corner of her eye Lenore could see them watching her with interest, and coldly she remembered Emma Lyddle, who had been passed on by her Baronet to Lord Wilsingame—and disappeared from London.

245

With a bright, fixed smile she presented the nosegay to a passing tiring-woman, who curtsied in astonishment. Around her the company tittered.

"Take this bauble back to Lord Wilsingame and tell him I have seen better." Lenore's tone was disdainful as she tossed the earrings back to the startled messenger with a light, contemptuous laugh. Around her the party of young dandies roared with merriment.

In his coach outside, Lord Wilsingame, benumbed with shock, studied his returned gift with glazed eyes.

Beside him one of his friends nudged another, heavy with gold lace. They exchanged droll looks, and a third, de Quincy, drawled, "She is playing with you, Wilsingame —like a cat with a mouse. Soon she will take you at a bite and be done with you!"

Wilsingame grew red with mortification.

"Come now, admit ye're outmatched!" coaxed de Quincy with a sadistic grin.

Wilsingame's discomfiture deepened. "I vow I will bed the wench!" he grated. "And no later than the morrow! Like other wenches, she has a price—and I'll meet it, for I mean to have her!"

His words could be heard by several others in the crush of coaches surrounding the theatre entrance, and by the next day word was all over London that Lord Wilsingame was in the market to buy Mistress Chastity's favors— indeed he had vowed to bed that Iron Virgin this very day!

Not surprisingly, a large and interested audience was on hand to watch Wilsingame's messenger—his face no longer sallow but flushed with importance—march up to Lenore in the tiring room after the play.

Lenore saw him coming out of the corner of her eye, but did not pause in rearranging her hair before the mirror.

"Mistress Frankford!" he cried.

"Yes?" murmured Lenore in a bored voice, concentrating all her attention on a recalcitrant curl that defied her comb.

"Mistress Frankford." His voice rose pompously, for he was well aware that he had an audience. "My Lord Wilsingame has instructed me to give you this."

He held out a handsome blue-enamelled box. Heads craned to see it.

Lenore sighed and laid down her comb. She turned and gave the boy a disinterested look but made no move to touch the box he tendered.

"Tell my Lord Wilsingame enamelled boxes do not interest me—I have several at home." It was a lie, but it had the ring of truth. In the tiring room, one could have heard a pin drop. Not even the spurs of the gentry jingled, for everyone was hanging breathlessly on her words.

"But mistress!" The boy's voice cracked in his excitement. "Please to look what's inside! My Lord Wilsingame said to tell you 'twould match your eyes."

Lenore raised her eyebrows and opened the box. She pulled out an amethyst necklace, each stone vivid and deep violet and ringed about with diamonds. A fabulous gift—scarce an actress in the theatre he could not have commanded for such a price! A collective sigh went over the assembly as Lenore let the diamonds and amethysts trickle like water through her fingers.

So Wilsingame thought he could buy her . . . and after his treatment of poor Emma! Lenore's expression hardened. Ah, he had played into her hands tonight! Bent on making him suffer, she held up the glittering necklace for all to see. The diamonds sparkled alluringly in the wavering candlelight, and the amethysts seemed to smoulder with a fire of their own. In the hush, everyone waited expectantly for her to capitulate before this handsome gift.

"Take this pretty trinket back to my Lord Wilsingame," she said negligently, dropping it back into the blue-enamelled box and shutting it with a snap. "For I doubt not he goes with the gift. Tell him I'll be no man's doxie— but if 'twere a role I chose, I'd be a *royal* doxie—not his!"

The story was so good it was repeated to the King, who was reported to have laughed over it uproariously.

Lenore did not admit to herself that by her cavalier treatment of Lord Wilsingame she was not only striking a blow for poor Emma, she was revenging herself on all men who would use a woman and leave her—she was making

Wilsingame pay for all the heartaches she had suffered when Geoffrey left her.

In selecting Wilsingame for her vengeance, she had made a dangerous choice. Made ridiculous at Whitehall—where he was inordinately jealous of his reputation, for he would have gone to any lengths to seek favor with the King—Wilsingame abruptly stopped his pursuit of Lenore . . . but he did not forget. Lenore knew that from the way he watched her from the pit, his cold, hard gaze insolently studying her breasts and hips and then flicking contemptuously over her face—hard as a slap.

Lenore only shrugged. What cared she how Wilsingame felt about her? She was one of the royal players and, as such, subject to discipline only by the Lord Chamberlain!

In any event, she had decided on a new path. She had written Lorena several long letters (much inflating her position in the theatre) and had scrupulously enclosed what little money she had been able to save. Come next summer she meant to go to Twainmere and claim her daughter, to bring Lorena back to London with her—yes, and to dress her well and educate her! She would need money to do that, and she meant to get it.

The road to Whitehall still lay open to her—she had but to reach out at the right moment and seize it!

She made that decision one night when her petticoat had been torn on one of the stage props and she realized she must buy a new one—for the actresses had to furnish their own petticoats as well as shoes and stockings, scarves and gloves. The price of a new petticoat would keep her on half rations for a week! Lenore glowered down on it—and called for a tirewoman. As she swept onto the stage in her mended petticoat and a handsome green satin gown trimmed in silver lace from the Great Wardrobe (a castoff of Lady Castlemaine's, the tirewoman had whispered) Lenore had reached an internal boiling point. What future was there for her in the theatre? She would never make enough on her meager "sharing dividends" to have Lorena with her! Ah, but she could mend her fortunes! She would do it as Nell Gwyn had—by taking a royal lover!

Having made that decision, Lenore lifted her head and

delivered her lines in such ringing tones that there was a small round of applause from the appreciative audience.

Lenore turned to acknowledge that applause with a smile—and froze in fury.

She was looking into the face of Gilbert Marnock.

For a moment her senses swam and she was submerged in memories. She was back again in her lodgings off Magpie Lane on a bitter cold winter night. She had waked to find herself bound by Gilbert's clutching arms, weighted down by his lean body. She could feel his hands impudently pawing her breasts and his hot breath searing her skin as she wrestled with him in her bed in Oxford.

From backstage Ainsley saw her shiver and reel on her feet. He wondered if she was coming down with some distemper, and would they all catch it? But she quickly recovered herself and went on with her lines.

"What ailed ye there as ye turned to the audience, mistress?" he asked her curiously as she stepped offstage. "For a space there, I thought ye would fall!"

"I remembered something," said Lenore grimly. "Something I'd prefer to forget." Her face was so pale and set that Ainsley, though curious, forbore to question her further.

That night Lenore wore a large black wig and a vizard mask when she went home from the theatre. She had no desire to encounter Gilbert again, and she had the uneasy feeling he might seek her out.

She was right. He sought her out at rehearsal the very next morning.

Lenore could not know with what care Gilbert had dressed for his planned confrontation. For two hours before, his hairdresser had been combing and pomading his caramel curls, which were more luxuriant than any wig and cascaded over his rose satin shoulders. He had cursed his barber, and he struck his valet when he discovered a spot on his satin knee breeches. Accepting the cuff with servility, the man—who wore Gilbert's livery—hastily brought Gilbert another suit, this one of violet taffety, and helped his cursing master into it.

Gilbert could afford these luxuries of temper. His parents had recently died, and he had come into a considerable inheritance. With more money than he had ever had before in his life, Gilbert had promptly hied him to London, that hub of iniquity for which his dissolute soul had hungered for years. He had arrived but last week, had busied himself with setting up a gentleman's establishment and hiring servants and ordering new clothes. This was the first time he had attended the theatre, and he had come in hopes of seeing the King so that he could later brag he was an intimate and back up what he said with a knowledgeable description of the monarch. But in that he had been disappointed, for the King had favored the cockfights instead of the play on that particular night.

It had been a mind-searing shock to Gilbert to see Lenore Frankford, seemingly more beautiful than ever and with a poise that even he did not remember, swish out upon the stage wearing Lady Castlemaine's cast-off green satin ballgown.

He had sat thunderstruck as she met his gaze and went rigid with shock. For a moment he had thought she would faint and had leaned forward tensely, but she had recovered herself and the play had gone on.

How wonderful she had looked with her flame-bright hair glowing beneath the myriad candles. Like a graceful flower she had swayed and turned as if blown about by the wind, while Gilbert's hard caramel eyes, hot with memory, had roved over her supple body. Her breasts were just as he remembered them, her waist as narrow. She still had that flaunting walk that drew men's eyes, that challenging smile. He remembered vividly what it had been like to hold her in his arms, to possess her. His heart thudded in his chest with his hot rememberings. He turned his head sharply as two seats away Lord Wilsingame leaned forward and muttered, "Damned vicious beauty! If I had my way, I'd have—" Gilbert did not hear what Lord Wilsingame would have done if he'd had his way, but he saw the vein standing out in Wilsingame's forehead, the way his jaw worked; he could *guess* what Wilsingame would have done if he'd had his way! Gilbert knew Wilsingame

250

but slightly, having met him at a gaming hall the night before, but he admired him enormously as a self-proclaimed court favorite—new to London, Gilbert had no way of knowing that Wilsingame was but one of a small army of hangers-on, eagerly finding any means to seek the King's favor.

About him in the pit, Gilbert could see London's wild young rakes lounging about on bulrush-covered benches; their eyes were filled with naked desire as they viewed the beautiful woman in green satin onstage, and more than one licked his lips. Gilbert turned thoughtfully to look at Lenore again. So she had made it to London, this woman he had meant to bend and humble—and enjoy . . . and now she was flaunting herself on the London stage!

She had escaped him, but not before she had marked him. His brows drew together in a malicious line. He would enjoy her yet, by God!

After the performance, he had shouldered his way through the milling crowd into the tiring rooms, but was told Lenore had already left. On the street outside he had searched for her, but she was nowhere to be found. He had felt a brief sense of panic—had she escaped him again?

But common sense had asserted itself. Lenore was a royal player; as such she was shackled to the London stage—as much a part of the theatre as the curtains or the green baize-covered floor. At the theatre he would find her, for like the other players she must rehearse!

Now with his hot blood somewhat cooled but with his hands still tingling at the memory of her flesh beneath his kneading fingers, he strolled through the crowd seething about during morning rehearsal at the Red Bull in Vere Street where Killigrew's company gave their performances. He was an elegant figure, faultlessly garbed in violet taffety (his clothing was the reason Lord Wilsingame had noticed him, believing him fresh from the country and wealthy enough that he could borrow money from him if he ran short of cash) and he tapped a tall beribboned cane as he walked. Onstage a new play was being rehearsed, but as Lenore would not appear until the second act, she was

251

sitting on a low stool across the room, studying her lines. She looked up to see Gilbert brush by an aspiring singer, wailing earnestly off-key, saw him wend his way past an eager young girl clad in doublet and trunk hose wavering along with a book on her head. Gilbert almost collided with her, and she dodged to avoid him, dropping the book with a groan. Ainsley, who was coaching her, gave Gilbert an irritable look and retrieved the book; he set it back upon the girl's head and urged her to walk gracefully, *gracefully,* make her hips *sway!*

Lenore sat, hypnotized, watching Gilbert approach with all the self-assurance of a Duke or a Prince. Every inch a fop, she thought contemptuously—lord, how she hated him! And to think that in Oxford for a time she had actually considered him attractive! Then Gilbert had passed Ainsley and stood before her, his handsome, scarred face lit by a smile of triumph.

Lenore rose warily, noting the cane in Gilbert's hand.

Gilbert saw the look on her face and waved his gloved hand with a lazy gesture that billowed his delicate point lace cuffs. "There is no need for alarm, Lenore."

"I know there is not—for I'm a royal player now, and under the King's protection!" But she moved a step away from him.

Ainsley noticed her backing away and turned from his young protégé with the book on her head. Frowning slightly, strolled toward them.

"Send yon graybeard away," said Gilbert in a low voice, indicating the approaching Ainsley. "I am not here to exact vengeance."

"No, nor will you! For I've a royal pardon!"

"Send him away," said Gilbert, his eyes threatening. "For we've much to talk about, you and I."

"We've naught to say to one another! Ainsley—"

With deliberate grace, Gilbert stepped between them with his back to Ainsley. He leaned upon his beribboned cane, hovering above her as if to overwhelm her with his masculinity. "Can it be ye've forgotten the night ye spent in my arms?" Gilbert's brows lifted mockingly. "But ye were hot for me then!"

252

Lenore paled and her hands balled into fists. "You raped me! And I marked your face for it—as you deserved!"

Gilbert shrugged. "I am magnanimous. I choose to forget that." Gilbert turned and waved Ainsley away with a disdainful flourish of lace cuffs. "You may go, sir. This is a private conversation." He turned back to Lenore as Ainsley hesitated, frowning. This would not be the first dandy Ainsley and others had had to eject from rehearsals; he placed his hand upon his sword.

"I will even allow you to make amends," Gilbert was saying expansively. "*In bed,* where amends should be made." He paused and smiled; Lenore did not like the look of that smile. She remembered it only too well. "If you do not come," he added softly; there was a threat behind the words, "you will have cause to regret it, I promise you."

Cause to regret it indeed! The blood flowed back to Lenore's pale cheeks in a hot surge. She drew herself up to her full height and looked at Gilbert with scorn. "Powerful you might have been in Oxford, Gilbert, playing both sides and able to blackmail poor women who feared for their lovers! But here even good Master Ainsley yonder"— she nodded toward Ainsley, who had now drawn his sword from its scabbard and was testing the edge with his fingers for sharpness while he studied Gilbert—"can mock you! As can I! For we're the King's players and sworn in, and not subject to arrest by any but the Lord Chamberlain himself!"

Gilbert gave her a lazy look from those caramel eyes. The face that had once been blindingly handsome now had a long weal down one cheek where she had burned him, and another mark, a deep pit in the other cheek. She could not know he had acquired that second scar when Geoffrey had hurled him from the window of his lodgings in Oxford.

"Did ye know I am paying my addresses to the Lord Chamberlain's daughter?" he drawled. It was untrue, but it was a thrust calculated to inspire terror.

Lenore's face grew a shade paler. She leaned forward.

"I care not if you are courting a princess of the blood!" she blazed. "If you so much as lay a finger upon me, Gilbert, I swear I will bring the matter before the King himself! And *then* we will hear again your explanation of why you did not fight for him at Worcester!"

If Gilbert was discomfited by this counter-thrust, he did not show it. None of his aplomb left him. "But I am your best friend, Lenore," he sneered in a voice that carried clearly to Ainsley. "Am I not always kind to my cast-off doxies?"

For a moment the world went red before Lenore, and she struck out savagely at his face, but Gilbert had been expecting the blow and dodged easily.

Ainsley, who had leaped forward at Lenore's sudden assault on this faultlessly garbed gentleman with the scarred face, was halted by Gilbert's words. Cast-off doxie? Who was he to come between a man and his doxie, cast-off or otherwise? He pressed the point of his sword into the floor and leaned upon the hilt.

"You have a nasty temper, Lenore," chided Gilbert. "Already you have been seen to assault me—by yon rough fellow there." He indicated Ainsley with a jerk of his head and swept Lenore a handsome bow. His voice rose mockingly. "I'll bid you good day, mistress. And I do regret that you cannot share my bed tonight, but I find myself otherwise engaged. Perhaps another time?" He turned arrogantly on his heel and was gone, weaving swiftly among groups of players toward the theatre entrance.

Lenore swung on Ainsley, who was looking after Gilbert, round-eyed. His expression said plainly: what, Mistress Chastity pleading to bed a cavalier? She must be his cast-off doxie indeed! "You saw that, Ainsley," cried Lenore. "He is a liar and worse. If he harms me, you must be my witness!"

"I saw no intent to harm you," Ainsley said dryly, sheathing his sword. "Indeed, I saw you strike out at him. But what provoked you, I could not say, for he had a smile on his face the whole time."

Lenore gave Ainsley a bitter look. Like so many others, he had lately fallen under the spell of Nell Gwyn, and Nell

Gwyn was certainly not one of *her* friends. But . . . in honesty, what had there been to see? Gilbert had been clever and had made her appear in the wrong. He had always been clever.

Shaken with bitter memories, she turned away; the second act had begun, and soon she must march on stage and speak her lines.

Gilbert left the theatre with a deep frown etched on his scarred face. He nodded his caramel curls absently to a passing lady in scarlet silk he thought he recognized—and then turned and gave her a swift, ingratiating smile, for he had recognized the King's new doxie, Nell Gwyn. A pretty piece, he thought, with her riotous chestnut hair and saucy face. But not so beautiful as Lenore with her deep expressive violet eyes and challenging smile. Lenore, who made him go hot and cold, who made his blood race in his veins. His jaw tightened. He would bring Lenore to heel. And punish her. Exquisitely.

But first he would humble her.

Deep in thought, Gilbert strolled along the Thames, with the salt breeze blowing stiff in his face. He paused, leaned on his beribboned cane, and watched the white-sailed merchantmen bringing "sea coal" from Newcastle, wine from Bordeaux and Cadiz, spices and rich carpets from the Levant, and salt from Scotland. About him roared and jingled a great city, filled with gaming houses and brothels, palaces and corruption. He filled his lungs with the lusty air of London—ah, this was home to him! Lucky Wilsingame, to have been able to reside here almost since the Restoration of the King! The night before last over a game of dice, Lord Wilsingame had regaled him with tales of the wild parties he held at his house on London Bridge. He had bandied names about, of famous bawds and courtesans, and behind his hand he had even muttered spicy tidbits about nights spent with Nell Gwyn.

Nell Gwyn! Suddenly Gilbert struck his thigh and laughed aloud, for the perfect way to humble Lenore had come to him.

So loud was his laughter that several seabirds perched nearby took wing and flew away, calling raucously. His mirth and the jaunty swinging of his cane as he left attracted the attention of several dirty little urchins from the docks who, seeing such a jolly gentleman, ran up and begged him for a penny. Contemptuously Gilbert struck at them with his cane, and they retreated, muttering. From a distance one picked up a rock and hurled it at the fine gentleman in violet taffety just turning the corner away from them.

Gilbert might have given chase, but he had a more urgent mission, one which set his blood to singing. He was headed for a tavern Wilsingame had warned him away from as being frequented by scenekeepers and lackeys from the theatre—especially did he wish to meet those who worked in the Great Wardrobe. There was malice in Gilbert's face as he swung through the tavern door and looked about him, for he had no doubt his plan would work.

Mistress Lenore, he promised himself grimly, would soon be removed from the King's protection, and would be impelled into *his*.

CHAPTER 16

Though the King had recently been patronizing cockfights
and bear-baiting, confining his playgoing almost exclusively to Davenant's company of players, who held their performances in the remodeled Lisle's Tennis Courts in Lincoln's Inn Fields—and naturally the Court trailed him—
Lenore's own star had been rising of late and she had once
again landed a "breeches part" in a new play. The play
had been written by Killigrew himself, and it was whispered that the King was sure to attend, for Nell Gwyn was
in it.

Up to now, vivacious Nell had been able to keep Lenore
out of plays in which she appeared, but she had had a falling out with Killigrew over her dialogue—she wanted it
lengthened—so this time Killigrew had ignored her de-
mands and cast Lenore in the "breeches part." The part
was indeed a juicy one, and Lenore's eyes had widened in
surprise and delight at the glamorous costume the woman
had been stitching her into. She turned about before the
mirror in the tiring room studying it. It was almost as

showy as the costume Nell had worn at Whitehall, of white and yellow satin, with amber silk trunk hose that clung to her lovely legs.

This morning was the dress rehearsal for the new play, and Lenore, finally free of the tirewoman, hurried forward on cue. Onstage she could see Nell Gwyn (who must have dressed for her part at home, because Lenore had not seen her in the tiring room), dressed as a shepherdess and waving a tall beribboned shepherd crook. Looking the saucy wench she was in her blue and white gown with its huge full skirt and bodice cut so low her round breasts seemed about to bounce out, Nell shook her chestnut curls and simpered roguishly in the direction of the royal box which Charles would occupy during the performance.

Everyone knew she was sleeping with the King.

Lady Castlemaine was absent from the city for a short time, and in her absence Nell was enjoying Whitehall—everyone wondered what would happen when spirited Lady Castlemaine returned.

Personally, Lenore hoped Lady Castlemaine turned Nell out. She strode onstage and spoke her opening line. "Ho there, varlet! What do you with yon maid?"

Nell, who had been absent from all the rehearsals, sending word insolently to Killigrew that she "already knew her lines," obviously had not known Lenore was to have a part in the play, for she turned sharply as she heard Lenore's voice and her hazel gaze swept over her would-be rival.

Nell did not like what she saw. Lenore was a sumptuous figure in tight amber silk trunk hose that clung like her own skin and displayed her lovely legs clear to the hips. The white and yellow satin jerkin did little to conceal Lenore's beautifully shaped outthrust bust, and her yellow satin sleeves were slashed and graceful. She wore shoes with high yellow heels (she had starved for a week to buy them) that gave her the advantage of height over the shorter Nell, and she had chosen to wear her own hair instead of a wig; it cascaded down around her slender shoulders in riotous red-gold splendor.

She was too beautiful, Nell saw that at once—such a

258

woman would surely arrest the gaze of the King. Nell, who hoped to supplant Lady Castlemaine and become first woman in King Charles's heart, was not pleased. She had been stumbling over her lines, for all she'd said she knew them. Now she abandoned her dialogue altogether and advanced on Lenore.

"Take off that costume and return it to the Great Wardrobe," she cried angrily. " 'Twas given by the Earl of Marford and promised to me for the play we do next week."

Lenore stopped where she was, rested her hands on her satin hips, and gave her rival a scornful look. "I'll not," she said. "Next week you may wear it and welcome, but for this performance the tirewoman gave it to me. She's been spending all morning altering it to fit me."

"Off, I say!" cried Nell, who'd not been getting much sleep, what with having such an amorous and athletic lover as King Charles. Her nerves were on edge, and her strident voice showed it.

"No!" Ignoring Nell's interruption, Lenore turned to continue her part. She waved a graceful slashed-sleeved arm. "Unhand the maiden—"

But she never finished her lines. With the fury of the street girl she was, hot-tempered Nell was upon her. She plummeted into Lenore from behind, ripping at Lenore's satin doublet, grasping Lenore's long hair and jerking her head backward. Lenore, who was taller than Nell and had a longer reach, stumbled forward gasping at the suddenness of this unexpected assault from the rear but recovered nicely, spinning around and striking Nell away from her. Nell struck out at Lenore with her shepherd's crook as she reeled backward into Blakelock's arms, propelled by the force of Lenore's blow. She was spitting curses and street language, and from all about the company ran to watch as Nell struck Blakelock's restraining arm away from her, knocked over a turkey-work chair and some tin candlesticks, and came at Lenore once again.

Lenore was ready for her this time. As Nell plunged at her, she sidestepped, but reached out to grasp a handful of delicate frilly bodice. She gave it a jerk, ripping away a

259

long ruffle. Nell shrieked with fury as she saw her bodice was torn and suddenly darted under Lenore's guard, seized her around the waist, and by the very momentum of her charge, knocked Lenore off her feet. They went down together in a flailing heap of yellow silk legs and voluminous pale blue shepherdess skirts. Around them the tire-women screamed, the actresses cried at them to desist and shouted for Killigrew, and the actors laughed and offered bets as to which would win—for though Lenore was taller, Nell was sturdy, and opinion was that they were evenly matched.

Lenore gasped as Nell's sharp nails raked her face, barely missing her eyes. In anger, she wound her fingers tightly in Nell's chestnut ringlets and gave her head a sharp bang on the green baize floor. Nell screeched and kicked Lenore's shins with her square-toed blue shoes. Lenore countered by stamping on Nell's instep with a punishing yellow heel. Nell bellowed and bit at Lenore. Over and over they rolled on the green baize floor as Lenore tried to avoid the other girl's sharp teeth.

Panting, Lenore had her rival pinned down when Killigrew arrived on the scene. He strode through the company, scattering players and tirewomen to right and left, and pulled the contestants apart amid scattered applause and raucous cries of "Encore! Encore!"

"Since the ladies are willing, perhaps we should incorporate that scene in tonight's play!" cried one jolly voice.

Killigrew, who was holding the two women apart, gave the speaker a scathing look. He ignored Lenore's scratched face and torn costume. "Are ye hurt, Mistress Gwyn?" he asked anxiously, standing Nell on her feet. Lenore, struggling to her feet without assistance, thought wryly that that bleat of worry was for the King's favorite—Killigrew dared not let Nell come to harm in his theatre.

Trembling with rage, Nell dashed his arm away. "I'm all right, but my costume is ruined!" She fairly spat the words at Killigrew, reaching up to smooth back her tousled hair—indeed a tuft of that hair, departed from the scalp, was still clutched in Lenore's fingers. Nell looked down in fury at her shepherdesss gown, sadly dirty and

260

torn. "That wench attacked me!" she shouted at Killigrew.

"I did not!" cried Lenore, incensed. " 'Twas *she* attacked me, for she wants my costume!"

"The costume was promised to me for next week's play, and I do not want her appearing in it before I do—'twas given to the company by the Earl of Marford that I might wear it!"

Killigrew looked pained. "I promise she will wear it only for this performance, Mistress Gwyn. There's no time to find her a new costume now. The tirewoman—"

"Devil take the tirewoman!" panted Nell, her face flushed. "She's not to wear it at all! Do you hear me?"

Killigrew bit his lip. Everyone could see that he was warring within himself. The possibility of feeling the King's displeasure if the current royal favorite was not appeased was very real. He straightened. He had made his decision. Although his face was pale, it was expressionless as he turned to Lenore. "Take off the costume, Mistress Frankford. The tirewoman will find you something else."

Lenore gave him a mutinous look. She opened her mouth and checked herself. Killigrew's decision in these matters was, after all, final.

"Ye can get your revenge this afternoon in the play, Mistress Lenore!" called a raffish voice after her. "When ye stab her in the second act!"

Nell sniffed and whirled away, trailing ripped ruffles, and Lenore stalked off to return her torn costume to the Great Wardrobe and to seek a new one.

The one they found for her was not nearly so nice, nor was there time to make it fit properly. But Lenore knew bitterly that there was no alternative, she would have to wear it.

That afternoon they played to a packed house. The King was in attendance, Lenore was told excitedly by a passing actress. As the First Music struck up, Lenore, who was dressing in the women's part of the baize-hung tiring room, looked down contemptuously at the dull gray trunk hose and cheap red doublet they had found for her. Gone were the handsome slashed sleeves. Only the shoes with their high yellow heels remained, for they were her own, but

261

they looked strange with those dull gray trunk hose. Lenore suspected them of deliberately seeking for her a shabby costume in order to pacify jealous Nell and dabbed angrily at her scratched face.

She rose for a last inspection of herself in the mirror—and that mirror told her that the red doublet clashed with her hair, that the gray trunk hose were too loose and sagged, making her legs appear awkward. She gave the stool on which she'd been sitting a kick that sent it skidding to the far end of the room, and several other actresses who were dressing in the room turned to stare at her. From the far end of the room came a burst of laughter, and Lenore shot an angry look in that direction. There Nell Gwyn was holding court, fluttered over by actresses and tire-women, who knew she was sleeping with the King and hoped to gain her favor.

Nell's costume was a wonder, Lenore noted bitterly. A most unlikely shepherdess's costume, made of silver gauze and trimmed in tinsel, but beautiful nonetheless. All eyes would be on her indeed!

Lenore was so angry she hoped she would be able to remember her lines. At least there was one part she was not likely to forget. In the second act—and unrehearsed, for this morning's dress rehearsal had broken down after Lenore's fight with Nell, Nell having refused to go on with the rehearsal in a torn costume and Killigrew throwing up his hands and stalking out—Lenore was supposed to give Nell a stab in the chest with a stage dagger. Lenore had used these stage daggers before—the blade would disappear into the hilt at the thrust, but the blow would burst a tiny pouch of sheep's blood which Nell would wear concealed between her breasts. With a realistic red stain spreading on her bodice, Nell would fall gracefully to the green baize floor—and die dramatically onstage.

Lenore looked down angrily at her ugly costume. She would give Mistress Nell such a blow as would burst the laces of her shepherdess's bodice!

Still furious, she waited by the curtain for her cue and strode onstage. In the blazing candlelight, Nell, in her tinseled silver gauze, looked lustrous.

"Ho there, varlet!" cried Lenore in a ringing voice to Blakelock, who had hold of Nell's white arm. "What do you with yon maid?"

" 'Tis naught to you," cried Blakelock sulkily, with an exaggerated stage gesture.

Out of the corner of her eye Lenore could see King Charles smiling sardonically from the audience, his gaze all for the lustrous Nell Gwyn, one white hand clutched to her bosom.

"Unhand the maiden and give her up to me!" cried Lenore furiously, drawing the knife and brandishing it.

Blakelock pretended to cower and ran away offstage. Nell rushed forward.

"My savior!" she cried.

"Nay," said Lenore grimly, as the plot called for her to do. "Not your savior, but your rival. 'Tis you who have seduced my lover!" She raised the knife.

"No, no!" cried Nell, with well-simulated panic. She turned gracefully to run, and Lenore grasped her by the wrist, spun her back and struck straight and true with the fake dagger—and with such force that Nell screamed and staggered backward, landing on the green baize with a thump instead of collapsing gracefully. The little pouch of sheep's blood hidden between her breasts broke under the assault as planned and stained her bodice red, but Nell did not spread her arms out fetchingly and "die." Instead she struggled up, her face contorted with pain. "She has killed me!" she shrieked hoarsely. " *'Twas a real dagger!*"

Pandemonium reigned in the audience as King Charles leaped to his feet, cavaliers vaulted onstage, actresses and actors came running from everywhere. Killigrew himself rushed onstage in the hubbub and tore from Lenore's paralyzed hand the dagger she had used on Nell.

" 'Tis a stage dagger," he said with relief, pressing the blade with some force back into the hilt, and Lenore fell back against Ainsley in relief. Her hands were shaking. She had meant to strike Nell—but certainly not to kill her!

"She has cut me!" cried Nell, giving her bodice an angry rip that exposed the white flesh between her breasts. There indeed was a small cut where the malfunctioning dagger

263

had penetrated through the bodice and pouch and gouged a quarter-inch into her white bosom. "She did it deliberately!" Her voice rose hysterically. "Dismiss her! I demand she be dismissed!"

Across the heads bent over Nell's prostrate body, Killigrew gave his frowning royal master a worried look. He took the knife and plunged it into the top of a trestle table onstage. The blade retracted. He tried again. It stuck.

"The knife may have been tampered with," he muttered.

"But I am not to blame for that!" cried Lenore. "I but took the knife the scenekeeper gave me!"

"She attacked me this morning and tore my costume!" shrilled Nell, aggrieved. "How do you know she did not substitute another knife with a rusty blade that would stick?"

King Charles's frown deepened.

Killigrew swallowed. Abruptly he seized Lenore and dragged her, protesting, from the stage. Nell, recumbent and watching, suddenly waved a graceful hand and insisted bravely that she would go on with the performance even though the pain was—here she batted her lashes and pressed a hand dramatically to her bared breast—"almost too much to bear."

Lenore thought Nell's whole performance over what was scarcely more than a scratch too much to bear. She could hear the cheers and applause that greeted this popular suggestion and looked back to see Nell being helped to her feet by half the gentlemen from the pit. She wondered if Nell could not have stabbed herself with a hatpin to draw attention to herself, but Killigrew brushed this suggestion aside as he dragged her along.

"I saw ye fighting with her this morning," he said grimly. "This is a theatre—not an arena. God's breath! The two of ye could get me hanged!"

" 'Twas not I who started the fight this morning—" began Lenore, but Killigrew thrust her from him.

"I care not who started it!" he bellowed. "Get ye gone! Ye are dismissed!"

Lenore stared back at him, her eyes wide and accusing. Then she turned on her heel and stalked back to the tiring

264

room to change into her street clothes. She knew there was no use arguing with Killigrew.

Nell had won.

Gilbert was standing by the door as Lenore, dressed in her own clothes and carrying a tapestry square that contained her belongings, emerged upon Vere Street into a thick, soupy fog. She started as his scarred face loomed up before her and would have brushed past him, but he stepped forward like a disembodied ghost and barred her way.

"I hear ye have been dismissed, Lenore."

Lenore paused in mid-stride. How could he have known so soon? Word could not be about yet.

"So it was you. . . ." she said bitterly.

His triumphant smile told her everything. Somehow Gilbert had arranged for the daggers to be switched—the wonder was that she had not killed Nell with that malfunctioning dagger! For a moment Lenore stood there indecisively. She wanted to run back and tell Killigrew that she had deliberately been given the wrong knife. But she knew it would make no difference, had seen it on Killigrew's set face as he dragged her offstage. Killigrew was looking to his own job, his own future; he had placated Nell by dismissing her, he would not take her back now—perhaps she could try later.

In the meantime there was Gilbert to be dealt with. Gilbert, who bent close to her. Shrouded in fog, they seemed to be alone in the world, and his voice held a strange wistful caress. "Ye can still turn to me, Lenore—*I* would protect you."

"Protect me? *Protect* me?" she cried on such a note of wild derision that she could see him wince. Her eyes narrowed. Gilbert had arranged her downfall, but she still had the power to make him suffer. "What did you do to Lally, Gilbert?" she shot at him. "That she left you so suddenly?"

"Lally?" Caught off guard, Gilbert gaped at her, his handsome scarred face made almost ridiculous by surprise.

"Was it the same thing that made 'Mother' Moseley bar you from her brothel?"

265

Gilbert paled.

Lenore laughed scornfully. "Did you think I would not know? But we players hear everything backstage! We know who sleeps with the King—and who does not. And who is thrown downstairs at 'Mother' Moseley's for . . . why did she have you thrown downstairs, Gilbert? Because of what you did to her best girl, Gertrude?"

"Gertrude is a whore," panted Gilbert. "What could it matter what I did to her?"

"Gossip has it poor Gertrude—now that she's up and about again—has promised to ease a dagger between your ribs if you return. Do you always wear out your welcome, Gilbert? Was it so in Oxford? What tale would Lally tell me, Gilbert, if I were to see her again?"

"We quarreled," he grated. "Nothing more."

"I've no doubt you quarreled," said Lenore relentlessly. "I could see plain evidence of the arguments she lost on her bruised face!"

" 'Twas impossible not to quarrel with her!" he burst out, "She'd no thought of anyone but Ned!"

It was probably true, but Lenore, smarting from her unfair dismissal, was hardly in a charitable mood with the man who had caused it. "One cannot blame Lally for preferring a better man," she sighed.

Gilbert seized her arm vengefully. "You will end up at 'Mother' Moseley's yourself before long," he hissed, "where you'll be glad enough of my favors—or anyone else's who has the price! Geoffrey knew you for what you were!"

At that mention of Geoffrey, Lenore's face paled. "What did you say?" she asked menacingly.

"I say he knew you for a whore!" shouted Gilbert, driven too far. "Why do you think he did not bring you to Oxford sooner?"

He saw the effect Geoffrey's name had on her, and a terrible light flashed in his eyes. He would give this insolent wench something to think about! "Did you not know Geoffrey's wife had died in France before your lying in? He learnt it on one of his journeys. Geoffrey could have wed you—but he would not."

Agony burst over her.

266

"It is a lie!" she cried fiercely.

"Not so," he gloated, enjoying her disarray. "All in Oxford knew of it—all but you."

Was *that* what they had been whispering that day she had gone with Gilbert and Lally to a play in a barn near Oxford? Those voices in the audience behind her that had been so suddenly hushed as she was recognized?

"It isn't true," she whispered.

He laughed scornfully. "Believe what you will. Geoffrey told me he would never wed you. Know you not why he was absent so often? He was seeking a rich bride to buy him a pardon!" He watched in triumph the shattering effect these lies had on her and smiled in demonic satisfaction as her face broke up.

"Geoffrey knew you for a whore," he taunted, raking the raw wound. "He had promised me that when he tired of you, *I* might have you." His sneering face loomed toward her eerily in the fog. "What think you of that, Mistress Chastity?"

For answer she brought up her knee and struck him in the groin. Gilbert gave a sharp barking cry and went down into the mist. At her feet he rolled on the cobbles, doubled up in agony, clawing at the hem of her skirt.

Ashen-faced, Lenore stared down at his writhing body, shrouded by the thick white fog. Her mind reeled. *Considered her a whore . . . seeking a rich bride . . . his wife already dead in France . . .* Gilbert was Geoffrey's cousin; he would have known if Letiche had died . . . and it was reasonable that he would tell her now to make her suffer. And she was suffering.

Oh God, she had thought Geoffrey had left her because of the child, but if he had been lying to her all along, if he had really meant to turn her over to Gilbert when he tired of her . . . ! She stared down at Gilbert's recumbent form without seeing him. She was seeing instead a bright vista of hell wavering at her through the fog, and the awfulness of that picture blurred her sight.

She stepped over the body of the satin-clad dandy who writhed and moaned on the cobbles and stumbled away into the fog. Somehow she made it home to the Spur.

Twice in the soupy fog she crashed into passersby, receiving a curse for her awkwardness. And once she blundered into a lamppost. She would not have cared if she had tumbled into the Thames and the dark waters had closed over her head. For she moved through a darkness of the soul that was absolute.

And when she climbed the wooden stairs to her room and barred the door, she fell upon the bed with great sobs wracking her body. Geoffrey had never loved her, never . . . she had been a toy, a plaything to be used and thrown away.

Rocking in an agony of the spirit, she faced it all that night in the darkness of her small room. The white moon rose and waned and still she lay there, filled with grief and pain. The next day she did not go back to the theatre to try to get her job back. She did not go out; she did not eat or sleep. It was a full week before she could command herself to go back to the theatre. She wandered in listlessly and asked to speak to Killigrew.

He kept her waiting, but at last he saw her. The waiting was no hardship to Lenore; she did not care how long she sat there. Killigrew was startled at the sight of her. She was thinner, pale, her hair unkempt, her dark-fringed violet eyes great gashes in a lovely face grown suddenly ethereal. She told him she had been ill, and he believed it —she looked ill enough now.

But—he would not consent to take her back. He was firm about that. She had been dismissed by the Lord Chamberlain.

He was relieved at the way she took it—apathetically. She did not seem to care. He wondered uneasily what had happened to this blazing beauty whose fire had put all the other actresses in the shade. Had his dismissal . . . ? No, surely not; he put the thought aside. Still he felt guilty, for in his secret heart he had considered Lenore the most beautiful of all the young women who had trod the boards in his theatre, and he would have cast her in leading roles long before this had it not been for the enmity of Nell Gwyn.

Killigrew coughed. She could, he suggested, work as an

268

orange girl. Lenore, who cared little what she did or where she went, agreed at once.

"Orange Moll will show ye the way," he told her.

Lenore nodded without interest. Orange Moll, she knew, was the fruitwoman and queen of the orange girls.

Soon Lenore had joined the buxom, brawling, good-looking group of young women who hawked their wares in the pit. She made only a fair living selling oranges, for she did not choose to respond in kind to the bawdy remarks the young bucks made to orange girls, and her swift bright smile flashed but seldom.

"Thinks she's above us, she does," said Orange Moll, aggrieved. "I wouldn't of taken her on except for Killigrew—he asked me."

The other girls agreed with Moll. They bawled their wares and shook their hips and flirted their skirts and wore their bodices cut so low they almost exposed breasts as big as juicy oranges. They jeered at Lenore for having been nicknamed "Mistress Chastity," and one or two tried to trip her in the crush.

Lenore did her best to ignore them. She was fallen low, but she hoped as best she could to preserve her dignity. Men looked at her with open curiosity as she struggled by them through the crowded pit, calling out her wares. But enough of them bought her oranges that she could live—though she had to move from the Spur into cheaper lodgings—and a bare existence was all she cared for in this period of despondency.

But as the days passed and she began to eat again, her beauty was restored, and she was soon the wistful target of all eyes as she swayed gracefully through the crowd in the steaming pit, selling China oranges for sixpence apiece. Around her the other orange girls bawled their wares so loudly they obliterated the sounds of the First Music, but Lenore kept her voice low. It was her beauty that made patrons call her over to them. They wanted to fill their eyes with her, and so they bought her oranges.

In time she might have become an actress again, but . . . at an evening performance she looked up and saw Gilbert again.

269

It was a hot night, a special performance, crowded with luminaries. Onstage between acts, the company was performing a lively jig. Lenore had been threading her way carefully through the boisterous crowd in the pit, trying to avoid a noisy quarrel that had broken out between some wild young bucks just in from the West Country and a group of London apprentices that threatened to break into a full-scale riot. Insults and curses flew about, the dancers stomped, the music pounded, and the orange girls tried to bawl their wares above the din.

Lenore's attention had been completely absorbed by the brawling that had erupted, and it was a shock to find herself looking directly into Gilbert Marnock's face.

She stepped back warily, treading on a booted toe and muttering an apology, scarce heard in the uproar. Gilbert did not speak, but naked hatred leaped out at her from his hard caramel eyes. All the lust with which he had always studied her seemed erased, all remnants of humanity had disappeared from his gaze, and Lenore was shaken by the sheer evil of his glare.

She turned away, having to clamber over a protruding satin knee, slapped away some impudent pinching fingers, and struggled between two fat gentlemen, almost wedged together at the ends of two bulrush-covered benches. She was tired, she could feel perspiriation dripping down her back causing her thin worn dress to stick to her, and the noise was giving her a headache. Last night fighting had broken out in the pit and erupted onto the stage when three half-drunk cavaliers had leaped onto the green baize, pushed aside the actors, and elected to fight it out with swords in full view of the audience. She hoped nothing like that would happen tonight. Some distance away one of the apprentices had leaped to his feet and was calling "To me!" Someone else pulled him down. If only she could sell her oranges and go home . . . She struggled on, ignoring Gilbert's smouldering glares, selling her oranges where she might, evading as best she could the surreptitious pinches and pats of the young bloods who thought orange girls easy prey.

Lenore would have done well to keep an eye on Gilbert.

But she was intent on keeping her ankles from being cut by the big spurs on the gentlemen's boots—they were so fashionable they were even worn in drawing rooms—and on avoiding the vicinity of the bristling apprentices.

So she did not see Gilbert get up and push his way through to the little clot of disreputable cavaliers who were the constant companions of Lord Wilsingame, did not see them part to admit Gilbert, did not see Gilbert bend over his lordship and engage him in conversation. At what he said, Lord Wilsingame's hard face registered first shock, then anger. He turned and spoke to the heavyset gallant who sat next to him, whose name was Bonnifly, and Bonnifly lurched to his feet and stared openly at Lenore's back until those behind him shouted at him to sit down. A place was hastily made for Gilbert beside Lord Wilsingame, by the simple expedient of pushing an elderly gentleman not of their party, who sat at the end of the bench, off onto the floor. He landed with a yelp, but Bonnifly gave him such a threatening look that he rose and fled through the crowd.

Lenore would have done well to note all of these things, for the group around Lord Wilsingame were drinking heavily this night, and Lord Wilsingame had been publicly humiliated by Lenore. She could not know that Gilbert, with his hypnotic voice and insinuating manner, was fanning Lord Wilsingame's erotic interest in Lenore to flame by describing strange, wild delights he'd enjoyed whilst sharing her bed in Oxford. She would have screamed in fury had she heard Gilbert recount the things he had done to her and the wanton passion she had displayed.

"Can it be true?" wondered Wilsingame. "Our Mistress Chastity a whore?"

" 'Tis true, I swear it," said Gilbert glibly. "In Oxford all knew of her exploits. In truth," he added on a lewd note, "in Oxford all knew *her!*"

Wilsingame frowned. "Then why so coy with us in London? Answer me that!"

Gilbert shrugged and took a pinch of snuff from an enamelled box. "Oxford is far from London. Here she could set herself up as a virgin—perhaps to entrap a King. As Nell has done."

271

Wilsingame drummed his fingers on his hard satin-cased thighs. "Then Mistress Lenore should be taught a lesson, it seems to me!"

"I doubt you can buy her," warned Gilbert. "She likes to keep up the fiction that she is a virgin."

"Buy her? I do not intend to try," said Wilsingame brutally. "It strikes me that I have been too nice with our Iron Virgin!"

These were the words Gilbert wanted to hear. He turned with a snicker to mutter some bestiality about Lenore into Wilsingame's ear. Wilsingame looked astonished. He smote his knee with his fist. "She'll do that for me, too!" he cried. "Aye, and for all of us!"

Gilbert sat back, well satisfied. "I doubt me there's a trick you could mention that Mistress Lenore does not know," he drawled. "Of amorous delights, she's a mistress! Though she'd never admit it. . . ."

"A taste of the whip will spur her memory," said Wilsingame heavily.

"Mistress Chastity has always bested you, Wilsingame," laughed the dissolute de Quincy, turning around from the seat just in front. "Take care that she does not best you this time!"

"That she will not!" Wilsingame rumbled an oath. "She will be taught a lesson this very night. No, not tonight." He looked irritable. "Tonight I must bide at home to waylay one who will be crossing London Bridge on the King's business."

Gilbert pricked up his ears. He had been learning London ways, and he now knew that hangers-on like Wilsingame waylaid passing notables whenever possible and urged hospitality upon them—in hopes of gaining a useful friend at Court. "But why not tonight?" he said craftily. "Provide your guest with ripe entertainment—Mistress Lenore herself!"

Wilsingame brightened. "Why not?" he muttered. "My manservant can watch for him as he crosses the Bridge and bring him in—no need for me to do it. We'll serve her up like a bird on a platter!"

272

"Ah, she'll not disappoint you," sighed Gilbert. "Though it may at first take some persuasion to urge her on."

"Come with us, Marnock," urged Wilsingame. "We'll have sport together."

Gilbert laughed, but dodged that neatly. "I'd like that, Wilsingame—but alas, I've a ripe wench of my own who waits for me at my lodgings. She'll grow restive if I'm late. But having heard you once fancied Mistress Lenore and that she had palmed herself off on you as a virgin, I thought 'twas only just you be apprised of her true nature. A veritable strumpet! In bed she is devastating!"

Wilsingame's heavy-lidded eyes widened enough to emit a lusty sparkle. "She will be put through all of her paces tonight," he growled. "You can rest assured of it! And I count it a favor that you have brought me this agreeable piece of news, Marnock. My door is always open to you." Graciously he offered Gilbert his gold snuffbox.

"Your lordship is too gracious." Delicately Gilbert took a pinch of snuff and sneezed. "Ah, a good blend!" He looked up to see that the jig was ending and the third act was about to begin. "Well, I've seen this play so often I think I'll take myself off before I start reciting the lines along with the players! Good health, gentlemen!"

Wilsingame's friends nodded affably and Gilbert got up and pushed his way over a tangle of booted feet, past a number of skirts and petticoats which he disarranged in struggling through, and made his way quickly down the long passage and out of the theatre.

He wanted to be well away from what was about to happen—in case Lenore should ever in future command the interest of the King, for he'd heard about her interview at Whitehall. Then, no matter what she said, no blame could be placed on him—'twould only be the hysterical accusation of a spiteful woman; he, Gilbert, would neatly escape the royal wrath.

The orange girl, he told himself with vicious emphasis as he rode home in a hackney coach, would not be so crisp and arrogant after tonight!

CHAPTER 17

Lenore, quite oblivious to these schemes, struggled through the unruly crowd, handing out an occasional orange, trying to make change—and knew a moment of gratitude when she looked back and saw Gilbert Marnock leaving the theatre. Then someone trod painfully on her foot and she groaned and forgot him.

But her progress through the pit was being surveyed grimly by Lord Wilsingame, who had lost all interest in the third act of the play—even though onstage a masked devil with a forked stick had just disappeared through a trapdoor in the floor and above the stage a tinseled angel was being flown about movable "clouds," maneuvered on ropes. Wilsingame drummed his fingers on his satin knee and stared at the lovely orange girl with such a combination of lust and vengefulness as would have chilled her blood had she but seen it—but her attention was elsewhere, on the apprentices who had settled down for the moment but might grow restive again.

Finally, having set his mind upon the object to be

gained, Wilsingame gave thought to how to go about it. He bethought him that this was a play with a loud thunderstorm near the end—and very loud thunder indeed would be produced by the scenekeepers backstage as they rolled great cannon balls over sticks and pounded wooden mustard bowls, whilst others flashed pans of gunpowder and musicians pounded out a rumble on big bass drums. A noisy ending for a noisy play. It occurred to him that the timing of the thunder would suit him perfectly. He leaned over and muttered a few words to the evil cronies with whom he surrounded himself. They laughed as at some great jest, and two of them heaved themselves to their feet amid cries of, "Sit down! Sit!" and wormed their way through the audience and out of the theatre.

Pleased with himself, Wilsingame sat back and watched the play proceed. He waited till it was near its end, and then when Lenore came weaving through the crush with her oranges, he leaned forward and snapped his fingers.

"Here—orange girl! To me!"

Lenore turned at the cry of "orange girl" and frowned slightly when she saw who the speaker was. Wilsingame smiled ingratiatingly.

"Mistress," he drawled in a bored tone, "I would buy all your oranges if you would but deliver them to my coach outside."

"Quiet!" someone yelled from behind. "And move aside, orange girl—you are obstructing my view of the players!"

Lenore moved aside a step, but she hesitated. Lord Wilsingame's unsavory reputation had grown even blacker of late. It was common gossip at the theatre that he bought virgins and that he gathered together groups of his friends and held mass deflowerings. Although wags at the theatre insisted most of the wenches were not virgins at all, but fakes palmed off on him by the knowing madams, most of those who were, ended up as prostitutes in their plush establishments, and it was rumored that two of the unfortunate wenches, ill-used, had died and their bodies had been tossed into the Thames from Wilsingame's upper windows. Lenore had no reason to doubt these bizarre stories, and gave silent thanks that young Emma had got away from him. But as she sold her oranges she had always been careful to give the unsavory Wilsingame a wide berth. She hated the very look of the man: those heavy-lidded dark eyes always seemed to crawl over her body like reptiles, chilling her very skin.

Tonight she saw that he sat among his friends—men whose company he was seldom without and who were known to her by reputation. Her uneasy gaze roved over them: de Quincy the swordsman, a dissolute brawler but reputed to be the best blade in London; tall and lean, he had turned to watch, and his narrow green eyes were licking over her body. Flemmons, with a cold reptilian look—a graceful dandy who'd been barred from half the bawdy-houses of London for his manhandling of their bawds; he frowned darkly at her because in better days Mistress Chastity had snubbed him. And Alverdice, a wealthy young lout newly in from York and eager to plumb the depths of depravity, who now considered her eagerly, as if she were an orange herself, ripe for peeling. And perhaps the worst of the lot—Bonnifly, a heavyset monster of a man with reaching fingers whose painful pinches Lenore had endured more than once as she tried to edge by the group who surrounded Wilsingame. Bonnifly was said to have smashed a young actress's jaw because she resisted his advances, and had been barred from Court. His surly face turned to watch the hesitant orange girl. She thought there'd been two others with Wilsingame, but they seemed to have gone.

Soberly Lenore considered the arrogant Wilsingame. He hated her, she knew, for having held him up to public ridicule. Still . . . that was some time ago and he'd undoubtedly debauched a number of virgins since then—and she had fallen low; he might consider that she had been punished enough for flaunting him. She did not regret humiliating him. She'd do it again, if she had to.

An angry bellow came from one of the apprentices. He turned and soundly cuffed the man behind him, yelling that he'd been struck from behind. Someone pulled him off his bench, and a moment later they were rolling among boots and spurs on the floor, locked in combat. There was a rising clamor between the West Countrymen and the apprentices. Lenore knew it was only a matter of time before large-scale fighting erupted—and the last time that had happened, all her oranges had got knocked to the floor and trampled to pulp.

Wilsingame yawned and deliberately took a pinch of snuff. "Well?" he asked testily, snapping his gold snuffbox shut. "Do I buy your oranges, mistress? Or do I procure them from another?"

Lenore disliked the idea of going outside at Wilsingame's behest. But the play had not yet ended, and it was doubtful either Wilsingame or his cronies would leave early—they never did. She was tempted . . . all her oranges. Let the apprentices and the West Countrymen fight it out in the pit! Having sold all her oranges, she could go home to her cheap lodgings in Southwark well ahead of the crowd and she could get some sleep—if sleep she could, for her lonely, restless nights were even more tormenting than her days.

"Give the oranges to my coachman." Wilsingame thumped the money into her hand as if it were a fact accomplished and turned back to give his rapt attention to the play.

That gesture of dismissal decided Lenore. Of course she would deliver them to his coach. No need to fear. Wilsingame and his cronies obviously were going to stay in the theatre. No doubt he was entertaining some doxie tonight and wished to favor her with high-priced oranges which she could bite into on the way to some other feast.

Lenore threaded her way out of the audience, where the noise of the combatants was fast drowning out the best efforts of the shouting players, and went swiftly through the long passageway that led out into Vere Street. She knew Wilsingame's coach by sight—all knew it because it was flaming red with much gilding and the green and gold Wilsingame arms emblazoned on the side. Ah, there it was now, just coming up to the door to wait for Wilsingame, who would be coming out as soon as the play ended—if he could make it through the brawlers. She

277

hurried toward it and reached up toward the coachman with the oranges.

As he reached down to take them, the door of the coach burst open, and two men jumped out. Lenore recognized them as Taggart and Lymond, the two missing members of the coterie that surrounded Wilsingame.

She screamed and turned to run, dropping her oranges. The oranges rolled over the cobbles as greyhound-lean Lymond, leaping forward, caught Lenore's shoulder in a punishing grip and spun her around. She would have lost her footing but that burly Taggart caught her other arm and together they dragged her back to the coach.

Lenore's screams might have attracted attention, but just as she opened her mouth the very building behind her began to boom with artificial thunder. As they dragged her to the coach, the warring apprentices and West Countrymen spilled out into the street exchanging blows and shouting curses—and Lymond and Taggart appeared to be rescuing a hysterical lady from the mob. They fairly threw Lenore into the coach, and Lymond promptly sat on her legs, pinning her down effectively while heavyset Taggart held onto her flailing arms.

Wilsingame had timed the attack exactly right.

Lenore was not going to give up without a struggle. Even though pinned down, she sank her teeth into Lymond's lean arm. He let out an angry oath as she bit him, grasped her arms from Taggart, and jerked them behind her so that she writhed in agony and a dark veil of pain descended over her eyes. When her vision cleared, she realized that she was twisted into a half-sitting position on the floor of the coach and surrounded on all sides by booted legs—and shiny spurs. She swung her head around. She stared upward and knew terror. Fearsome Bonnifly had joined Taggart and Lymond, and the heavy-lidded eyes above those loose cruel lips that smiled down at her belonged to Wilsingame himself.

"If you scream again, Mistress Lenore," Wilsingame said in a voice so polite he might have been asking her to share a glass of malmsey with him, "Bonnifly here will cuff you hard enough that you'll lose your senses—and that would be a pity, for there's another coachful of gentlemen following close behind us, all of them as interested in your charms as we are!"

At that chilling statement, the bold courage that had never failed her came back to Lenore. Haughtily she lifted her head. "Lord Wilsingame," she said defiantly, "if you do me harm, the King shall hear of it!"

"Ah, but you are not in the King's favor—'tis Nell who sleeps in his bed," pointed out Wilsingame calmly. "Besides, who said we meant to harm you? We mean to *enjoy* you. Surely the King himself would approve of that!"

Lenore returned that relentless stare with an insolence she did not feel. She had heard too many stories of Wilsingame's sport with women not to believe some of them were true.

"Where are you taking me?" she demanded.

"Home—where else?"

Stonily, Lenore turned her face away from him and inspected the large spurs on Lymond's boots. She would not let them see the terror she felt.

In silence the coach jogged along toward Wilsingame's house perched in the middle of London Bridge. Lenore tried to scream once when she saw a pair of sturdy gentlemen edging by the coach as they entered onto the Bridge, and Bonnifly clapped a rough hand over her mouth, seizing her around her slender waist and laying rude hands upon her breasts. She tried to wriggle away from him and kicked out, managing only to tear her stocking on Lymond's spurs. Bonnifly raised a threatening hamlike fist, but Wilsingame lifted his hand.

"Enough, Bonnifly, enough," he said mildly. "Remember I've a gentleman coming by this evening that I wish to impress—'twould not do to mark the wench."

Bonnifly subsided, grumbling, and Lenore was left trembling on the floor of the coach as they passed through first one and then another short tunnel where the houses that lined the bridge met overhead.

She made one last attempt to break free as she alighted from the coach, to fling herself down to the cobbles and take off running down the narrow way. But even as she took flight she was snatched up in a mighty bear hug that drove the breath from her lungs, and Bonnifly carried her lightly through the oaken door that opened discreetly to admit them. She had a brief glimpse of the impassive face of the manservant who had told her Emma had left London and gone to the country.

Behind her she could hear the clatter of feet from a second coach that alighted before the house, and the occupants hurried in to cluster around her. Several of them she did not even recognize. God, there were so many of them —nine or ten all told! Two were very drunk, swaying on their feet, and one lurched toward her and peered down into her face.

"I know this wench," he muttered fuzzily.

"So will we all soon," snickered Bonnifly.

Lenore gave him back a defiant look, but she offered no resistance as Bonnifly carried her up the stairs with Wilsingame close behind. The manservant unlocked a door at the head of the stairs, and Lenore was thrust inside; the door slammed and locked behind her.

She had a swift impression of a candlelit square bedroom painted with fat rosy cupids in the French manner and dominated by a large canopied bed. The canopy parted suddenly, and a face peered out, to be swiftly followed by a thin female body. Across an expanse of worn carpet Lenore saw a fragile blond girl in a low-cut pink satin dress trimmed in black lace. The girl was emaciated, and her eyes appeared sunken and suffering in her white face that brightened suddenly in recognition.

"Emma!" gasped Lenore. "Oh, Emma, what has he done to you?"

Emma ran forward with a cry and impulsively threw her arms about Lenore. She seemed to collapse like a broken doll. "It's been terrible!" she sobbed. "You wouldn't believe—" Sobs choked her voice.

Lenore pushed her away and studied that pretty tear-stained face. "They told me you'd left London, Emma."

Emma shook her head, sobbing.

280

"What has he done to you?" Lenore demanded sternly. "And what happened to your Baronet?"

"At first—at first he was kind," Emma faltered. "And I even thought I loved him. But then one night he drove me here and—and left me. Lord Wilsingame said I was payment for a gambling debt!"

"But you're so thin! Doesn't he feed you?"

" 'Tis my own fault I'm thin," sighed Emma. "I thought —I thought that if I did not eat, maybe I would die the sooner."

Lenore looked at her sad little friend, appalled. "Surely it cannot be that bad!"

" 'Tis worse," Emma said simply. She looked down in misery. " 'Tis not only *him,*" she whispered. " 'Tis his friends. They hold big parties sometimes two or three nights a week, and young virgins are brought here to be 'broken in,' they say! Some are no more than thirteen— one was only twelve! Lord Wilsingame and his friends frighten them into submission by . . . by doing terrible things to me, Lenore. In . . . in public where all can watch!" Her eyes filled again with tears.

"Don't talk about it," said Lenore harshly, moving to the window. "Is there no way out of this place?"

"None. All the doors are locked—and that great footman, Bales, guards the halls. Once when I tried to run, he near broke my arm—and then he had his way with me on the stairs while Lord Wilsingame watched. He—he laughed, Lenore, and said Bales could have either me or his wages but not both—and Bales took me!" She shivered. "How did you come here, Lenore?"

"His friends abducted me from the front of the theatre."

Emma gaped at her; then hope sprang up in her eyes. "Then they will come looking for you!" she cried. "We will be saved!"

"Don't count on it," said Lenore grimly. Orange Moll hated her for being "above herself." Killigrew and the rest would assume she'd found a "protector" and gone off with him. She doubted she'd even be missed!

Emma's face fell. "You are right," she sighed. "I thought somebody might come looking for me—but nobody did."

"I came looking for you," said Lenore, "but I was told you'd left the City."

"Would that I could! Lord Wilsingame has circulated a story that he has a mad sister locked up in here and that her screams rend the night, and that sometimes they are joined by the screams of serving-women she attacks. But there is no mad sister. Mine are the screams they hear—mine and the poor virgins' who are dragged in here for deflowering and for . . . for terrible games that are played downstairs."

Lenore did not ask what games those were. "Have you no weapon?" she asked sharply.

Emma went over and lifted a corner of the carpet that stretched under the edge of the bed. She pulled out a small kitchen knife. "Elsie, who brings my food, forgot this one day, and I kept it and hid it. I meant to plunge it into Lord Wilsingame's chest the next time he tormented me—but I had not the courage. Then I thought as they dragged me back from the games downstairs and flung me into my room—for I could not walk, so badly had they treated me—that I would plunge it into my own breast and be free of them. But I had not the courage for that, either." She stood looking down at the knife in forlorn fascination. "Perhaps one day I will find the strength to use it," she sighed.

"Give me the knife." Lenore reached out and took it from Emma's limp fingers. " 'Tis not much against so many, and I doubt we can do much damage with it, but it might serve for surprise so that we can dart past that large footman."

"Bales? He always stays in the hall outside. 'Tis only Elsie comes into this room. 'Tis long since Lord Wilsingame visited me here—he prefers to make me come downstairs so that he may make sport of me with his friends."

Lenore tried the casement. To her surprise, it was not locked. She opened it and peered out. This building over-

282

hung the river, and she found herself looking down into the black waters of the Thames.

"There is no need to keep the window locked," mourned Emma, "for there is only the river below. Sometimes I have thought of hurling myself out and ending this wicked life I am condemned to—for I do not swim. But I have always so feared the water. My sister died by drowning."

"You're not going to drown," said Lenore energetically. "Nor submit to that evil pack again, either! Here, help me drag this—heavy—cupboard against the door," she panted, setting her shoulder to the work. Emma heaved her pitifully slight weight against it. It moved protestingly over the floor. "And now this—great—chest!" Panting, Lenore stood back and surveyed her handiwork. "Where does that other door lead?"

"Only into a small dressing room. But—they'll break down the door, Lenore."

"We'll gain time by making it harder for them to get in. Have you any possessions? Tie them into a bundle—quickly." She moved again to the window. "And I'll need that necklace you're wearing—unless you've money?" She reached out for it.

"I've no money," said Emma, bewildered. "And I think—I think the stones are glass."

"No matter," said Lenore. "They'll look real enough in the moonlight! Hurry!" Behind her she could hear Emma open a chest. She glanced back to see her bundling her clothing into a sheet which she tied at the top.

They could hear feet ascending the stair, and a key turned in the lock—but Lenore had seen what she wanted on the river below: a rowboat with a single oarsman had just slipped from under the bridge. She leaned out and called down to him. "This necklace if you'll take us downriver to safety!"

He looked up, startled, his face pale in the moonlight. Lenore dangled the brilliants temptingly. They had an expensive glitter. Behind her now there was a thundering on the door and Wilsingame's voice cried, "They've blocked the door somehow—Bales!"

From below the boatman bobbed his head. "Aye,

mistress, I'll take you where you want to go. Toss down the necklace!"

" 'Twill be on this lady's neck!" said Lenore, clasping it quickly around Emma's neck—the girl had just stuck out her head. "You must fish her out of the river for it! And here are her possessions!" She tossed down the bundle of clothes, and the boatman caught it and rowed rapidly back to position as the current swept him away.

Behind her Lenore heard Wilsingame say, "They've pushed something against the door, Bales. Bend your back, man!"

"Jump, Emma!" she cried. "I'll be right behind you!"

Emma clambered onto the windowsill and looked down fearfully. "I cannot do it," she cried hysterically. "I cannot jump into the water!"

"You must!" Feverishly Lenore sought to free the girl's clutching hands from the sill. "Emma, jump!"

Behind her she heard the great chest move, and the heavy cupboard toppled over with a crash that shook the house. At the sound of that crash, Emma's hands suddenly were loosed in fright, and Lenore gave her a strong push. With a shriek Emma went plummeting into the water and the boatman reached out and grasped her by the arm to pull her into the boat just as Lenore leaped to the windowsill poised to jump.

But it was a jump she was never to make. Even as she would have spun off into space, a pair of strong hands clutched her around the waist, and she was jerked backward into the room.

"Row!" she screamed to the boatman. "Bring help!"

Even as she spoke, she knew how futile that appeal was. Poor exhausted Emma would be lucky if she got away herself, would be lucky if the boatman actually delivered her to some place of safety downstream. But— even if he did not, her fate would be no worse.

"The wench Emma has escaped!" cried Bales, keeping his grip on Lenore's waist as he leaned out the window. "Milord, she is being rowed away in a boat!"

Wilsingame's cold voice cut in contemptuously. "No matter, Bales. I was about to get rid of her anyway—

284

she'd no spirit left in her. I want a woman, not a wooden doll! We've a better wench here, Bales."

"But milord, suppose she tells—"

"She'll tell no one anything, Bales. She'll fear to! She'll hide in fright that I may get her back!" He chuckled, and Lenore realized the chilling truth of that—Emma would probably fear to speak up in any event.

Wilsingame turned to Lenore. "Behave yourself, mistress. If you please my important guest from Kent, so that he speaks well of me to the King, I may reward you by letting you drive about London with me in my coach. Release her, Bales."

As Bales's fingers loosened their grip on her waist, Lenore tore free and clawed at the window, but the casement was inexorably pulled shut against her best efforts and a heavy body pushed her aside. Big Bonnifly had come into the room and was leaning against the window grinning at her. He reached out and gave her a shove, and she found herself standing unsteadily on her two feet, facing Wilsingame.

"I will not entertain your guests—or yourself!" she panted. "I warn you, Wilsingame, that if you force me, I will give you no pleasure!"

Wilsingame's hand lashed out, and Lenore reeled back as he gave her cheek a stinging slap. "On the contrary," he sneered, his expression turning as bleak as his eyes. "You will give me great pleasure, orange girl—aye, and my guests, too! We will sport with you as long as it pleases us, and when we've done with you, 'Mother' Moseley can have you—with my compliments!" He took a threatening step forward.

Lenore would have prudently backed away, but from behind her Bonnifly's big hand pressed against the small of her back and propelled her forward. Before Lenore was aware what he was about, Wilsingame had grasped the front of her bodice. He gave it a violent jerk that split the fabric to the waist and—combined with her forward momentum from Bonnifly's shove—tumbled her to the floor at his feet.

Lenore scrambled back away from his boots, aware

285

that her white flesh showed in a cleavage that now reached to her waist. Desperately she clutched the material around her with one hand and managed to regain her feet.

Boots planted, Wilsingame towered above her. She thought hopelessly that she had never seen a more ruthless face.

"See that she puts this on," he said in a colorless voice, jerking his head toward a black silk gown trimmed in creamy lace that was tossed over a chair. "Where've ye been?" Lenore saw that he was speaking to a frightened-looking gray-haired serving-woman who was just staggering into the room burdened down by a large metal tub partially filled with water.

"Bales said ye'd brought in a woman, milord," she faltered, almost groveling before Wilsingame as she set the tub down and straightened up with difficulty. "And I've been heating a bath for her. I thought you'd want—"

"Very well." He cut her words off contemptuously, and she scurried away for towels and soap. "Nail the window shut, Bales," he ordered his burly manservant, and Bales hurried away for hammer and nails. "Bonnifly, you might guard this door to see that our pretty bird does not fly away before we've clipped her wings. You'll doubtless enjoy watching her in her bath."

Bonnifly grinned, moved to the doorway, and lounged against the jamb. Lenore edged toward the window, meaning to jerk it open and hurl herself out and take her chances on swimming to safety, but Wilsingame guessed her intention and seized her wrist.

"Not so fast, mistress!"

"I feel faint," she complained, noting that the kitchen knife Emma had meant to use on herself had been dropped below the sill as she tried to urge Emma through the window.

But Bonnifly's keen eye had spotted it, too. "Ho!" he cried from the doorway. "The wench seeks a claw to scratch us with!" He sauntered over and picked up the knife, tossed it in the air, and caught it by the hilt. " 'Tis a kitchen knife, Wilsingame. Your serving-woman should be careful not to leave sharp things lying about."

Lenore felt her heart sag to her worn slippers. That kitchen knife had been her last hope.

Glowering, Wilsingame waited until the serving-woman came back, carrying linen towels and soap. Bonnifly handed her the knife, and she blanched.

"How do you explain this, Elsie?" Wilsingame asked gently.

Elsie shrank back. "I—I do not know how it came to be here, sir!" she stuttered.

"Another example of your carelessness," barked Wilsingame, giving Elsie an angry shove that sent her skittering across the room, dropping her towels and soap. "One more such blunder and I'll dismiss you!"

"Please, milord!" Elsie fell to weeping. "I've seven children at home, and my husband's hurt and can't work!"

She went about picking up the scattered towels and soap and was still weeping as Bales hurried by, hammered the window shut with stout nails, and left.

"See that Mistress Lenore is well prepared, Elsie," Wilsingame told the old serving-woman sternly, at last letting go of Lenore's arm. She rubbed it against her hip, for it was almost numb from his harsh grip. "She must look very fetching, for I've a guest riding in from Kent tonight."

"A guest?" laughed Bonnifly. "That's hardly the word for it! Does he know he's coming here?"

"Bales will waylay him outside as he crosses the Bridge, unless he misses him in the darkness. You may soon laugh on the other side of your mouth, Bonnifly, for this man has the King's confidence. If we woo him well, he may gain for us a Royal Patent to trading rights in the Indies. 'Tis my plan that our orange girl here will give him such entertainment this night as he's not enjoyed before!" He laughed discordantly, on a note of mounting excitement, and Lenore cringed inwardly. " 'Tis only a pity we've no time to teach her special tricks, for I doubt me she's the expert Marnock claims her to be."

Marnock! Lenore gasped.

"A novice is better, anyway," stated Bonnifly.

"You may be right. She looks to be a hot wench, and

287

from what Marnock said, she was a whore in Oxford—before becoming a virgin on the London stage!"

"He lied!" gasped Lenore, clutching her torn bodice around her. "Gilbert Marnock raped me in Oxford! I was never his willingly!"

"Ah, so you admit you've lain with him?" Wilsingame's short, unpleasant laugh chilled her. "Yet you returned my gifts as if you were some mewling virgin newly come to town! Well, tonight we shall play games with the Iron Virgin! Tell me now, Mistress Chastity, how many men have you known?"

"Three!" flashed Lenore. "And *you* shall not be my fourth!"

Wilsingame's contemptuous laugh seemed to linger in the air as he brushed past Bonnifly and clattered down the stairs.

"Your bath, mistress," whined Elsie, who had dried her eyes on her apron. "We don't want it to get cold, you might catch a distemper!"

"I will not bathe while this man watches!" stormed Lenore, backing away, clutching her torn bodice with both hands.

"Please, mistress," coaxed the old serving-woman, trying to take hold of her hand. "His lordship will dismiss me if you refuse to bathe!"

"Then jump out this window after me when I smash this small chair through the panes," muttered Lenore in a voice too low for Bonnifly to hear. She took her right hand from her bodice and rested it casually on the back of a small straight chair. One spring and she could be at the window smashing with the chair. No matter if she was cut by broken glass, if she could but leap through . . . !

The old serving-woman shook her gray head sadly. "You heard me say I've seven small ones at home, for my sister just died leaving me her brood, and there's few will hire one so old as me—I must find work where I can. For years I did work for 'Mother' Moseley, making up the featherbeds for her young ladies to tumble in—but she dismissed me because I was no longer young and spry enough. 'Tis lucky I am to find any work at all."

"Then trip Bonnifly as I smash the window, and I'll find work for you myself—at better pay," muttered Lenore.

Elsie looked tempted, but she hesitated. "I am afraid, mistress."

From the doorway Bonnifly guessed her intention and leered at Lenore. "That chair will not break through the window, mistress, but if ye try it, I promise I'll have ye first—on yon big bed—before the rest of them have ye downstairs! 'Twill be my reward for preventing your escape."

Lenore removed her hand carefully from the back of the small chair. Bonnifly was probably right, the little chair was too frail to break the stoutly nailed casement before Bonnifly would be upon her. He was a big hulking man, and she had no desire to push him too far, for she had no doubt at all that he would make good his threat and not be pulled off of her, not even by Wilsingame, until he had achieved his purpose. No, she'd best take her chances downstairs. Perhaps, she thought forlornly, she could find a way to slip past them, make it out the front door onto the Bridge, and throw herself on the mercy of some passerby—if there were any crossing the Bridge at this time of night.

"Please take your bath and put the pretty dress on, mistress," pleaded old Elsie. " 'Twill not aid your cause to wear a torn dress!"

No, that it would not. "I will wear the dress," agreed Lenore with spirit. "Since your master has seen fit to destroy mine! But I will don it behind the hangings of yon bed. And I will bathe only if *you*"— she glared at the serving-woman—"will hold those hangings betwixt this man's evil gaze and the tub!"

"Mistress, mistress—"

"If you do not do it," said Lenore in as brutal a tone as she could muster, "I will take these sharp fingernails of mine—see them?" She held them up. "And I will tear at my face and neck and breasts until I am all scratched and bleeding. And I will tangle and rend my hair so that I will look like a woman who has slept in the gutter for

289

a week, instead of the 'juicy morsel' my Lord Wilsingame expects!"

So white and determined was her face that the serving-woman fell back in alarm. "I'd best do as she says, Mister Bonnifly," she muttered. "Else she might do herself some injury and then Lord Wilsingame would blame us that we let her mar her beauty!"

In the doorway, Bonnifly shrugged. His nasty gaze said he would be viewing her naked body soon enough.

Looking resigned at this duty, Elsie the serving-woman held out the heavy bed-draperies as a shield behind which Lenore disrobed, pinned up her long hair, and stepped into the warm water. It felt good, and she sank down into a sitting position with her knees drawn up before her because of the shortness of the metal tub. She saw that she had been provided with expensive scented soap ("Soap like 'Mother' Moseley's girls use," bragged Elsie proudly) and she lathered it soberly down her white arms and across her breasts.

She bathed slowly, moodily, remembering another bath —one taken on a day of sun and wind in the raw wilds of Dartmoor. She had stood naked on a rock in the sunshine in a clear swift-running mountain brook, and Geoffrey, his gray eyes alight and laughing, had dipped water from the stream with his hat and poured it over her bare shoulders until her white body glistened and her round breasts pinked with the coldness of it and her pink nipples hardened under his provocative touch. He had bathed her with loving hands and dried her tenderly with his shirt. He had kissed her bare back and her gleaming shoulders, and his lips had roved exploringly over her breasts and stomach. And then his arms had tightened and he had taken her to him and there beside the gurgling brook they had lain together in the soft grass, their arms and limbs intimately entwined as he led her on to passion and fulfilled all her dreams of womanhood.

Tears misted her violet eyes. Love to her was a sacred thing, worth fighting for, worth dying for. All these years she had endured hardship and humiliation when she could easily have become somebody's kept doxie, making

290

men pay dearly for her favors. She had done that because she felt her body was her own and should be freely given —not bartered or sold. Nor would she easily brook the taking of her by force.

She thought of Emma, who had been so young and so pretty and so full of foolish dreams when first she'd seen her in Killigrew's outer chamber—now Emma was broken and spiritless. Poor Emma, who had been used for cruel sport and tortured to frighten the young virgins Wilsingame "bought" from "Mother" Moseley into submission.

Well, *she* would not be used so! The hurtful memories of her beautiful days with Geoffrey—those days that had opened the floodgates of her heart and then when he had gone become an ice jam locked around that heart—came back to taunt her. She would not see Geoffrey again; he was dead or he'd have returned with the King—and perhaps he'd never loved her. No need to live for him.

And Flora had written that young Lorena was "lovelier than even you could have dreamed" and that all the best catches in the village were but waiting for her to grow up. A sad smile crossed Lenore's face. That lovely young daughter she had not seen since she was a baby . . . At first they'd been kept apart because she feared to endanger her child, feared she might end up in prison or a harsh orphanage, her young life ruined. And then when she received her royal pardon, she'd written lying letters of her new affluence, her success—lies she'd meant to make come true—and her stupid pride had kept her from going back to Twainmere to visit her, for Lorena would see at once that her mother was but one step from the almshouse.

No, she need not live for her daughter. . . .

Sitting pensively in the soapy water, she brooded—and suddenly Bonnifly's big hand jerked away the bed-hangings from Elsie's grasp and he laughed down at her.

With an angry shriek, Lenore brought up both her hands filled with soapy water and dashed it into Bonnifly's grinning face. The soapy water struck him in the eyes and he fell back, rubbing at them, unable to see.

"Lor, mistress," muttered the shocked serving-woman. "Ye'd best mend your manners, or they'll do terrible things to ye downstairs! They'll brook no interference with their sport. One poor girl fought them and kept fighting, and they did hurt her so bad she later died!" She stopped abruptly, as if fearful she had said too much. "I do but warn you," she muttered. "Even poor little Emma, who was afraid to deny them anything—"

"I am not Emma," cut in Lenore curtly.

She rose and suffered Elsie to pour a pitcher of warm water over her body to rinse off the soap. Her head was lifted now, her chin held high, for she had made up her mind. An arrogant naked figure, lovely as a water sprite and gleaming in the candlelight, she stepped from the bath and toweled herself dry with clean linen cloths. Then she climbed into the dainty black silk chemise trimmed in lace that Elsie had brought, sat down on the bed and smoothed on her long lovely legs a pair of sheer black silk stockings, and fastened them with the garters of silver tinsel that lay at hand.

Never in the theatre had she worn underthings or stockings so fine—and perhaps it was fitting that she should, for this, her last performance.

She looked up with an odd little smile. "Dress me well, Elsie," she said grimly, "for I would look my best this night."

Elsie gave her a frightened, uncertain look from her watery eyes. Could it be that this beauty's mind had come unhinged from fright? Here she was about to become the single victim of a mass sport—mauled by a pack from whose rough caresses she would emerge as the others had, trembling and screaming with fear and pain—and she wanted to *look her best* for the ordeal?

Lenore stood up. The black chemise was cut artfully low so that the tops of her white breasts gleamed. She no longer cared that Bonnifly, the soap cleared from his eyes, was staring at her hungrily. Let him rest his covetous gaze on what he would never possess!

CHAPTER 18

"And now to comb out your long hair," crooned the serving-woman. "I used to comb hair for 'Mother' Moseley's young ladies—ah, but you've prettier hair than any of them!"

Lenore, sitting bolt upright on the small chair she had intended to use to smash the window, suffered the old woman to comb her hair down around her shoulders.

"We could pile it up but—they would only pull out the pins and it would be worse tangled," advised the serving-woman. "First you will walk down the stairs—slowly, like a bride, mistress. Milord likes that. Bonnifly will walk with you, and you mustn't hang back, even if you're frightened. They're harder on them that's scared."

"No one will have to drag me!"

"If you don't walk down proper, I'll plant my boot on your round bottom and send you down amongst them sprawling," warned Bonnifly in a surly voice. He felt he'd been robbed of his fine private showing and angrily eyed the cooling bath water.

"When you get downstairs," continued Elsie, "Bonnifly will lead you into the drawing room, and there you'll take off your clothes—slowly like. The gentlemen like to lounge about on the benches and watch."

Lenore's throat felt dry. She kept her gaze steady and serene in the mirror, while her heart pounded. "And then?"

"They may make you dance a bit—first." Elsie was reluctant to upset the beautiful doll she had been ordered to gown.

"We'll tell you what to do!" snickered Bonnifly. "For me you'll—"

"I could fix your hair real cunning like," Elsie quickly interposed, with a frown at Bonnifly. "I could put little satin flowers in it. There's some in the chest there. Oh, I was a real ladies' hairdresser at 'Mother' Moseley's—let me show you."

"I've no doubt you're an expert, Elsie," said Lenore with a composure she did not feel. "But we will not seek for fashion tonight, since it seems I'm to wear this gown so briefly—we will seek instead for beauty. We will dispense with the flowers. Think you, is this dress cut low enough?" She held it up for critical inspection—it was artfully cut, she saw, and frothing with creamy lace at the top. "I would have it reveal my bosom, which is very white, don't you think?"

Elsie choked and looked frightened. " 'Tis indeed white as milk," she agreed. " 'Twill inflame them," she added timidly.

Lenore peered into the mirror. "I will pinch my cheeks to give them a high color, but my hair—no, my hair is my best feature. I will wear it combed down about my shoulders so that it will swing like a great shining shawl as I walk. Elsie, these shoes I'm wearing won't do, don't you have something better?"

"I—I might have," gasped Elsie. She padded out and brought back a pair of dainty black satin slippers with high red satin heels.

"Ah, that's better," purred Lenore, who now stood up

in the black silk chemise trimmed with a froth of black lace that barely concealed her nipples.

Awed, Elsie helped her slip into the clinging black gown trimmed at the bosom with creamy lace. It fitted Lenore's round breasts and clung to her narrow waist like her own skin and then flared out into a huge billowing skirt. The cream-colored lace frothed around her bare shoulders and hid part of her plunging bosom.

"I like not that lace," murmured Lenore, frowning as she turned about before the dressing mirror. It was so large she wondered if Wilsingame had got it from some theatre. No matter, it was the last looking-glass in which she would ever see her reflection. "Bring scissors that I may trim it away."

"Trim it away?" Elsie gaped at her. Of all the frightened women who had been dragged into this house, none had ever asked to cut their necklines lower.

Lenore nodded. "And a fan—I will need a fan, Elsie. Lord Wilsingame will wish me to appear as a great court lady, not as an abandoned wench from the streets. Am I to go bare-handed like a serving maid? Are there no black gloves?"

Elsie ran out and returned with scissors, a lovely fan of carved ivory and black ostrich plumes with a dainty mirror in its base, and a pair of black silk gloves. She watched in fascination as Lenore promptly cut away the offending froth of lace so that the daring dress now possessed not only a plunging neckline but a regal dignity.

Lenore studied her reflection grimly. All black . . . save for her white shoulders and the pearly tops of her breasts gleaming pale and her high red heels, she might almost be in mourning. And in a way she was. Mourning for her lost love, her lost lovely life that had somehow slipped through her clever fingers.

She set down the scissors and before Elsie could pick them up again she distracted her by saying, "My hair—it has become tangled again as I turned about, and I want it to fall as truly as running water. Comb it out again while I struggle into these gloves. And be quick about it, for I think I heard the front door open."

Downstairs there was indeed some commotion. A door slammed and they could hear a hubbub of voices downstairs, and over them all Wilsingame's booming, "Ah, but ye must stay—at least for a while. We've an entertainment planned, and 'tis about to start!"

Lenore controlled a shiver. An entertainment! *Herself!*

She picked up the black silk gloves, fragile and delicate —and recoiled from their smooth touch. To whom had they belonged, and was their owner dead? Or cast out upon the streets or into some brothel to make her way? She straightened up, getting control of herself again, and eased the tight gloves over her fingers.

For a long moment she stared into the mirror. A vivid beautiful reflection, violet eyes alight, stared back at her. She could hardly believe she was doing this!

"You do be beautiful," sighed Elsie, laying down the comb and stepping back with a wistful look to view her handiwork.

"Yes, I want Lord Wilsingame to admire me," said Lenore in a level tone. "This effect should please him, don't you think?" She picked up the mirrored ostrich feather fan—and with it the scissors—and wafted it gently, careful to conceal the scissors from their gaze.

Elsie stood as if hypnotized, spellbound before this magnificent creation. She nodded her head in dumb approval. "I do think he don't deserve such," she muttered huskily. " 'Mother' Moseley would pay a packet to get hold of you!"

"But 'Mother' Moseley shall not have me, Elsie!"

Elsie's eyes widened. So that was this beautiful wench's game! She meant to *win* Wilsingame! She gazed at Lenore in admiration. None had so far done it, but . . . none had looked like Lenore!

From the doorway, Bonnifly, too, watched her—with avid soap-reddened eyes. She must keep his heavy hands from her—somehow. She turned arrogantly to Elsie. "I do not wish to have Bonnifly jerk me downstairs as if I were some kitchen wench squalling at her fate," she said in a cold voice. "Go and tell Lord Wilsingame that I wish to make a grand entrance. Tell him I wish to trail down the stairs all alone—without Bonnifly to mar the picture. Go and tell him how I look, Elsie. Make him grant me this request."

Elsie bobbed her head and scuttled away. She'd give odds she was looking at her new mistress here! And when she whispered to Lord Wilsingame that the saucy wench upstairs wanted only to *please* him . . . !

Lenore waited, wafting her fan and turning about to keep Bonnifly's eyes occupied, to keep him from thinking about where the scissors might now repose. Downstairs there was a shuffle of boots and a clank of spurs. She could hear Wilsingame call, "Bring her down, Bonnifly."

Bonnifly surged forward to seize her, and Lenore stepped back to elude him. "You heard me say I wanted to go down alone!"

"What ye want don't matter!" grated Bonnifly, grabbing her by her left arm. In her right reposed the plumed and mirrored fan—and concealed in it the precious scissors. She had studied them well as she trimmed away the creamy lace—one plunge into her breast should be enough!

Bonnifly had dragged her protesting to the door when Elsie came running back. "The master says ye're to let her come down the stairs alone, Mister Bonnifly. If she's bent on bein' tractable, he don't want her upset again. He says you're to stand well back—he don't want the scene destroyed. He wants to impress his guest!"

Bonnifly let Lenore's arm go with a curse and lounged sulkily back in the doorway, and Lenore came out on the landing. A long flight of stairs yawned at her satin-shod feet. She drew a ragged breath. Life, which she had been so willing to throw away a moment ago, seemed suddenly sweet and dear to her.

But . . . in the wide hallway below, clustered at the foot of the stairs leering upward, was a knot of men. In the forefront she saw faces she recognized, those who had been with Lord Wilsingame at the theatre: the lean de Quincy, lounging against the newel post as if to be in position to seize her first; reptilian Flemmons with his elegant yellow wig and his elegant rose satin ruffles;

297

young Alverdice, his heavy face flushed from wine, swaying on his feet, mouthing newly learned obscenities; Lymond, Taggart, they were all here. Indeed the nine or ten seemed to have swelled to beyond a dozen. Mingled among those she knew were some she did not recognize by name, but at least four of them she had seen about the theatre; they were a vicious lot, known for their shocking exploits. Several faces she could not see behind the great plumed hats and enormous curled periwigs, but there were many, *so many!* It seemed to her anguished view that Lord Wilsingame had invited all of London to witness her shame—and partake in it.

"Ye must start down now," hissed Elsie, crouched behind her lest she spoil the effect. "Remember, walk right past them into the big room at your left. 'Tis there they'll have their sport with ye."

Lenore swallowed. Life was not that dear! She did not reply to Elsie but gripped the mirrored plumed fan—and the concealed scissors—the tighter. Her delicate jaw had a grim line. The elegantly dressed gentlemen below would be disappointed if they hoped to have sport with her tonight!

With a regal gesture she lifted her head and tossed back her lovely hair so that it rippled about her back and shoulders like shimmering silk. She made a startling picture in the clinging, low-cut black silk gown, with her large grave violet eyes shadowed by long thick lashes, her brows dark wings against her white forehead, her slightly parted mouth seeming to promise so much. A pulse beat in her slender throat, and the candlelight gleamed on her white shoulders and arms, dramatic against the black silk gloves. The eyes below feasted on that throat and on the pearly tops of her round, beautifully molded breasts—almost fully exposed against the rich clinging black silk of her seductive gown—that rose and fell with her rapid breathing.

Lenore no longer hesitated, for she knew what she must do. Somewhere down the Thames, poor destroyed Emma quaked—she had gone through all this, and it had broken her. Now was her own moment of trial—and it would not find her wanting. Long ago Geoffrey had called her brave. Tonight she would prove it. She would take her own life before she would let this evil pack have her for a plaything.

Some fierce female instinct deep within her made her determined to flaunt before them the beauty that would never be theirs. To make them hunger and burn for what they would never enjoy. To snatch the cup just as they were about to drain it.

With a provocative, swaying walk she moved on her black satin slippers lightly down the stairs. Below her, rapt and avid, the pack waited.

"Gentlemen, our evening's entertainment approaches," observed Lord Wilsingame. "Is Mistress Lenore not a delicate repast to whet the most jaded palate?"

Midway down the stairs Lenore paused and gave Wilsingame a mocking smile. From the landing above, Bonnifly frowned. Was the wench going to balk at this point and have to be dragged downstairs, after all? Others had tried to flee back upstairs when they saw how many awaited them below!

Resting a hand gracefully on the railing, Lenore wafted her plumed fan with an airy gesture. She posed there so that her elegant shoulders and plunging neckline showed to best advantage. So arrogant was her stance that she might have been a princess about to greet her subjects. Below her rose a collective sigh.

Cold and hard, her voice rang out. "You will have to kill me, Wilsingame. For I will not submit to you while I live!"

"Kill you?" From below Wilsingame laughed unpleasantly. "We but wish you to provide us with an evening's entertainment such as Marnock says was your custom in Oxford."

Her flung challenge had been answered. Lenore dropped the ostrich fan, which swung from a ribbon around her wrist, and the scissors flashed in the candlelight as she raised them high. "Then throw another dead woman into the Thames!"

"No!" shouted a voice from below.

But Bonnifly had crept soft-footed down the stairs behind her. Even ·as she brought the scissors down he arrested their flashing flight with a wild leap and pinned her to the balustrade with his heavy body. The scissors were torn from her grasp and clattered down the stairs into the hallway below.

"There'll be no gainsaying us, mistress," growled Bonnifly. " 'Tis not," he mocked, pulling her down the stairs with him, "as if ye had a champion!"

"*I* am her champion!" cried a ringing voice, and Lenore twisted about in Bonnifly's grasp. Her eyes were staring in her head at the sound of that voice. Before her paralyzed gaze a dark head reared up topped by a wide plumed hat above a great black periwig, and a tall, lean, russet-clad body swept impetuously past Wilsingame and up the stairs. Swiftly drawn, a naked blade flashed in his sinewy hand, and Lenore stood rigid as the·point of that cruelly sharp blade was suddenly pressed against Bonnifly's throat.

"Release her!" roared a voice calculated to strike terror into the bravest. Hastily, before the menace of that dark, saturnine face so near his own, and the blade that already had drawn a drop of blood from his pulsing throat, Bonnifly dropped Lenore's arm and stepped back, almost tripping over his own feet in his haste.

"Geoffrey!" whispered Lenore, and sagged against him even as his long left arm reached out to catch her.

From the hallway below, Lord Wilsingame let out a bleat of dismay. "Wyndham—man, are ye mad? 'Tis but an orange girl from the theatre! We intended her no harm!"

Grimly, back to the wall, Geoffrey came down the stairs supporting Lenore with one arm. "Not only will ye do her no harm this night or any other—we will have your apologies to the lady, as well!"

Lord Wilsingame's face suffused with color. He appeared to be choking. "Ye have my apologies, Mistress Lenore," he said in a stifled voice, and then burst out, "but *why,* Wyndham?"

300

"This woman is mine," said Geoffrey tersely, sweeping by him.

"By what right?" From the shuffling group, de Quincy's cold voice rang out.

Geoffrey turned on him a face so threatening that Wilsingame and the others fell back a step. "She is mine by right of possession," he said coolly, making steadily for the door.

They had almost reached the door when de Quincy's sword flashed from its scabbard and he leaped forward. "I challenge that right!"

"Gentlemen, gentlemen!" Wilsingame was dismayed. "Let us not quarrel! Wyndham is our honored guest. All can be resolved! You may have the wench first, Wyndham —all can be appeased."

"Nay, *I* will have her first!" cried de Quincy insultingly, making his blade sing in an arc through the air.

"You will not have her at all!" Geoffrey roared, pushing Lenore behind him. Her heart was beating so hard she thought it would fly out from her chest. *Geoffrey!* her soul sang.

"De Quincy, remember Wyndham is a court favorite!" pleaded Wilsingame in a tragic voice.

"De Quincy is the best blade in London." Flemmons's laugh jarred. "He will kill you, Wyndham—court favorite or no!"

"And if he does not," chimed in Bonnifly heavily from the stairs, his gaze passing Geoffrey to rest on Lenore's white bosom, "the rest of us will bring you down."

"There are too many of them, Geoffrey," Lenore whispered. "If you kill de Quincy, they will be on you in a pack."

He turned his head, keeping his wary eyes trained on de Quincy. His voice, barely a whisper, reached only her ears. "Flash your fan mirror in his eyes when I lead him back to the door."

The mirror in her plumed fan! She had forgotten that. Tense, she watched Geoffrey step forward, presenting his naked blade to de- Quincy. De Quincy's blade snaked forward to meet it. Blade slid along blade; for a moment

301

their faces were close, they were smiling grimly into each other's eyes—then both sprang back.

But for a moment Lenore had seen surprise in de Quincy's face—he had thought his sudden thrust would bring Geoffrey down, she realized. Now they circled each other, making sudden thrusts and parries, both wary antagonists, for each knew the other's reputation with a sword.

There was rapt attention on the faces of the men, and Lenore shrank back toward the door, surreptitiously testing the mirrored fan, which she held tensely in her black-gloved hand, to see exactly where it threw the light from the crystal chandelier overhead. Ah . . . there it was, a circle of light on that bust of Plato. Now she flashed the light on the eye—there, she had it, a flick of her fingers could control its beam.

The swordsmen were evenly matched, and as they lunged and withdrew, the company fell back to give them room lest they be pinked in passing. Scant attention was paid to Lenore, although from the back of the hall the footman Bales kept an eye on her lest she try to escape. But Lenore knew they would bring her down within moments—and Geoffrey, too, for all the swords would be unsheathed then and they would hack him to pieces. Stiffly she stood there, giving them no cause to think her in flight.

The swordsmen were too evenly matched. Their blades clashed, they sprang back—feints, parries, lunges. Once de Quincy stumbled over a footstool, cursed, and recovered as Geoffrey's blade brushed his hair; once Geoffrey slipped on a corner of the carpet and righted himself in time to let de Quincy's singing blade sweep harmlessly by. Geoffrey, ever attacking, had pressed de Quincy back and back, almost to where the footman stood. Now he seemed to weaken and de Quincy, pressing his advantage against an apparently tiring opponent, was leaping forward in renewed attack, pressing Geoffrey back and back toward the front door whence he'd come.

"A bit rusty, Wyndham?" taunted de Quincy with sinister emphasis.

302

"I may be, but my blade is not," panted Geoffrey. He was imperturbable, but to all present he gave plain evidence of tiring.

De Quincy chuckled; he was a cool executioner. "I will have you the next time," he boasted. "I will split you like a chicken just as we reach the wench!"

Geoffrey's back was to Lenore, who was pressed against the wall. Slashing, striking, de Quincy pressed his opponent. Geoffrey parried, but his blade seemed a trifle lower. De Quincy's cold eyes gleamed. Soon he would finish this!

Borne back, Geoffrey had almost reached the door. Oh, God, she must time this exactly right! She could do it but once, for de Quincy would cry out and someone would leap forward and wrest the mirrored fan from her grasp. Geoffrey had fallen back—de Quincy was about to lunge forward for the kill!

With a tiny twist of her wrist she flashed the shining light directly into de Quincy's triumphant eyes.

Instinctively he jerked his head to the right. A slight movement, but it deflected his aim at the moment of making his thrust. A matter of delicate timing, and at the crucial moment the light had blinded him.

Geoffrey took full advantage of it.

Suddenly not tired in the least, he brought up his sword and swept de Quincy's blade from his hand. As it clattered across the floor and de Quincy—who had disemboweled so many men—stood before him rigidly, waiting to be impaled, Geoffrey suddenly grasped his tall opponent and flung him with all his force at the others who had crowded forward to watch the finish—and to kill the victor.

As de Quincy's flung body bore them backward in a tangled heap of satin knees and elbows, boots and spurs, Geoffrey whirled—but Lenore already had the door open and was running through it. Geoffrey went through it like a shadow and slammed it behind him.

Outside a stable boy—the same sallow-faced messenger Wilsingame had sent to Lenore—was holding Geoffrey's horse, for Geoffrey had agreed to come in "for but a moment" at Wilsingame's urging.

Snatching the reins from the amazed stable boy, who

retreated before that naked blade, Geoffrey landed in the saddle in one smooth leap, swept Lenore up before him and tossed a golden coin to the stable boy. "That's for tripping the first man to clear the door!" he called—and they had swept past the gaping boy and were thundering down the narrow track through the maze of tunnels between the houses that bestrode London Bridge.

Clinging to him, Lenore could not believe it. Geoffrey! This moment had been dreamed of, prayed for. . . . For a wild moment she could almost believe she felt the pain of the scissors biting deep into her breast—and that she had died and gone to heaven.

For it was sheer heaven to cling to Geoffrey as she had in the days of their wanderings when they were perpetually on the run, to sway with the strong horse galloping beneath them, to feel the wind in her face and blowing her long silky hair—and pressed tightly against her breasts Geoffrey's broad back, pressed tight against her inner thighs Geoffrey's lean thighs, reminding her, reminding her . . . of long, wild nights with the cry of the loon and a feeling of Eden before the Fall and fierce primeval delights.

Behind them now there was a muffled howl as men spilled cursing out of Wilsingame's house and shouted for the stable boy to bring their horses—but Geoffrey and Lenore now had a long lead. Though they were traveling double, none would catch them now before they reached Southwark and the safety of an inn.

Lenore floated back to earth as Geoffrey galloped into the courtyard of the Tabard Inn in Borough High Street and dismounted. He swung her down from the big black horse, holding her a little longer than was necessary while she thrilled against his hard body.

A bright-eyed stable boy with a shock of tow hair hurried up, and Geoffrey tossed the boy a coin. "Mount up and ride my horse through the streets until you lose the rabble who follow me here—be about it, man!"

The stable boy blinked down at the gold coin in his hand. He did not hesitate. In a bound he had leaped astride Geoffrey's horse and a moment later had cleared the courtyard, clattering fast away. Geoffrey drew Lenore back under the shadow of a pillar as Lord Wilsingame and his disappointed guests straggled by, their hooves thundering on the cobbles, their voices raised in an assortment of complaints and curses.

"The boy knows how to ride—they'll not catch him," said Geoffrey with satisfaction. "Nor will they know where we went. By tomorrow, when they've had time to think about it, they'll become frightened—we'll have no more trouble with them." He turned a stern visage to Lenore in the deserted courtyard. The moonlight gleamed down on his great periwig and plumed hat, caressed his broad shoulders, and shadowed his eyes. "Where is Michael," he growled, "that he would allow this to happen?"

"Michael?" Lenore was staggered. "Michael is dead, Geoffrey!"

"You are a widow, then?"

"A *widow?* Michael was killed by robbers before we reached Banbury—I fled, for 'twas claimed I murdered him!"

Geoffrey's head lifted abruptly, and in the moonlight she saw that his dark face had gone blank with astonishment. "But I searched for you on the road to Banbury, at Coventry—everywhere. When I could not find you, I believed you fled with Michael to America."

She just stared at him. He had *searched* for her?

And then the ice jam about her cold heart melted and she felt warm again, free again, in love again. *Geoffrey had not deserted her—he had searched for her!* Her happy heart sang the words like a refrain, it was she who had deserted him—not the other way around! Gilbert had lied, Gilbert had lied!

"And all this time"— her soft voice caught—"you did not forget me?"

"Lenore," he said huskily, "your face has haunted me. Though I thought you had fled me, you were always there destroying my delight in other women."

Ah, so he had not gone back to Letiche . . . Her heart leaped. "So it has been for me, Geoffrey," she whispered. *"Always."*

He took her face in his hands and looked deep into her eyes. "Lenore, I was wrong in Oxford, wrong about the child—I came back to tell you so, but found you gone. Gone with Michael, they said. Come inside, Lenore—Wilsingame's crowd may ride back this way." He opened the inn door and as she went through it, a bell above the door tinkled. They found themselves in a spacious, empty room filled with rugged tables and chairs and benches, and facing a large stone hearth where banked coals glowed. Geoffrey turned to her again. "When my search proved vain, I came back to Oxford to wring the truth from whoever knew it—and was jailed by the Ironsides. But forget you—never!"

She gave him a soft look and touched gentle fingers to his lips. Time enough for explanations tomorrow; but for now . . . she had him back! Back after the years of pain and loneliness. Back in her arms; for he was always in her heart. "Hush, Geoffrey—the innkeeper is approaching."

"Your pleasure, sir?" Rubbing sleepy eyes, the fat innkeeper bustled forward.

Geoffrey looked fondly down at Lenore. "A room for the night."

"Aye, sir. What name?"

Lenore spoke up. "Daunt. We are the Daunts of Williamsburg—in the American Colonies."

Something flamed up in Geoffrey's eyes, and she lifted her head proudly and looked back at him, a splendrous woman in the candlelight with her white shoulders gleaming, her half-bared bosom seductive against the low-cut black silk. Her violet eyes were lustrous and slanted at him provocatively through dark lashes, their flickering light promising reckless delights. She smiled up at him, that swift, blinding smile that was like summer sunshine breaking through the clouds, and in that smile was a sweet promise of what was to come. Of what had always been there . . . just for him.

From the street came two rollicking male voices singing a raucous drinking song off-key, and from the stableyard came the giggles of a kitchen maid meeting one of the grooms in a dark corner—giggles and a sharp slap and

306

an aggrieved feminine voice crying, "You promised you wouldn't!"

Lenore smiled to herself. This was wild, unbridled London—the London of Frost Fairs and theatre brawls and maypoles and wild court parties. But it was also a great and busy port, and tomorrow they could begin their plans to make an old dream come true, they would embark on a tall white ship and sail to the American Colonies. They would become indeed the Daunts of Williamsburg, and Lorena, her lovely daughter, would be with them!

In the Colonies, with all their mistakes behind them, they could start a new life, better than the old. They could forget the past and become at last the people they were born to be . . . ah, she would make Geoffrey such a good wife!

But for tonight—and this was a part of the promise her reckless violet eyes foretold—tonight as Geoffrey's lean body sank into his warm bath, she would—very slowly—remove her black silk gloves, one by one, easing them down her lovely arms. With a tantalizing smile she would unfasten the hooks of her black silk bodice, plunging its daring neckline even lower, until—with a twist that would make her breasts bounce—she would drop the heavy silk dress to the floor and step out of it.

And while he watched she would ease out of her elegant black chemise, letting the lace rasp delicately down her smooth white skin until the black silk whispered to the floor at her feet and she stood before him clad only in her red-heeled black satin shoes and sheer black hose.

As he leaped from the tub and eagerly toweled dry—with his glowing eyes never leaving her!—she would kick off her high-heeled shoes, plant a foot upon the footboard of the great fourposter and with great concentration remove her silver-tinseled garters, slide the sheer black silk stockings down her elegant legs and toss them like smoke rings toward the cold hearth.

That hearth would be the only cold thing in their room tonight!

Tomorrow was time enough to talk of sailing, of a new

307

life—but tonight was for twining naked arms and limbs, for soft murmurings and ardent caresses, for seeking the wild, free heights of love's stormy passions. Tomorrow they could plan to sail to the American Colonies, but tonight—tonight was for lovers!